A MOVEABLE VERDICT

A NOVEL

by

David R. Cudlip

Pen & Pencil Press ♦Tryon, North Carolina
www.penandpencilpress.com

Revised Edition published by Pen & Pencil Press LLC

Retitled as A MOVEABLE VERDICT

ISBN 9780984621019

"To the living we owe respect; to the dead we owe the truth..."

Voltaire

Author's Note

The trial-gunners of America may take exception to the manner in which I've presented the courtroom scenes in this story. Still, stories have a mind of their own and often go wherever they wish to go...which is why it's so much fun to conjure them.

Prologue

Excerpted from a Midwestern newspaper, an updating of The People of California vs. Romaine Brook.

(Los Angeles)—Tempers flared yesterday as Assistant Attorney General Lloyd Pritter submitted into evidence a threatening letter written by Romaine Brook, who stands accused of murdering Marc Sterne this past November. This is the most damning evidence yet offered in a trial pitting the celebrated actress against the state, over the alleged killing of the son of Julio Sterne, a top-tier California industrialist.

Outside, here in this City of Angels it swelters as Santa Ana winds blow their furnace-like breath across the Los Angeles basin. And here, inside this jammed courtroom, another kind of heat is chasing Ms. Brook, who's supporting role in *Tonight or Never,* in which she starts out as an ingénue and ends up as a nun with a gun, won wide acclaim and subsequently earned her an Academy Award. Many rank her as the most gifted American film-actress since Meryl Streep.

The lithesome Ms. Brook, a blondish emerald-eyed beauty, seems to mesmerize the packed courtroom. Even though she sits in her shroud of silence, she somehow manages to upstage her assailants with occasional subtle gestures. She seems possessed of an extraordinary power to draw attention, as if somehow bathed by radiance from above. Indeed, no matter the verbal clashes of the opposing attorneys, it is only by concentrated effort that one can avert the temptation to gaze and gaze again at the accused, who often comes across as the flower of innocence.

How, one may ask, is that remotely possible when she has yet to utter a single syllable in her own defense?

Marc Sterne, who she is accused of killing, was found dead eight months ago, sprawled across a four-poster bed at his family's Malibu Pointe estate. A subsequent examination by the coroner revealed the body was "inundated with enough heroin and other ingredients to fell an ox".

A companion forensic exam by the Los Angeles Sheriff's Department concluded that the sheets from the bed, where the body was found, revealed

1

DNA that matched perfectly with both the deceased Sterne and the accused, Romaine Brook, thus linking both to the crime scene.

The state's theory is that young Sterne had no reason to wipe away his own fingerprints from the heroin-syringe, even if contemplating suicide, which so far is not an issue in the trial.

As no prints were found on the syringe, his or anyone else's, a homicide presumably took place. No gloves, no cloths were found at the death-scene, which might explain the absence of prints. It is, of course, possible that Sterne wiped the syringe clean before dying, but the question persists as to why would he perform such an act, unless he was purposefully trying to throw blame on Ms. Brook?

If so, then for what reason? Was that reason, whatever it is, the basis of a motive for her to kill?

"She did away with him," argued Lloyd Pritter, the lead prosecutor, in his opening remarks eight weeks ago, "and then she wiped away the traces of her criminal act. We intend to make it diamond-clear why she committed a vile murder in the first-degree..."

Raye Wheeler, the wily veteran who represents the young actress, objected strongly to the manner in which the letter was introduced by the prosecution yesterday. A Vesuvius moment quickly erupted. At one point, the attorneys were nose-to-nose, parting only when the threat of a contempt citation was issued by an obviously upset judge.

Based on the prosecutor's remarks, one could readily infer the letter itself detailed a scheme to recover certain photos, allegedly of bizarre sexual acts, that likely could prove damaging to Brook's career. The judge, having read the letter's contents, placed it under seal, awaiting a later ruling as to whether the jury would also be permitted to see it. Already, the jury has seen photos that allegedly show Ms. Brook in a compromising state.

For at least a year prior to young Sterne's death, he and Miss Brook had been romantically linked, and were often seen at Hollywood events and parties. Sterne, scion of one of California's wealthiest families, was employed by Parthenon Studios, where *Tonight or Never,* one of the leading box-office draws of past years, was produced. Parthenon is controlled by Sterne's father, Julio Sterne, a top industrialist.

It is widely known that the younger Sterne traveled in fast company. Earlier, at the trial, several of his acquaintances admitted to their own run-ins with the Los Angeles police over the use of illegal substances, and, in the case of two lesser known actors, statements were made they had appeared in pornographic films financed by young Sterne.

This publicity-riven clash continues to grip the nation's attention. So much so, that Cliff Rhodes, the presiding judge, found it necessary to sequester the jury at the downtown Biltmore Hotel, where they have been cooped up for the past several weeks. There, the jurors are isolated from the flood of ink and heavy television coverage attending the trial, as they weigh the fate of Ms. Brook.

The trial has become something of a Hollywood saga. Off to a balky start, lately it has picked up pace. Observers credit this to Judge Rhodes, who, until assuming his judicial robes two years ago, ranked as one of the West Coast's top trial lawyers. Prior to his appointment to the Criminal Court, Rhodes, in addition to his flourishing legal practice, had served as president of the International Academy of Trial Lawyers. Only three months ago, he was nominated for a seat on the Supreme Court of California, this state's highest tribunal, a rare occurrence for criminal attorneys who are thought to be too specialized and too controversial for...

PART I

Chapter One

Day sixty-seven.

You could walk the entire China coast in less time, Rhodes was thinking, or even make a dozen trips to the moon. Inwardly, he was groaning, waiting for the fireworks sure to come as soon as the prosecution took its turn. His cat-sense told him the woman was fibbing. A lie, but how important? Everyone hid something—past sins, a serious fault or two, wrongs against others, insults made in the heat of argument, thefts, lies. Lies probably topped the list. Still, the truth could ruin people as fast as a lie, sometimes faster.

And what was she hiding?

His foot had gone to sleep. He wiggled it a few times to awaken the circulation, then leaned forward, waiting.

"On the night Marc Stone met his death, you saw Romaine Brook. Correct?" Raye Wheeler was asking his witness.

"That's right."

"And do you remember what time that was?"

"Around ten or so at night."

"Why do you say that hour?"

"Because the evening news was on television when she arrived at my apartment."

"You watch the evening news show every night?" asked Wheeler, who, suddenly bent over in a coughing fit. His head shook, as if someone had unexpectedly punched his neck.

Waiting for him to recover, the woman said, "I watch the news most nights."

"Let's agree it was ten o'clock or so at night. Miss Brook comes home, then to your apartment. Tell us what you saw or recalled that night. Was there anything unusual? "Nothing. She just stopped in. We talked and she asked for a glass of milk."

"Milk?"

"She likes milk with egg in it."

6

"Did she appear strange? Upset? Shaken? As if she'd just come from the scene of a murder?"

Pritter struggled to his feet, waving one thick arm. "Objection! He's not only leading the witness, he's asking for a conclusion that—"

"Sustained," said Rhodes. He shook his head, smiling wanly. "You'll have to fix that question," he said to Wheeler.

Wheeler nodded, returning to his witness. Drawing two or three deep breaths, he patted his mouth with a blue hanky pulled from his back pocket. Then he bowed with mock courtesy to Lloyd Ritter, the heavy gun sent in to add firepower to the state's case.

"How did Miss Brook appear to you that night?" Wheeler continued.

"Just fine. Lovely as she always is, you know."

"No noticeable marks? No rips in her clothes? No bruises that you could detect?"

"To me, she looked fresh as next Friday."

"Did she tell you where she'd been?"

"No."

"Did you ask her?"

"No."

"Did Miss Brook look as if she was running away from a crime?"

"Objection." Getting up, Pritter knocked against the table and a sheaf of papers flew across the floor. An aide bent over to pick them up.

Two or three of the front row press rose halfway out of their seats. Stretching, gazing down on the spilled papers, they were hoping to see the notorious photos of Romaine Brook previously admitted into evidence but unseen so far by the either the press or the public.

"Up to the bench, please," Rhodes said, motioning both attorneys forward. He waited. "C'mon. You both know better. Do it the right way."

Crossing glances, the attorneys ambled away, each in a perfect contrast to the other: Pritter, large and slope bellied, his face full of blood pressure; Wheeler, features haggard and worn, his suit drooping badly around his thin, brittle-looking frame.

When Raye Wheeler faces his witness once more, he changed his tack slightly. "And how would you describe Miss Brook's moral character?"

"Why, I'd say it was just excellent. Outstanding. Just look at her," said the witness—as some of the jurors did for the hundredth time that day. "She is thoughtful, kind, terribly honest."

7

"Ever known Miss Brook to do anything immoral? Break a law, anything of that sort?

"Well, I paid a parking ticket for her once when she was out of town."

A quick volley of laughs from somewhere among the spectators.

"Thank you, mam...your witness," said Raye Wheeler, walking away as he gestured to Lloyd Pritter.

"A moment, may I?" requested Pritter. He looked up at Rhodes, asking for a pause before his cross-examination.

"All right. How much time?" Rhodes replied.

"A minute or so. Not more."

Rhodes nodded.

Pritter shifted around in his chair. Motioning his two colleagues closer, he cupped one hand to the side of' his mouth to muffle his bull-lunged voice. The juror nearest Pritter peered intently at him, as if trying to lip-read him.

A trial where time seemed to tiptoe, occasionally quicken, then all too suddenly stop in a freeze-frame. But in murder trials, you never hurried the clock. You slow it down to expose every fact worth pinning down to get at half-truths, to let the jury hear everything so they could sift what was important. You were doubly careful of every statement, every exhibit. You let the whole wheel of evidence turn and turn again until it wore itself out.

That was Rhodes's formula. Murder trials depressed him. He'd done too much killing with his own hands. Done away with nameless foes in war and, now that he looked at them, done away with a long row of juries, too.

Catching Pritter's eye, Rhodes pointed at the clock. The attorney made a quick gesture, asking for a few more moments.

This day and every day, the courtroom was filled to capacity. Bodies cramped together, bodies eager to see what lurid sparks might fly. And the press in the front row, scribbling notes, waiting avidly for the damning words that would be the perfect lead in tomorrow's newspapers.

Go away, play with someone else today, Rhodes implored them silently as he ran a thumb under his collar in a futile attempt to let some air under his robe. He sweated uncomfortably in the stuffy courtroom, in part, he supposed, because the trial was beginning to gnaw on his nerves. He'd been criticized for its snail-like pace. Recently nominated to fill an opening on the California Supreme Court, he wanted to finish his tenure in the lower court, and get this publicity-heated trial behind him, with no further problems and no more complaints.

A faint rustling from the witness stand and Rhodes swerved his attention to the witness. She was fortyish, he guessed; robust and with the strong looking arms of a farmwoman that ended in curiously delicate hands clasped on her lap.

Wheeler had cruised her across the better sides of Romaine Brook's character, and had smiled after finishing with her. Still, he looked old today, even exhausted, as if all the worries of the world were invisibly lashed to his back.

Ill, though. Coughing too often in those deep wracking spasms. Rhodes knew the older man's lungs were in sad shape: emphysema, a hard mile for anyone to travel, but fatal for a man who earned his daily bread with his mouth. Still, it might gain him some sympathy with the jurors. God knows he needed it, the way the trial was going for his client.

Rhodes was fond of the older man. Very fond. They'd been colleagues once.

Wheeler, with the young celebrity at his side, his fetching client, the fated Academy Award winner, in a rigorous duel attempting to beat a murder rap. The young woman was acting nicely here, too, Rhodes thought; almost as if she were an onlooker instead of the person facing a murder-one charge. Calm, composed—even detached from the proceedings that could mean a life behind bars instead of one looking into the lens of a camera.

Glancing at her again, noting how her posture made her seem taller. She was tall, but the way she sat, so erect, imparted a regal line to her body. An alert, intelligence face, one that fell short of the purely beautiful but a face with very clean planes: money-bones is how they called that look in the film game. A face that a camera loved, in any light.

Tawny hair rolling to her shoulders, direct and doe-like eyes, wide mouth, high breasts and legs for making a bishop jump.

Scurrilous photos of her had been offered into evidence not long ago. Naked, with the mouth of another woman hanging on her breast, hands of a man or men fondling her. Others, worse. Hard to believe it was the defendant sitting here so demurely in the courtroom. Most of the photos seemed to suggest a look, however vague, of resistance. Eyes closed, lips in a tight scowl, the jaw taut along its fine lines.

Had she been coerced somehow? Or was it a pose?

9

Hard to tell, and Rhodes was left to wonder. As he also wondered about one particular photo—where her face had apparently been slathered with caviar? The shot had been labeled accordingly: face, frontal view, streaked with caviar eggs. Odd. Kinky? Whoever did that with expensive caviar? Or was it used as some form of cosmetic?

He'd heard of stranger things; a skin specialist in Beverly Hills had once explained to him the uses of bull's sperm to tighten a woman's facial texture.

Wondering and watching, as Pritter approached the stand, placing one meaty paw against its molding. The witness leaned forward in her chair, an intensely suspicious look on her face. Rhodes guessed that Pritter would plow up the earlier testimony and reveal the small lie. But he guessed wrongly, was wide of the mark.

"We're going to go over a few things, if you don't mind," Pritter began, his voice booming like a drill sergeant's.

"Oh, I don't mind. Not at all, no sir."

"You said earlier that you've known the defendant for two years."

"Yes, that's right. Two years and two months now."

"And first met her when she rented a room in your boarding house?"

"It's not a *boardinghouse*. I lease out three small apartments in my triplex to young women from the School of Drama over at the university." Incensed, she spoke in a wounded tone.

"Very well...Miss Brook rented from you two years ago. So now you know her quite well?"

"I get to know all my girls quite well."

"What do you mean by *my girls*?"

"My paying guests. I don't accept just anybody, you know."

"So I'm told." Pritter looked over at the jury and slowly repeated, "Yes, that's what I've been told."

Rhodes saw Raye Wheeler come halfway out of his seat. His hand went up and down before he sank back into his chair. Coughing again, shaking his head, choking. The young lawyer next to Wheeler rubbed the older man's back. Romaine Brook turned away, and, for the first time in weeks, Rhodes saw a pleading look on her face. She's in a fright, Rhodes thought sympathetically, as Pritter went to work again on his prey.

Are you familiar with the film Miss Brook appeared in? Her second one, I believe--"

"Yes. Marvelous, wasn't she?"

"Do you have any idea what she was paid for appearing in it?"

"Objection!" Wheeler's young assistant nearly catapulted out of his chair. Rhodes agreed, saying, "Sustained. Where're you taking us, counselor?" he asked Pritter.

"I'm about to impeach the earlier testimony of this witness, your Honor. It needs airing, we think."

"Get to it, then."

At the word *impeach*, uttered so forcibly by Pritter, the woman in the witness stand blushed. Her eyes narrowed. As Pritter watched her face harden, his own neck squeezed down into his shoulders the way a pit bull does before attacking.

"Madam," he said, "how much rent did Miss Brook pay to stay in your triplex? Monthly rent?"

"Five hundred dollars. Same as the others."

"Why does she stay there?"

"She likes it and told me so. Many times...and there's a waiting list. Did you know that?"

"No doubt it's wonderful," Pritter agreed. "But Miss Brook could presumably afford her own home somewhere. More privacy, a garden, perhaps a pool."

"You'd have to ask her. I'm not her accountant."

"But you were something else, weren't you?"

The woman looked up, sharp-eyed. "What's that supposed to mean?"

"What I mean is that occasionally Miss Brook spent her nights with you. Isn't that correct?"

"Not really."

"Never?"

"Sometimes I'd rehearse her lines with her if she had a class the next day. I enjoyed doing it."

"Enjoyed what? Her spending the whole night with you in your...your room?"

"I beg your pardon, mister."

"Did Miss Brook ever stay the night with you in *your* bedroom?"

"Sometimes she might have fallen asleep. She worked so hard and—"

"How many times?"

"I don't know exactly?"

"More than ten?"

"I can't remember," said the woman slowly.

"Twenty?"

The woman shrugged. She swiveled her head to look up at Rhodes who told her she must answer the question.

"Possibly ten times, I can't remember...sometimes she was lonely and she'd stay."

"And?"

"And nothing. Well, sometimes we would talk the way women do when they're by themselves."

"That's all?"

"Of course, that's all. What're you driving at?"

"Now, isn't it a fact that you're involved in the Women's Gay Liberation movement here in Los Angeles?"

"Yes, I am. No law against it, either."

"Your privilege naturally," Pritter said as he scanned the jurors for a reaction. "But you testified only minutes ago to the good character of Miss Brook. And now you want us to believe your statements are made in good faith. Are objective and not tainted by more intimate and personal feelings. She is presumably paid well for her film appearances. She didn't have to live with you and I suggest she did so because on the ten or more nights she spent in your bedroom something else was going on—"

"Objection! Object-shun!" Raye Wheeler could barely get it out, furiously waving a frail arm.

"You, you're a lying bastard," the woman shouted at Pritter.

Hurriedly, Pritter threw his deep voice at the jury. "And it was something other than rehearsals, wasn't it, unless they've got a new name for it?"

Gasping, the woman's mouth opened, closed, flopped open again. She glared at Pritter, visibly paling. Then her eyes fluttered, rolling upward until they turned into fading white disks. She tilted, in sections, tumbling forward onto the floor in a splayed heap. She went down so fast and hard her blue skirt twisted up over her hips.

The jury craned like storks, as if on cue, with their stunned faces glued to the unconscious woman.

What they saw, what everyone nearby saw, was a large blue and red rosette tattooed on her upper thigh. Very near to her shaved and exposed groin.

The room seemed to shudder nervously. People milled around in the aisles as reporters tried to elbow their way closer to the fallen witness. A bailiff knelt by the woman, tugging her skirt down, patting her face gently.

Rhodes waved another bailiff over. "Clear it out. Everyone. Get the jury out of here, and tell Pritter to be in my chambers in five minutes...hear me?"

Goddamn it anyway, Rhodes swore to himself.

As another yell echoed from somewhere out in the throng of pushing spectators, Rhodes glanced around quickly. He saw Raye Wheeler and his assistant, the gawky young lawyer, hovering around a quite composed Romaine Brook who seemed, oddly, to be smiling. Propped on her elbows, the witness was trying to sit up, apparently recovering, and with enough modesty to ensure her dress covered her where she was supposed to be covered. Rhodes absorbed the scene, then departed as the last of the jurors filed out of the jury box.

In his chambers, he pulled off his robe and draped it on the wooden clothes tree next to his work desk. Leaning on it, his balled fists supporting his weight, is the way Macklin Price found him as she came in with a glass of iced tea.

"What happened out there? Everybody buzzin' again out in the office."

"Pritter cooled Wheeler's witness right to the floor. She actually fainted."

"Gawd, really? I heard all the commotion. Everyone did."

"Yes, really it happened."

"Well, don't blame me."

Moving closer, Macklin Price saw that Rhodes's shirt was wet and his unruly sun-streaked hair was mussed again. Tufts curled over the back of his collar. Time for a haircut. She handed him the tea and he drank half of it down in one long gulp.

"What's in this?"

"Jose Cuervo, the Golden. Figured you might need one," Macklin replied.

"You're an everything with ribbons." Sending her a grateful smile.

"You know me, God's chosen child...You want your messages? A stack of em. One from the governor's office—urgent as diarrhea."

13

"Later, Pritter's due in here any minute."

"Can I listen in?"

"Sorry." He smiled though.

Hearing a knock, they both turned to see Pritter looming at the open door. Rhodes looked coldly at him. Pritter wore a gray suit cut by some tailor of sufficient genius to almost hide his massive girth, but the clever stitching couldn't hide a double chin, or the rolls of flesh on the back of his neck.

"Interrupting anything?" Pritter asked.

"No. Come on in," Rhodes said, and then to Macklin, "This won't take long. I'll be with you in a few minutes."

The door closed as Pritter asked, "Is it sit or stand today?"

Rhodes pointed toward a leather sofa, and heard the cushions squawk as Pritter dropped his freight there.

"When Raye Wheeler is feeling better, we're going to have to repeat this conversation in his presence, right?" Pritter nodded as Rhodes continued, "I'm close to lowering on you, Lloyd. I thought you ought to know...you've gotten all the dance floor you're going to get here," said Rhodes, sitting down at his desk, lighting a cigar at the same time.

"Frosty in here, isn't it?"

"And slippery too."

"Are we informal today, or what?"

"Informal?"

"Can we talk plainly?"

"I am certainly, and you're going to listen—"

"Good then—"

"No, not so good," Rhodes stopped him.

"Look, I can't help who they put on as witnesses. If they can't come up with better than floozies like that, then that's Wheeler's worry," Pritter complained.

"We've got a powder keg smoking here—"

"She doesn't even put on underwear. In a courthouse, even."

"That doesn't give you the right to—"

"I came down on her because that's my job. You know it is."

"You can impeach any testimony, I agree. But this is the third time you've tried to bulldoze witnesses so you can impress the jury." Rhodes floated a stream of smoke over his desk. "You're trying to jam the jury, and do the same with the record using slurs you knew Raye Wheeler would've objected to. I would have sustained him, too."

"I didn't hear any objections from Wheeler."

"He never had a decent chance. That's why."

"You know how it is out there. You've been in it a hundred times. I get excited—"

"You're getting me pretty excited. Notice?"

Cigar smoke hazed Pritter's face. He waved it away only to find one more billow coming at him.

"You pulled that stunt for the last time. You're trying to slant the jury with what comes damn close to slander," Rhodes said.

"I've got a right to go after Wheeler's witnesses...besides, I may have a few of my own to tell about the lovey-dovey that went on between Brook and that—"

"You've got witnesses who'll actually testify that way?" Rhodes asked, surprised.

"I said I *may*."

"*May* isn't good enough. You've alleged homosexual acts between the defendant and the witness. You tried to slam it into the jury's ears before Raye Wheeler could react and I could act."

"Well, Wheeler ought to sharpen up. Not my fault, is it? I've got the clear right to demolish any defense witness's statements. Of all people, you should—"

"You're accusing witnesses of things that don't matter here. You're playing to the prejudices of the jury and sucking up to the press, too."

Pritter shifted. The davenport creaked as he handed away more cigar smoke.

"Putting on a medicine show out there, aren't you?" continued Rhodes. "Hell you will. Not in my courtroom."

"You gagged us with the press. Now you want to gag me when I cross-examine."

"Not quite."

'Then what?"

"Have you got someone lined up who knows there was some sort of affair going on between those two women? Have you?"

"We're looking into it."

"You think you can show, absolutely show, the woman was involved with Romaine Brook?"

"I...I don't know for sure." Pritter faltered.

"Here's what's for sure then. Tomorrow I'm going to strike your statements from the record." Rhodes picked up a yellow pencil, snapping it in half easily between two fingers. "And I'm probably going to remind the press again of their forgotten-duty *not* to publish crap trumped by the prosecutor...and you...you know what you're going to do, Pritter?'

"I can't even imagine."

"You'll apologize to the witness and the jury."

"Hell, I will. You can't do that." Prying himself off the couch, Pritter lunged toward the desk, then stopped abruptly as if a knife had pinked his belly. "I can file a complaint with the Superior Court, too."

"Sure you can. But not before I shut the book on you and toss it to Kingdom Come."

"Stretching it, aren't you?"

"I'm going to stretch the record back into shape. You're going to help by apologizing."

"Supposing I produce a witness who knows what was going on?"

"I'll want the name first thing tomorrow."

Glowering, Pritter retorted, "Is that it?"

Rhodes nodded as Pritter got up, heading for the door. He thought of how the press would play up the fracas. A witness fainting under duress, a witness who was jaybird naked under her skirt. And the jury, there were seven women on that jury. Pritter must know they wouldn't be overjoyed with his sort of hammering at one of their own. Still, those same women were unlikely to forget the tattooed thigh of that witness who had likely nose-dived her way onto tomorrow's front page.

Another knock on the door signaled the arrival of one of the bailiffs. A lanky man, stony faced, with a strong nose and cropped black hair, and he had come, Rhodes knew, looking for guidance.

The jury was about to leave for the Biltmore, he reminded Rhodes. Tonight was one of their nights to go out for dinner and a private room had been reserved in a Chinatown restaurant. All right? *Yes, fine.* The hotel manager had agreed to open the health club at 6 a.m. as a special favor. But it'll cost in overtime. Is there enough money for it? *"Somehow, yes. Just see to it they don't get near a newspaper stand"* Then the little bomb: "some of

16

the male jurors," said the bailiff, "are up to some light housekeeping with two of the women—the redhead and that other one, the rangy brunette wearing the horn-rims. *"That's your department, you handle it."* But it's six weeks now, these things happen, and there's no rule to go by. They're all side-by-side at the end of one floor. *"I know."* We can't exactly stop it, your honor. *"No one ever could, and I can't issue chastity belts either."*

The bailiff left, no wiser, resentful at being reduced to baby-sitting chores with this locked-up jury. Several weeks of being cloistered and they had turned surly, bitchy, as much imprisoned as the accused Romaine Brook. They sounded out with every imaginable complaint: threatened to get sick, quit; wanting to return to their own worlds. "What's happening in the outside world, fr' chrissakes?"—"Hey bailiff, this steak, I wouldn't sole your goddamn shoe with it."—"What breed of donkey did they strain this vodka through?"—"My dog gets washed with better soap..."

Everything, endlessly.

&#x08;

Raining again.

A knot of people crowded against the front doors of the courthouse, waited for the drizzle to let up. Lloyd Pritter turned sideways and pushed his way through the bystanders.

Apologize to the jury? He fumed. The press would jump all over him, and the thought of it doubled his rage. Just when he had the newspapers hooked, too; the trial was going his way; in a couple of weeks, he would have it sewn up, all but put on ice.

Out on his feet, ready to kiss the canvas, the great Raye Wheeler wasn't even smart enough to know when to take down his shingle. Probably made ten million in his time. Now it's my time, Pritter thought. That was the word coming over from Oldes & Farnham. "Win this one, Lloyd boy, and we've got a cushy office waiting for you. Three-hundred and fifty-thousand sound about right for starters? You've labored in the public vineyard long enough, eh?"

Weight. Strength. Julio Sterne's strength, the nice heavy smooth force of money talking in green-papered words through Sterne's personal lawyers. But the high Mandarins of Oldes & Farnham wouldn't be so pleased if he had to apologize before the entire courtroom. He'd have to figure out how to duck that one before court opened tomorrow.

 CR

In Rhodes's chambers.

"Lawdy-dawdy," Macklin Price sang out. "No panties I hear, and all barbered up like—"

"C'mon Macklin, just let me have the messages," Rhodes extended his hand, waiting for the sheaf of paperwork.

"I'll read them...here's one from the inimitable Alonzo Fahey waiting to know if you're on for poker Thursday night." She flipped to the next pink slip, batting her eyes comically. "Fritzi called, needs to talk with you." Then she scowled. "And I already told you about the governor's office."

"Call Fahey, tell him I'll see him Thursday."

"And Fritzi?"

"I'll do her myself."

"You'd better," Macklin advised. "She sounds like what you'd call *neglect-ed*."

Rhodes raised his eyes. "She say that?"

"She didn't have to. She's a smiler but there ain't no tinkle-bell in that voice today."

Send flowers? A present? He hadn't seen her in days, too preoccupied with the trial, dividing himself as if he were an amoeba. Fritzi was a gift, a love, but she'd have to be patient with him. And in weeks past he'd become unsettled, emotionally tripped ever since Audrey Sterne had boomeranged into his life again.

"You need a haircut."

"Schedule me somewhere," he replied absently.

"I can cut it for you."

"Even better, if you wouldn't mind.

"I wouldn't mind. Not ever."

Rhodes missed the benign look on Macklin's face as he flipped through the papers on his desk. One stack, daunting to him, contained forms to o complete before his nomination to the State Supreme Court could move forward. You'd think you were replacing an unknown god for the amount of information they demanded of you. Taxes. Financial holdings. Security clearances, if any. Mother, father, spouse, children. Nothing for dogs and cats, but everything about your homes and schools, all of them. Records and dispositions of any arrests. Military service and rank, much of which in his case remained classified. Your whole life neatly checked off in small squares or lines to fill in.

"What did the governor's office want?" he asked. "Wanting to know when all this stuff will be ready."

"Didn't say. They want you to call back though. His assistant."

"Let's handle that one first."

Macklin nodded and looked down at her notepad. "There're those speech dates. B'nai Brith and Town Hall Meeting. What about those?"

"Tell 'em thanks, but not while the trial is still on. Draft a thank you letter and let me have a look at it."

"And you're lecturing tonight at the law school," she reminded him.

"I know."

"I could call and cancel."

"You'd ruin the only fun I can count on this week. Besides, it's a new class."

"Okay, I'll get the calls going."

He watched her move off. A gazelle of a woman, with a café au lait complexion, she rolled as smoothly as a ball bearing when she walked. He had defended her sister against charges of running a call-girl operation in West Los Angeles. Gotten the sister off, too, but not in time to collect his fee before she had waltzed off to Rome. Macklin had offered to pay if he halved the fee and agreed to employ her. She was so helpful and talented he canceled the debt after two months. They had worked together amiably for ten years, singing over the victories, cursing the defeats. She ran half of his life, kept his calendar sorted out, and excelled at keeping the bureaucracy of law and order off his back.

A light blinked on his phone console.

He spoke to a governor's assistant, the man who was assigned to handle the larger errands. This was the third time he'd called about the trial, checking on its progress, dropping veiled, unpleasant, inapt suggestions. "The Sternes are good friends of the governor and his wife," the assistant reminded Rhodes, who needed no reminding. "The trial ought to move along a better pace, and we're getting concerned about the rather dismal press reports."

Counting to five, then to ten, Rhodes was in a near fury. "Tell the governor to stay away from it. We could both get into trouble, I'm sure you're aware of that, or I hope you're aware."

"Sure thing, judge," said the assistant. "I don't think you want it said quite that way, though."

"What way is that?"

"So stridently."

"I'd like it said as stridently as you can stridently say it."

"Look here, it's the governor who is nominating you to the high court and—"

"And I'm grateful," Rhodes said. "But this trial doesn't need any more kibitzers."

"I resent that, I really do." The voice suddenly chilly.

"Drop the heat then, and we'll all feel better."

"There's no pressure at all from this end. I merely make an occasional comment from time to time."

"Three times," Rhodes said. "That's not what I call occasional."

"I'll be sure to tell the governor."

Rhodes decided to back off, offering a scant apology. "This thing is full of booby traps, you know. The Sternes seem to be kissing the press up to a white heat, and it's nothing the governor should mix into. For his own good."

"The governor," said the assistant, "does not forget his friends, either."

"Are you one of them?"

A pause. "I don't think that's fun—"

"Neither do I. Not funny at all. So let's forget this conversation."

"Perhaps."

"I'll get on with your forms."

"And the trial, let's not forget the trial."

Rhodes slipped the phone on to its cradle, then pressed his fingertips to his cheekbones where blood was heating his skin. Trying mightily to stall his temper before it ruled him. Had he screwed it for good now? He wanted that high bench appointment badly. Criminal lawyers rarely made it to the Supreme Court. Other lawyers, yes, of course. Who else? But not a trial-gunner who freed people the public wanted jailed or hung or both.

He resented the very hell out of the Sternes sending messages to him this way; through the governor's office, no less. Incredible. Didn't they know a jury is the only real judge in a murder trial?

He was barely acquainted with Julio Sterne, the industrialist and film impresario, and never had met the dead son, Marc. But he had known Audrey Sterne as surely as if she were the everyday air in his life. Knew that look of warmth in her, like a candle's flame in winter, and a body that went from fire to wildfire faster than any he'd ever known. Remembering that, and more at this most untidy moment.

Quite a social animal nowadays, cavorting with the high-born, and a fashion-hound, her own personal fitness trainer he'd read somewhere, the best hairdressers in Beverly Hills, showing up for the season in London or Paris, attending jet-set charity balls in Monte Carlo. A real swan, and as pure-looking, and she moved like one—gliding about, forever unruffled. He had seen her only a few times in the past twenty years. The last time right out there in his own courtroom on the day she'd come to tell about seeing her stepson's body after the houseman had discovered him in a bedroom. She'd been one of the state's leadoff witnesses, acquitting herself quite well and quite matter-of-factly.

To see her again, this way, so close, had jolted him. Got him going again, made him remember things he thought were cleansed by the scrub-brush of time. But time hadn't brushed it all away, and it bothered him.

An hour later, he left to lecture at the law school. He was still thinking of Audrey Sterne, and why Raye Wheeler wanted to recall her to the witness stand. Be interesting to see what that old magician had up his sleeve the next time out.

Weeks ago, when it came his turn to cross-examine, Wheeler had barely sparred with her. A featherweight bout, letting her off easy, but exerting his right to recall her. Setting her up, probably, before he dropped the hammer on her. Had Wheeler learned something crucial? Another surprise, was it? to titillate the newshawks?

Chapter Two

Romaine Brook shoved the tray away. More starchy food. Enough starch, she thought, to run the laundry here in the county detention center. Almost gagging at the sight of it. She'd gained five pounds during her incarceration, was unable to shed them no matter how much she exercised.

Standing up, stretching and yawning, she went over to her bed and lay down, listless and bored.

I must stop thinking about the night when the world emptied itself of Marc. Still it all comes back, in darkness and light. A horror story that put me here.

All that pulls me through this is the feeling that I'm rehearsing a new part. Living it, learning the reality of what it's like in the slammer. That it goes on. But the script is lost. The director is on a binge somewhere. I must act it out, keep cool, look put upon, look wronged, look as innocent as the moon.

Keep my eyes as much as possible on the jury. They are the lens intently focused on me. The judge is interesting. I think of him as my producer. One of those steady faces with deep lonely eyes. Where did he get that scar over his left eyebrow? He's cute—clean, neat, masculine. Christ, how I'd like a man right now. Someone straight, someone not too dangerous.

All these gawkers at the trial and it's all I can do to ignore the press. A year ago, or so ago, after Tonight or Never *was released, I was their golden girl. The whole world, my friend. Now I'm the princess who turned into a toad.*

Pritter is the frog-lizard. Which reptile he is depends on which day. Hopping his fat ass around and tormenting me with his forked tongue. Me, his one winged fly. He's one for loathing, after what he did to my landlady. Yes, I did stay with her at times. She was like a mother. But made love with her? What a laugh!

God, I'm only twenty-three and my career is so much faded confetti now Shit is more like it. Raye Wheeler has to put me on the stand...he has to... I'll make him do it, somehow.

By the time I'm through, they'll think they're seeing Joan of Arc at the stake again. I can act. I know how.

Poor old Raye. His face is white as salt and he can hardly breathe. Goes through three hankies every morning. Drops pills like a junkie. But he was the only name lawyer who would take me. Owns me now. I'll be paying him off for the next century.

Men always get the breaks. Never seem to learn what it's like for women. Just use you. Have to play men like harps. You must, to survive. Why does it take us so long to learn that?

A rapping at the bars of her cell brought her back to where she was and wasn't—to the lumpy mattress, the orange stained sink, the cold floor, and a toilet that flushed only when it felt like it.

The matron wanted the tray back. Romaine stirred herself, swinging her legs off the bed, a movement she'd been doing for months. A routine, a habit, an autonomic response as if she were Pavlovian dog. They appeared, they spoke, she complied. *Hang on*, she told herself. *It can't get much worse. Not this week anyway.*

But then she knew it could and likely it would; and she didn't like much that look on the matron's face, either. The matron was making eyes at her, had already made several veiled suggestions. They were nuts here, depraved and totally out of their skulls.

Chapter Three

Usually thirty or so students attended these sessions. This evening two or three more had come, new faces. Rhodes never gave lectures. He simply met with those wanting to talk shop, with plenty of give-and-take. A free look around the corner for some; for others, it reinforced feelings there were better ways to draw your pay in this life than by defending criminals.

"A good trial lawyer," Rhodes was saying to the gathering, "has to think like a really competent crook. You have to plot, plan, look for angles. Hidden meanings, hidden bogeys. Otherwise, you may never know if your client is yanking your chain. It's against human nature to confess to large crimes—"

"Be a crook yourself?" interjected a young woman. She sat midway up in the small auditorium.

"I never said that."

"Even so, a lot of people think criminal lawyers are the grubs of the law."

"Do you care what they think?"

"I don't want to be thought of as a grub."

"Well, let's see about being a grub. What if it was you, your siblings, a close friend accused of a crime. *Wrongly accused*. If you knew how to defend them, wouldn't you?"

"Of course."

"Is that being a grub, as you put it?"

No reply

Rhodes shrugged. "Maybe you'd prefer to practice in another part of the law. Great. Go to it. Criminal law is there to help the accused. To carry out the meanings of the Constitution. Yes, there are and there always will be some who get off and who ought to be in prison. That's the price we pay for our freedoms. For our right to a fair trial and to be represented in that trial."

"Especially, if you're rich."

"It definitely tilts the table that way, you're right. Most things do. Money speaks and always has."

"You think we're too easy on criminals here in the United States?" another asked him.

"Outside of Russia and China," said Rhodes, "we've got the stiffest conviction rate in the world."

"I don't believe it."

"Look it up and you will believe it."

Another query: "What did you mean when you said only poets should write our laws?

"Where'd you see that?"

"In a back issue of the *Law Review*. I forget which edition."

"I was just making a point, I guess."

"But what point?"

"Laws are too hard to understand for the average person," Rhodes said. "You really can't expect people to respect what they can't understand. I think that's a failing in how we make law. An example is the tax code. That's law and no single person in America professes to understand all of it. That's terrible law on its face."

"Then what's the answer?" asked the same student.

"I don't know, but it's worth working on. The Ten Commandments are on one page, and they've stood for a couple thousand years. No changes. Everyone knows the score. Everyone understands the Gettysburg Address, too. It's simply written in the once case, and simply said in the other."

He beckoned to a heavy-faced young man, a few rows higher up. "This one's off the wall," said the student.

"Go ahead."

"You think it's unethical for lawyers to sleep with their clients?"

Guffaws crisscrossed the room. Rhodes smiled slowly. Every session produced at least one bell-ringer, part of a game the students cooked up to test his reactions.

"Up to you," he said. "But that's how you can get arrested for bravery."

"How often does all the truth come out in a criminal trial?" asked someone else.

"Rarely," he said. "No more often, I suppose, than it does in a divorce. A trial is a dispute. No one tells all he or she knows. Some of it you're not allowed to tell. A wife can't testify against her husband, for example. Or vice versa. But they know lots of things, and often it's probably the truth."

"You think that's right? That they're not allowed to testify?"

"I think that's life. And I know it's the law. It minimizes perjury."

Tensing up, he was tiring. He had skipped lunch, trying to catch up on some personal mail. And he hadn't slept well the night before, thinking about her again.

"Just a couple more, okay?" he said. "Then I gotta run." He nodded at a student who was circling one raised finger in the air.

"Why did you quit practicing and go on the bench?"

"I wonder myself sometimes."

"But you quit."

He shrugged. "Maybe I burned out."

"Don't you miss all the publicity?" he persisted. "I mean, you were the Dance-Master and everything. So don't you miss all that?"

Rhodes blushed slightly. "Not much. I'm getting more press than I want right now"—and went on quickly—"and I want to leave you with a little problem...discuss it next week...everyone ready?" Waiting, then, until he saw enough faces nod agreement.

All right," he said. "If I were to hit you with a pipe and break your arm, that's assault and battery. You press charges and the law is coming after me now. But what if I say I love you, when I don't, even though you believe me. You give me yourself. Your heart. All your sentiments and feelings. I don't even have to touch you to break your heart and soul. But you can't really press charges, can you? Why not? And what causes more damage—a broken arm for a month or two or a fractures heart for years, or even a lifetime? Think on that. What's the remedy in law? And don't be telling me it's a breach of promise."

Up next to a pillar in one of the highest rows, a fuzzy-haired man waved energetically. "On your current trial, Judge?"

"Yes?"

"You under any political pressure?"

Rhodes had seen this man before. Wearing a three-piece business suit, he seemed older than the others. Rhodes tried to get a fix on the man's face.

"Do I know you from somewhere?" he asked.

"I've been to your court."

"In what capacity?"

"I substitute once in a while for the regular reporter from the *Times.*"

Now he remembered. This reporter leaned against a pillar, staring expectantly at Rhodes. Some of the students swiveled in their seats aiming sour looks at the gatecrasher. A few hisses sounded.

"Got to take off," Rhodes said. "See you next week...be careful which professors you *don't* kiss."

Walking away from the lectern, he went through a door to the faculty room. Usually he would stay longer, answer whatever he could, loving the fun it gave him. Always trying to spot any budding talents. Someone with a fleet brain, healthy ego, an idealist, the aggressive ones and others who bore the earmarks of sonsofbitches.

CR

Gravel crunched under the old Bentley's tires as Rhodes pulled into his driveway. He pushed a dash button, watched as the light flooded out from under the lifting garage door, then drove in and quietly sat there. His hands never left the wheel while pondering the reporter's question.

Political pressure on the trial? Most certainly. Meddling? Signals coming down from Sacramento: get the actor convicted or you can forget about your Supreme Court appointment. Was that the implication?

The governor owed him. But the governor owed Julio Sterne more. A bundle more.

Rhodes had campaigned hard for the governor, making the effort when his reputation as a trial lawyer was at its peak, and when his own name was known just about everywhere in the state. With the timing nearly perfect, he'd raised buckets of money in a very tight race.

But this was Julio Sterne country, too. A very big tuna in these parts, not just the kingpin of a major film studio, but one of the top industrialists in the west. A man who had lost his only son, now wanting Romaine Brook's blood in exchange for the son's blood.

The trial was beginning to smell like a hot brake, thought Rhodes, as he lifted his foot off the pedal in the Bentley. The state didn't have an overly strong a case against the girl, and they must be aware of the heat coming down from Sacramento. Sterne behind it all?

Leaving the garage, he lingered on the flagstone walkway to catch the cooling breeze and get a glance at the starlit sky. On the higher ledges of Bel Air the soft night air drifting in from the ocean would clear his head. If only it would clear away his doubts, too.

He came to the door and fished in his pocket for the key. An overhead light cast his shadow against the white brick of the house. Suddenly the door flew open, startling him. He jerked sideways before seeing Consuelo Ramirez, his housekeeper, the front of her white apron wound nervously around her plump brown hands. Small and dark, her graying-hair seemed even grayer in the half-light, and even the brown eyes a size larger now in her round Mexican face.

"Now what you do?" she asked opaquely. "You come in quick."

He grinned. "I will come in, get a drink and have your dinner. What's the *comida* tonight?"

Consuelo stood in the foyer as Rhodes stepped in, licking her lips nervously.

"What's the matter? You hear from your ghost or something?"

"On tee-veeah few minutes ago."

"What is?"

The *abogado*, your friend. He got sick, they say, and go to hospital."

"Who?"

"The *hombre*...the one who fight for the girl...Wheela—"

"Raye Wheeler?"

"*Si*! Him, your *amigo*."

Consuelo tapped her head, her belly, and both sagging breasts, making the sign of the cross, praying up her saints to forgive Rhodes his oaths.

Throwing his briefcase on a bench, he bolted for the phone in the library. Calling the local CBS station, he identified himself to the news desk and asked which hospital had admitted Raye Wheeler.

Cedars-Sinai.

Dialing again, he was put through to a floor nurse whose rundown on Wheeler's condition was as clipped as her sharp tone. He asked for Wheeler's doctor, who was unavailable. Rhodes left a request for a callback, any hour.

He tried another call to Macklin Price, but no answer. Another one to his law clerk, to whom he gave instructions as fast as he could reel them off. Then to the Biltmore and to the bailiff there, telling him to advise the jurors of a pending delay. And no, there wasn't time now to discuss more juror complaints. Finally, a call to Pritter who seemed almost enthusiastic. Rhodes guessed it was because the prosecutor wouldn't have to make his apologies to the jury after all.

Calling around had taken up most of an hour. Consuelo brought his dinner, setting it on a small table: soup, enchiladas gummy with crabmeat and cheese, a pot of steaming coffee. He snatched a few bites, drank two coffees, and waited for the phone to ring.

He thought, thought again, and became certain the defense would ask for a delay. Days of it, possibly.

Rhodes swore.

He stifled his nerves with a cigar, pacing the room. He spent more time in the library than in any other place in the house. Some of his best memories were locked up here. Shelves halfway up one wall held leather scrapbooks with clippings of court fights he'd won, and some he'd lost, too. Macklin had kept them as dutifully as a museum archivist. His trombone, in a faux crocodile case, was propped up in the far corner.

The walls were painted in Ferrari-red lacquer that glowed softly in the subdued light of brass table lamps. A fun room, bright and cheerful, banked with deep padded couches and chairs covered in three hues of Brazilian leather.

The room meant comfort, where he could do as he damn well pleased, whenever he pleased. Read his favorite poets—Blake and 'Tennyson and Burns. Study some little known point of law; drink with his pals; dream of court battles he would never fight and of loves he would never know.

But no poetry tonight. Still mired in deep thought, he opened the French doors and went out to the terrace.

Burke? Was that the name of Wheeler's assistant? Just a rookie who looked fragile as a hummingbird. A clumsy looking boy with a ripe girlish mouth. Pritter would blow him away. If a new lawyer were called in, any delay could roll into weeks.

Waiting for the doctor's call, he prayed once and silently for Raye Wheeler, who had taught him so much about the finer art of getting juries to see only white, even when the facts seemed colored in anything but white.

လ

Audrey Sterne was saying goodbye to the last of the guests at her home in Malibu Pointe. Not the sort of guests who were socially close, but just a handful of volunteers who offered to help her with the Motion Picture Relief Fund ball. They'd come by for after-dinner coffee and cake to discuss last minute details: table layouts, flower arrangements, the souvenir program, a change in the hors d'oeuvres selections. Last minute naggers and they all had to be settled quickly.

This upcoming Friday, she would accompany her husband Julio to Masquers for dinner with the other studio chieftains. She would be ready for them, have her end of the planning as neatly tied up as a wedding gift.

Back inside, at the end of the mirrored front hallway she walked a few steps to a drawing room rarely used except for nights like this one.

Kardas was cleaning up the cups and saucers and plates. Black hair, thick, wavy and beautiful. High Magyar cheekbones and a complexion most women slaved for. Dark eyes that followed her like a dog's. He was the houseman and doubled as her husband's valet.

"Ferenc," she said, stopping at the door, "this can all wait until tomorrow."

"I do it now. Very easy."

"Suit yourself. But I'm going up."

"Perhaps later?"

"Later what?" But she knew.

Ferenc Kardas looked at her brazenly. He looked at her in a way that no woman ever mistakes, not even once. Folding his arms across his white linen butler's jacket, he said: "Later, I come to you. He's away for two more days. Why waste them? I know you like what I do."

"Julio's apt to come home without warning"—and Audrey caught herself—"besides, Ferenc, it's over. Totally over. We made a stupid mistake and we have to put it in the past."

"But you must think how happy we were for—"

"*Over.* Please get that absolutely straight, Ferenc. Will you turn out the lights, please?"

Without waiting for his answer, she left the room, her ash-blond hair swinging against her stiffening shoulders.

Ferenc Kardas stood quietly, musing to himself. So much, she didn't know. Probably nothing at all of the arrangement he had with her husband. To keep her content, pleased, served, especially when Julio Sterne was away on his everlasting business trips. So she wouldn't stray, fall into some embarrassing affair that drew attention and idle but perhaps damaging gossip.

No, she knew nothing. Still, it wouldn't do to press her, not now. Better to keep a watch on her. She'd give in, eventually.

He owed the old man. Kardas had owed him ever since Julio Sterne had found him—an ex-captain in the Hungarian army, a refugee who had crossed illegally into America from Canada. An actor with some skill but not enough of it to earn a living. Sterne had taken him on as a valet, and, after the marriage to Audrey, paid him considerably more to double as houseman. Sterne had secured a green card for him so that he was employed legitimately; two more years and he could apply for U.S. citizenship.

Though very grateful to Julio Sterne, Kardas wanted the wife again, the leggy blonde with that magazine-cover face, and a body built for the night. Many of which nights he could recall at this precise moment, as lust gathered in him. Having if off with her was all right with the old man, but not so, it seemed, with the old man's wife. Not anymore, making Kardas wonder why the cut-off, what had he done?

Nothing, so far as he knew.

Had she taken up with someone else? Julio Sterne would blow his feathers, if he learned of anything going on between his wife and some interloper. Kardas liked his work, the pay, the place, the vast blue ocean greeting him every morning. Besides, Malibu gave him access to people with expensive habits and the money to pay for them.

He didn't care to be aced out of any of it. He still awaited his big score; and since that no-account kid, Marc had gone down, no real scoring opportunities seemed near at hand. He couldn't afford the risk of dealing by himself. He had needed the cover, a sucker like a kid from a rich family. But a sucker able to access clout; his old man's clout. The kid accessed the drugs, Kardas did the Malibu Pointe peddling.

And then her; Audrey Sterne could make his life too chancy, too uncomfortable. She could, if she chose, run him off. How to curry her favor again? Something had to be done. Soon, too, before his nerves whittled him into pieces and he did something foolish.

And this fucking murder trial wasn't helping any. Where was that awkward business headed? The sheriff wanted yet another interview. Why?

Trouble with the law, and he'd be kissing his green card goodbye, also the best sex he'd ever known, and, as for Sterne himself—a mighty protector if ever things became really complicated.

Chapter Four

Arriving at Cedars-Sinai, Rhodes scurried through a maze of corridors, had a brief visit with the doctor, then was escorted by a nurse to Raye Wheeler's room. He stayed clear of hospitals. After spending months in two of them in Germany and Texas, any reminder of those days still made his spine wiggle. He'd not have done this for most colleagues from the bar. But Ray Wheeler was like family, a prince, someone very special and easy to rate, both as a friend and as one of the best legal minds Rhodes had ever known.

Bending closer, he could see webs upon webs of tiny lines in Raye Wheeler's sunken face, as if a hairnet had been pressed into the grayish skin.

"Raye," he was saying, "you won't be on the cover of *Sports Illustrated* next week, but we'll have you out of here before you know it."

A quivering smile from Wheeler, who could still make a good guess at how he looked. Like a mummy and feeling too weak to banter now.

"They only gave me a few minutes, Raye. Anything I can do for you? Look in on your house, anything like that?"

"Taken care of…" murmured Wheeler. One bony hand opened its fingers, in a gesture perhaps of resignation. The hand's veins stood out, greenish, like a larger one pulsing near his ear "No good at all. Me like this, with everything up in the air." Wheeler began to wheeze, his teeth clicking as his head rose a few inches.

"Easy now. Let me do the talking," Rhodes said. "That's partly why I'm here, Raye. Can't hold the trial up much longer, as long as your client is represented in court. They say your colleague Tommy Burke is going to stand in for you. Is that the way you want it?"

Wheeler nodded.

"Looks to me like he's still got diaper rash. Pritter'll walk him over the edge. I'm concerned about Miss Brook."

"S'alright. Has to start somewhere, doesn't he? You did, I did."

"You're not thinking of calling in someone else?"

From the back of Wheeler's mouth came a sound like two drumsticks clacking together, then, "No mon-*mon-ey*. I took the case for a song."

Rhodes sat back. "Well, I didn't know. Do what I can to help, but I have to keep things from drifting."

Wheeler's eyes glinted, sharp as two needles. "Can you get Fahey to help us?"

"Fahey? Why Fahey?"

"S'good, that's why. I need that berserker for a few days. He already begged off once."

"You want more investigating done? Late in the day for that, I'd think."

Wheeler winced as he tried shaking his head. "Loose ends. Couldn't get to them all and look where I am now."

"Sure, I can try talking to Fahey, or send him to see Burke. But that's all I can do."

"Need him..."

"Okay, I'll ask. Anything I should know about?"

She's adopted. Find her family. Fahey's good at—"

"For money help? For that?"

Wheeler nodded weakly again. "Unless you can get us a police investigation."

"I can't, Raye. Your client doesn't qualify. You know that...and besides no one else is charged with anything. The police wouldn't touch it, and I can't make them."

"She's broke."

"Sorry, but no go. Not for simply finding a family."

Wheeler's head fell away and his chest seemed to flatten. His head lifted off the pillow once more, as he sucked air before expelling a sob. Pink foam oozed from his mouth.

Rhodes reached swiftly up to a cord dangling at the head of the bed. He pressed the button for the nurse three times. To the side, on a cabinet, he saw a kidney-shaped steel dish full of gauze pads. Taking one, he patted away the stringy drool on Wheeler's chin.

"Relax now and don't talk, Raye. Everything'll be fine. Be up in no time."

Looks like a ghost, Rhodes thought, held together only by loose wires. A battered fighter struggling for to go another round, yet unable to answer the bell. Wheeler's hands shook, a shoulder twitched, and then, with a moan, he passed out.

The nurse came in. "You rang?" she asked.

"He's been coughing up—"

"It's past time for you to leave." Striding to the bed, she straightened the covers and smoothed back a scarf of white hair from Wheeler's forehead.

"How can I find out how he's getting on? Rhodes asked. "The doctors here are almost unreachable."

"Call the desk on this floor," the nurse replied tartly, without shifting her intent look from Wheeler.

Rhodes leaned over and opened a briefcase. He pulled out a pint of Jack Daniel's Black, walked over and placed it on a windowsill. The nurse looked up, a sour frown scrunching her face, her lips disappearing instantly. Hand on hip, ice in her eyes, waiting for him to leave.

"Guests, you know," Rhodes said haplessly.

"He can't have anything like that." She pulled on the chromed arm of an oxygen tent, draping the plastic hood over Wheeler's pale face.

"He'll like knowing it's here, believe me."

"I'd like knowing you're out the door this very minute," she snapped.

"Sure, on my way. He was head of the varsity, you know. Take the best care of—"

"We always do our best." In an annoyed tone.

Rhodes walked slowly to the elevator, pausing to look at several framed prints on the pastel walls. One was a Picasso copy, another a Cyrik, further down a Matisse. The place could pass for a good hotel, was famous, had the best and hired the best, and took care of half the Hollywood clan.

And none of them more colorful than Raye Wheeler in his time. There weren't half a dozen lawyers alive who could quarry rock alongside the man.

Grim lipped, Rhodes waited for the elevator, certain that Wheeler would never go into the pit again. The pressure would be too great. He'd never withstand it in his condition.

Rhodes remembered a time when he had been just a beginner trying to unravel the mysteries of the courts: who the stricter judges were; where the real talent was in the DA's office; how to butter up the court clerks who seemed to run his whole world of law. He had nearly starved while learning his way around. Who needed a rookie to solve their legal problems anyway?

No one, that's who. And he thought again about the fledgling Burke, who'd be carrying the load now, fumbling, screwing up the proceedings and the record that accounted for them.

And then remembering how one day in his own career the widow of a police officer had asked him to defend her daughter on an embezzlement charge. Against the odds, he had won.

He had caught Raye Wheeler's benevolent eye, and Wheeler threw a few small cases his way. More wins. Then the older lawyer had asked him to help at fifty bucks an hour in some really important cases, carefully watching him. Cuffing him with sharp words when mistakes were made, but showing him the craft: how to read a jury, how *not* to cross-examine, how to learn a judge and play to the judge's style of thinking. How to talk with soft nails in your words. Where and when to set traps for untruthful witnesses.

Rhodes reached the street. His eyes stung, thinking about Wheeler and his generosity. He wanted to offer his hand to an old friend. Both hands if he could. But this time other kinds of hands were needed. He would try to persuade Fahey to take a look around, do it for Wheeler, do it for the sake of old times. This trial was getting so much attention that Rhodes was ready to bend over backward. He had to.

He had thrown his last big trial out of court. And the press had bared their fangs, chewing him to shreds.

Child molesters, a ring of Catholic priests, the worst dregs, but he'd rejected the case because the police had come by their evidence illegally. Stolen it almost. Rhodes could still hear the public outcry—mothers had called, fathers too, railing and cursing at him. The police were praised, naturally. He had done what he had done because it was the right thing; the wrong thing ethically, perhaps, but the right thing legally. No regrets there, yet at times the press still chewed on him.

He needed a good, tight, fair trial, and he'd like to take his leave here, go up to the Supreme Court knowing he'd done his best. He'd already locked up the jury and gagged the lawyers so they wouldn't try their case in the news media.

How much further could he go? Wisely go?

Events during the trial touched on the bizarre. Peripherally, very peripherally, it had reconnected him to an old and lost love. It had drawn an uncommon amount of media play. It had come to his docket on the advent of his Supreme Court nomination and just as he'd been about to resign from the Criminal Court. The senior judges, coping with a temporary shortage of adjudicators, had begged him to stay on, preside; believing it as his duty, and it was, so he acquiesced.

He could do many things as a judge, especially in a murder trial, as long as he kept within tolerable bounds. But getting Fahey to run an investigation, *gratis*? Why should Fahey do that? Or anyone? Nothing wrong, Rhodes supposed, in asking an old friend who was also a pal of Raye Wheeler's.

At least, a dinner with Alonzo Fahey was always good for a laugh——a true tenant of Oz, or so thought his wife who knew her husband stem to stern.

And Rhodes needed a laugh, ignorant that it would be his last one for a long time.

෨

At the Jonathan Club in downtown Los Angeles, Lloyd Pritter helped himself to his third smoked trout. He had already put away a large fruit salad and a round of sourdough bread spread thickly with butter. After lunch, he planned to get a haircut, pay a visit to his tailor, and then, if there was time, negotiate a mortgage for a condominium he intended buying.

He was about to loosen his belt buckle when his waiter hurried over to advise him of a phone call awaiting him in one of the cubicles down the hall. Pritter told the waiter not to clear the table, and charged off. It was his boss, the Attorney General, the state government's highest-ranking lawyer.

"Going to be a long holdup over this Wheeler thing?" Pritter was asked.

"A few days, I'd guess."

"How's it looking?"

"No different than last week. The fish is tight on the hook," replied Pritter, thinking of the trout awaiting his return to the table.

"Who's going take over for Wheeler?"

"Some junior who's been helping him. Fellow named Burke. No one ever heard of him before."

"Well, okay then. Keep your foot on it."

"Don't worry, we've got it wrapped with ribbons. I figure her for thirty years at least."

"Been in touch with Sterne lately?"

"Some. Mostly his lawyers over at Oldes and Farnham."

"And their view is?"

"Same as ours. It's going our way."

"There's real interest up here, as you know."

Pritter became petulant. "Yes indeed, been hearing about *that* for months now."

"Hold your horses, Lloyd. I work for the same man as you. When I get a call, I make a call."

Hanging up, the Attorney General called the governor's assistant, filled him in, and then offered a suggestion: "Drop a little weight on Rhodes's head," he said. "Why not goose him along and threaten to cancel his nomination?"

Chapter Five

*T*ommy Burke came by this morning. They'll delay my trial at least a week so I can rot in here some more. Tommy is sweet. Thin as a vanilla bean, pink as a baby's butt. He stuttered when he asked if I would allow him to take over my defense—now that dear old Raye is incapacitated.

There's no more money to hire a new gladiator. Made that clear. So it's all Tommy now and God help me.

He brought some newspapers and the Hollywood trades. So far, I've counted fifty-nine articles on the trial in the Los Angeles papers alone. Made Time magazine three times and twice in Newsweek. Mostly sly innuendo.

That letter. Tommy is worried about it. God, how I wish I hadn't lost my head and sent it to Marc, that prince of all bastards. Nasty as I could write one, and Pritter waved it in front of the courtroom like it was my white flag of surrender.

Raye Wheeler told me before the trial began that it's always a contest for truth. I tried not to laugh. No one can stand the sound of truth for very long. Hollywood truth is the biggest illusion since the Resurrection or something. Celluloid truth. Takes one lit match to make it disappear.

The truth about the Bastard will never be known. Too slimy. They'll never get it out of me. If I tried, they'd twist me into a liar, and send me up for sure. I have no real proof anyway.

Pritter—that Eel—has it all screwy. I never knew about those disgusting photos. But I know where they were taken and why. Pritter thinks I was threatening Marc Sterne over them. And that I trashed him out of revenge.

But the letter was only to get my money back. Forty-eight thousand I loaned him like an idiot from my last payment for Tonight or Never. And then the other money for a screenplay idea that Parthenon bought from us. My idea, the whole thing. Bastard goes and puts his name on it. Collects the hundred-thousand in option money we were supposed to split.

I got taken. But who can I tell that to. They'd for sure think I had a motive to get him. Me versus the Sternes, what a joke.

Tommy Burke doesn't know what I've got cooked up on my abortion angle. That'll take care of those awful photos. I've been rehearsing and rehearsing it, getting it down pat. And practicing my voice, which I do when no one's within hearing.

I can use any of four voices. I like the one of the wronged woman, best of all. Complete with the sniffles.

Chapter Six

Unrelenting rain rinsed Los Angeles all the next day, the sky guzzly, unable to wring itself dry. Streets flooding to the curb tops, the traffic crawling along like armies of wounded caterpillars.

Rhodes drove impatiently. Spotting an opening, be ripped the wheel over, and sped his chocolate colored Bentley up an off ramp. The going was somewhat easier on the side streets. Half an hour later he had slugged his way across Sunset Boulevard, out beyond Brentwood, then finally to Lost Canyon Road heading up toward Masquers.

Leaving the keys with the doorman, he took the steps two at a time until he reached the double oak doors of the club.

Just past seven in the evening.

Behind a front desk sat Ginty Jellicoe, working his way through a racing form. A friendly man, once ranked third in the light-heavyweight division, he showed the wear and tear of his years in the ring. His battered face was missing half of one eyebrow, and the left ear was folded into a knob, the target for too many right hooks. Two of his front teeth were whiter than the others. He had been at Masquers for ten years, keeping the riffraff out, and he ran a betting book on the side. Ginty was also the man to see for a ride home, if you'd lingered too long at the bar.

Marking his place with a pencil, he rose to greet Rhodes. "You been a stranger, Judge. Wet out there, eh?" He flicked a few drops off Rhodes's shoulder.

"Like someone pushed the whole Pacific our way. Your horse come in today?"

"Things are swell," evaded Ginty Jellicoe with a grin that threw his twice-broken jaw to one side. "There's an underpriced filly in the fourth tomorrow at Hollywood Park. Looks real nice on form. Speed. Like some of her action?"

"Me? I'd only bet on your side of the sheet, Ginty."

"Judge, I just give with a little advice here and there. Customer service is all."

"It's okay by me, Ginty. I never issue warrants when it rains."

They laughed.

"Six-to-one, and that girl'll go wire-to-wire. Got real speed there," Ginty urged.

Never yet had he induced Rhodes into a bet. Talking to him openly about the ponies gave the impression they did some wagering together. Ginty made certain the word got around, and, though untrue, it was good for business. Rhodes let him get away with it because Ginty did him small favors and never asked questions.

"Tell you what, Ginty. I'll give you six-to-one the filly doesn't make it out of the gate first... how's that?'

Ginty lifted his scarred eyebrows. "That ain't good for anyone's reputation, Judge. You gotta know that."

Laughing again, Rhodes asked, "Fritzi around?"

"In her office. Will I ring in for you?" Ginty reached for the desk phone.

"No, no, don't bother her. I'll be at the bar."

"She comes out, I'll give her the word first thing."

"Good luck on your filly."

"You need luck with fillies, especially them that wear skirts." Ginty winked with the eye having the half-gone eyebrow.

Across the red-carpeted lobby, past the coat checkroom, Rhodes stopped at the cigar counter. He asked for a few Honduran Panatella 6's. To the counter's side a screen flashed stock market prices and banner news. Another one showed photo clips and out-takes of current film productions underway. The content was fed by private wire from various studios. It was cheap publicity. Masquers was a hangout for Hollywood big-shots—the top agents, producers, actors and directors—and it was never too early to start the buzz on film releases soon to appear in theaters across America.

Suddenly, she was there, as if risen like a vapor: Audrey Sterne stood just inside the curve of the long bar. Moving a step, he could see Julio Sterne too; a mingling of studio moguls—the top-level *honchos* of Twentieth-Century, Paramount, MGM. Rhodes supposed the women standing around were their wives.

Wishing he had not seen her, but he kept looking right at her as if she were an optical magnet. Inside himself, he felt a strong movement he could not identify.

Polite waves a few times at a distance were all they had managed since she had returned to California from England. But then they traveled in very different lanes. She had lived in London for years, married to some earl or lord until a messy divorce had dropped its axe. Twin boys. He remembered reading about them in the papers, when she had married Julio Sterne several years ago.

Polite waves, that is, until the day she had appeared in his court. Merely some very polite words then, as she took the stand and stopped his heart, all in a single flashing moment. A helpless sensation. And he knew he ought to know better and behave better—a lot better. But if you couldn't conquer it, then you simply accepted it. It either burned itself out, or it didn't. And it hadn't, not even after twenty-odd years.

The sultry tint of a Damascus rose under her skin, swept back ash-blond hair falling to her shoulders, Arabesque lips. The eyes glinting gray and green; and sparkling so you wondered if they were hooked up to a private battery. A thirty-year-old face on a forty-three-old neck and still very nice scenery from the feet all the way up. He knew women who would trade teeth to look like Audrey Sterne for only one night.

She had left the bar and come to where he was standing. "Cliff," she said. "Well, how nice to see you. Here you are…"

"You look lovely, Audrey."

"Thanks, really."

"Having dinner?"

"Beastly night to be out," she said. "Yes, it's a get-together for the Motion Picture Relief Fund. Julio is chairman this year."

"Busy man, I hear."

Rhodes thought about his recent dust-up with the governor's assistant. How Sterne, he believed, was busy backstage, putting heat on the trial. Or was he?

"I'd invite you for a drink with us," said Audrey, "but I suppose that wouldn't look right, would it?"

"No, I don't think so." Rhodes smiled. "But thanks anyway."

Still looking at her, remembering things now long past between them, and he nearly failed to see her husband approaching.

Audrey had braved it out, coming up to him, wanting terribly to find out if she were nervy enough. She had overcome her anxiety of encountering him, and was proud of herself.

"We're going in to dinner now," said Julio Sterne coming up, his words more like an order than a suggestion they join their party.

"Yes, of course," Audrey spoke softly. "Julio, you know Cliff Rhodes, I'm sure," Her fingers fluttered nervously to her throat. A diamond, big enough to skate on shone brightly on one finger.

"'We've met once or twice before, haven't we?' said Sterne tersely. He gave Rhodes a tight smile, a smile made by a plastic surgeon.

Rhodes nodded. "Mr. Sterne, I'm terribly sorry about your son. I've never had an opportunity to say so."

"No one is sorrier than me."

"Naturally," said Rhodes, distinctly uncomfortable now.

Sterne slid his hand under Audrey's elbow, guiding her away. Tall, much older, but ramrod straight, he had an aquiline nose centered on a blade-like, tight-skinned face. A full head of white hair streaked its wings over his ears. Supposedly, a tough operator and he looked it. He certainly seemed to know how to keep a tow- rope on his wife.

Rhodes watched as Audrey disappeared, still struck at how she could stir feelings in him. Immediate feelings, as if he'd been hammered by an unexpected blow, dazing his senses. He headed for the bar.

Shaped like an inverted bow, the bar had an overhead bridge of stained glass that ran its full length, and under the bridge were racks of upside-down snifter glasses, the only type used at Masquers. At the bar's rear, beveled mirrors were separated by six hand-carved figurines of satyrs and maidens. A quick look into those mirrors and you saw double the number of people actually there; triple if you hung around long enough to have yourself a real outing.

Two old-timers, black men wearing red waistcoats and black bow ties, made the drinks. They had been there as long as Rhodes could remember, and were one of Masquers' many traditions. He liked it here, the very good bar, the waiters, the rhythms of the place, the superb music. The atmosphere appealed to women and men.

Rhodes asked for a double José Cuervo Gold, no ice, from a nearby waiter. The drink was in his hand within a minute. Wonderful service—you paid for it—but it was the best anywhere. He stopped to say hello to some people he knew, and then went over to the baby grand, where he sometimes swapped one-liners with Sweetpear Porter, a musician out of Memphis with the bluest of blood in his musical veins.

And watched, fascinated, as Sweetpear's fingers moved like fast mice up and down the keyboard. Beautiful Gershwin stuff. Once in a while, they played together for fun but Rhodes never kidded himself. Sweetpear was in another class, a natural, and, like the great Errol Garner, did his magic by ear alone.

Rhodes ran some of the drink into the back of his throat. He was partial to José Cuervo Gold, whenever his drinking hour arrived. Tonic for his banging nerves when they banged, and a couple of deep conversations with old José usually had a nice effect. When turning forty, he had upped his daily cigar ration to two and lowered the Cuervo intake to no more than four ounces. Which usually meant one, or at most two, high-octane drinks from sundown to sundown.

Tonight would be an exception: Fahey was soon to arrive; Fahey, an ex-police officer, a five star dreamer, and an eminent chaser of lost or stolen art. Good at it, too. He charged one-percent of the appraised value on anything recovered, but if he didn't much like the client, he had no compunction about running it up to five-percent, even higher if you were in the armaments game. He had once charged the CEO of Lockheed-Marietta twenty-percent on a burgled Monet, earning himself a raging roar and threats of a lawsuit. Worried about publicity, Fahey had slashed the fee in half, hired a publicist, and made sure that all of Los Angeles knew he'd given his reduced fee to the Girl Scouts. A wholly unpredictable type, he was great fun to be with, though with a dangerous side to him, if in the mood.

He had taken a seat by the fireplace, listening to Sweetpear, then heard Fritzi's laugh rolling across the room. Lips brushed his ear as he inhaled an exotic waft of her perfume.

He stood up, she sat down.

"So where've you been for the past century?"

"Waiting here for my love, and to see if you smell as good as you look, and you do."

"I mean for the entire last week, lug."

"You're always so beautiful when you're upset."

"I could get a little steamed, you know."

"Been a very busy time, Fritzi."

"You're not forgiven. You look tired, and I've missed hell out of you, Cliff."

Rhodes sat again. His hand was on her knee, and his eyes never swerved from hers. She smiled finally, but be knew she'd be rubbing more scolding into him for a while.

"Seen Raye?" she asked. "How is he?"

"The doc says the emphysema is bad, and there're other pulmonary complications. A mild stroke maybe."

"Oh God, really? You know what?" Fritzi's face lit up. "I'll send his dinners over while he's there. Be a lot better than that hospital fodder."

"Better call first. I think they've got him on the tubes."

"I'll find out. What happens for you now?'

"Monkey-wrenched again. Have to delay the trial for a few days. We have to keep going. Got a locked-up jury who's screaming for one thing."

"That poor girl too," Fritzi said. "She must be ready to smash down the walls. It's been months now, hasn't it? I think anyone would go crazy in all that time. I would anyway. Be a wreck by know."

"About eight or nine months," Rhodes said, hoisting his drink. He looked up briefly over the fireplace to a Frank Tenney Johnson painting of a lone cowboy night-hawking his herd on some windswept prairie. A painting he greatly admired, reminding him of his youth in Montana, where his father had been the ramrod on a big spread near Livingston.

"You think she did it? I don't believe it somehow."

"I can't talk about that, love."

"I feel sorry for her anyway. Are you going to break training and come over tonight?" asked Fritzi pointedly.

"Soon as dinner with Alonzo is over, I'm there. And you're shameless," he said, reaching for her hand again.

"Well, I'm liberated now, along with the rest of the girls. I can ask for what I want. It's legal now, Mr. Prude."

"You care to shout that around in here? Maybe write it on the wall a few times."

"Owner's privilege. You can say anything you want in your own joint, can't you?" She smiled, having her fun.

Fritzi's gaze swept over the bar. Her eyes became intent and far off. She looked back at Cliff again, her mouth taut, her cheeks flaring.

A raucous shout rang across the room; loud enough to startle a waiter, who was pushing a silver cart laden with smoked salmon by their table.

"Look at her, will you," Fritzi said in a low voice.

"By the bar?"

"The one getting fresh with Robert De Niro. Six months behind on her bill...the nerve of some people." Her eyes narrowing again.

A tall redhead wearing a safari jacket with matching pants had her arms looped around the actor. A wide-brimmed olive-hued hat with a leopard band partly shadowed her tan face.

"Looks like she's having fun anyway," said Rhodes.

"On my nickel, too. I'm going to toss her the hell out of here."

"Easy, sweetheart. Maybe she went to Kenya and just forgot."

Fritzi was already off her chair, and she blew him a kiss as she moved away. She possessed what Rhodes liked to think of as a mellow figure: a well-slung front, haunchy at the hips, flat bellied, and lovely long legs. She moved well. And midnight dark hair always shone like stilled night water.

Those were only her assets for show. The interior qualities, the ones you had to learn about, gave her a glow and a natural pulling power that touched almost everyone who knew her. A woman in balance, he thought, very much in tune with her world.

Other women, as far as Rhodes could tell, rarely seemed threatened by Fritzi. They liked her, as men did, and the few times he had noticed any bitchery directed her way; she either ignored it or foiled it with her easy laugh.

Theirs was an affair that had traveled safely for several years now. Arguments? Awkward moments? Plenty of both, but they had never sloped off the way so many affairs do. At times, he wondered why. His work was necessarily of the day, hers of the night. As a judge, he had to run his life with a modicum of restraint, at least publicly, while Fritzi adored the romp of an active social calendar. Her nature begged for attention; his, however, needed more privacy, more air, the freedom to thrive by himself, like the cowboy up there in Johnson's painting.

Rhodes looked at the drinking crowd by the bar, and then across the room spotted Alonzo Fahey. Rhodes got up, glad to park his thoughts elsewhere, and went over to intercept him.

Threading his way through the tables, Fahey waved openly at everyone he had never met or seen before, pausing to talk with two women he knew well. Very well, apparently. One grabbed his arm, trying to tug him into an empty chair.

Fahey had his ways: one was that angled, guilty grin he often wore, hinting he had just been somewhere he didn't belong. If you were to ask him his birthplace, he was liable to admit to anything. But likely, from the way he used vowels, it was up near Galway in the land of the green, and the bridge fairies who only danced on moon-splashed nights.

Fascinating to watch in action and Rhodes would lay money Fahey could take any woman here, waltz her outside into the rain, and somehow persuade her the wet drops dribbling down her cheeks were the lost tears of angels.

Lean and deceptively strong, Fahey had earned a shattered elbow one night when chasing a thief in Beverly Hills. The man had suddenly swung around, pulled a gun, and almost put some daylight through Fahey who had plowed on, knocking the gunman over and breaking his neck. Cited for valor by the police chief, Fahey was given a medal, but that all happened before his other troubles with the Police Commission.

"Boyo, h'lo there. A bit late, we are. Traffic end by fucking end all the way out Sunset. Had a drink for me, have you?" said Alonzo Fahey coming up, flashing a smile bright as a new penny.

"One with Fritzi," replied Rhodes.

They shook hands.

"God, will you look at all the gash in here tonight," said Fahey. A low whistle sung through his teeth.

"You're married. Off limits."

"No one's that married, Rhodes-ey boy, no one. It's an institutional mirage, eh?"

"C'mon I'll buy you some of that sewage you drink."

"I mean Jesus," said Fahey, as if hard of hearing, "all we'd have to do is kick a few husbands out to the alley, and there's enough here to last us till Easter."

Fahey stood there, absorbing the view. Women adored him, fell like cut timber for his darkly handsome Irish looks, and the lyrics he spun so shamelessly. "Can't believe a word of him," they would say, begging for more of the same. He had a gift for giving women a sense of place. Put them

47

on a very high billboard, and, like kittens, they lapped up the warm milk of his flattery. When Fahey was off the scene for a time—Fritzi had once told Rhodes—some of the women who frequented Masquers became noticeably uneasy. Started talking a little too loud and fretting about. They missed their confidant who knew more of their secrets than did their hairdressers. He was good for business, and Fritzi let him go on the tab for three months before asking for a little relief.

"C'mon, let's go," Rhodes urged, sensing Fahey was on the roam tonight.

"See the one in uniform. The one with big melons there?"

"Yep, I see."

It was the playgirl in the safari rig; she was back on station at the end of the bar.

"I could go stamp her parking ticket while you're slopping yourself at dinner."

"You know who she is?"

"I don't, but I'm going to find out."

Fahey started his move. Rhodes grabbed a handful of his sleeve, telling the detective, "She's trouble. She cruises around here and forgets to pay her bill. One of those."

"Looks to me like she needs a friend. A face like that ought to be on a holy card."

"I've some business to go over, Alonzo. That's why we're here."

"Jesus, relax. A true traitor you were to marry me off so young."

"You had it coming, too."

Fahey rocked back and forth on his heels. A woman down the bar, next to the one wearing the safari rig, kept eyeing him. He smiled back, winking, before his fingers suddenly locked into fists. "I'm starved. I could take a whole cow down, honest I could," he side-mouthed to Rhodes. "Let's fr'chissakes get our bibs on."

In the main dining room a maître d' greeted Rhodes politely, and tried without success to hide his dismay at Fahey's outlandish garb. Tonight the detective *nonpareil*—Fahey's description of himself—was gussied up in a gray lodencloth jacket with a green velvet collar, yellow corduroy slacks, a white ruffled shirt, and a red bolo tie. Rhodes was so used to the wild combinations he hardly noticed them anymore. The maître d' showed them to a small private room, at the center of which was a small round mahogany dining table, along with a private wet bar off to one side. Softly lit, and with more western art hanging on the walls, the room boasted a notable chandelier made from the racks of two caribous.

Most of the hour passed with eating and catching up. Rhodes asked about Fahey's wife, Wanda, then news of the darker side of the art market, Fahey's specialty. He learned little of Wanda but heard reams s about Fahey's theory that all the hot art worth real money was ending up in the Vatican's vaults or private Arabian collections. Business was soft; all the good second-story pros were either lying low, waiting for the next big score, or had already been put away in the slammer. "You judges ought to let up a little. Ought to let some of the boys out for some air, Cliff. Better for business. I'll be starving this year. And you know we've some friends who're buffed-off that we canceled out on the poker tonight," complained Fahey, adding this notation in a fresh swerve of thought.

"Couldn't be helped." Rhodes leaned across the table and poured more Cabernet in Fahey's outstretched goblet. "I know another friend who could use your help, if you can spare the time. It has to do with the Brook trial."

"Oh, that ditty? Raye Wheeler already asked me once and—"

"I know. But he's extremely ill and he's asking for your help again. He can't ask, so I am asking."

"Been away from that line of country for a while, laddie."

"You did plenty of it, when we were together."

"Other years and other star movements, my friend."

The pupils of Fahey's eyes began to glint, so Rhodes went ahead with, "Couldn't you give them a few days?"

"What's it to you?"

Rhodes shrugged. 'It's a murder-one trial, as I'm sure you must know. Nothing beats holding a fair one."

"Something specific, is there? A little hint or two, perhaps, for old friend Fahey?"

"Raye's trying to find out who Brook's natural parents are. If they're alive and so forth? Are they in California? I went in to see how Raye was getting along, and that's when he asked me to ask you. I could hardly refuse him. He's on the ropes, Alonzo."

Ignoring the wine Rhodes had poured, Fahey chugged on a tumbler half-full of Bushmills whiskey. The Saint's water, he called it. A steady drinker, Fahey managed to keep an unending flow of the stuff near to hand.

"You want me to poke around for you. That it? All of it?"

"No, not for me," Rhodes said. "I'd like you to think about going to see a young lawyer, name of Burke. He's in Raye Wheeler's office."

"They're in the old corner are they? Gasping?"

Rhodes nodded. "Don't you read the papers?"

"Not if I can help it. Wanda does. A regular dustpan for news, she is...last time Raye called, they couldn't pay anything. All on the come-line," said Fahey.

"They're short on money, I was told. Expensive, this kind of a trial. One reason why they'd like to find her biological parents."

"What've they really got on that girl?"

With his thumb moving from one finger to the next Rhodes ticked off the evidence against Romaine Brook. "A tantrum letter that doesn't sound so good if you read it in a certain way. Some lurid photos that may or may not be relevant. Definitely present on the night Marc Sterne was killed; two gate-guards had confirmed it. The most contentious evidence is that hypodermic syringe. No fingerprints were found on it, according to the forensics, and that one is hard to figure when you think about it. Mostly, it boils down to circumstantial evidence. That's about where we are..."

Fahey pondered a moment, his eyes wandering to the far end of the room. Screwed into a door there was a brass plaque with black letters on it read: FOR BOYS ONLY. A momento from Fritzi, who had personally fixed up the next room for the stag poker games held there every other Thursday night.

"Not so bad a situation for her?" he said, eyeing Rhodes again.

"Getting political, though. Someone's worried about something."

"The Sterne family, you mean?"

"Maybe."

"Was this...a what...a lover's spat ending with that kid juicing himself?"

"I don't know. We haven't heard her side of it yet. And may never. Depends on whether she testifies or not."

"Blackmail? Reverse blackmail? The photos?"

"Possibly."

"Or she didn't do it at all. Snow White with her ass caught in in a sling."

"I really don't know," Rhodes answered. "We'll see, or I hope we'll see."

"So why do you care?" asked Fahey in a cynical tone.

"Of course, I care." Rhodes stiffened. "This thing is a damn potboiler. She deserves a square shake, at least. If she loses, it'll go up on appeal, and I don't especially want to get reversed on any errors I made or might make. I'd like to get the trial back on its wheels again, and soon, and over with even sooner."

"And you don't want to be up there on that Supreme Court, and find out you were reversed on appeal?"

Rhodes admitted, "Who would?"

"You shouldn't be asking me to do this."

"I shouldn't but I am, Alonzo. Raye Wheeler got me started in the law and he helped you when the police commissioners were about to hang your tail for you. He needs your help and, frankly, so do I. I've enough latitude to ask you. I can make requests, I can even appoint a public defender if come to that."

"You think I'm the Red Cross, do you? I've got bread to put on the table, boyo. Fees, I need my green fees. Not the golf kind, the paper kind. Green, crisp, starting with the number one-hundred. Twenty of those'll do as a retainer. "

"Do a pro bono."

"Pro my ass. That's my pro. Besides, I told wifey we'd go down to Cabo San Lucas for a week of the marlin," said Fahey. "Getting cranky again she is, I'll tell you that for free."

"Delay it, can you?"

"We've got a good price on a boat. Have to tickle her up. She's a fisher, you know?"

"Wanda'll do the right thing."

"Be the end of me, that girl. Be the end of us all, if we don't keep a leash on her…so, you want a favor, do you?"

"Of sorts, yes."

"At no pay?"

"Possibly not. But it's only a day or two, Alonzo."

A temperate sigh before Fahey said, "Let you know tomorrow, that be good enough?"

Rhodes saw a mixture of pity and disdain now in Fahey's razor-blue eyes. Everything was there of the man, and yet nothing. The bloodhound in him, the quixotic nature, his big exuberant heart, the remorse at what he saw of this god-forgotten world. Yet a man loyal to his lowest bone, always watching for you and that side of yourself you never could see.

"Like another?" Rhodes raised his glass.

"Had my barrel for tonight." Fahey looked pensive. "But I've got the hell of an idea for you to hear."

"I'm listening," Rhodes said, getting up, heading for the small bar on the other side of the dining table. Splashing some Cuervo into a tumbler, he studied a painting of an Arabian ebony-haired nude reclining on a pile of tasseled burgundy rugs. He hadn't seen this one before. One of Fritzi's latest touches, he guessed. Fetching, too.

"You listening, are you?"

"I am, Alonzo. Both ears."

"Then look at me."

"In a minute." Still taking in the nude. "Go ahead."

Rhodes made a shrewd idea as to what was coming. An old refrain by now, and he tuned out slightly, while viewing the nude's turban and its single gleaming ruby. Slave bracelets adorned the nude's ankles and wrists. A baby ocelot nestled against one breast, its tiny pink tongue licking close to the nipple.

"Why do you need to go up there?" Fahey was asking. "I mean, Christ, Sacramento is a bean pot. Have they an airport yet? We could do it again, Cliff. You'll go straight to your death in one of those black robes. That's why they're black. For sinners and those fucking priests who're the worst sinners of all."

"For those priests in *your* church, remember."

"Who are the worst! Six of them just got caught for keeping a young girl. Barely fourteen, the kid is, and they started in on her."

"Don't go into it. I'm still recovering from the last bunch, the ones I had to let off. Sacramento, you were asking why there? I want to try it up there

for a while, Alonzo," Rhodes said patiently. "It's the top rung in my business. They rarely appoint criminal lawyers."

"Do what you were born for." Fahey's voice was much closer now. "Throwing it all away, why the hell ever for?"

"You know how many lawyers with a reputation like mine ever made it up to the Supreme Court?"

"Nor do I give a swift shit."

52

"Not one. That's how many."

"You looking for Christmas in July again? Trying to put two suns in the sky when only one fits."

Sighing, Rhodes sipped his drink, tired of explaining himself, tired of people on his back, even his friend Fahey. "Jesus, Alonzo, let up will you?"

"Don't *Jesus* me. I get enough of that on Sundays when Wanda drags me to her pew. Quit running is what I say."

"What's there to run from?" Rhodes still stared at the painting.

"Yourself."

Fahey now stood very close, too close, with his breath warming Rhodes's cheek.

"I'm not fast enough to run from myself," said Rhodes, turning away from Fahey. "Let's go home."

"You said after a couple of years we'd be back together."

"I know. But I've got some ideas I want to try out, and the high court is the place to go."

"Cat crap. You're afraid to fight again. Pillar of Jello is what you—"

"Alonzo. I'm me. And all I want for me is to be the best I can. Now what in hell is the matter with that?"

"You were already the best."

"Let's adios."

Fahey stalled. Inspired by a crasher of an idea, he wanted to float it by Rhodes. It had popped right out of the side of his brain in the shower one morning, delighting him. He plunged ahead, as if what they'd just been discussing was a lost fragment of history.

"And there's the new regiment to provision," he said out of nowhere. "Takes time to organize one. Be busier than ever with the logistics."

"A regiment?"

"For you and me, we can have it."

"You don't say." Rhodes knew what was coming now—a newly harvested figment of the man's bottomless imagination.

"A whole gorgeous regiment. Ours. Think of it, Cliff. A marching band, a general staff. Everything. Uniforms tailored on Savile Row."

"Call me if you get orders to go overseas."

Pain gathered around Alonzo Fahey's mouth. Black curls had tumbled across his forehead. "Okay," he said. "You want to be the general? You can be the general."

53

"Regiments only go as high as colonels."

"This one is different. Better than the Queen's own. Jesus! She never even sent me a birthday card this year, the old hag."

Fahey's face glistened. Excitement poured from his eyes as he began his spiel, the necessity for more law and order, his aggrieved sense of right and wrong, most notably the wrong. Of how the labor unions had gone sour. Crooked police commissioners. Churches filching funds from the poorest and the weakest. Politicians conjuring new and unpardonable lies. What was needed was a regiment of Medieval-type crusaders to protect the public's soul. A regiment with the finest of camp followers, first-line troops chosen from the ranks of Olympic athletes. Every man mounted on an Appaloosa. Russian batboys to slop the latrines.

"Listen, Jesus, Cliff," Fahey went on. "We can bivouac up in the vineyards of Napa Valley. Cabernet and Zinfandel by the bucket, and we'll have it by the fires at night, there where the women'll be wearing their velvet capes and feeding us oysters." Fahey stopped suddenly, breathing hard and excitedly as if he'd made a strong finish after a ten-mile run.

"Send me a regimental tie and I'll wear it to your hanging."

"You don't care at all, do you?"

"About you I do."

"Look into it, will you? Imagine the fun. You get the White House permit or whatever it is we need."

Rhodes started to laugh. "Can't be done, Alonzo. I doubt it anyway."

"Hell, I can't. That Frenchie Lafayette did it, and so can we." Fahey teetered, his upper body assuming a diagonal line, his face aglow while caught up in his latest inspiration.

"We gotta get out of here, before you fall on the floor," Rhodes said as he turned toward the door. He thought he heard Fahey behind him, but it was only the noise of the great investigator resuming his chair. When reaching the door, Rhodes turned once more and saw Fahey gripping the neck of the Bushmills bottle, pouring a steady stream into a large tumbler.

It was the true Fahey tonight, he thought, the great dreamer who was playing at taming a world he found so very off course.

Sacked by the Police Commission for telling the truth too loudly about corruption rife in the department. And lest it ever be forgotten, for shacking up with one commissioner's wife, while Fahey had been assigned to the

54

department's internal affairs...looking into those lower and higher sins of the police department. He was a talented investigator but the worst possible man to pick for that job. He had no compunctions about stepping on toes. He hated liars, cheats, favoritism, sneakiness (unless for himself), and if the higher-ups needed a dose of detergents, he was ready for them.

Charged with unbecoming conduct, and for all the hell he constantly raised, Fahey had been suspended without pay. Rhodes had agreed to defend him for nothing. Fahey was legend in police circles. But at the special hearing the Commission convened, Rhodes never got a chance to wage a fight. Fahey took care of everything himself in one of the utmost performances Rhodes had ever witnessed.

There Fahey had stood, ready for all comers, undaunted against an array of those wise men who dared to judge him. Confessing them, it almost seemed. Barraging them with nervy questions about delicate confidential items so conveniently buried under the dust of the past.

And as the hearing drew to its close, with Fahey coolly reminding the Commissioners that: "Yes indeed, I am your insulted, aggrieved internal affairs officer. That poor wife I bedded," he had shouted, "was criminally neglected. She had craved me. Approved it was, too, by the Holy Mother Church..."

On that point, Fahey said he had checked and double-checked with his own conscience and a few priests who must remain nameless. And because he was an internal-affairs specialist, who else was better qualified to look after the affairs of the Commissioners' wives? "Fahey, gentlemen, that's the only *who* on this day in this temple of debauchery and crime you oversee. Yes? I've appointed myself as the Avenging Angel. How much of your underhanded, sordid activities do you care to read about in next week's papers? I can keep a full-fledged serial going for the rest of the year. Or there's always this—who among you wants your confession heard? Fahey, and only Fahey, is here to wash away the worst of your sins. I'll have the lot of you bastards in jail, after I sing my songs..."

They had wanted to crucify him, but ended up by dropping all charges if he would only agree to clam up. About everything. And Fahey knew a gift whether wrapped in tinsel or not.

It had been some show to behold, straight out of Cervantes.

"See you later, Alonzo," Rhodes said, shaking off his reverie.

"Hold on, and I'll find us some nice tarts," promised Fahey, for he was night people all the way through. "I'm reserving that safari princess for myself."

"Already got my bed, thanks. Call Burke, will you? Please do it, Alonzo."

Rhodes stepped through the door to a hallway. He'd done what he could do for Raye Wheeler, and there was Fritzi to see. He'd promised her, a promise he had best keep.

Chapter Seven

Rhodes stood on Fritzi Jagoda's front lawn, listening to the quiet dark and looking down over the hills to the endless strings of freeway traffic, the miles and miles of car lights resembling strings of electric spaghetti. So many people on the move at this hour, and then remembered he, too, was a good five miles from his own home. Smiling, he went up to the door, stepped through, entering a large foyer.

Everywhere, a fragrance of flowers. Red roses in bowls on a side table; in the living room yellow blossoms on either end of two sofas; white chrysanthemums poking out of vases on the fireplace mantel. The colors of the flowers blended with the chintz drapery that all but covered the outsized windows.

He found her in her bedroom. "You sure do this place up right," said Rhodes admiringly. "The flowers fill the air."

"The gardens are really fabulous now. I hope the rain hasn't spoiled everything. I'll have to check in the morning." She placed her book on the bedside table.

"Rain's on the run. Going south."

Rhodes sat next to her, then sprawled across her bed, his hand wandering across her lush breasts. Leaning closer until their noses met, then their mouths as they kissed deeply.

When he broke away, he whispered, "I'll change, be right back."

"Do that, and I'll brush your teeth later."

"But with what kind of brush?"

"Ah, the clown tonight." Fritzi made a face, then giggled.

Rhodes changed into a red flannel robe he kept there along with a few suits, some shirts and ties. They were handy on the mornings after he stayed over and, pressed for time, unable to get by his own home. Coming back, he switched off the light on his side of the bed, waiting for her to do the same.

"Come on," said Fritzi, "I'm over here, remember?"

"Flip the light."

"Undo your robe, then I will."

"This is silly."

"You're *the* silly," said Fritzi.

"Head games are not on the menu tonight."

"Really? I was sort of looking forward to some head."

Rhodes's smile left before it arrived. Peeling off the robe, burning a little inside, he slid under the covers. Fritzi snapped out her light, then snuggled close.

"I don't know why it bothers you," she said, "after all this time. I mean we've been in the shower, naked in the pool, God knows where, and you—"

"Innate modesty. I'm really one of Fahey's lost priests. I only pretend to be a public servant."

"Wouldn't it be easier just to face up to it...look at all the women with mastectomies. People with no arms or legs—"

"Write me an essay sometime on how to go to bed with you."

'Why not just face it."

Rhodes lifted his head from the pillow. "Fahey and you must be reading from the same song sheet. Are you sending notes to each other?"

"Not about this."

"That's nice."

"You're really in a great mood, I can see."

"I'm okay. A long, unfruitful day. I hope not too unfruitful..."

"Just a little black and blue inside, where we can't see it and kiss it," Fritzi kidded him. Nothing from Rhodes, though. Only an audible exhale. "Sometimes," said Fritzi, "I think you use your cock as an excuse for everything."

"I really don't need much of this, if that's okay."

"You know what?"

"Tell me, sweet one."

"You can't stand it when you're not the best at everything you do. Isn't that so?"

Rhodes's outflung hand grazed the mahogany headboard, making a noise that startled Fritzi. Low and throaty, she laughed but it was a laugh with nervous notes. "Easy. Don't go violent on me."

"Are you still sore, because I've been tied up and scarce all week?"

"And don't even call me. I'm supposed to do what? Wait and worry? Look for you on TV? Do it with the cat, when I get lonely?"

"How, for Christ, can you get lonely? You're surrounded by droves every night."

"Never mind, if you have to ask."

She was about to touch him and show by her touch that his penile wound didn't matter to her. That it never had mattered to her, only to him. Yet an invisible wall had descended from somewhere. She took his last remarks as a rebuff, when in her own mind all she had tried to convey again was that he shouldn't be so sensitive. So touchy because he was disfigured there, for it didn't bother her in the slightest. Surprised her at first, but she had known and loved him for five years. They all but lived together, full-time.

What upset her was his failure all last week to call and find out how she was, what she was up to, doing what, her lesser and greater worries? Taking her for granted, and she wouldn't, by God, take that from any man. A call took five minutes, less even. Maybe a big deal lawyer and judge, but she dealt with rainmakers every day and night.

Down came his arm, sliding across her belly. His legs entwined with hers and he started to play. She began to feel better though more tense now that her nipples tightened. Fritzi felt herself rise when, later, his mouth searched her thighs. She held him very hard with both hands, and could feel the small ridges of scar on his upper shoulders.

Much as she tried to excite him, she couldn't, and she tried everything but finally gave up. "You're tired, baby," she murmured.

"Sorry," he said, trying to shuck Audrey Sterne from his thoughts.

"We've got all night and then some."

They moved apart and Fritzi shook out the covers and spread them evenly. Shallow breathing, a stirring of limbs against the sheets, a breeze from the opened window lapping at the drapes was all that could be heard.

Rhodes bit the inside of his lower lip. His neck swelled and his skin began to feel like wet rubber. He should apologize but the words died in the back of his throat. His thoughts drifted back to the Army major, a psychiatrist, who nursed his mind after the surgeons had fixed him up with half a new *pico*. "Any size and shape you want," they had told him, full of good

59

cheer and humor. Rhodes had hit one of them so hard he broke his own thumb, and was damn near brought up on charges for his outburst and the damage he'd caused the surgeon.

The major, who had been so nice, older and a healer, had tutored him, even in bed, to believe that he was still a man and not a freak. He remembered her now, and remembered her frequently all through the years.

Just as he still remembered the clunking sound of the grenade. How it bounced down the dirt path inside the cave where he had lived for months in Afghanistan. A bursting flash, a whomp of thunder that knocked him flat, the shrapnel splitting him apart in three places.

It was always easier, he knew, to blame the fighting days, whenever he didn't work right in bed, especially now that Audrey Sterne had invaded his senses again, making him ask himself what Fritzi really meant to him anymore. He shouldn't be here with her, the worst kind of cheating against her. Touching her, feeling her, while thinking of another woman. Immoral, wasn't it? What else could it be, other than a stark betrayal?

೮೩

Fritzi rolled to her side of the bed. She had known other nights like this one, forty or fifty perhaps, and they always seemed to happen when she needed him most, when her natural urges were pitched up so high.

Another of those soft killings inside the soul. Worse, she thought, than an exchange of angry words. You could always take those back, but how could you take back the sex you were supposed to have but didn't have when you wanted it most? A little piece of death that stayed buried in you until some unlikely moment when your dam burst and you start spewing awful things to the man you loved.

Fritzi sensed him trembling. She knew he wasn't crying. He never cried and she rated that as a flaw in anyone. She began rubbing his back gently, surprised at the wetness on the smooth cords of standing muscle. He was barely a foot away, yet it seemed like the width of the Grand Canyon.

Sex and the male ego. Dear God, she thought—will there never be a solution to that one?

છ

Raye Wheeler formed a small hole with his mouth, sucking hard for air. A feeble effort, though; his bronchial tubes had withered and his lungs had begun the slow, frightening process of collapsing. Sometimes, as now, it felt as if his breaths had first passed through a furnace before he could force them down his throat.

Seventy-one years of the best times a man could hope for were reaching their last day. The vents were all worn out and no spares existed to fix them.

Strange images visited him, then suddenly disappeared. Once a shadow waved at him, and, nearing him, it seemed to be Romaine Brook. Saying something. Straining to hear her words, but no sounds came forth. There she came, closer with every step, then arranging herself on his bony knees. She was naked as she'd been in those shocking photos that Pritter had put into evidence at the trial.

Her whispered words, and he heard those words this time, the soft and imploring words. Suddenly, instinctively he knew it all. It wasn't his past life wending through him; it was the sinister side of truth, its revelation in all but its cold proof. Something acquired after forty-odd years in criminal courtrooms. Not proof, not yet, but the road that ultimately got you to truth's doorway.

It was his turn to shout but the shout was not louder than a canary's chirp. No one heard him, not the nurses down the hall, not Tommy Burke, who had no idea of Wheeler's game plan for winning the case, not even Cliff Rhodes, who was about to be cleaved in ways he never remotely imagined.

In one feeble last rattle, his plan for Romaine Brook's defense, along with everything else he hadn't gotten around to doing in his life, died right along with whatever else was left of him.

છ

Crossing town the next morning, thinking of Fritzi, Rhodes stopped on a whim at a pet shop. He sent her a pair of plump lovebirds in a large gilded cage as a peace offering. Afterward, driving off, he came to a stoplight, turning on a favorite radio-station for some music. What he heard was a news bulletin announcing Raye Wheeler's death. Memories, hundreds of them, at once flooded him. Swamped by them. A horn blared, then another while he blocked traffic, thinking slowly, thinking that a great coach and gladiator was gone now, that the world was poorer off now by one superb gent. Raye Wheeler had been a constant in his life, a second father, a measured and deliberate quantity, something like a Greek alpha or sigma letter in a mathematical formula.

Rhodes's thoughts moved to Romaine Brook, then to the jury locked up at the Biltmore. They'd find out about Raye Wheeler soon enough and probably go into a red lather at the prospect of more delays, longer separation from their families and jobs. Longer everything.

Yet another concern made its leap forward—was Burke up to it? Lloyd Pritter was no cakewalk. He knew his way around a courtroom. Burke was, at best, a tyro. He'd need help and what about Alonzo, was he off to Cabo San Lucas for a fish with Wanda?

Chapter Eight

At the dock on the oceanside of the Sterne home, Ferenc Kardas unhitched a bowline and helped guide the *Paloma* out of her slip. The cabin cruiser slid out smooth and straight, churning up the barest froth of wake as it eased into the Pacific.

Thirty yards from the dock, Julio Sterne swung the boat around and headed for deeper waters, waving at Kardas. Ferenc saw no sign of Audrey. She was probably below, fixing drinks or getting the cold supper ready.

A late afternoon cruise, California style, nice. On Mondays and Fridays nobody went to work in Malibu Pointe as far as he could tell, except, that is, for Julio Sterne who rarely missed a day of toil looking after his many enterprises. Today was different. Very different, when the old man had come home at noon, ordered a lunch of two soft-boiled eggs and a slice of toast, then busied himself by barking orders into the library phone, likely to one of his four secretaries. Then, abruptly telling his wife she was about to go boating, to change her outfit and instruct the kitchen staff to prepare food.

Watching the *Paloma* gain distance, Kardas's dark eyes narrowed with envy. He intended getting a bigger slice of this life for himself one day. He already had some of its beginnings—a small suite of comfortably appointed rooms over a five-car garage; upwards of a hundred-thousand dollars on deposit in different banks; and, for a time, the pleasures provided by an old man's succulent wife.

Why was Sterne taking his wife out for cruise so suddenly? A tête-ê-tête? About himself, was it? Were his days numbered?

The old man knew all about Ferenc's dalliances with his wife, indeed had encouraged it beginning on the day of his employment, also deliberately advising him that Audrey Sterne was to be kept quite unaware of what he, Julio Sterne, was privy to. Ferenc had never uttered the barest hint about the arrangement to her. Was today the day for ventilating all; for a Mr.-and-Mrs. dust-up in the seclusion of a vast ocean? Perhaps so. Perhaps a better choice than in the sprawling glass-sided Sterne home, where one had as much daytime privacy as a goldfish, with all the household help scurrying about.

He climbed the thirty-two steps to the house, the same number he had climbed on the night they had found Marc Sterne's sprawled body—eyes white and unseeing, one hand barely covering his genitals, the other splayed next to a hypodermic syringe. And with Audrey Sterne looking over his shoulder, stifling a scream with the back of her hand.

A hard way to die.

But then, thought Ferenc, are there any good ones? He hurried along. While the Sternes were out boating, he had a few hours to contact some of the other butlers and housemen on the Pointe. His pushers.

Already he had lost Marc Sterne, his prime supplier. If he didn't come up with a top quality source soon, he'd forfeit his market. He had to find that missing stash, and had a fair notion of where to go looking, if the cops hadn't gotten there ahead of him.

He fed the noses and arteries of some very rich people: a life insurance tycoon, several well-known actors, three film producers, the number-three rock-and-roller on the charts, and a dozen but well-off lesser lights. Quiet action, with a turnover of about twenty-thousand dollars weekly, if he hustled hard enough.

Too nice a thing to give up, worrying him. He had already lost thousands on one missing bag of Columbian Jewel #1 that Marc Sterne had never delivered. Some of the other butlers and housemen had chipped in for the buy. Growling, they wanted either their money returned or more brain powder, and they wanted it very soon. Two of them had cornered him a few nights ago, as he walked the beach. Irate, they had shoved him around, making threats, and he knew they hadn't been joking.

He was being boxed, but where to turn next and where to find help? He was a Hunkie, given a break by Julio Sterne. He had no other contacts with movers and shakers, and fear set in. He had even lost the wife, and was unsure how that had come about…she'd not help, of that he was dead certain. She had gone unaccountably cold; a woman's moods, he supposed, and after all that pleasure she'd given. A woman born for the night, born for day or night.

CR

It was the right place, but Fahey looked twice anyway. It seemed like something out of Tijuana North. The building was an old-timer, still sturdy yet tired looking, located on one corner of the Broadway intersection near the law courts. Once this had been the most fashionable office area in Los Angeles. But then Little Tokyo had edged closer. Soon Chinatown crept in; finally a swarm of Latinos had made it into their own camping ground.

If you stopped to listen, as Fahey did, the sounds of the streets were embroidered with a dozen tongues.

He couldn't begin to guess why a lawyer of Raye Wheeler's rank had stayed on when so many others had left years ago. Maybe, thought Fahey, it was plain sentiment, or the proximity to the courts, and maybe it was only a dose of superstition—that if old Raye had left, his mojo would've left with him.

In the front of the lobby, a computer dating service promised bliss for twenty bucks a throw; a money-changing cage was located in the back shadows; and on a whitewashed window a tattered and outdated poster advertised a week in Acapulco for five-hundred dollars, air fare included.

Fahey rang the elevator. Overcoming a nibble of fear, he stepped in as the rickety gate closed, and prayed for the first time all year.

Coming through the door of Wheeler's office, he was eyed suspiciously by an elderly woman, who gave him a look hard enough to scratch a match on. She stopped tapping the keys of a typewriter to ask him what he wanted, perhaps figuring him for a salesman.

When he told her, she sent him on his way with a few curt directions. Manners. He would tell her some things about manners later.

Perched on a stepladder, his head buried in a law book, Tommy Burke failed to notice Fahey at first. The room was a smallish library with a high ceiling covered in motif-tin, shelves sagged under the weight of books, dark paneling, and the room itself smelling like a musty cellar.

Fahey tapped his knuckles on a square of the paneling. Burke looked down, startled as a feeding deer.

"I'm Fahey. At your service. And you're younger than I thought."

"Twenty-eight."

"Barely off the nipple, are we?"

"Nipp—? Hah! I'm afraid you're wrong there...by the way, can you show me your ticket?" asked Tommy politely, marking his place in the book with a length of string.

Fahey reached for his billfold and then showed a laminated photostat of his private investigator's license. Burke handed it back, saying, "You look different in this picture."

"I got older, hanging around too many lawyers."

"You don't like lawyers, Mr. Fahey?"

"Eighty thousand of 'em in this state. That's a lot of troublemakers. Call me Alonzo, incidentally."

"I'm Tommy."

"I know. Irish. What part?"

"County Sligo. Two generations back."

"Sligo, eh? Not like Maghera, but passable. Puts you in the right pew anyway."

As they talked, Fahey began to absorb the younger man. Awkward looking, as if a few vital pieces were missing. Defined by too many protruding bones. A puckering, thick-lipped mouth, a long and freckled face with a pale glow of blood under a translucent skin. By his left eye, a purple birthmark stood out, the size and shape of a shirt button.

"You think my shoes are funny," Tommy Burke said, aware that Fahey was inspecting him.

"Boots, aren't they? Climbing boots. You ever been in a regiment?"

"Everybody jokes about my footwear." Tommy Burke's mouth turned into a sheepish grin.

"You a climber?"

"No, it's my weak ankles. Grew too fast, and the boots support my ankles better."

"You up to talking about this trial?"

"Sure. We can talk right here."

"You can maybe. But my neck is going stiff looking up at you."

"Oh, sorry." Burke's voice, already high, crept a note higher. The knob in his slender neck bobbed twice.

He came down off the ladder, legs and arms working as if they were each getting a different brain message. Burke was double-jointed. He reminded Fahey of a stick-figure in a cartoon drawn with a sharp pen almost out of ink.

Still, Fahey could feel for the younger lawyer. A natural cripple, born that way, and Fahey thought of his own shot-up elbow. He understood, partly anyway.

"So what made you change your mind?"

"About this case?" Fahey asked.

Burke nodded. He was a full head taller than Fahey, who measured six feet without his shoes.

"When Raye Wheeler first asked me, I couldn't do it. I was busy on something else."

"I thought you didn't do trial investigations anymore."

"I haven't for a while...I'm an art man now," said Fahey with mock pomposity.

"Now you're ready again?"

"Help you if I can, my son. I liked Raye."

"Everyone did."

"And you're in charge of the whole bus now. Is that it? No one else coming in?"

"Just me. You're looking at it. We're short of funds."

"Right, an old refrain."

"I can't make any promises about paying you. I'm probably on my own, too. If you want a fee up front, I guess I'll be seeing you around."

Fahey rubbed his eyes before they wandered up to the ceiling again. He was here only at the bidding of Rhodes and, indirectly, Raye Wheeler. Calling Burke yesterday, telling him he could spare one week and not a day more. That the trial looked interesting and the investigative work by the police, as far as he was able to tell, looked shaky.

"Look," said Fahey, "I'll trust you. I'll do it on the cuff. One week, as I said, and not a minute more."

"No way can I guarantee you anything. Now or later on." Burke shook his head vigorously until copper-colored ringlets spilled almost to his eyebrows.

"Then I'm free to walk whenever I want. Right?"

"Yes. Certainly."

"So how do you get paid, if that's not too invasive of me?"

"When we win, Romaine'll pay us. She promised."

"Win, you say? Okay, a man with the glory of confidence in his bones. That's the stuff. Let's get on with it," Fahey urged.

"Any place special you want to start?"

Fahey yawned. Then he told Burke what he'd like to know about Romaine Brook. What Burke thought of her? How she responded to hard-edged questions? How she grew up? Where? Her discernible habits? A score of things, all adding up to—*who is she, inside and out.*

Fahey asked for everything they had that linked the young actress to the crime—the sheriff's confidential reports, other police records, the coroner's findings—all the data the state had collected, and, by law, must turn over to the defense.

"Like to meet her myself. Soon as you can arrange it," Fahey also requested.

"That's easy. Tomorrow? After the funeral?"

"Good. But I want a look at those evidence files first."

"That it? Nothing else?"

"I'll need to see those photos," added Fahey in an afterthought. "You've got copies?"

"Yes," said Tommy, frowning.

"Lots of skin, eh?"

"I suppose. But you don't really need those pictures."

"I do if you need me, boyo. We either work this thing together or I go home. You tell me which."

Tommy shrugged, then quickly averted his face so Fahey couldn't see how upset he was. Those photos gave him nightmares. She wasn't like that; she was beautiful, a delivered dream, a wonder of the earth. Marc Sterne had tried to stain her. It drove Burke almost crazy whenever he thought about what cameras had done to Romaine. One kind had made her famous, and another kind had made her out to be a sluttish porno actor.

They walked down a hall to a small conference room between Wheeler's office and the one Tommy used, and Fahey said it was just what he had in mind. "Quarters fit for an admiral. Exactly adequate. Better than I've ever had before," he lied very pleasantly.

Burke lingered, looking uneasy. Fahey wondered if the younger lawyer had yet to shave that pink freckled baby skin.

"You going to work tonight? Here?"

"A few hours anyway." Fahey closed the desk drawer he'd been exploring. "Learn my way through your files."

"Want to join me for dinner later?"

"Sure. Is it on the client?"

Burke laughed. "Not this month."

"You running a branch of the Legal Aid Society here or what?"

"I said she'll pay. We'll just have to wait for it, till she gets working again."

Fahey's grin disappeared. "Supposing she gets the iron bars or worse?"

"I don't think about it," said Tommy, his voice nervously rising again.

"I was right. You're young, all right, young as next New Year's."

If Tommy was insulted or miffed, he hid his feelings. He was trying to get the feel of Alonzo Fahey. He knew the man carried a gold-plated reputation as an investigator who almost always delivered for his clients. But he looked so off-center, so impulsive—so something. Hard to define at any rate: what kind of detective wore an electric-blue shirt and a scarlet bow tie with orange polka dots? Takes all kinds, Tommy thought, including Fahey who looked like a human neon sign.

Tommy started for the door, then hesitated and spun around on one spindly leg. "I know you worked with Judge Rhodes at one time. Raye told me so."

"Raye had it right."

"What's he really like?"

Fahey itched the stubble on his cheek, a darkening shadow climbing up to his sideburns. The blue-black of the windows behind him and his shirt gave him a sinister appearance. Now he squinted, his jaw hardening, looking bothered and as if might pounce at any second.

Burke waited for a reply.

"A minor poet," said Fahey after a moment. "Fights filthy, a dirty one, mean as a pissed-off woman in a divorce court. Seen him do it."

"You mean with his hands or something?"

"Jay-*sus*. With his ghost. He fights with his ghost and it *ain't* the fair thing, is it now?"

Tommy tilted his head, confusion clouding his face, the coppery curls dancing against his forehead again. Heading out the door without another word, he went back to his law books. If he was worried about the sobriety of the detective, he was also doubly concerned for himself. He had hardly slept the night before, so jumpy at the prospect of standing in front of all those people in the courtroom; about the way he came across to others, his high-pitched voice, and never having represented a client by himself, not ever, let

69

alone in a murder-one trial. He was scared, and he knew he'd be scared again, full of a flopping belly and the jitters.

Would they laugh at him? Snicker, too?

Fahey had called him out of nowhere, offering help. A man who talked like a lunatic, but Tommy was ready to clutch at anything.

Three hours passed, as if rolled into one. It was after eight, when Tommy led Fahey to a noisy Mexican cantina around the corner from the office. They sat in a booth in the back, away from the mariachi music blaring out of the sound system up front by the register.

Fahey ordered a Bushmills and was told they didn't stock it. Asking for another brand, he got the same answer, so settled for a margarita with extra limes. "And for pure love of Christ turn down that music," he implored the waiter, and then he began a closer inspection of the environs. Seedy. A second-level bean and nacho joint, hardly a woman in the place. Women knew where to eat, were the best litmus test of where to buy the evening's fare.

The Peninsula tomorrow, Fahey decided, and fuck the expense. He'd take it out of the wife's dress money.

"Las Infantas," Fahey said a few minutes later over the lip of his margarita glass. "What is it, a sacrament?" The thought had zinged into him like a rifle shot from an unknown direction. "I saw it in your files."

"It's where Romaine was put up for adoption," Tommy said. "A foundling home run by a religious order."

"Adopted? Does she know it?"

"Yes, she does."

"Does she know who her real parents are?"

"No, she's tried to find out but sort of gave up. That's my impression. Would you go up there one day? Soon, if you can swing it."

"What for?"

"Before the trial actually began, Raye tried to track down Romaine's natural parents. To see if they might be willing to help financially. But Las Infantas wouldn't give us the time of day. We sort of dropped it. Ran out of time. And who knows where her parents are anyway. Maybe they're gone and buried."

"Places like that are pretty touchy," Fahey said. "Doubt if I could help you on that one."

"Worth a try. Maybe if someone went to see them, told them what a spot we're in. The expenses just keep climbing and we simply can't afford to mount a trace."

"We'll see, eh? Tell me about her. Start me on the bird, and let's see how far we get," said Fahey, his courageous bow tie skewed at an acute angle, making him look clownish.

Burke began.

But Fahey was thinking about the photos he had seen an hour before at the office. Romaine Brook's body, naked and quite an aristocratic assembly, if you possessed the knowing eye. She had a pedigreed-look of a countess, at least. A dozen prints of her on film. A healthy-looking damsel, fit for a soapsuds ad. Another woman's hands, holding a black dildo, showed up in some of the photos and at least one pair of male hands. In one shot there was even a dog mounting her. The photos were of good quality, but it was the· look on the face that mystified him. He couldn't tell whether she was asleep or on a sexual moon-ray ride.

Why would a newly heralded actress get herself into that situation? None of it figured, intriguing Fahey. Had she been doped? Had the photos been part of an extortion attempt? Blackmail?

Alonso Fahey, sleuth of all he surveyed, would be disturbed again in a very few moments. He listened raptly as Burke outlined the twists and turns of Romaine Brook's young yet eventful life.

Of how she had been adopted from Las Infantas by Josephine and Chatham Brook. The mother had died of double pneumonia when Romaine was only ten.

"And the father, where's he gone to?" asked Fahey.

"Went out for a beer one night," Burke advised. "He was last heard of in Morocco or someplace. Turned Arab, I imagine."

"Abandoned the kid? Who was he?"

"British type, an immigrant. Arranged and composed music for movie soundtracks."

"How'd she get along?"

"The family had lived in the Valley. Encino. A tract home, fully mortgaged and sold to pay debts. Romaine was taken in by her high-school principal and his wife. She lived with them for three or four years. Oddly, sort of oddly, they schooled her under Catholic nuns."

"Is that odd?"

"Search me, but they were Mormons."

"You a Catholic?"

"Sometimes," Tommy admitted.

"Ah, we're brothers then…and then what happened?"

"She competed for and won a scholarship to the California School of Drama. She had small parts before getting her big break in *Tonight or Never*."

Encino? A slant, perhaps a trail-marker—Fahey wanted more of her background. What her day-to-day life had been made of.

From the way Tommy Burke talked, Fahey was fairly sure the young attorney had fallen for her. Eager of expression, a slight blush in his cheeks, his high quick voice. The signs of a nervous suffering lover were scribbled all over his face.

Wondering again who had taken those photos, Fahey asked, "You think she's innocent?"

"I know she has to be," Tommy answered.

"Where the hell's our dinner?"

"They're a little slow here, I admit."

Fahey pushed himself up from the booth, throwing a few crumpled bills on the table.

"Where're you going?"

"I'm off for my time of meditation, a new alphabet I'm working on."

"Can you drive me to Raye's funeral tomorrow?"

"Drive you?"

"Please."

"Can't you drive, chrissakes?"

"I never learned. Never could afford a car, either," said Tommy Burke, making it sound like a high recommendation.

"Jesus, man, this is Los Angeles. Everyone drives. I don't know…I'm to be the chauffer, too?" Fahey started to leave. "How do you get around, by the way? You got some white wings for us?"

"I use the bus. I like the bus, I'm a people-watcher."

"You don't say? The bus…the bus? I'm damned. See you around, Tom-Tom."

Fahey turned and went down the bar. He'd go to Masquers, where he had credit, and order a decent whiskey and a dinner to go with it. Chat up the ladies. Needed time to think, graze on a solid mug or two of Bushmills to clarify all the murk. Whatever had he been thinking of, when immersing himself in this quirky business?

And he chewed on that notion till past eleven, when he left two women he'd been gassing with at the end of the bar, then found his way home where he fell into the tolerant arms of his quite ravishing, long-suffering Wanda.

Chapter Nine

The half-light made the corridor seem like a tomb for the living, nor did the faint carbolic smell appeal to Fahey. The clop of his heels against the linoleum floor sounded too mechanical and deadening to him; all so eerie, especially after Raye Wheeler's dreary funeral.

He'd been a cop once; he knew these places for what they were—sump pits. Dog dungeons. If they had any balls, the Health Department would shut them down.

When they had entered the building, Burke passed through a screening gate immediately, but Fahey, was directed to step aside. A quick frisking by the desk guard uncovered a silver flask in his hip pocket. Told he could pick it up on his way out, Fahey, grossly insulted, had shouted at the guard, being a woman of heft who nearly ejected him. He had stunned her with his reaction, and had stunned Tommy Burke with his attire worn for Raye Wheeler's burial earlier that morning: a green suit, a candy-striped shirt, with a tie, loud as a siren that seemed to change color with the light. On one lapel, an odd-looking golden medal hung from a daring crimson ribbon.

They had come to a stop. Fahey gripped his black beret in one hand, ready for a fight to keep it.

Their uniformed escort unlocked a door, then showed them to a small visitors' room that was as lifeless as a moonscape. The walls were a dingy gray and one small barred window gave little light. Fahey felt trapped. Much too somber a cubicle for his liking, and his face showed strain as he paced around. He sailed a joke over to Burke, who was arranging a legal pad and pencils on the table.

There she wasn't, then there she was, arriving as noiselessly as an ethereal spirit passing through the wall. She wore a loose-fitting drab gray shift, its hemline reaching her knees. Her feet were shod in open-toed sandals. Tommy Burke scrambled up, nearly knocking his chair over, and, flustered, he turned to see Fahey advancing like a prophet with arms spread wide.

"Hi, Tommy," she said softly.

"Hello, Romaine. This is Alonzo Fahey."

"A new lawyer?"

"No," Tommy said. "A sort of specialist, who used to be with the Los Angeles police. He's here to help us."

"There's no money for any more of you, Tommy. You have to believe me. I'm stone broke, and if I don't get out of here I'll be stone everything else."

Taken with her silky voice, Fahey was also impressed by her welcoming smile. Noting her calm manner, too, and her clean scrubbed looks. She looked nothing at all like those sordid photo images.

"To no one in particular, Fahey said, "We'll get up a church collection for our cause. Burke and I may rob a chapel or two tonight. The stars are just right, and we're here to finish the plans to get you home safe and sound, my darling angel. A gorgeous thing, you are, lovey...I'd make a run at you myself but it won't do. I'm married this year and she won't let go. A real strangler. Got to keep an eye on her round the clock. "

Romaine giggled.

"You'll get to know him. It takes a while," Tommy said, mildly exasperated.

She had extended a hand toward Fahey, who continued to regard her in rare silence. He held her hand a moment, liking the warmth of it, and surprised at her strong grip. Even in the ratty shift, she looked appealing--a golden Madonna, he thought, and took a deep breath as she smiled again at him.

"Tonight or Never," he said. "A great one, and now you're here in person. I'm near breathless. Heart jumping everywhere."

"Oh! You saw it?"

"I've not seen it, but now I shall," Fahey replied. "The matinee variety, soon as I find one where the popcorn hasn't gone stale."

"Alonzo is an investigator," Burke clarified. "He's going to check on some things. Like to ask you a few questions."

"What sort of questions?" asked Romaine, her voice churlish, defensive. "All I ever get are questions."

Fahey said evenly. "Just testing the winds a bit. Nothing much, then again who knows, love? We'll be fine, just you wait."

"Things you might've discussed with Raye," added Tommy. "Loose bits and pieces that Alonzo can look into."

"Poor Raye. I don't know what more can happen." Romaine's eyes, green and steady, seemed to mist. A faint blush creeping into her cheeks. Fahey was tempted to lean over and feel its warmth. "You've got to get me out of this awful hole, Tommy. I just can't stand it much longer," she said in what sounded like rising despair.

"You've got to be patient a while longer."

Romaine snatched a quick glance at Fahey. He seemed strong as a dockworker, she thought. And very flirty with his sudden blue eyes.

"You hurt your arm somehow?" she asked him

"Many nights ago."

"I'm sorry. Excuse me for—"

"S'alright. I'm used to the damn thing by now." Fahey had been massaging his elbow. Tender there today, and supposed it would rain again tonight. "Now then; let me advise you what I can and can't do for you." After briefly telling her what the law allowed a private investigator to do, he wanted to hear a few things from her. "Absolutely straight, straight and clear for my own ears. It might give me a feel for something. Make me hear things. Things you don't want your own soul to know."

This last remark caused a stir of alarm in Romaine. What did he mean? She started to speak but her mind raced everywhere. "Yes. Naturally I'll answer anything."

"You want me to take a stab at finding your father?"

"Thank you, no. I do not."

"Why?"

"He ran out years ago. Somewhere. North Africa is what I heard. I don't ever want him near me."

"You're sure?"

"Perfectly."

"Maybe he can help you with money," Fahey pressed.

"I want nothing to do with him or his money, if he has any."

She had turned her head away; obviously, he had touched a frayed nerve. Tommy Burke broke in, "Romaine, prudence says we need a more experienced litigator than I am. I'm not a trial lawyer, and we really need one. I'll do my best but you need a real pro. You see that, don't you? For that, we need money. Possibly from your father."

"He didn't need me, did he? If he's in California, and wanted to stand with me, do anything for me, we'd've heard by now."

"Possibly. That's hard to know."

"I'll go with you, Tommy. You're loyal, at least. You can represent me, I know you can."

Fahey took a turn. "There're notes in the files saying that you claimed Marc Sterne was into drugs. Heroin, even."

Romaine nodded. "Was he ever!"

"He spent time in some rehabilitation clinic?"

"I think about three months," Romaine said. "It was before I knew him."

"Did he talk about it?"

'Never. Well, hardly ever."

"So lf he got eased off the drugs, why do you say he was on them again?"

"How he died, for one thing."

"What else?"

"He dealt, you know. He dealt to a lot of people in the industry, and I think some of the residents in Malibu Pointe. Lots of entertainment people live there, and they do recreation drugs."

"You're meaning the film business, when you say entertainment people?"

"Yes," said Romaine. "And the recording companies too. Music people, the executives. He knew all those people. All kinds of them."

"You ever see him peddling anything?"

"At a few parties we went to. He would disappear, and I'd go looking for him and he had those packets. Glassine packets full of the white stuff."

"Lots of loose cash?"

Romaine shrugged. "I guess so. But he was always short. His father kept him on a tight salary."

"How tight?"

"A hundred and fifty-thousand, I think."

"What's so tight about that?"

"In the world he lived in? Are you kidding, Mr. Fahey?"

"Alonzo. I'm Alonzo. Don't go formal on me or I'll up my rates."

"Alonzo," she repeated, smiling slightly.

"So he was a pusher? Heroin, cocaine, all that?"

She nodded again.

"Where'd he keep it?"

"I don't know."

"Were you fucking this guy? Hot and heavy, were you?"

A flying pencil hit Fahey in the chest. He looked across the table to an enraged Tommy Burke, whose mouth opened and closed, a sort of strangled sound coming forth.

"Where the hell do you get off talking like that to her?" Burke remonstrated, when he regained himself.

"It's all right, Tommy," said Romaine. She leaned over, touching his knee. "I don't mind."

"Look, you want a tea party, then I'm not your man. I gotta find out what was happening, that's all," Fahey stated, then continued: "You don't know where he kept his merchandise? Or who he bought from?"

Romaine hesitated. She knew the answer she would give; she just didn't want to give it too easily. "I'm not exactly sure where he kept it," she said after a pause. "And I've no idea who he bought it from."

"Okay. Where do you suppose he might've stashed it?"

"Somewhere in the living room of his apartment. Near a long couch there. When he needed some he'd always send me out of the room, and when he let me back in, one section of the couch was askew or sometimes the lamp was out of place."

Fahey jotted some notes, then made a rough sketch of a sectional couch. As he drew, he asked Burke: "Place was searched, right?"

"And sealed afterward. It still is. That's where they found that letter Romaine wrote."

"The photos were there, too?" Fahey asked.

Romaine averted his eyes as Tommy replied, "Yes, along with the letter."

Fahey lay down the pencil. Bothered suddenly by a rush of prickly heat, he rubbed his nose and the side of his mouth. The girl, he had only shaken her hand, no more, and yet she was seizing him somehow. He eyed her. "Are you into drugs? Ever?"

"Never."

"You sure? This is us, remember. I'm on your side."

"I swear," Romaine protested. "Please, you must believe me, when I tell you something."

"I will. But I'm also trying to make sure of your answers. Can you tell me how you met Marc?"

"I already told Raye Wheeler once."

"Raye's not with us anymore," reminded Fahey. "I'm the new boy, so please tell me."

Romaine knew she must be very careful. She got up from her chair and walked slowly to a corner of the room. Gazing at her, Fahey felt a surge of admiration at what he could see of her legs.

"Give me a minute, and I'll tell you," Romaine said. It was the same, almost, as remembering lines from a script, trawling her memory as she had so many times. As if on stage, she began her lines:

And she began:

"Nothing ever excited me more than getting the supporting role in *Tonight or Never*. Like a trip straight to paradise. The cast and crew were great. My role was fabulous, the lines terrific, everything. His stepmother introduced us one day at a lunch she gave. Marc was an assistant producer, and he was assigned to my film. Wow! He had this deep voice. Musical, sort of. It was as if I had opened my eyes for the very first time, and then looked and looked again at all this man. He was tall, with a great body and periwinkle eyes, and dark wavy hair…and then every day when we were shooting, a small wicker basket arrived in my dressing room. One pink rose. One split of Moet. Even on location in New Orleans, the same thing. I was so flattered. And his manners were perfect always. 'Did I have everything I needed? Was my hotel room all right?' Little things, nice things. We went everywhere together: Beverly Hills parties, had our own special table at Ma Maison. I was on the magic carpet ride and felt so beautiful, so alive. Even the gossip columns called me "a radiant Cinderella." A couple of months or so after the shooting ended, things started to change. At first, I sort of ignored it. But then I discovered another side of Marc when he took me to those parties with dope and coke and those medical or chemical names I never even heard of before. Metha—something. He'd leave me at odd times for five or ten minutes. No one seemed to bat an eyelash, and that's when I learned he was dealing and I got mad at him. If he were arrested, and I was with him, it could be extremely damaging…then things smoothed out again. The charm oozed, flowers arrived, no more crazy antics. He asked me for lunch one day at the studio commissary. Half the big brass stopped by our table. Everything but the band was rolled out. Marc had been given his own film project to produce, and I was offered the lead this time. I'd arrived! Finally, I had arrived. His father had approved a substantial increase in my fee, too, and I wanted the money. It was still a smaller budget movie, but that didn't bother me at all. I was really excited. But that's the last I ever heard of the film. Never saw the script and neither did my agent. A ruse of some kind? I really can't say. Film projects get killed all the time, you know..."

Still standing serenely in the corner, her hands laced together, she rested them against one thigh. She had done her remembering all over again, her eyes shining as she spoke her piece, as if performing on stage. Not a hitch, not a stammer.

One moment, she seemed an ingénue of, perhaps twelve years in age; the next she seemed thirty, an artful experienced woman who might have been through peril. Fahey had observed her closely—no question, he thought, she was the real deal—a happening. Truth, was it? Or a mix of the truth laced with imaginings?

An actress, so how could you tell?

Maybe Romaine really is a star, he thought. I mean, Christ, here we are in a cement cell. She's got little more than a shirt on, and yet she can still make you believe you're hearing her life as you're walking a forest's leafy trail together. Her face interested him. It hadn't fully set. She was too young for worry lines, and he speculated how she'd look ten years down the line. And what would her capacities be like then? At this rate, extraordinary, he supposed.

"You want to tell me about the photos," Fahey suggested.

"I never knew about them before this trial."

"How come?"

"I was drugged and—"

"You said you didn't take drugs."

"I don't," Romaine said abruptly. "Please don't try to confuse my words either...I was slipped drugs in a drink, I'm pretty sure of that."

"Where?"

"Palm Springs."

"Would you tell me—"Fahey broke off, glancing over at Burke, saying, "You heard this before?" he asked. Burke shook his head. "You tell this to Wheeler?" he asked Romaine.

"Yes."

"But he didn't tell you," Fahey asked Burke.

"No. Remember, I was just researching and that sort of thing before Raye died."

Fahey frowned. "Can we hear about it? The photo session? That same nice way as you told us earlier. Don't try to measure your words."

"There wasn't any *session*. I really don't appreciate that word, Mr. Fahey. What do you think I am?"

"Please go ahead," Tommy consoled, his voice notching up a note.

Romaine still stood in the corner, straight-shouldered, almost regal-looking even if dressed like a Dickensian street waif. Her toes were pointed outward, making her pelvis arch forward. At second glance, she looked a seductress. How could that be: appearing as two women, in seconds? To himself, Fahey swore on saints who never existed that she had an actual aura about her. Perhaps it was only a fragment of light from the barred window playing a trick on her blondish hair. Somehow he didn't think so, somehow she was different—a changeling, like a chameleon. An imaginary creature, who spoke. But she was real enough—alive, breathing, muddling him.

Listening raptly then as Romaine, her eyes closed, began to talk again.

"We drove down early, the sun just rising, and I remember we were going to make up. For the second time, he promised there'd be no more drugs. He wanted to go over another film idea. We went up some road that overlooked a canyon and then pulled up at a curve-shaped house so low it seemed almost hidden against the rocks. It was still cool outside and I remember seeing steam rise from the swimming pool. A really nice place. It belonged to his parents, I found out

later. He told me his parents were arriving later, but they never did…a couple came out from the house. Mexicans, I think. Young and very good-looking…we swam and sunned and swam some more. I wore a bikini, and Marc took pictures of me with his Apple iPhone. And then some other shots of the Mexican couple; the woman, Rafaela, had stripped and she was bare-ass. She wanted me that way, too, but I told her no-go.

81

"By afternoon," Romaine went on, "I was lazing around and enjoying myself. Marc made me a white wine and soda. A spritzer...right, it was a spritzer. At first, I guess I thought I was getting dizzy from all the sun. But then I saw colors, every color of the rainbow swirling together. Crazy. And then nothing, a blank.

"I don't remember the rest. I don't even remember where the big dog came from that was in those awful pictures. I mentioned the Mexican couple. I think they were in the pictures, doing those filthy things to me...the trip back to Los Angeles was a total blur. It must have been the day after, I guess, but I don't really know. I was drugged so deep and I never take drugs so whatever it was must've really knocked me flat out. I woke up in Marc's apartment in the Hollywood Hills. He was gone and had left a note saying he was at the studio.

"My breasts and neck were covered with splotches. I could hardly get up. I stumbled into the bathroom, sat down, and found blood dripping into the toilet bowl.

"All I could think of, when I could think at all, were those times when that priest, the one at my high school went after me. Forced himself up my backside, exploding in me. Telling me that this is how adolescent girls learned about it. Made me sick. Made me puke.

"When I cried out, he muffled me with his hand. I thought I'd suffocate. God, how he hurt me and shamed me. I hated him! Oh, you have to understand, both of you. I was so afraid and felt so dirty, I couldn't tell anyone about it. Not the nuns, the nuns would deny

everything, say I was crazy. That's what I thought, too, that I'd go crazy..."

Romaine opened her eyes, then, as an empty look crossed on her face.

Tommy Burke had noticed that, though dry, her eyes seemed full with fear, and she had trembled noticeably as she spoke. Rage welled up in him at her terrible, ugly story. He wanted to lash out with his fists, his feet, anything, at Marc Sterne and that unnamed priest—wherever the bastard was now. He recalled how Raye Wheeler had said, "That girl's been through a real patch of hell and then some."

Burke yanked himself off the chair, wanting to sweep his arms around her. But she had moved, tugging at her shift as she returned to the table before he could reach her.

Fahey sat still, numbed. He picked up his pencil again and doodled. A raped angel, he thought, and he drew a double halo.

"Pritter know any of this?" he asked Burke.

"How could he?"

"You never mentioned this to anyone except Wheeler?" Fahey asked Romaine.

"I could never," Romaine said, her voice faltering.

A pause then, as they gathered their separate thoughts, until Tommy Burke finally said, "Can't use any of it in the trial, either. Sure as toot the jury would think Romaine was out for revenge."

"I just want to forget," Romaine said aimlessly.

"We're going to put you on the stand, Romaine," Tommy told her. "You know that, don't you? You'll just have to deny you had anything to do with Marc Sterne's death."

"One thing I haven't heard," Fahey said, dropping his pencil. He met Romaine's bewildered look with a hard one of his own. "Why, after all this, did you ever see the guy again? Go out to Malibu that night? I'd think you'd never want anything to do with him."

"I already told Raye. I wanted my money back, the money I loaned Marc. He said he'd have it in cash."

"What money?" Tommy asked.

"Marc owed me money that I had loaned him. And other money I was owed from a story treatment we sold to Parthenon. I told Raye all this—"

"That right?" Fahey asked, looking at Burke.

"I suppose," said Tommy. "Raye didn't tell me everything."

"I swear I told him," Romaine protested.

It was the first of three lies she'd already planned in her cell during those long and monotonous hours with all the time in the world to pull them apart and put them back together. Seamless, perfect lies that couldn't be checked. She'd act her way through the whole grim charade, scene by scene, if that's what it took. No one would ever catch on, and Romaine had been scanning Fahey and Burke to see how they reacted, how her story was playing. So far, they seemed to be biting.

"How much money are we talking about?" Fahey wondered aloud. "The loan?"

"Close to a hundred-and-ten thousand. A little over."

"He borrowed that?"

"Yes," Romaine said, evenly. "My last paycheck from the film, and he owed me a share of the story money besides."

"He was broke?"

"Nearly always. He spent money like he printed it in the basement."

Fahey blew a low whistle under his breath. "Can't use that, in the trial either, can you, old son?"

"Not a chance," Burke agreed.

"You see," Romaine said, "I went out to Malibu to see his parents. I was going to ask them to talk to Marc and help me get my money back."

"You called them?" asked Fahey.

"Before. A day or two, I think, and asked if I could come out."

"And spoke to whom?"

"Ferenc. He's the houseman."

"He testified, right? Was that in there? In the transcript?"

Burke said no, it wasn't. That Wheeler might have decided not to press that angle. Pritter might pounce on it eagerly, opening the way for a money motive as a reason for the murder.

"I didn't kill him...I didn't, *didn't*. Can't you believe me? Any of you?" Romaine wailed as she buried her face in her hands.

Fahey examined the ceiling. His thoughts hopped everywhere on the grayness up there. He tried catching them all in his mind, ever suspicious but still inclined to believe her. He did and he didn't. What could he fit together that might bear a clue or two, a clue to the as yet unknown or perhaps, with massive good luck, to the unknowable.

Burke intervened. "Romaine, they said you could come out to Malibu? The Sternes?"

"Oh yes, Tommy. Ferenc asked Mr. Sterne, and then told me it was just fine." Her second maiming of the truth on that afternoon. She knew fear now, the fear that neither of these men could ultimately protect her from Pritter or a man with the swat-power of Julio Sterne.

A lengthy, telling silence had descended. Romaine's eyes seemed so intimate, so searching and eager and playful that Fahey had to blink several times to keep a steady gaze aimed her way. "Be wanting to have a look up there at that Hollywood apartment," he said to Burke. "What do we need? An order from Rhodes?"

"Yes, and Pritter will have to know."

"What good does that do?" Romaine asked.

84

"Maybe some, maybe none." Fahey replied absently. "Look around, check the pipes. See what the cockroaches are up to. I don't know what. But if you don't snoop, you don't get."

"You wanted to ask about those sounds out on the water," Burke reminded him.

Fahey looked at Romaine. "You know what a sheriff's confidential report is?"

"Not really."

"It's what they write up when they're making an investigation."

Romaine nodded. "Got it, thanks."

"The night Marc Sterne died the neighbors questioned by the sheriff said they heard sounds out on the water. Did you recall hearing anything like that?"

"Yes, I think I did. A motor sound, like a boat, I suppose."

Fahey smiled. "For how long did you hear it?"

"I don't remember," said Romaine, shrugging.

Fahey liked that answer. It rang true. No one could remember something like that, not in a time of stress that had occurred months ago.

"The Sternes have a boat, I hear. Think it might've been theirs?"

"Maybe. I don't know. All I know is Mr. and Mrs. Sterne were out on the boat. With Ferenc Kardas, the houseman. The day help were all gone."

'You didn't see their boat at the dock when you arrived?"

"I didn't look, either," Romaine said. "But if I'd known they'd be out on their boat, I'd never have gone to the house that night. Tommy," she pleaded; "you're going to help me, aren't you? You just have to. I can't stay here." Her eyes clouding over again.

"You've got to hold on," Burke said. "Pritter has to prove everything. And the jury's got to believe him."

"Or me."

"Or you. Right. I'll be coming back. We'll go over everything, again and again, and you won't have to worry about anything."

"Oh, thanks, Tommy, thanks. I adore you, I do.".."

Burke blushed the blush of a man ready to scale any rampart ever built or imagined. The sound of her vibrant voice rang in his ears before it was swallowed up by his heart.

"You, too, Alonzo. I know you'll help me," Romaine said.

"Another thing," Fahey said. "Who did you say was on the Sterne's boat that night?"

"I guess the two of them and Kardas."

"You guess? You didn't see anyone or see the boat?"

"No. I just assumed." Instinctively knowing she had better go no further.

"Okay, we'll go looking. This is a grim joint, so keep your stars lit and, as Tommy says, hang on to your rompers."

She reached out and squeezed both their hands. Fahey looked down at the double halo he had doodled on the pad. He knew he was back in the pond, back in the murder trial business again.

"So, are you going to hold out one me?"

"I'm not."

"I asked you earlier, were you humping this Sterne kid? The druggist?"

"None of your business."

"You *are* my business, angel. Best you know that. And the answer is?"

"I'm of an age. I'm healthy. I have a vagina and I'm not a nun."

"I'd never ever make that mistake, love."

The assaulted angel, Fahey mused. On the way out of the detention center, he retrieved his pocket flask. Jiggling it a few times, he accused the woman guard of nipping from it. Burke, taller and more confident now that Romaine Brook "adored him," pulled Fahey out the door.

"You're not just capricious, you're all the way crazy," he told Fahey.

"The bitch. See the hair on her lip? Ought to see a barber for Chrissakes."

"Look, I have to stay on even terms with those people."

"Kick her in the ass is what you ought to do. You wear the boots for it."

"Alonzo, you're nuts."

"Let's find us a drink. Have one for old Raye."

"Sorry, but I've got to get back to the office."

"Some girl, that one." Fahey watched for Burke's reaction. "Ought to put her on Austrian television. Has the right looks."

"Romaine?"

"Sure Romaine. Who the fuck else? You see how she looks when she talks? Like she's keeping a private vision of Jesus in her soul. Got some class, she has."

"Trouble class. She's the head of that class, I'd say."

86

But Fahey's mind traveled elsewhere. Burke had turned down an all-expenses paid offer to visit one of Fahey's favorite gin mills, where they raced turtles on afternoons of odd numbered days. A grave error in the usage of one's limited time on earth. Fahey jumped the conversation to his great Gypsy whore, a spectacular find. She knew particular things. Where to look for stolen art. Told the future, she did that too, and read all your hours with her tealeaves, often consulting her secret star charts written in ancient Bulgarian. Weighed in at an even two-hundred pounds, a real formation of a woman with one ebony eye and the other of amber. Possessing the strength of a Sumo wrestler. "Going to put her in charge of the Regiment's Intelligence Section." Fahey stopped suddenly, pulling on Tommy's arm. "Gave me this medal," Fahey said proudly, pointing to a colorful but obsolete Turkish military medal dangling on his lapel. "Wear it to remember the fallen people like Raye. I'll see if I can find one for you. Lucky, these medals. Talismans, you see."

Tommy stepped away as soon as he could, telling Fahey he needed a leash, if not a straitjacket.

Fahey grinned as he savored a swig from his flask—"emergency reserves" he was calling it today. He pointed across the way at several boys tossing a football, and then pleaded with Tommy to find a store that sold red berets. A bloody winter was coming up, and Fahey was going into survival training in the San Gabriel Mountains. "One day, Tom-Tom, we'll have a grand outfit. And you know what? Listen to me, they'll all be mounted on camels with those Moroccan silken saddles. Think of it."

"I better not."

"Oh, Tommy, laugh for Chrissakes. It's only one life, so fly your heart, man. It's all God's joke on us, so let's play one back." Fahey looked at him with mock scorn, then flew to a newer thought. "You keep an extra gun anywhere?"

"A gun?"

"A. Luger or a Colt, either one'll do. Not sure I know where mine is anymore."

"I don't keep guns."

"Too bad. I'll have to knock over a cop on the way to the Gypsy's."

"Alonzo, I swear I don't understand you half the time."

"Doesn't matter, does it? Life is mostly smoke signals. The Comanches made the best ones. Got it down to a fineness, they say."

Grabbing him again in a powerful one-arm hug, he kissed Tommy on his birthmark. Recoiling, Burke pulled away, wiping his cheek and hurrying off, hoping no one had noticed.

Fahey needed certain credentials for tomorrow, when calling on the nuns at Las Infantas. Instinct informed him he should borrow a rosary to charm God's living virgins, vacant of all the men ever meant for them. A long, long interval had separated him from those ladies in black. Must do it, he thought, make a stab at getting to her father, if he were somewhere findable. Money was needed for everyone—even the Gypsy. He owed her for last month's frolics and her other lessons she'd imparted in that freezing bathtub of hers.

∝

Fritzi's had the painters at her home, freshening up her kitchen and the living room. A rarity: she was staying at Rhodes's home in Bel-Air for the week. In bed one night, he couldn't make love with her again; her misunderstanding of the situation was as complete as it was unnerving. She attributed it to the war wounds he had incurred, requiring a re-make of his male member. But he knew the problem for what it was: whenever they were lovemaking, guilt suffused him. Audrey came to his thoughts and when she did, and he could not shuck the desire for her, he wilted. He was utterly conflicted. When with Fritzi in bed, he felt pangs of guilt that he was somehow being unfaithful to Audrey Sterne, who had been no real part of his life for twenty-odd years. But the reality was, and he well knew it, that his infidelity, at least the one of desire, was not aimed at Fritzi.

Making him sick at himself.

Fritzi wanted him to see a doctor. She meant a shrink, but had delicately avoided that term of reference. No shrink he knew of could fix what ailed him: his soul was going through a slow burn, and it was for him alone to extinguish the fire.

He was now involved with two women: one, a figment that had never really left his heart, the other now at his side. He hadn't the guts to tell Fritzi of this, try to explain it. How could he explain it to her, when he couldn't explain it to himself or barely admit it to himself? Audrey Sterne was an episode from the ever-deepening past. Still, she was there, she was real, and had been so ever since Lloyd Pritter had brought her into the trial as a witness on behalf of the state.

He had always, in the past, slept like a buried state secret; then, two months ago the trial had ensnared him and there came Audrey Sterne, re-entering his days as if she had been there all along. Ever since, the many remembrances of her kept him awake far into night as yearning burned inside him with the red heat of a branding iron.

Ridiculous, even unimaginable.

He was beginning to despise the trial, and what it was doing, but knew he had to see it through, get it done with, and now this—his emotions blocking him from making love with a woman he'd gladly have as a wife after all these years as a bachelor. Little was making much sense to him. Nothing beats the truth, and he ought to tell it all to Fritzi. But he'd almost rather become a mute than reveal himself to the discontented woman sleeping three feet away.

With so much on his plate to deal with: the trial, the pending nomination to the Supreme Court, the media who could cause him principal trouble, and Fritzi, and Audrey—he had also begun to think that the harder you pursued happiness, the more evasive it became.

ଓଃ

In her third floor cell at the detention center, Romaine Brook struggled with an ever-strangling bout of loneliness. She was segregated from the others, at Judge Rhodes's orders. Raye Wheeler had pled that because of who she was, the dykes in the detention center would make prey of her. Rhodes's had bought Wheeler's argument. Still, segregated meant she was usually alone. Too much so, and after the session with Burke and Fahey, she had been returned to her cell, lay down and began another round of figuring her future: *that Fahey, him I've got to watch. A tricky one. He's got more people inside him than I do.*

Letting that one tumble around till she tired of it, and it was time to escape to a little enjoyment, get away from this sump in the only way she knew how to get away.

So she traveled into one of her solo séances. And in a little while she connected with her beyond, her other world, where she heard nothing but her other selves.

"I hear voices talking with my other self. I call upon that self, and I channel my Muse, when I'm learning a film part so I know how to step into the skin of someone else. Be them, and yet be myself. It's like playing that game called imaginary people. You need an artist's imagination and perception and a great memory, and I have all three and I know how to use them. I've a spirit guide, who holds my hand in the dark of night and takes me places only she can find. Fantastic. She journeyed me into her vagina once. Incredible. Unless you're a gynecologist or the coroner, you can't believe what's in there. Enzymes and chemicals and bacteria with unreal shapes. I saw sperm swimming, then invading an egg. Pop!

No one will believe me, were I to tell them. Not important. It's only important that I believe in where I go, what I see, what it makes me do.

I know how to be Marie Antoinette, Marilyn Monroe, Jean d'Arc, and do them all in one day. Even in one hour. In fact, I've done it. Some refer to it as the theater-of-the-mind, but I call it what it is: The World According To Romaine Brook. I'm actress, director, producer, writer, all wrapped up in one enchilada.

If I could wangle a couple of days and nights with that cute judge, I could end this trial fast. He's older but he's not that old.

We'll see.

It's so woefully boring sitting next to Tommy all day, listening to the endless bullshit in the courtroom...what a chicken-dance, you'd think these characters would have better things to do, or better parts to play...it's the way it is, in life, with everyone wearing a mask to conceal who they really are. Hiding, and probably quaking that they'll be found out one day.

Actors all, just like me. At least, I'm honest about it. People don't know what I am but they know who I am.

Poor Tommy. He's really got it for me. One day, while we were alone doing legal stuff, I told him I wasn't wearing a single thread of anything under this despicable jail uniform. He almost panted like a winded dog. Tommy's fixed; he's on my side, totally so. The bumbler supreme, though, and I need to juice up his act, or Pritter—that fat-assed Eel—he might get to the jury before I do.

Sometimes it's the canary that must eat the cat. A director told me that, and it's beginning to sink in. When I'm called to the witness stand, who shall I be? I need time to rehearse...this one is for all the marbles. My life— and I want it back!

Chapter Ten

Balmy air drifted over the fruit-laden groves of San Timoteo. Yesterday, Fahey had made a quick reconnaissance of the small coastal valley. It had changed little since last he'd been here: still a haven for rich Eastern hobbyists dallying at small-scale ranching, while scooping up fat agriculture tax deductions as they acquired their winter tans. It had dodged developers' bulldozers because the local gentry made it nearly impossible to obtain building permits, and because the price of local land kept it safe from the invaders.

After eggs and bacon at a country inn, he called the orphanage to say he was on his way. The same standoffish voice reluctantly gave him directions, hinting they were not overly thrilled about his visit. A voice fit for a fishmonger's wife, he thought, when hanging up. She'd not get so much as a cent from the regiment's mess accounts.

Still, a smile was never far from Fahey's face, and this, after all, was a new day with its specter of fresh adventures beckoning. He had already envisioned the regiment of his waking dreams on bivouac here in this sun-drenched valley. Hills and gullies and streambeds everywhere—a fighting general's delight.

He loved it.

And the town with all its clapboard-faced shops had a cleansing evergreen smell to it. Probably too clean, Fahey thought, as he left the inn for another stroll down the main street of San Timoteo. Hushed as a cathedral at midnight, and having an ear for such things, he knew for what it was: the sort of quiet that could always be arranged by old and heavy money. Though it was barely eight in the morning, he counted seven Mercedes SUVs and four Rolls Royces parked along the stone curbs of the street, He was tempted to spit on the spotless walks just to see if an alarm might go off somewhere.

He ambled over to where he had parked his Buick near the local tavern. His silver flask needed refilling. He had time to kill, and needed to locate a flower shop, then check his appearance again.

He wore his twice -a-year church clothes today. A blue tie against a pale blue shirt tucked into his dark blue suit. Had even brushed the suit carefully before slipping it into its travel bag. Around his waist, as a sort of a belt, he had folded and tied a pink headscarf belonging to his wife.

He was quite well set to make his mark on the day that lay ahead. Dressed, as he always was, to be remembered. It was cheap marketing.

In the tavern, he sat on a cowhide stool, having an early one along with a cup of Ecuadorian coffee. The bartender remarked on the pink of Fahey's belt and the hip-holster with the .38 poking out of it. Deep in thought, readying himself, Fahey merely replied, "I'm having my last drink for a while. Been sent orders to report for training to the regiment bivouacked up this way. A Vatican outfit. Amphibious troops. Water-walkers. Getting rid of the Swiss guards over there..."

The bartender had backed away when Fahey asked where he could buy a machine-gun at that hour. Flowers, as well; an incongruous request.

He tarried in the tavern for an hour, then left to find the florist. He bought a box of them, then consulting his hastily scribbled notes, he headed for the edge of town and then to a back road. Cloudy with dust, the road was overhung by great live oaks that almost hid the hills that were all in feather with daffodils.

Fahey had expected a quite different set-up, when pulling up to a ten-foot high front gate. On both sides of the gate, decaying stonewalls snaked across a slope of lovely verdant land.

A defunct brewery, he wagered; perfect camouflage for a nunnery, they always had a trick or two up their sleeves. Through the slightly bent bars of the padlocked gate, he saw the main building—low slung, a patchy slate roof and thick-trunked oaks towering against the bluish stone facade. A marl driveway full of deep ruts and potholes as far as he could see.

Wonderful, be thought. Be perfect for a headquarters, yet the concept of a microbrewery held a certain appeal. Perhaps the good sisters would sell on generous terms: a payout, say, of forty years at a Christian rate of interest. How does one go about applying for a license to brew rare ales? Rhodes might know and Fahey made a mental note to ask him.

He warmed up by humming a fighting ballad the Gypsy had taught him one day when they'd been in a sauna sweating it out. Suddenly he let out a deep buffalo-like bellow aimed at a hunched over figure faraway at the driveway's end.

Shaking the gate, he saw the figure rise and shuffle his way down the driveway. Fahey went back to his convertible and slid the long green florist's box off the back seat.

Peace offerings.

A dark-skinned man drew nearer. He had a flat and unlucky face with no teeth visible when opening his mouth to speak. A groundskeeper, Fahey guessed, spotting streaks of dirt on the man's overalls.

"I'm Fahey," he said calmly. "They expect me."

"Señor?"

"An appointment. Me...and the Sister Marius."

"*Si*. You to please move the car, señor?"

"How about you watch it for me? Don't drive it over that tank course either," said Fahey, pointing to the rutted driveway.

""I busy, señor. You must move own car."

"Speak Italian?"

"No, señor."

"Parlez-vous Francais?"

The man shook his head.

"Russian? You must speak Russian fr'Chrissakes, it's Monday today. Revolutions are best done on Mondays. Ask anyone in Moscow. Lenin was a Monday man. You can ask Stalin if you can find him."

A droopy-eyed look crossed the Mexican's face. All he could think about was the gun on Fahey's hip, and the fumes of liquor on the shouting breath.

Fahey rattled the gate again. "Little man, I important. Come straight from Roma. Orders from the Vatican...Office of Lost Souls, you wonderful little mother." He shifted the flower box and opened his jacket far enough so the groundskeeper could glimpse the gun, then pulled a tenner from his pocket, handing it through the gate. "Here. Now open the fucking gate, Gomez, or I'll be coming over the wall for you."

A hundred yards later, Fahey looked into colorless eyes on the other side of a Judas window He stated his business again. The Judas window closed with the raspy sound made by old and warped wood.

93

A bolt slid back and the wide oak door of Las Infantas opened. He was allowed in by a young fresh-faced woman, a postulant, he would later learn, about to vow her eternal life to an even more eternal God. Great insurance, he thought, though no one really knew if it ever paid off. He felt a massive urge to kiss her, showing her she had other options, if she cared to do a bit of exploring.

He was asked to sit. Fahey let his eyes roam the foyer. He could have his office right here, he thought, and be keeper of the keys to the vast storage cellar of the brewery. Greet the important customers, chase away the bill collectors and any unbidden Treasury agents.

Up high, the ceiling was cross-braced with aged timbers. A rose window was cut into one wall and an intricately carved choir screen, like a balcony, stood out on the opposite wall. He could use it to deliver pep talks to the good nuns who he'd enlist to sell his brews. They sold for God, why not for Fahey's Heavenly Ales? Put them on a special commission and excuse them from their Lenten fasts.

His busy mind tinkered with two or three sales slogans until the postulant returned to guide him into the deeper recesses of this sanctuary. Walking along, he noted walls of irregularly cut granite. Can't be another like it anywhere, he decided, as he followed the musical sway of the postulant's chaste hips. Somewhere around her fifth sway, he knew she would be just right to conduct tours for the paying public.

Make a fortune. Can't miss if God smiles on this place of very cold bed sheets.

Brimming with enthusiasm, he handed the box of two dozen roses to Sister Marius in her small office. She thanked him politely and remarked on the pink ones. Sixtyish, he guessed and a bit rotund under the flowing blue habit that almost concealed her black lace-up boots. Her skin was the color of rose pearl, hardly lined at all, and dark eyes glowing like lasers out of the gray shadows. Lots of woman there, he speculated.

Fahey feigned with: "Quite a gardener you've got here. A linguist, eh?"

"I hardly think so. Pedro's been with us for years. He barely speaks English."

"Caught a trace of Russian there under the Spanish. Rare combination, you know. Not the same lip muscles."

"You're a linguist, Mr. Fahey?"

"Gaelic. But I've a few minor languages like French and German."

94

"I see." Sister Marius sniffed daintily. "Are you drinking so early today, Mr. Fahey?"

"Doctor insists on it. Touch of insomnia...say, Sister, have you ever thought of selling Las Infantas? For a worthy purpose, of course."

"Why, never, Mr. Fahey. It's our home."

"But it's no longer a foundling home."

"Not for some years, that's true. They changed the laws and we didn't have the funds to change with them."

"Sodders," murmured Fahey, delighted at the news.

"Beg your pardon?"

"Plodders. Fools in government, you know. Be our ruin, they will. You need to keep kicking them."

"Well, we've managed all the same. But we miss our little ones...now, Mr. Fahey, you'll have to tell me your business. We don't allow visitors on the premises very often and—"

"Surely." Fahey's smile competed with the sun. "You won't sell it? The place, I mean?"

"Where would we go? Of course not, Mr. Fahey. Why would you want it anyhow?"

Fahey crossed his legs. His coat slipped open. "A restaurant is what I had in mind. Country inn. Religious lore and that sort of thing. Be a nice change, wouldn't it?"

"This is consecrated ground." Sister Marius's eyes locked on Fahey's gun as he had meant them to. She blinked twice, startled. "You're here, I believe, on some confidential matter. Isn't that what you phoned about?"

"Ah, yes. Glad you reminded me. One of your own, I gather. The Brook girl."

"And how may we help?" the Marius voice a little querulous now.

"She was adopted from Las Infantas?"

"That's quite correct."

"I'm told her adoptive parents are either dead or missing." Fahey said. "We're trying to locate her real parents and we knew you'd want to help."

"Excuse me, but who is this *we* you're referring to?"

"Thought I explained, when I called for this appointment. Sorry. I'm employed by Romaine Brook's defense counsel."

"Well, Mr. Fahey, that may be so. But I wouldn't have any way of knowing that, would I?"

Fahey pulled out a breast-pocket-wallet. As he opened it, one side dangled down to reveal a scrolled honorary sheriff's badge made of gilded silver. A jeweler friend had embossed the shield with a few extra touches, one being a non-existent badge number. He slipped out a letter written by Tommy Burke and handed it over to Sister Marius.

As she reached for it, the cowl of her sleeve slipped back to reveal an Ace bandage, wrapped around her elbow. For arthritis, Fahey supposed. She moved stiffly at times, yet her serene face never betrayed the slightest grimace. A God-given discipline for suppressing one's pains in this often unforgiving world. He'd have to ask her for her recipes.

Sister Marius read the letter. Then she looked up, saying, "Well, that's all very interesting. Quite interesting. But I still don't see how we can assist you."

"Let's just try for an answer or two. Then I'm off like the fairest of winds. Besides, you'd not want a subpoena and all that sort of foolishness." Having made his opening gambit, he retrieved the letter from Sister Marius's slightly trembling hand.

"I wouldn't expect anything like that. A subpoena, did you say?"

"A real nuisance, those are. You'll be hiring dollar-hungry lawyers and all the rest of it." Fahey went on, explaining that he was new to the case. He understood that Raye Wheeler had requested information from Las Infantas on the identity and whereabouts, if known, of Romaine Brook's biological parents. Wheeler's request had gone unanswered. And now at the eleventh hour, Fahey was pleased to repeat the same inquiry.

"The defense, you see, needs money to defray costs. Perhaps, her real parents, if they could be contacted, might help. No obligation naturally. Yet," Fahey conceded, "worth a try, isn't it?"

As he talked, Fahey noticed a faint bobbing, up and down, of one of Sister Marius's feet. Suddenly it stopped. A signal of unease, he was sure of it. He had long ago trained himself to observe such frailties.

"Mr. Fahey," she said when he'd finished, "the information you seek is held in the strictest of confidence. I'm sure you can appreciate why—"

"I think, Sister, begging your pardon, those laws, too, have changed somewhat."

"But the policies of Las Infantas haven't," she stated adamantly.

"I got it. You don't want to help us. Such a shame. You want that poor young woman on your conscience...but not really, Sister Marius, do you? After all, Miss Brook was an alumnus of sorts, eh?"

"I'm quite sorry you've gone to all this trouble—"

"Well, then." Fahey stood up. He adjusted the pink headscarf around his waist, and saw her staring at it. "I'll tell the lawyer Burke and you might be expecting that subpoena any day now. I was hoping we could make it easy on everyone. You'll likely have to come to Los Angeles and appear at the trial for questioning. Produce your records, and so on. Be all over the newspapers, I imagine."

"Please, Mr. Fahey. You must understand a few things. Romaine Brook was born out of wedlock. I was here, and I remember the circumstances well enough..."And at this, Fahey sat down again..."and the mother of Romaine Brook was herself a young woman at the time. From a very prominent family, who were deeply upset about the situation. Often it's the best thing," persuaded Sister Marius, "to let these regrettable incidents to, uh, well, remain undisturbed. Naturally, we would like to help Romaine Brook. We're a Christian community. But we must also respect the wishes of others."

Fahey had kept quiet. He looked around the almost scruffy room, absorbing some of the religious objects: a crucifix surrounded by a wreath of palm fronds; a glass case enclosing a carved Madonna; a missal with a tattered leather cover resting on a small side table. Then he regarded Sister Marius again, with her earnest face that seemed to fear nothing and know everything.

"You see," he said, "it's a trial about murder. Her lawyer has to fight hard as he can for her. Go to any lengths. I do not think he'll succumb to your, ah, protective ethics. No fun, you know, being hammered to a pulp in one of those witness chairs. The press hanging on your every word and ready to hang you soon as they find some angle. Poke you right in the eye, they do. Never apologize for it, either. Louts, the bunch of them."

"Well, I'm sure you're wrong about one thing, Mr. Fahey."

"Please tell me, Sister." Paying out with a winsome smile.

"I don't think any judge would approve a subpoena, if it meant stirring up the past for innocent people."

"Who's so innocent?" Fahey said. "I'm pretty sure this judge, and I happen to know him, would do whatever's fair. As I say, it's all about murder, isn't it? When it's about murder, they don't care overly about the feelings of the innocent. Or the religious," he added somewhat forcibly, and giving her a look she'd remember for more than just this day.

"Supposing we no longer have the records?"

"Won't make any difference. You were here, you said a moment ago. So they'll just subpoena you, bring you to court, and force it out of you. If you don't answer, you'll be ruled in contempt. That could mean jail until you see God's light shining, messaging you to tell the truth. Then what? More sins to confess and you don't look to me like a sinner. Not you, dear Sister. Were you an artist's model at one time, you've the angelic virtuous face for it."

Alarm tightened Sister Marius's face. She'd never expected anything like this in her day. Las Infantas was indebted for those donations, much-needed ones, received on condition it kept to a strict silence about Romaine Brook.

"Suppose, Mr. Fahey," suggested Sister Marius after dueling with her conscience, "that we compromised?"

"I'd love it. Wonderful!" A ray of hope in his voice.

"Then suppose I contact the, er, mother and ask if she'd like to help in some way...that is, if I can contact her at all," Sister Marius hedged. "I can call you later. Perhaps you'll leave me the letter?"

Fishing the letter from his pocket, he handed it back to her. "That'd be fine. Delighted, you'll cooperate. Be best for all, that's how I see it." Happy with himself, but concealing it; the good sister had lent him a clue—the birth mother was alive somewhere.

"And there'll be no subpoena?"

"Won't be necessary, if you'll help us."

"That's not quite what I said."

"Ah, but it's what I heard. Let's just see what happens, Sister. I'm not the one trying the case. Lawyers, you know. They're liable to do anything. Shakespeare knew it and told us so. Henry the Fourth as I recall."

Sister Marius grimaced, and her voice, so even and clear before, had suddenly become ragged and hesitant. As if her chest had heaved, the silver crucifix shifted places on her bosom. "I'd like—um, I wish—well, you see—don't you see we need to know for certain that we can reveal confidences."

98

Fahey took note of her angst, as he replied, "You can have the subpoena or not. But why deal with all that inconvenience? Having process servers camped at your gate. Frightening your charges. And they'll be a nuisance to Gomez and—"

"Gomez?"

"That groundskeeper who's so hard of hearing…all you have to do is lead us to the parents or parent and all will be forgiven, shining and bright, and we'll end your troubles in an instant. God will grant both of us a river of new graces."

"We are not the ones making trouble," Sister Marius said firmly.

"Remember, I'm there trying to help Miss Brook. What would Christ do? I'm on the same side as she, and she's the victim, we think, of a foul act of miscarried justice. Or I'd not be here in your blessed sanctuary."

"These matters of compromised birth are very, very confidential," repeated Sister Marius. "Surely you understand that innocent people have a right to privacy and—"

"You keep saying *innocent*. I don't know how innocent they are, Sister. They had babies and without the sacrament of marriage, but then there are worse things."

"It was a long time ago, and they've atoned."

"Atoned, have they? I wonder how. That, also, is exactly why I've come here, so whoever they are can do some real expiation. Stand and be counted at a time of peril for a young lady who may be falsely accused. There is God's undone work here, Sister. Time for clean hands."

"But that would only reveal what others prefer to be kept silent. We cannot violate a trust, Mr. Fahey, as I've said twice."

"One or two names, and I shall promise to keep you out of everything. No subpoena. And then we're all mum as a mummy." Fahey pressed her, throwing down his bluff. He unwound from his chair, slightly flushed and slightly frustrated at all the runaround.

"Mr. Fahey, I've no right to be personal, but are you Catholic?"

"Sometimes. I've a habit of going in and then out. My wife is devout as Magdalene, and with several of Magdalene's habits. I might send her up her to see what you can do with her. Lovely woman…got everything…"

"Does that mean you are uncertain of your faith?"

"When I'm in a bad corner, I'm very certain of it. You see, Sister, I've been searching for a long time for the truth of eternity. Whenever I get close, I see to get run over."

"Run over? By what?"

"By myself."

She shook her head. She was being trifled with, and resentment was building in her. A mistake had been made, allowing him anywhere near this office. Where, she wondered, had he ever come across such an odd-looking belt? And why a gun brought into a religious home, for heaven's sake? Not knowing, of course, that Fahey had various costumes for various occasions.

Fahey was warming to her, though it was nearing time to leave. He had gotten more than he expected at the first go-around. Sister Marius had a confident tough way about her, the sort of authority that reminded him of a blackjack tapping on glass. She probably had a lot to deal with—a crowd of women, her nuns, and no men around to keep them in line, and right then he was wishing he had her job.

"You've been most kind, Sister Marius," he told her as he buttoned his jacket, though the knot in the headscarf-belt still showed.

"Oh, not at all. Not at all. I assume we have a meeting of the minds."

"Spot on, or very close. And you'll let me know if you ever want to sell this citadel of hope and reverence?"

"You're really quite foolish to keep bringing that up."

"Must cost the sky to keep it up."

"Oh, we manage."

Leaving her office, they ambled to the large foyer with its vaulted ceiling. Sister Marius unbolted the great oak door, holding it ajar.

"You know," Fahey said while making his goodbyes, "if you weren't already spoken for, I know a place we could go for a luscious dinner, champagne and all. Would they let you out for a breath of air? I'd even post collateral, I really would."

"It's time you left us, Mr. Fahey."

Bolting the door once more, Sister Marius leaned against it, silently assembling her troubles. Another mortgage payment to meet, new habits for the nuns who had already re-sewn their frayed garments several times, medical bills, broken plumbing to repair. A new cold-locker for the kitchen, and the stove had failed so they were cooking with split oak. Now this, a threat of a subpoena, and very likely more difficulties to contend with.

She must make a call of surpassing urgency. But dear Lord, she thought, what will happen to Romaine Brook now? Guilt pressed its thorns on her roundish but no longer serene countenance.

∞

A brassy hot twilight surrounded Fahey, as he reached the outskirts of Los Angeles. The convertible's top was down, and the smoggy congested air smarted his eyes and dried his throat. He took a deep pull from his emergency reserves. Stopping for gas fifty miles back, he had tried to call Tommy Burke but learned the lawyer was over at the detention center again. He had tried the Rhode's chambers, kidded around some with Macklin Price, then learned Rhodes had also left for the day.

In Bel Air an hour later, he parked in the driveway, off to one side, and saw the Bentley in the garage. Fahey heard a low melodic sound, partly muted, as he circled the house.

Rhodes was standing on the terrace, one foot upon the stone balustrade, filling the air with notes from his trombone; a synthesizer played background sounds of a piano and a snare drum. The music came together, full and smooth, then was interrupted abruptly when Fahey clapped his hands.

"Scaring the owls again. The Humane Society'll be after you."

"H'lo, Alonzo."

"And yourself. Thought I'd try you here. Mackey-girl said you were splitting up the payoffs for the other judges."

"That's right. Everybody made plenty today...I just got home. C'mon up."

Rhodes rested his trombone across the arms of a white wicker chair. Flicking off the tape recorder, he dipped into his shirt pocket for a Honduran cigar.

"Like one?" he asked.

"Can't, thanks all the same. Ruins my taste for what's good for me."

Rhodes looked out over the lawn. "Sun's across the trees, Alonzo. Feel like a drink—"

"Thought you'd never ask. We'll have to do something about your manners, old son."

"You just got here," Rhodes said, a little uneasily "What're you wearing there? That pink thing—"

"Need a new color image. An experiment of mine. The women have it all over us on color...can't let'em have everything, can we?"

"Why not?" Rhodes smiled. "Hells bells, they got *everything* else you seem to want."

"When they're supine you mean?"

"I'll never quote you, Alonzo, I promise. You want the usual Bushmills?"

Fahey nodded as he removed his sunglasses. Seeing the look on Rhodes's face, he decided to explain himself.

"I know you told me to stay scarce until this work for Burke is over. I couldn't get him earlier on the phone. He's with the girl, or he was anyway. I'm trying to find out if we can get the okay to look around Marc Sterne's apartment." Fahey stepped onto the terrace.

"Burke called me about it. I told Pritter to call the sheriff and take care of it. If he resisted that suggestion, I'll take a motion from the defense."

"Good. I'll get over there tomorrow then."

Rhodes saw redness in the rims of Fahey's eyes and knew he'd been slurping already. "You want a short one or the long kind?"

"Long. Why walk when you can stagger is what I always say."

Pausing to light his cigar, Rhodes exhaled and saw Fahey dissolve for a moment, blanketed by the white gauze of smoke.

"Found a lovely little tavern today up by San Timoteo. Nice lay-by. Bartender needs a little disciplining, but we ought to buy it. Be just the place when we retire—"

"What's in San Timoteo? A new girl?"

"Not so new to you."

"What's that supposed to mean?"

Fahey repeated, more or less, what he had learned at Las Infantas as they passed through a terrace door into the red walled library.

Going to the bar, Rhodes asked a little testily, "What's with that gun you're wearing, Alonzo?"

"Not loaded, so don't worry."

"See that it stays that way. Hope you've got a license for—"

"Don't go up in flames. Cliff, it's just for dress, when I need impressions made."

"With a nun?"

"The one I saw could run the Marines. I use whatever I can, as you know. What're you, today? The first Bishop of Munich or somewhere?"

A pause, as both man tried to avoid argument.

"Well, Romaine Brook's birth, or the identity of her parents, has nothing to do with nothing," said Rhodes after thinking over what Fahey had related.

"Except, maybe money."

"Yes, maybe that. That's where we started, isn't it?"

"It was, and it is. Would your court ever issue a subpoena to help find out who the real parents were?"

"Have to think about that. I doubt it, though." Rhodes began to fix the drinks. "Not if it's only for the purpose of finding payment for legal fees. No, I think we'd steer clear of that idea. If that *is* the idea."

"Well, the nun may come across without one. I bluffed her a bit, told her you'd issue a subpoena if it came to that."

"That was really very very good of you, Alonzo. Maybe you'd like to take over the trial, too."

"Jesus, aren't you the one. Who'n hell asked me to come into this thing anyway? This nun had a mouth on her tight as a mail slot until I got her to sing a little. Had to lean on her, and I bet she's going to call the birth mother. The mother is alive, according to this Sister Marius. Now, we know something we didn't know before."

Rhodes stirred ice into Fahey's drink. "You're right there. I did ask you to get involved. But you can't go throwing threats of subpoenas around, willy-nilly," said Rhodes, handing over Fahey's drink.

"You look all in, you know that?" Rhodes's face seemed drawn tight, and without his usual color.

"Sleeping funny. Raye's funeral got to me. Anyway, cheers."

Politely but definitely Rhodes meant to get rid of Fahey. Find some lame excuse. Any other time and he'd gladly ask him to stay for dinner. Call his wife, Wanda, and have her come as well and laugh over past times when he and Fahey had been closer than two crossed fingers. But now it was different. And it was not such a hot idea for Fahey, while working for the defense, to be dropping by for private ex-parte talks.

Irregular as if could be; and with Fahey's wild mouth, no telling who might hear of it.

They gabbed a while. After one more rendezvous with the bar, Alonzo Fahey left for his own home. Very early in the day for Fahey to be thinking of going home, Rhodes thought, as he put the trombone away, went to his desk, shut off the phone, and then removed a sheaf of papers from one drawer. He could put in a few hours now. With time to whittle away for a change, he would work harder on a pet project: his ideas for improving the state's criminal justice system. Streamline it, cut back on the red tape. A year ago he'd gotten the governor's go ahead to draft proposals for the Legislature. California was different from most other states; a place in constant flux, a nation apart it often seemed.

Rapes, murders, scams, frauds, embezzlements—the courts perennially jammed to the gills. Cases awaiting trial for four and five years. Witnesses died, so did felons. Innocent people were caught in a time trap waiting their turn, facing a rising river of legal bills and with no way to dam the flood.

If you were in money, you could hunt the law down—instead of the other way around—by hiring the best guns. But it always took money, amounts far beyond the reach of most claimants or defendants.

Rhodes knew all about it. He'd played on the course many times, been in the fray as a hired shooter himself. And usually for hefty fees, sometimes for amounts in excess of two or three millions. Money was the poison in the system. Wrong way, but a good way to cave in the ribs of fair law and a fair system for applying it.

So, he had worked on sketching his ideas, devising what he thought would be a better path. One day, up on the high court, he would try to persuade others that the law was basically sound but needed a newer engine to make it work better. A hard sell to negotiate, eventually calling for the backing of the highest court in California to have the slightest of chances.

Well, he would try. What good was the law, if the courts were tangled up?

He had no illusions as to how trial lawyers would react to his ideas. Getting his way meant a slashing of their fat fees. They'd raise a howl for his hide.

Lost in thought, looking down at his scrawl illuminated by a pale cone of light, he heard Consuelo Ramirez waddle in. Scolding him about something, twice in the same breath, then telling him of the urgent call he should answer.

Picking up the phone, remembering that he had shut it off earlier so he could work in quiet. The voice surprised him, so nice at first, then pleading with him, almost begging—but not with a beggar's words. Audrey Sterne seemed on the verge of desperation.

"Yes," he quickly agreed, "of course, you can come over," and gave her directions. Laying down the phone, asking himself what was up, why the big rush? Thrill speared him from the toes up.

Chapter Eleven

Checking the number twice on one of the stone pillars, Audrey let up on the brake and turned into the driveway. With hardly more noise than a butterfly, her white Maserati Quattroporte coasted to a stop in front of Rhodes's home. Giving it the once over: the gray slate roof, vines of grape ivy climbing the white brick walls, red geraniums abloom in window boxes, a black front door set back into a high turret that ended in a cone-shaped crown above the roof-line.

Elegant, she thought—who would have ever guessed it of a ranch foreman's son?

A glance into the vanity mirror, then, checking her lipstick, trying to calm her nerves; nerves that had jangled ever since the call she'd made two hours earlier, hot-wiring her into a near frenzy.

Lipstick was fine, she saw, while primping her ash-blond hair. Outside the car, she smoothed down her peach colored dress and slid her hand through the straps of a Hermès alligator handbag dyed to match her dress.

She was tempted to jump back in the Maserati, but it was a drive of over an hour from Malibu into the city and she knew that if she didn't see him now, privately, very privately, she'd only prolong her agony. Hoping he wouldn't do anything abrupt or foolish, and would understand what it cost her, in fear and all else, to come here.

About to press the bell, she was startled as the door to her newest hell opened so suddenly.

"Heard you pull in," said Cliff Rhodes, his voice forcing its way through a grin. "Wow! You always look so marvelous, Audrey."

Returning his grin with a smile so wide you could hang laundry on it, she said, "Oh, Cliff, yes, thanks so much. Nice of you to say it." She sighed softly, suddenly relieved.

"Come in, please." He backed away and gestured her forward. "Right straight ahead. We'll go out and sit on the terrace. It's pleasant at this hour. I just found out we're having Chicken Diablo for dinner. Or we can go down to the club, if you'd rather."

"Right here is absolutely divine."

Her eyes roamed the high-ceiling hallway with its winding staircase and a banister of polished teak. "Quite lovely, your home, Cliff. Very, very nice. All the Lowestoft Export and Staffordshire. Reminds me of England."

"Reminds me of the bill I was handed by the decorator."

Looking at her mouth as she spoke, that mouth for breaking your heart, slightly drawn up at one comer so that it always seemed as if an invisible cigarette dangled there. You were mine once, he thought.

Audrey paused by an antique table. Guiding one finger along its inlaid design of satinwood, she asked, "Sheraton period?"

"I think so."

"Neat."

Hoping for some faint signal to suggest the reason for the visit, he stood there filled with expectancy. But when she said nothing more, they went out to the terrace, where Audrey arranged herself on a blue and white striped chaise-longue. Rhodes leaned against a stone rail a few paces away. Talking away, gauging each other, attempting the impossible task of sifting through so many years since they had last been together by themselves. There had been the greetings at Masquers recently, but now this, the two of them alone in the privacy of his home.

Easy questions, then vague ones and the vague answers to accompany them. She mentioned her twin boys by her previous marriage to a lord of the British realm. "My London Incident," she termed it, referring to the marriage. The boys, she said, were in their second year at Eton and summered with her in California or at Cap Ferrat.

Then, almost deftly, Audrey shifted gears. "A strange way for us to come together again, isn't it?"

"The trial you mean?"

"Yes, you running the trial and everything. That's quite strange, I feel."

"Unfortunately, it is. Even stranger than you might think."

Rhodes told her how the trial had been assigned to him almost by fluke. His calendar had opened up when two cases he'd been hearing were settled by plea bargains, and he was taking advantage of the situation to tender his resignation in anticipation of being confirmed to an opening on the Supreme

Court. He had agreed to remain, however, and preside, when another judge, originally slated to hear the charges against Romaine Brook, had been in an auto accident. "So, the trial fell into my lap almost by sheer chance."

Audrey turned her face at the sound of Consuelo Ramirez shuffling across the terrace. Rhodes introduced them, with Consuelo smiling politely yet gravely at the beautifully attired visitor. "Ees all right for eating soon, señor?" she asked.

"Anytime. All right with you, Audrey?" Rhodes looked at her.

"Would you mind if we wait for a...no, all right let's go ahead," she answered, changing her mind.

"I open wine now?" asked Consuelo.

"*Muy bien.*"

As Consuelo padded away, Audrey went on: "Where were we?" she sighed once more. "Julio was devastated when Marc was killed. Bitter, God! He barely talked to anyone for weeks."

"You could hardly blame him. But I don't think we can talk about the trial, Audrey."

"I'm afraid we must."

"That's all but against the law. So I'm afraid we can't. That's one of the rules of the road. My road anyway."

"Tell me, Cliff," she said, "what would you say if I told you I needed your help. Badly needed it."

"I'd say I'd give it to you if I can. But not on the trial, if that's why you came here."

"Well, that's exactly why I came," Audrey tossed her head back and her hair flew. "And what would you say if I told you it's you who might need the most help of all."

The way she said it unnerved him. Across the terrace, Consuelo fussed with the dishes at a serving table; hearing the clatter, he smiled and motioned to Audrey.

They sat at an umbrella table to a first course of gazpacho soup. To their side the green neck of a bottle poked its nose out of a silver wine cooler. A spray of roses lifted their faces from a crystal vase near to where Audrey sat.

He would wait her out. Rhodes wondered if this were some new ploy, some new game of pressure. Julio Sterne working another angle, an angle dealing with Rhodes's pending appointment to the high court. A political shot? Something else? But then he doubted if Julio Sterne had an idea of what had gone on between his wife and himself years ago.

Her spoon poised hallway to her mouth, Audrey said, "You remember, Cliff, when you were being sent to Afghanistan. When I took off from school for a week, and we went up to Pebble Beach?"

"Sure, I remember. How would I ever forget?"

Audrey sipped from her spoon. "I still don't know where to begin this."

"Start anywhere."

"You don't know it, were never told, but I...well, I got pregnant up there. Had a daughter, *we* had a daughter, I should say. That's who Romaine Brook is...our daughter." There, she had said it, straight out, and Audrey was relieved to find out her bones weren't flying apart.

The first thing leaving Rhodes was his spoon dropping into the soup bowl. The blood inside his head seemed to race to his feet. The tiny creases around his eyes went smooth, his eyes shut, and his mouth became thin as a matchstick. When he peeled open his eyes, they had flared wide with surprise.

Like millions of other men faced with paternity out of wedlock, his instant reaction was: it must be someone else's, not mine. He'd seen Romaine Brook's birth date in the trial record somewhere. Furiously, he tried recalling it. But his memory blanked on him now as surely as if an anvil had suddenly dropped on his skull.

"You don't believe me?" Audrey asked.

Rhodes shook his head, his mouth half-agape. "What can I say? I have to believe you. I'm trying to absorb the...the, uh, news."

"She was born in the night," said Audrey as she began to work out all the arithmetic for Rhodes. Their week in Pebble beach together, the birth nine months later, the twenty-odd years in between. Bing, bing, bing, like an adding machine tape counting up an overdue bill.

Searching his face as she talked, Audrey could tell he was busy trying to tack down the edges of his flapping nerves. "I'm sorry to have to tell you now, after all this time. But you had to know," she said sadly, worriedly.

Confused, and listing inside, he somehow knew—if only by her manner in telling him so evenly and so dourly—that this bullet of a stunning truth had finally found its mark.

"Why now?" he asked hoarsely. "Telling me this now?"

"Because something happened earlier today, Cliff. At Las Infantas, that's where Romaine was sent for adoption...someone went there and threatened a subpoena, or whatever, to find out whom her real parents are. That's why I'm here, why I called you. If it ever came out—"

But he heard no more. His mind thrashed around again. Fahey, of course. Oh, my Christ! How could it be! There'd be no subpoena. He'd all but told Fahey so.

"Audrey, there'll be no subpoena."

"But I don't know those things, how subpoenas work. Sister Marius, she's a nun at Las Infantas, called me, really shaken up, and told me a subpoena was coming. I had to see you, Cliff. My name is on the original birth record."

"And mine?"

Audrey nodded and Rhodes face froze.

"Why in hell didn't you tell me? A long time ago, I mean. Or when the trial began at least?"

"A long time ago, I tried. You were overseas and I couldn't find you, and then my parent insisted that, um, everything be hushed up," Audrey replied, and began to tell him of that wretched stretch in her life.

Of how, discovering she was pregnant, she finally broke down and told her mother, who wasted about ten minutes before telling Audrey's father. Their rage had been historical, volcanic. Abortion was against the law then, and it wouldn't have made a whit of difference anyway. As Rhodes knew, her family were devout Catholics.

They tried to locate you," she told him, "but the Army wouldn't say where you were. For months and months, they stalled us. Said you were missing, possibly dead. How was I to know? I really crashed. I was nearly disowned, and my parents forced me to put the baby up for adoption. At Las Infantas, where my father gave free medical care to the nuns...I couldn't tell you. I couldn't find you. I loved you, Cliff, but I couldn't find you anywhere. I was sure you were dead because they wouldn't tell us anything...so I was sent to England, and a year later, I married, trying to blot out the pain and misery and missing you. Oh Christ, I thought I'd put it all behind me. But found I couldn't do that either."

Audrey stopped.

My daughter—Romaine Brook? Rhodes thought. This woman lost to me, and then my daughter, all because of that goddamn war.

"Who else knows about us?" he asked solemnly. "That we're the parents."

"Me. You now. Of course, Sister Marius at Las Infantas. That's everyone."

"Not your husband?"

"That would be the final noose for me," Audrey said. "Marc was his only child. If he ever knew it was my daughter who—" she stopped abruptly. It was too horrible, too unbelievable, to even try talking about it.

"Your parents, but they're dead?"

"Yes."

"That's everyone, you're sure of it?"

"Everyone, Cliff."

Was the loop really closed? Maybe, maybe not. His brain thrummed away. He was still spinning on air, the rule of gravity somehow thrown aside for him.

"Audrey, how did you ever find her again? What happened?" Rhodes's face deepened again.

"I hate to even think. At one time, I cared very much. But now I have much less trouble working off that feeling. I just don't know what to feel."

"Tell me." Rhodes poured some wine. The bottle almost slipped from his moist, fumbling fingers before he caught it.

She began.

It wasn't at all what he'd heard Audrey explain in court on the day she'd come there, as the state's witness, to blister Romaine. Of how after eighteen years she'd divorced Lord Robert Huibbard-Hewes, a famed and quite notorious London theatrical producer. They had come to the end of their arguing over his constant affairs with every actress in England and places beyond. She met Julio in Surrey at a weekend house party and one thing led to another until they decided to marry. But the British courts insisted her twins be allowed to finish their schooling in England.

After she and Julio had come back to California, she found herself missing the boys unbearably. She had always wanted a daughter, though at Julio's age that was awkward, if not impossible.

But Audrey knew where to go looking for her abandoned daughter.

She befriended Sister Marius at Las Infantas. Gave money, gave quite a lot of it, and in return she learned the identity of Romaine's adoptive parents. Waited for a time, setting up a plan, then she had hired an investigator to conduct a search.

A month went by. One day the investigator's information came in a sudden, unexpected flash, almost like a bolt of summer lightning. Her missing daughter, she was informed, was Romaine Brook, an actress who was a student at the California School of Drama.

She went on explaining how she had persuaded Julio to make a heavy donation in the name of Parthenon Studios to the school. She was allowed to audit classes, as a courtesy. Weeks went by. She began to make casual inquiries, as a veil, about three of the drama students, and then two of them, and finally just one—Romaine, her daughter. Who would never, if Audrey could help it, learn of the extremely inconvenient identity of her birth parents.

The rest was easy.

She had invited Romaine to lunches at nicer restaurants. They were seen, occasionally, with Julio at Sunday polo matches or the glitzier tennis tournaments, at dinners and parties in Beverly Hills and Malibu where Audrey arranged for Romaine to be added to the guest lists.

Other nights Romaine, all sweetness and devotion, came for dinner at the Sterne's Malibu Pointe house. In time, Audrey, who had no particular feel for acting talent, saw what the teachers and coaches knew all along: Romaine had the makings. She had the money-bones, a photogenic face and she slipped into roles as if she had invented them.

"One of the rare ones," they said, "born for the stage. I was so proud of her. And I began to quietly back a few small productions so she could appear at the Santa Monica Playhouse," Audrey went on. "Audiences loved her. The reviews were often excellent, and then came the inquiries from Broadway producers and Hollywood studios. I wanted to showcase her, though I never told her I was an angel, an investor. I had her meet people of social position, the real kind and the Hollywood kind. It was lots of fun at first. She bowled people over with that deadly charm." Audrey's voice faltered and she stared out at the hills and ravines below the terrace, struggling with her emotions.

He waited for her to go on, not wanting to interrupt, and, besides, it was one of those moments you can do nothing about—a woman with her tears— and it was better never to try.

"I—well, you know, I wanted to look out for her, help her, assist her future," Audrey blurted, wet-eyed. "My own daughter, still and always a stranger. I came to love her, then fear her, and now I often feel hatred for her. For my own child." Audrey shook her head as more tears spilled down her cheeks. "But that came much, much later."

Wiping her eyes with the napkin. "When Julio approved Romaine's role in *Tonight or Never* everything seemed to change. Practically overnight, it changed. Somehow, the sunshine of Romaine turned into black clouds. She became moody, tricky, sly, even more of a stranger. I was furious after all we'd done. Her behavior was outrageous and she manipulated shamelessly...my mistake was failing to put a flat stop to Romaine's chase after Marc. I was the one who had introduced them. Before I knew it, a casual friendship blossomed into a raging affair. Talk of marriage, of a new world, of love everlasting, you know what I mean...and Marc Sterne had to have her. I nearly died twice every day just thinking about what'd happen, if Julio found out I was her mother. He still reminds me, digs at me is more like it, that I was the one who introduced Marc to the woman who killed him. If Julio finds out the rest, I'll be the next one on the trash pile. It's unbelievable, isn't it?"

"Your husband, he approved of the two kids being with each other?"

"Marc was all bright and starlight in Julio's eyes, and if Marc wanted Romaine, what could Julio say or I say? But on the business of marriage, Julio smartened up; there was a lot to think about, he agreed—and not the smallest of those intricacies...problems was seven-hundred million dollars or so of Sterne money that needed guarding. And Julio knew Marc was meddling in drugs and thought Romaine might be a good influence on him. What a laugh...influence...*some* influence...it was all a big boomerang," Audrey confessed, "and I could never bring myself to explain the truth to Julio. Not before Marc died, and *certainly* not afterward. It was one of those times when you never, never can be wholly truthful. There's no sane way I could explain to my husband that his only son was killed by my daughter that he never knew was my daughter. And after that, I couldn't believe she was my daughter, either. It's been impossible to believe. The whole mess is too fantastic, and I don't know what to do about it. I'd kill myself if it ever got into the newspapers."

Rhodes was silent. He let her tale seep into his bones, believing he was actually hearing what otherwise seemed too incredible to be realistic, that it was no dream, yet nonetheless it couldn't have happened. The odds were too astronomical that a daughter he never knew about until five minutes ago was now a defendant in his court. He admired Audrey for telling him what she had, knowing it couldn't be easy. And not knowing, and probably never to know, if there were more to the story.

As to his end of it, he smelled rigid trouble. Ethically, he must recuse himself from the trial. The conflicts were unmistakable, would be apparent to anyone who possessed eyes and ears. But he couldn't see an easy way to recuse himself.

"I'm so sorry, Cliff," said Audrey, breaking the silence "But my life is so filled with torture that the idea of a subpoena nearly drove me nutty. I don't think you can understand what it's been like, and will be like for me."

"I'm still trying to touch earth. I can't get used to the idea of a daughter."

"You haven't eaten anything."

"Not sure I could hold anything down, frankly."

"Me, neither."

Another pause. "A dead letter finally got delivered, didn't it?" he said, shaking his head, "My God Almighty."

"You can't send it back either."

"And you came here because some nun thought I'd subpoena her records?"

"Yes, she is terribly frightened. She knew if it all came out, it'd be a mess beyond belief."

"Do you know Alonzo Fahey?"

"No, should I?"

"Not necessarily. He was here earlier, that's when I first heard about a subpoena. I told him it wasn't in the cards. Now, it's in all fifty-two cards…all this over a damn subpoena." Rhodes went blank-faced, shaking his head aimlessly.

"You've got to stop it. For your own good as well as mine."

"There's nothing to stop. It'll never happen. It's not relevant to any issues in the case itself. But you've told me a thing I'll be living with the rest of my life. Now, I'll return the favor, which is not favor to you at all. I was the one who got Fahey to try to find out if Romaine's parents, her real parents, were still alive and, if so, would they be willing to help her with her legal costs. In a very direct way, I'm responsible for what's going on here."

"Making matters worse, in a sense."

"Making me involved, whether I like it or not. I sort of pulled the trigger on this situation." Rhodes was still pale from the strength it took to keep his insides together. "Would you consider Romaine at all dangerous?"

"I can't say, not really. But I put nothing past her. And I mean nothing." Audrey shrugged. "You just never know who she is, day to day."

"A split personality?"

"Maybe. An accomplished operator and user, that's for sure."

"Tell me more."

"Well, you see her every day, don't you?"

"See her, yes, that's right I do. I've never talked to her though. Never yet heard her utter a word."

"Go see her movie. She's quite unreal. She actually plays a nun. A *nun*, and if that isn't irony, what is? She plays this nun who does crime on the side." Seeing Rhodes's eyes traveling over her, Audrey shifted in her chair, pulling on the hem of her skirt. "A female shark," she continued in an empty voice. "You think she's so naive. So innocent and vulnerable. I was fooled. A sorceress. I got so afraid of her, I never turned my back when she was near. She made me paranoid, and I'm not kidding you, Cliff."

Night had descended. The cicadas had set up their incessant chatter. The light at the table, where they were sitting, came from four flickering candles, veiling Audrey in the dancing shadows, yet he noticed two white patches emerge on either side of her mouth, as if frostbite had set in.

"She stole something from me," Audrey told him. "Something dear and damn valuable, too."

"Stole what?

"An emerald bracelet. A Bulgari piece Julio gave me for our anniversary."

"Are you sure?"

"I couldn't prove it. I just know, that's all."

"Then you shouldn't accuse her."

"Oh please, Cliff. I'm just a woman, not a lawyer or a cop. I just feel, then I know...and Romaine knows I know."

"But why would she steal from you?"

Audrey went back to the time when they were on the *Paloma*, Julio, herself, Marc and Romaine. They'd been swimming one afternoon in a small cove on Catalina Island. Audrey had left the bracelet, a week or so earlier, in a locked safe embedded in a cabinet located just above the galley. She had removed it shortly after leaving the dock on the way to Catalina, so she'd not forget it again. But she'd taken it off while changing into her bathing suit in the owner's cabin, leaving it on a bedside table. Later, on the way back to Malibu Pointe, she couldn't find it anywhere after searching every nook of the boat. She could hardly accuse anyone there of stealing it…not then, not ever till now.

"I just know," Audrey repeated after thinking and talking about it again. 'There're things you simply know. She's full of guile. And she's a thief, damn it all."

"Not a helluva lot to go on," Rhodes observed drily.

"Oh, she's always so clever. Afterward, she said she saw me go in swimming with it on. Tried to warn me, even."

"Maybe you did."

"I get careless sometimes, but not that careless, not with a Bulgari bracelet. Julio was apoplectic. It cost a bomb. All matched eight-carat stones and my initial done in pavé diamonds on the clasp."

"Hope you were insured at least."

"That's why Julio was so angry. It wasn't."

"Ah."

"I can't bear to even think about it anymore," said Audrey, tears flooding her eyes again. "I'd like to wring her damn neck, but she's still my daughter."

"*Our* daughter."

"Right, Cliff. Our daughter and you can have full title to her."

Rhodes had been nursing his wine. He put his glass on the table. Thinking at speed, he attempted to pin the corners of the problem together so Audrey would be sure to grasp its collapsing sides.

"If I stay in the trial and Romaine is found innocent, and then later I'm discovered to be her father, it'll seem like I put the fix in somehow. And also if I stay on and I'm found out, that I had learned the accused was my daughter, I'll be disbarred for sure. I could even get jail for judicial misconduct. On the other hand, if I recuse myself at this stage, I'd have to have some beaut of a reason for doing it. That I'd been hit by the bus or something. If I state the facts to the other judges, it's bound to get out at some point and there goes everything, including my next stop in life.

Sacramento. That'll have no chance of happening. You're dead-on right, Audrey, it's a mess beyond redemption. I'm boxed, either way."

"I didn't realize it could be that bad. For you, I mean. They'd never pry it out of Sister Marius. So, if there's no subpoena, then who's to know other than you and me? "

"Are you willing to take that chance?"

Audrey thought a moment. "Is there another choice."

"Face the music, we can always do that. If we do that, then gird yourself for a month-long invasion of your privacy. Probably more."

Her face went hectic again. "God, what'll—what can we possibly do? Julio would go insane. He's got a lulu of a temper at times…oh, Cliff, you've got to get us out of this. You have to!"

"I don't know what anyone can do. This trial's cost a million bucks already. If it ever turns into a mistrial, they'll hang us. Me, at least." And there goes the Supreme Court appointment, he thought. All his work down the chute; indeed, a hefty chunk of his future.

"Cliff? That lawyer who died, Wheeler, the one who said he might recall me as a witness?"

"Yes."

"You've got to get me out of that."

"It's all up to them. The state. You're their witness."

"You must, though. You're the judge, aren't you?"

"Only a judge, not Caesar. There's no way I can prevent the defense from making you appear. You're already sworn as a witness. They have every right to recall you. And if you refuse to come to court, I'd have to issue a warrant. Please don't make me yank that cord, but be aware I'd otherwise have to."

"What if I'm asked the wrong questions?"

"Answer them. You have to answer them, and don't do any games when you do answer."

"Speaking of games, Julio is sort of doing things. I've heard him on the phone talking to the governor."

"He may one day regret it, too."

"It's only because she killed Marc. You must know that, don't you?"

"That's for the jury to say."

"Help me, you said you would. You did say it, Cliff."

"I didn't say I'd absolve you of making a court appearance, if you're recalled."

"Well, shit on everyone! Why don't I have some rights? You're always told about democracy and freedom. A hollow promise, I think. I'm sick of it all."

"One day this'll all be over."

"I wish that day were yesterday."

She stood and he stood with her. She ran to him and clung with both arms locked around his neck. Every organ inside him seemed to move a full foot.

"Audrey, you've got to hold up. You're the kind who can. You must do it. I need time to sort this out…if I can sort it out…"

Though the words were somewhat muffled by his shoulder, she let go with, "I can't stand it anymore. Julio or Ferenc Kardas, the whole crazy wild bloody mess. S'breaking me apart, Cliff. I can't go on like this, don't you see? No one sees *anything* anymore."

"This Kardas. Is he the one who testified earlier?"

"That's him. He's a Hungarian."

"I could tell he wasn't from around here," Rhodes replied.

But what he was seeing were the flaming pits of Dante's Inferno. His thoughts had shot a mile into space, or perhaps it was a mile downward toward the middle of the earth, and he had paid no attention to her mention of a Ferenc, whom he had never heard of. They held together for a time, very close, as he attempted to solace her. He smelled her perfumed scent, and felt her hair against his cheek. One leg moved against him, and he had a rowdy urge to lift her face and kiss her. Then he saw a moving shadow. It was Consuelo coming out of the terrace door and quickly she turned and scurried back inside.

Audrey pulled away, saying, "I'm all right now, I think. Don't look at me, I know I look like hell. I'm sorry I broke down but I'm at my wit's end. I guess I'd better be leaving you now."

"That's a long drive back to Malibu," he suggested. "Frankly, I don't think you should do it. Wait till morning, you'll feel more like it."

"Go to a hotel? I'm too well known. They'll think I'm having an assignation or something. No thanks."

"Stay here. I've got three empty bedrooms and you can choose whichever one you like. We'd better call your husband. Or have him send a car for you, if you're dead-set on going home."

"Julio's out of town. He's always out of town."

"Then, it's up to you."

Suddenly, it occurred to him Fritzi would be staying here till her own house was ready. He could never explain Audrey's presence, if she were to stay the night. So he said, "Look, I know the people at the Hotel Bel-Air. It's just done the road over on Stone Canyon. I'll put the room in my name, sign the register and retrieve the key. It'll be a key to one of the villas, so you don't even have to go through the lobby. It ought to work just fine."

"What're those villas, a thousand or so a night?"

"Something like that, I suppose."

"I'll pay you back."

"You already have."

"I didn't mean it that way."

"Neither did I, Audrey, neither did I. Excuse me a moment, and I'll see to the hotel arrangements. I hoped they're not booked solid. Not all the villas anyway. I'll find out."

They looked at each other, as if they were both waiting for the other one to say something more. Perhaps, a hint, or more than a hint, that they might spend the night together. Ordinarily, he would leap at the chance, or at least be sorely tempted. But no, not tonight and likely not on any other night. If there was to any such suggestion, it ought first to come from him. He said nothing, and soon the act of looking at each other became a vanished moment. One more paragraph in their slender memory book.

Later, he accompanied her in her car to the hotel, less than a mile away, and then legged it back home. As he made the uphill climb, he thought it remarkable how a couple of decades could be jammed into less than two hours. Shockingly so, still confused by it. He remembered their paradisiac week in Pebble Beach, recalling it now as easily as his own street address. Nor was nine months of gestation hard to add up after that glorious, flesh-sodden stay at a small beachside inn. Romaine must've been born just about the time he'd been wounded, with the shrapnel from the grenade ending any hope of fathering another child.

He had fought for nearly everything he had in this life: in wars, in getting to the top of his profession, in successfully defending scores of clients, some innocent, but most not.

What kind of man wouldn't fight for his only child? He could beat Pritter, he knew he could, if only he were down there with Burke instead of sitting up there in the chair.

The thought drummed and drummed again: how much of Romaine Brook was of him? Half, anyway. Half, gene-wise. Should he make sure? Call for a DNA test? How absurd to be thinking that, when a hundred people would ask why it was needed.

Was she a murderer, a thief? And those photos, how did Marc Sterne come to possess those? What had really been happening between them, things even unknown to Audrey? Rhodes began to wonder if anyone really knew all the truth—or was telling it, if they did.

Had Marc Sterne abused Romaine, taken sheer advantage of her in some despicable way? The young man sounded like something of a fast-living bounder. Were the photos a scheme of blackmail? Had his daughter lost her senses, and done him in over a threat he posed? Was she capable of killing? She looked as innocent as a nursery rhyme. Your looks, how you really look, always meant a lot in a murder trial—to a jury, the press, and especially the public.

Should he openly admit his past, get free of the trial, face the public clamor, take his licking? Tell the world he had a swell sleep-in many years ago with a beautiful girl, and then a billion-to-one shot had turned up. They'd have to start the trial all over again, just as he'd be forced to find ways to re-starting his own life again.

He could always return to the practice of criminal law, where clients ignored everything about you except your skills in getting them safe and dry. Yet he aimed for more out of his profession: he wanted to leave something worthwhile behind, wanted the administration of criminal justice to be bettered for the sake of all. He had no money worries, not in the slightest. Yet he would always have the usual worries of any man, be thinking about the future, wanting to have friends and look after those friends, be Fritzi's love while loving her in return, be viewed as a solid citizen and a respected contributor to his community.

Why should a man wanting to protect his daughter pay such a stiff price for it? Yet if he hid the facts, blithely went on, and were found out, he'd be done for; and he knew it for what it was—an indisputable certainty.

As he reached his driveway, Rhodes was hit by a funny feeling: that whatever was going to happen had already happened. And there was damn-all he could really do about any of it, without wrecking too many lives.

His own, for starters.

Chapter Twelve

Fahey waited, dueling with impatience. Did this louter think his time was for free? That he was paid by the government, or the like? World in a fucking mess like every day, and no wonder.

He stood near a short upslope of road, Upper Alta Street, cut into one of the smaller Hollywood hills. The road curved at its bottom and ended at the driveway of one of the better apartment houses in the area: pseudo-Spanish in style, tiled roofs, stucco walls. Here at the top of the road, where he waited, the street was lined with one-level bungalows and magnolia trees. All expect for the three-level apartment house.

He leaned casually against one fender of his Buick, glancing at his scribbled notes; the ones penciled at the detention center when he and Burke had seen the girl. One note reminded him: *In the living room somewhere by the back of a couch.*

She had told him how Marc Sterne always sent her from the room, whenever he went foraging for his drug-stash. A strange maneuver, Fahey thought, his instincts in overdrive at this moment.

A black and white vehicle nosed over the rise of the street. Fahey put his notepad away as the car drew to the curb.

Scrambling out the car door, a man hurried over, almost at a half trot. He had a tough leathery face like a baseball mitt used for too many seasons. He wore an off-white suit, a very white shirt, and a black knit tie speckled with white dots.

"Hello, you Fahey" the man said. "I'm Redd Cullis."

Fahey shook hands. Cullis was tapered and wiry, with quick darting eyes. Skin as black as a domino and the white suit crisp as an altar cloth.

"How'd you come up with Red for a name? Someone colorblind?"

Cullis chuckled softly. "R-E-D-D. Everyone asks...and you're the one, aren't you?"

"One of the what?

"The guy who got busted by the Commissioners. For donging one of 'ems wife. What I heard anyway. That story still travels."

"Wonderful woman. Great ears. Shaded like the pink of a conch shell."

"Ears?"

"Could hear my heart beat for her when she was a whole county away."

"Wasn't she the runner-up Miss California once? What I heard anyway," said Cullis, his eyes covering Fahey like a searchlight.

"She's Miss Tahiti now. Ran off with a priest I once knew. Abyssinian, I think. You're a lieutenant, right?"

Cullis nodded. "Three more years to go. Then me and my brother'll be in the haberdashery business."

"I can see you've got a flair for it. Born in Panama, were you? They dress like that down there."

"You come down and see us when you need something decent to wear. Get you all rated out on real friendly terms."

"You make uniforms? Pale blue with red flashes on the collar. Crossed keys, like the Vatican has, sewn on the front pockets..."

"You gonna be a doorman? Shit, no, we don't make uniforms. No uniforms for me either for five, count'em, five years."

"Been a loo-ey that long, eh?"

"S'right. Change their luck, I said to 'em. Get yourself a sharp black man. Redd Cullis reportin' in for his gold bars, I told 'em that."

"You really did all that, eh?"

"I did, Fahey. And I didn't have the Commissioner's office come down on me neither...so tell me what's a dude like you do all day long?"

"Make babies. Mulattos, when they let me. I specialize in two-toners."

"You a smart-ass, ain'tcha?"

Fahey smiled as they made their way down the curved driveway to the apartment house, with Cullis moving swiftly as a scat-back. He reached the manager's ground level door ahead of Fahey, who never hurried unless something notorious was about to happen. Cullis knocked near a bright brass plate with the name: A. Noor, Manager.

When the door opened, a frumpish woman stepped outside. She seemed to sag everywhere, with heavy jowls and jet-black hair gathered in a bun pierced by an ivory needle. Her medium-dark features and the hook of her nose suggested she was of the Middle East.

The woman already knew Cullis, and she smiled at him, but when he introduced her to Fahey, she scowled. Fahey slipped out a different wallet this time, palming it in one hand behind his leg.

"I've still got a key," Cullis was explaining to the woman.

"No-e-no," the woman protected. "I let you in, is bett-or."

The woman closed her door as Cullis led the way up a small flight of stairs. When Cullis's back was turned, Fahey flipped open his wallet so the woman could see his bogus sheriff's badge. She sent him a fresh copy of her scowl, and he privileged her with a smooth smile. Better to seem harmless, thought Fahey. Later he would need her, if not quite as a friend, at least not as a bitchy harridan.

A fetid smell greeted them as they entered Marc Sterne's apartment. Withered plants drooped over the sides of their clay pots. Cullis switched on the lights. Fahey moved over to a wrought-iron railing and looked down into a sunken living room. Behind him, the woman fussed about, muttering.

"Don't you air this place out?" Cullis asked her.

"I see sign you put there. Bad for me," she said indignantly, and pointed to the open door with its sheriff's seal, advising of legal penalties for entering the apartment without lawful permission. "When you take that down for me? I loose-a the money every week."

Cullis sent her off. "Some joint, ain't it?' he asked Fahey.

Other than a few scattered pieces of white upholstered furniture, everything was cast in shades of lavender. The walls were painted in winter lilac; the carpet almost the same hue; the long, closed drapes were of a bluish purple. The entire ceiling was paved with smoked glass and, in the corner of the room, white pedestals supported fake Grecian statuary.

"This a cathouse?" asked Fahey, "or an upstairs massage parlor?" He blew one of his low whistles.

"You like it, huh?"

"I never...you've been here before, of course."

"Oh, yeah. A few times. A few of my men swept it the day after our Malibu station started the investigation."

'When exactly was that, Lieutenant?"

"When the Sterne boy went down. They went right at it that night out in Malibu. Next day we got asked to look this place over, then seal it up."

"That letter and those photos, where'd..."

"Right here. Dresser drawer in his bedroom."

"You see them?"

Cullis laughed. "Yeah. Everyone here did. Some piece, ain't she?"

Fahey didn't answer, glad that Burke wasn't present. He went on looking around, getting a feel for the place, noting things to store in his mind. He noticed the position of the long white couch, the chairs at either end, the side tables, and the white floor lamps that arched over at their tops like the necks of two swans.

"Can we see the rest of it?"

"Right this way," said Cullis, hovering close by.

"You know anything about Marc Sterne and his drug dealing?"

"Let's take you where you want to go," said Cullis evasively, turning away.

They went through a small kitchen, where Fahey opened and closed some drawers. The refrigerator held a dozen cans of Budweiser, a cut of moldering cheese, and a carton of spoiled fruit juice. It smelled like an unkempt dog kennel. After a look at the dining room, they came out to a hall with bedrooms at either end.

Cullis still dogged Fahey, never leaving his side.

Marc Sterne's bedroom was a smaller version of the purple living room, only this time the color was brown, with more of the smoked glass on the ceiling.

"Liked his glass, didn't he?"

"Awful lookin', ain't it?" Cullis said.

"Wonder what the Noor lady gets for it?"

"You ain't gonna tell me you'd want to have this—"

"I was wondering if she took anything off the top of his narc deals. Ever ask her?" Fahey waited, listening very closely for Cullis's reaction.

"You seem mighty fixed on that business."

"Aren't you, lieutenant? The kid has a reputation as a dealer. Maybe he forgot to pay the wrong man once or twice."

"And that means?"

"Could mean anything, couldn't it?"

Cullis spread his mouth slightly. He seemed ready to speak, but he only scratched behind his ear somewhere, as if puzzled about the way his day was going.

"Couldn't it?" Fahey repeated.

"You tell me."

"I might at that, lieutenant. I just might."

Fahey walked over to a SONY TV mounted on a cabinet. He rummaged through a rack of DVDs, read some titles and replaced them. Porno films. He opened two closets and found twenty or more suits, shelves filled with every style of shoe, and several other shelves piled with sweaters. Some of the sweaters still had price tags and most were cashmere knits.

Out in the hallway again, Cullis asked, "You lookin' for anything special?"

"Know of anything special, do you?"

"Nothing that isn't in our reports, Fahey."

"Maybe you missed something."

"Like what?'

"Who Marc Sterne really *is* or *was*. How he lived, functioned, fucked, shaved, who he stole from...his brain-workings if he had any brains, who he hung out with, where he accessed his drugs, how he got along with his old man. You want more. You ever go to school, did you?"

"We combed this place out all the way."

"And found only photos and a letter."

"I told you that once, Fahey."

"What I'm interested in is what you haven't told me. Or told anyone else that you should have told."

Even in the semi-darkened hallway, Fahey could see the lieutenant's face grow stronger, more chiseled. His eyes widened and they looked yellowish in the faint light.

"Just a goddamn minute," Cullis said softly. "I don't have to take shit from you."

"You might have to take it from the lawyer I'm working with. Wears mountain boots. Might put one up your tailpipe."

"What're you gettin' at?"

"That there's more than what's in your reports. Always is, and you're keeping it under your hat that you don't wear."

"You're goin' way out of line, Fahey."

"Am I? You want to be in the regiment you'd better get your eyes checked."

"What in hell does that—"

But Fahey had already pushed by him. He had to shake Cullis somehow. Get out of range for a moment so that he could leave something behind.

Something he'd be coming back for. He whipped around suddenly, knowing Cullis would probably bump into him.

"Any closer," Fahey said "and you could share my socks."

"Or fix your mouth for you," he answered, coming even closer.

"Remove your hands, Cullis, or I'll cripple you."

The man was so close, Fahey could smell his breath. Like any other breath, neither sweet nor sour, just a man's mouth smell. But too close for Fahey's liking, and he knew the lieutenant was ragging him on purpose. He knew why, too; Cullis was troubled about something.

On the way back to the living room, Fahey felt for his pen. He plunked himself down on the long white sofa, opened his notepad and scribbled a few lines of nothingness.

"You know Tommy Burke?" he asked, as he made a ceremony of clipping his pen to his inside coat pocket, then unobtrusively shoved his small notebook down between the couch's cushions.

"What you been writin' down?"

"My maid's address in Madagascar. She's due for a demotion."

"You're a real smartass, you are. No wonder they ran your butt off he force."

"Did me a favor, too." Fahey clasped his hands over one knee. "You know I've been reading all those confidential reports put together by the Malibu sheriff. Then some others by the Attorney General's crowd. Nothing whatsoever on Marc Sterne's dope traffic. It tickles my curiosity, Cullis. A cover-up, is it? You boys into someone's wallet, beefing up your paychecks while the rest of us starve?"

"Narcotics wasn't ever the point of our investigation."

"Narcotics is part of any investigation, old son. Especially, when it's murder."

Cullis shrugged. "I stay away from the narco detail. I wouldn't know."

"Would your memory get better if Burke threw you up on the stand? Tear you up a bit. Put a spot of blood on your teeth?"

"Who in hell'd'ya think you are, coming at me this way? Intimadatin' an officer of the law. I could run you in."

"You'd need a witness to make anything stand up. Call the landlady, she'd be a big help. She can barely pronounce her own name."

"You got a mouth on you, Fahey. A real loose mouth."

"I can make it looser."

Obviously, Cullis had been told to cooperate, but only vaguely, offer nothing more than a minimum. Fahey decided to push him hard, just once, to see what would happen.

"Tommy Burke, that's the girl's lawyer. I really came here to get a gander at you so I could tell Burke."

"Tell him what?"

"How you'd come across when he puts you on the stand. Starts frying your black ass for you."

"They ain't gonna call me, no-how, no-way."

"Sure they are, Lieutenant. Burke will want to find out a few things. Like why your Malibu people and then you—the Hollywood sheriff's station—got stepped on. Wasn't that what happened? The State Bureau of Investigation came in, looked at your crummy work and threw you all to hell out of their way."

Cullis was too dark-skinned to show a blush. But his neck seemed to widen over his white shirt collar, and he cleared his throat twice before his eyes began showing more white than brown.

"Political crap," said Cullis eventually. "A big case, big folks, those Sternes, and the State people insisted on—"

"Like Jesus clearing out the temple, eh? Rolled you right over and out the door. Amateur night, eh?"

"State always has precedence, you know that."

"And the handy part is they can shut things up more easily. Or forgot they saw or heard something...so Burke may want you, Cullis. He may want your black hide and see how good you are at perjury."

"They don't need me, goddamn you. I'm looking after this apartment till it's over and that's it." So easy and sure of himself until a few minutes ago, now Cullis's face wobbled slightly.

"Save yourself a long day downtown at court and tell me what you know," Fahey said.

In the round brown irises of Cullis's eyes, a warning light appeared; it stayed there for a long moment until a few blinks washed it away.

"We got a real smart narcotics squad at our station. Most of that is handled by LAPD. We help out, naturally. Best you try your crap with them."

"Maybe I will. But you're the one who's here, aren't you?"

"I could come down on you, Fahey." Cullis simmered noticeably.

"Personally or officially?"

"Both ways."

Tread gently, Fahey advised his more sensitive side. Look at Cullis, then look away. Keep your voice of all voices casual, not one decibel louder than necessary.

"Been a lovely morning, hasn't it?" Fahey began to rise from the couch, careful not to push the pillows down.

"I really don't know that much," Collis griped. "It's all done above me. You know what I mean."

Fahey sank back in the couch.

He guessed correctly that Cullis, like Sister Marius before him, shared a fear of becoming involved in a murder trial. High-octane trials were notorious for making people dumb with fright. You could so easily be made a fool of, be kissed by trouble when the cold wind of an even-odder lawyer blew your story apart, and the press decided you were fair game for a mauling. Better to shut up. And if they wouldn't let you shut up, then say as little as possible.

Fahey waited for Cullis to begin again. He wanted to wet his drying throat with a pull from his flask, but fought the urge. Cullis might use it against him somehow.

"There's talk going around," Cullis said, turning his face slightly so that his line of vision came diagonally. "Lot of it's just shit you ain't never gonna prove. Those Hollywood big people are behind tall walls, man. Big goddamn walls. You got to go real soft and take 'em down fast or you're in for some high shit. Know what I mean?"

"I know," Fahey said. "But what is it that *you* know?'

"Yeah, I hear that Sterne was movin' some snow and brown sugar around. Movie people and to them music people. Some with big names, you always hearin' that jive."

"And nobody went after him?"

"You sound stoked now." Cullis relaxed into a chuckle. "You think you just walk into some big time studio and ask 'em to hand over some rock star or one of them tight-ass blonde bitches pullin' down ten-million a picture. You need yourself a bench warrant and a truck of facts to get one, and then you got to get by studio security without them yellin' upstairs before you're outta the car."

129

"But he was in it? Peddling? Sterne was?"

"S'what they say. The boy, not his old man. Never heard any talk about the father."

"That doesn't mean anything."

"I wouldn't try that fishpond, if I was you, Fahey. They make you into no-find-ems fast."

"No-find-ems?"

"Little bones. Real little. You're messin' with the big weight there."

"That why no one talks about the son's action?"

"See, you got to talk to the State Bureau of Investigations, don'tcha. Anything left out of those reports, that's their lookout."

Fahey knuckled his chin, feeling the stubble there. A longer than usual inning in bed that morning with Wanda, and he hadn't found time for the razor.

"What was he? Small time, middle size—"

"You wanna know for sure?"

Fahey nodded.

"Better you call the undertaker then, 'cause I don't know. And nobody ever bought stuff from him is going to tell you nothin', not nothin'."

"You never found anything here or anywhere else? Photos and the letter, that's the whole haul."

Cullis nodded.

Fahey got all the way up from the couch. He straightened his red blazer, buttoned it, then gazed sorrowfully at his shoes, dusty from his walk down the road. He wiped them off on the back of his yellow pants, leaving dust smears. Cullis grimaced. Then Fahey stretched his arms, saying, "Know what?"

"What?"

"Your shit's so high it ought to be in the Getty Museum."

"Look here, Fahey, I said to you what you asked. You got no reason to get on me!"

"Wouldn't try, Lieutenant. Wouldn't even think of it. I don't snap garter-belts anymore."

Fed up, Fahey left. Closing the door, Cullis tested the knob, then smoothed down the edges of the yellow tape securing the sheriff's seal.

03

Lloyd Pritter waved a cheery goodbye to the receptionist at Oldes & Farnham. He had just finished a three-hour session with two partners who oversaw one of the top litigation departments in Los Angeles.

A courtesy visit, and one for figuring out the next series of courtroom tactics. Julio. Sterne, out of his own pocket, had made available the services of his personal lawyers. Pritter had spent part of the morning ticking off the options available to the defense, if and when Burke put Romaine Brook on the stand.

The meeting over, he shoved his way into an elevator jammed with others, stood there uncomfortably close to a big-bellied Latino, yet still he was tingling with excitement. When the trial was over, he would be sending in his resignation as Assistant Attorney General. The next time he waved to the receptionist, it would be as an about-to-be senior member of Oldes & Farnham's litigation staff. Nice. A hard promise. All he needed to do is get the job done, wring a thirty-year sentence out of Rhodes once the jury voted a guilty verdict.

Real money for the first time in his life.

Burke, they had all agreed, would be forced to put his client on the witness stand. What else could he do? The facts of the trial, even if largely circumstantial, were running against her. Hungry at the prospect of dicing her up, Pritter almost rubbed his hands together at the specter of forcing her into lies or into admissions that would lead to a conviction.

That conviction was the gold-plated ticket to Pritter's future.

Burke was no Wheeler, not even a wheezing, frail, failing Wheeler who had said, before dying, he intended to recall Audrey Sterne for added cross-examination. Still, what pieces of her earlier testimony had he been planning to discredit? A ruse, was it? No worry there, thought Pritter, having previously agreed on the situation with the Oldes & Farnham attorneys. Still, the thought badgered him, and he knew not why.

Leaving the elevator, he stepped clumsily on a woman's foot, but he was so afloat in his future that he failed to hear her pained cry. Only one woman, a young one, occupied his thinking at that moment.

CR

The walk to the visitor's room to see Tommy Burke is the best walk of the day. And the walk back is the loneliest most awful in this world. Like lining up for the gas chamber. But we're close now and he is so sweet with his attempts to encourage me, "Chin up" and all that rot. He held my hand twice, smiling at me. Lovely eyes, he has.

He brought a letter from my agent, who is really the dearest man. A magazine is making me an offer for a serial—to tell all—when the trial is over. I might do it, too. God knows I need the money.

I'm depressed. My period's coming on. But I can't wait to get on that stand. It's the illusion you create, making them believe you, and I can act circles around the Barrymores, if that's what it takes to get out of prison.

One thing about Marc Sterne—he gave me a post-graduate course in the fine art of sticking it to people.

Have to go over that part about the photos again. Rehearse a few more times. I'm almost there.

Pritter, that Eel, is stalking me. I wouldn't give him a kiss on my ankle, but one day while I was sitting at our table, I did manage to show him plenty of thigh. His eyes gleamed like hot black marbles. He does remind me of a fat slithery eel. All that greasy black hair and those beady little eyes.

When I look over at him, my blood turns to red ice. What is there to do but defend myself in any way I can? Even lie, when I must. It's my life at stake! I'd do a Brody out the window before spending my life inside a cement cave. Mr. Wheeler once said that half the witnesses who go up on the stand usually lie at different times. That's why they have those cross-examinations, where they try to mince you into smithereens.

Mrs. Sterne was lying about her and that Hunkie houseman, Kardas. She'll lie more, too, so why can't I? If I have to, I will. I can't gamble everything on Tommy Burke. He's nice enough but there's no real throw-weight there. I need real muscle, but haven't the do-re-mi.

CR

The next night, hunched over a console, a television director spoke softly into a head-microphone. He sat on a low stool inside a small cubicle overlooking the main ballroom at the Beverly Wilshire Hotel.

"Four, three, two...we're on," he intoned, chopping his flattened hand at the cameraman, signaling him to pan the ballroom. Nothing more he could do now, though he wasn't worried. Those were all pros down there, in the audience, the best in town; and that made them the best in the world.

Blue and white spotlights swept the audience of over a three-hundred luminaries seated at tables of twelve. The gala had reached its high point. The dinner had been endless—five courses—and the live show, broadcasted throughout America, was running late.

The cameras swung to the stage and caught the orchestra playing a few bars of music as the standing Julio Sterne bowed to loud, loyal applause.

His speech closed with a short, almost predictable ending: "And I'm so very pleased to say we have raised another seven-million dollars for our Motion Picture charities this year...that does not include, ladies and gentlemen, all the private donations of the members of our industry, or especially the time given by our outstanding actors and actresses to countless causes...fair to say, and I think you'll agree, that no other industry in America does so much for the needy...so I thank you, one and all..."

Taking her cue, Audrey stood and hugged her husband when he returned to the table. They were bathed instantly in a flood of white light as the cameras whirred away.

"Just perfect," said Audrey with one of her diamond-spray smiles.

"Short enough?" he asked.

"I think too short."

"Hate these damn speeches." He wiped his forehead with a red square of silk.

The orchestra struck up a new medley, with Michael Buble singing "Moon River." Audrey pulled Julio off to the dance floor. They twirled around in the crowd, fielding compliments, a rash joke or two. Julio unpasted himself from Audrey as they found more dance space and told her: "You did most of this. Proud of you, Audrey, very proud..."

"Your name, your fame."

"Nothing without organization and elbow grease."

"It did get a little heavy there at the end, I guess."

"I could tell. You haven't been yourself for the past few days."

Audrey smiled again. "I didn't know it showed."

"Showed?" he grunted. "You've been pacing the night away. For two, three nights anyway."

The orchestra played "Stardust." They danced off to the edge of the crowd.

"Julio?"

"Umm-hh."

"I need a real rest."

"Good idea. Check into the hospital for a few days," he suggested. "Get some sleep. I'll have the office take care—"

"No. I mean get away. Maybe to Main Chance or perhaps go over to see the boys in England."

"Not now."

"Why not? I'm really bushed." She drew him closer. He resisted.

"Slow down. You deserve it," Julio told her.

"I expect to. That's why I need to get away before I split in half."

"When the trial is over, we'll run off to Hong Kong, perhaps. I've business there to look after. Or Hawaii, how's that? Or would you prefer Cap Ferrat?"

"By myself, Julio. I need plain rest. I've had it with the ef-fing trial." Audrey's face stiffened. Her mouth parted and her teeth were tight enough to be slightly off center.

"Oh, you have, have you? That's almost interesting...it was only my son—"

"Darling, I know! I know it *all* by now. By heart, I know it. By the everyday news, I know it. I'll collapse, damn it, if I hear any more of it."

They stopped dancing. Sterne's hand moved up to her shoulder, and he dug his fingers into her soft flesh.

"You're hurting me."

"You'd be better off learning your place," Julio warned her.

"Stop it. That hurts! You're making a fool out of—"

"You want to get away, do you? With Ferenc, I suppose. A little tryst for two. Maybe Budapest—"

"Julio, how dare—"

"You think I'm blind. He tells me everything I want to know anyway."

"He doesn't! He never would," she blurted, instantly knowing she'd made a gross error in her choice of words.

A cruel and knowing smile, a smile for hardening arteries, twisted Julio Sterne's mouth. "And frankly I don't care as long as it stays in the house."

"People are watching us."

"Let them. They've been watching us all night."

"Possibly, Julio, you should remember a thing or two about Ferenc."

"Such as?"

"Such as the night when the police were there. And you weren't home again. And Ferenc had to lie that we'd all been on the boat. You had gone upstairs and fainted dead away when finding out about Marc, and that you couldn't come down for a...well, you know, to answer anything. Make a statement or whatever."

"So they wouldn't find out about your bed jumping. That's what you mean. That's why you lied, Audrey. So the police wouldn't get suspicious about you and our Hungarian cocksman out on the boat."

"That's not true, dammit. Stop that! Just stop it!"

"Who in hell do you think pays Kardas? I know everything that goes on."

As she began to breathe heavily, nervously, the upper spheres of her breasts swelled over her low cut Versace; a gold sequined gown and with the blond upsweep of her hair, she seemed like a bejeweled mannequin escaped from Cartier's window for the night.

"He tells me you're the best lay this side of Jerusalem."

"I'm leaving, Julio. People are looking." Spinning away, she dodged her way through the tables, her bare shoulders raised and rigid from anger.

Julio saw some of the bystanders staring at him. The music seemed louder, too loud. He needed air. Get away, at least from this cloying mob. Standing there like some befuddled waiter, he felt like a fool and the feeling upset him.

She could find her own way home. His blood was up. She had never cared all that much for Marc, and the blow he suffered when losing his son...well, she could have offered more of her heart, more consolation. She had once told him, "Your son spies on me, and I wish you'd talk to him." A flagrantly rude, fallacious remark. She had never elaborated, and even if she had, he wouldn't have listened. She had never shown much affection for Marc, was tolerant perhaps yet standoffish. It irked him, and tonight, for some reason, it irked him even more.

Outside the hotel, he asked the doorman to call for his car and driver. Hell with it, he thought. He'd send the driver back for her. It would look better. How did she think she was going to leave town before the trial was over? They were going to recall her, his lawyers at Oldes & Farnham had advised. Better her than me, he thought. Slumped in the back seat, Julio still smoldered. Ingrates. The whole lot of them. His wife, too. Suck his blood dry if he wasn't careful.

He thought about Marc, the son he never really understood. Plenty of men he knew said the same thing about their own sons. Maybe it was every son's duty to understand his father rather than the other way around.

Marc never had. He was born when Julio was already forty-six and that was more than a quarter century ago.

Too big of a leap in age differences. The boy had never liked work, only wanting to play around, screw actresses, dog it at the beach, drive expensive cars. Marc had liked the life at Parthenon Studios, all the deference paid him, the easy access to the starlets, yet had exhibited no interest in the banks, the ranches, the food companies, the chemical works, the largest carwash chain in the U.S., and two manufacturers of aerospace parts—all that Julio Sterne had worked so hard to amass. Not bad for a Jew who had left Loyola University in his sophomore year with a hundred dollars to last him for the rest of his life.

He had built a mid-size empire with his brains, with super-human effort, with sacrifice and a dose of luck here and there. Now he had no heir to groom, bring along, or to inherit his wealth. It made him unbearably despondent.

Marc was barely cold in his grave before a half-dozen Jewish charities had contacted him for consideration in his will and testament.

Memory's reality was tapping hard on Julio at that moment. He recalled vividly how Marc had joined the useless flotsam of the drug generation. Julio had spent tens of thousands on clinics and therapy for the boy. For a while, the therapy had worked, before Marc went crazy on the murderous stuff all over again. The Brook girl, she'd had been a good ally for a time. She wasn't a user, Julio knew, because Parthenon Studio's Medical Department had run all the usual tests required for insurance coverage.

Bewitching Marc for months, then an argument had interfered and she had dumped him. So Marc had claimed. He moped, acted withdrawn, pulled fast ones, was irritable as hell for weeks. As irritable as Audrey had become recently,

The girl, she had killed Marc. One way or the other, she had sent him swimming back into that sea of drugs again. The boy's future, and his own plans for him, wiped out with the single malicious plunging of a syringe.

Nearing the Santa Monica hills, he began to recall the night, really the day, when he had learned of Marc's death. He'd been in Seattle at a board meeting of a chemical company in which he owned a one-third interest. He would've been there in Malibu that night had his private jet not been grounded with a hydraulic problem. The pilot wouldn't fly—which was why he was still the pilot—and Julio had stayed one more night, calling Audrey to tell her he'd be back early in the morning.

Returning to Malibu, at six the next morning, he had walked right into a brilliant sunrise and a nightmare at the same time. He was senseless with shock for hours. Brooding, weeping, then raging. And it was then he had begun his questioning of Audrey and Kardas. He sensed he needed a story for himself, and that meant knowing their story.

Why were they away, when Marc was by himself at the house?

What was Marc doing there anyway?

Had he called to say he was coming?

Why was the girl in the house? Hadn't she and Marc called it quits?

Where had Audrey and Kardas been anyway? *Out in the boat!*

And other questions, plenty of them and he demanded some answers before meeting with the sheriff's detectives. The bedroom where Marc had died was roped off; coffee cups and sandwich dregs were everywhere; stale cigarette smoke had spoiled the air.

Audrey, then Ferenc, had explained what they'd already told the sheriff the night before. That all three of them, including Julio, were out on the boat. Wouldn't that look better, sound so much better? Julio Sterne's new wife, relatively new anyway, wouldn't go larking off on a boat ride with the hired help—a single man—while her husband was away. Surely, Julio could see the wisdom of going along with that story.

A day later, Julio had shut the pilot up. That was easy, only a promise of a raise. Plus, a couple of thousand and a trip to Mexico for a weeklong vacation. Seemingly, it was the smart choice at the time. Whatever he did would never bring his son back, and he hadn't wanted any loose gossip flying around about Audrey and Kardas. The Malibu sheriff had swallowed the story—that Julio had been upstairs that night, in shock. No statement was possible until he sufficiently recovered from tragedy.

Audrey. She had her virtues and her faults, and he had thirty years of age on her. She was a vibrant, red-blooded beauty—the classic Los Angeles trophy wife. Wasn't it better if she had a willing servant to bed her rather than some Beverly Hills stud of a blabbermouth? He'd rescued the beautiful bitch from a broken marriage with Lord What's-his-name, and what was he getting in return?

Bills, more bills. Plenty of pictures in the tabloids that, admittedly, enhanced his own image. Still, if she had stayed home, where she belonged when he was away, there would've been no death, no loss, no funeral. Marc would be alive. All of them—the girl and Audrey and the Hunkie—had, in their own way, been responsible for his death.

With all the young actresses in Los Angeles, why had Audrey—at least for a time—befriended Romaine Brook? How the fuck could that happen?

Ferenc Kardas was another dice-roll. Kardas, of course, knew now that a lie was on the loose. A smallish lie but nevertheless a lie. The sheriff, if he got wind of it, would most certainly want to know the reasons for the deceit. And what else wasn't on the up-and-up?

Was that an advantage for Kardas? If so, how much of one? And what about running him off to some safe haven, where no Malibu sheriff could get the bright idea to interview him. One slip and Audrey would've been seen to perjure herself, and Julio knew he'd be dragged into the melee, into the maw of the press, into endless questions and all of it blanketed by nasty, lascivious gossip. And, for all he knew, collateral investigations into his highly guarded business affairs. If for no other reason than to pressure him, get him talking, get him to fall into their tricky traps.

Julio supposed he had at least ten years left, if he was lucky and took care of himself.

He had one younger sister in Dallas. His accountants said his net worth was close to eight-hundred hundred millions, given this year's jump in the stock market. No other real heirs now, none except Audrey. Well, his sister but he didn't much care for his sister.

Back to her, his goddess. Had he made the greatest mistake of his life, throwing Audrey and Kardas together? He no longer cared about sex, but knew she still had a fulsome appetite. He had devised that arrangement discreetly, he thought, just as he had spent a lifetime fixing up so many other things.

Had she some sort of a black deal going on with Kardas? Possible, wasn't it? What the hell did he owe either of them?

In his present frame of mind, Julio Sterne would put nothing past anyone, especially her. She was half the time living in worried silence whenever he was around her. Very unlike her; usually as effervescent as a flute full of champagne bubbles. Nowadays acting so strangely, up half the night. He could hear her footsteps out in the hall at two, three, four in the morning, doing the sleepless walk of the damned and the guilty.

Guessing, then, what it would take to pack her off to anywhere but here? A couple of lies, a couple of revelations, even the whole truth that might lead to an indictment of her for misleading the sheriff.

It could cut any divorce costs by millions, putting her in jail. Might work, might be just the ticket.

He was a little happier now that he could see the lights to the gates that guarded the entry to Malibu Pointe. He bet himself a thousand that Audrey would arrive home within an hour, probably by taxi; mad as a swatted wasp.

But he knew exactly how to cut her act in half.

Make a threat of one call to the sheriff is about all it would take. That, or a call to Oldes & Farnham where he'd drop a few questions which they, in turn, could feed to that fellow Pritter. She'd be paying her own lawyer's tariff—likely, given who she was, it would run two-million or so—and she hadn't that kind of money to her name. Nowhere near it.

He would chew on the idea again in the morning. Penalties for lying or making misrepresentations to law enforcement officials were severe; and he wasn't going to put his head in the noose for Audrey, for Ferenc Kardas, or for anyone.

As the limousine rolled through the fluid night, his thoughts kept roving over some options; what might happen if Audrey was found guilty of interfering with the investigation of a homicide? If she had lied as she had certainly lied, as had Kardas had lied, then you were interfering, was that not so?

But then if he hung them out to dry, would he be aiding Romaine Brook? He would have to rinse out that possibility, too. And then what of himself, for he hadn't corrected the facts with the sheriff's people? He thought he might have an excusable defense. Quite possibly so, and his angered nerves were assuaged the longer he lingered on the idea.

Chapter Thirteen

Fahey rapped sharply on the manager's door. Waiting till dark the next day before coming back to the apartment, thinking it wouldn't do to appear too obvious. This was the right hour to go scouting for what he wanted. Cullis would be off duty, safely out of the way.

The door parted and Fahey sniffed fish and garlic cooking. Mrs. Noor poked her head around the edge of the door. She yawned, and in the faded light Fahey saw dull flashes of gold in her gawping mouth.

"Sorry if I'm troubling you, dear Princess."

She peered closely.

"I'm Fahey. Remember? I was here yesterday with *my* lieutenant. Cullis, you know."

"Ya-ess."

"Are you Iranian? Great country."

"Lebanese. Why you ask-*a* this of me?"

"Ah, yes of course, Lebanese. Gorgeous women, the best. Should've known right off."

"A-what you want, Mr. Fah-hay?"

"Left something upstairs yesterday. Forgot all about it until an hour or two ago. Came right over to fetch it."

"Why you don't call first?"

"I should have, Mrs. Noor. I was out in my car and didn't have your number handy."

She seemed to juggle the idea. Fahey wanted to slam her door before the fish odor passed him out cold.

"I have dinner now," she said.

"You'll be a good woman, won't you, and let me borrow your keys?"

"Cullis have key."

"I know. He'll be here later. I thought I'd just run up to the apartment and wait."

"He come."

"Within the hour for sure."

"Why he come, too?'"

Fahey thought fast, hard. "We're going to look around once more. You see, Mrs. Noor, we're trying to get out of your way...turn the apartment back, get your rents up again. Pull down that sheriff's paper." He made a paper ripping motion with his hands just below her hawk's beak of a nose.

"Es-ss so?"

"Is very much so, Mrs. Noor. Your dinner, you better not let that burn. Smells delicious."

She nodded. "I get you key. You stay here."

Fahey waited. He heard a drawer shut, then a shuffle of feet before Mrs. Noor was back dangling her ring of keys. With one bitten fingernail, she tapped on the key to Sterne's apartment. It had a lilac dot painted on its upper part.

"You never lose the-ese."

"I'll just be upstairs."

"Cullis. He get my apartment back for me?"

"He's fantastico, Mrs. Noor. An iron man." Fahey flexed his arm. "Black magic, you know."

Her mouth showed more gold this time.

Upstairs at the apartment, Fahey switched on the lights. The fish smell had temporarily flooded his nostrils, so the mildew odor of the apartment he knew was there, wasn't there this time.

Ten minutes went somewhere as Fahey tipped the floor lamps upside down and shook them. Nothing there, and the same with the sectional couch. He had pulled it out from the wall and patted it down. Flipping the sections over, he examined their bottoms, and found nothing. Nor could he find anything behind the chrome-framed art posters. He picked up a phone from one of the side tables and saw the line was no longer plugged into the wall-jack.

Then he checked the shag carpet for torn seams. A floor safe? Looking and looking. Again, nothing. He hadn't expected to find drugs. But he might learn where they'd been hidden away.

After a while, it looked like a fight had taken place. Fahey had things littered everywhere, and began to replace them.

He shoved the last couch section against the wall when he saw his notepad on the floor. How had he forgotten that? Blessing his luck as he stooped to pick it up, he saw one of the wall outlets slightly askew, its metal plate angled and loosened from the baseboard. He counted three other sockets.

Pulling at the loose one, he found it stuck but still movable. He looked more closely. The screw heads ware fake, and he pulled again but the plate wouldn't budge. Taking Mrs. Noor's keys from his pocket, he tried jimmying one of them behind an edge of the plate.

Not enough leverage. He leaned back. The kitchen, he thought, would have something better. Then he remembered the knife in the side table drawer. A moment later, he squatted near the wall plate, and slowly levered it away.

A bent metal track began to appear. He pried harder until he saw a small metal drawer, working on it till enough of it showed so he could yank it, and he did so as the drawer slid fully into view.

What he saw made him smile. In the back of the drawer, a plastic bag was fastened at the top with a wire twist. A tag on it read: Ferenc Kardas. A smaller bag underneath it was marked: A. Noor.

Fahey opened the smaller one, wet his finger and sunk it into the crystallized powder. White as a fresh snowdrift, and he tasted it, and then again. Re-wiring the neck of the bag, he put it back, and shoved the wall-plate flush against the wall.

Bingo.

A second plate came out more easily. The bag in this drawer was three times heavier. No name tag—Marc Sterne's, he guessed. Private stock, a fortune there at street value. Once more, he pushed the plate home till it was mostly secured.

Christ and Mary! he thought. A whole bank there, enough to fund the regiment for years.

Sweating, doing most of the work with his good arm, Fahey was about to stand up. His brain whirled around like the spots on a slot machine, and seemed to go even faster as he stood up, hearing his name called out.

Mrs. Noor came down the three steps to the living room, a look of hand-tooled suspicion on her alarmed face. She stopped on the lowest step, resting a hand on the iron banister.

"Where Cullis?"

"Should be here. Any time now. Have to dock his pay, won't we?"

"What you do?"

"Oh, me?" Fahey laughed nervously. "Well, I—you see, ah, the phone. Was going to call Cullis. Trying to plug the phone in..."

"Es-connected."

"So I found out." Fahey wiped his brow. "Hot as your old good granny in here, isn't it? Let's kick a window out. Cullis won't mind."

Coughing loudly to cover the sound, he let the knife drop on the shag carpet as he came out from behind the couch.

"You find what you want?" she asked.

"Right here on the couch, Mrs. Noor. Dumb of me, wasn't it? Pressure of the job, you know. A muddled mind is the devil's workshop, eh?"

"You stay here or you go now?"

"Be going soon. Just waiting for old Cullis." said Fahey, advancing on her now. "You know, Mrs. Noor, I'm new on this Brook case. The girl, you know, you ever meet her?"

"Many times I see her. I tell police so."

"You ever talk with her? Have tea? A bit of girl gossip? Pass the time?"

Noor nodded.

"What's she like? Friendly? Happy?"

"Actress. Strange peoples. She dress ver-ah nice."

"Any trouble between her and Marc Sterne?"

"He es-sa dead. How you need more trouble than that?"

"Parties here? People coming here all the time, I suppose. That sort of thing?"

Fahey was right on her, two feet away, noticing a glitter of amber beads against her neck. He detected the aroma of fish again.

"Young people," she said. "They have party, but not so much."

"Hard worker, Marc Sterne?"

"Nice good man. Very polite. Always pay he-esa rent on time."

Pay you with *what,* Fahey wanted to ask. But that might tip her off and he couldn't see how she fit in anyway, not really. Hustling some action on the side, that was more likely her style. He was certain of one thing, though. She obviously had no idea where Marc Sterne kept his treasure chest, or those bags of hot sugar would have been long gone by now.

"I'll be going," he said. He handed her keys back. "Can't thank you enough."

"I go with you."

She locked the door, clucking strange words to herself that Fahey didn't grasp. No fish cookers in the regiment, he thought. Red meat only. She had small feet besides, pig trotters that could never keep up with the assault troops. Not quite the right shape to qualify as a camp follower, either.

"What I say if Cullis come here?"

"Tell him he's to quick march the square in full battle gear. Till dawn."

"I—es-what?"

"That I've been here and gone," he said, giving her his most pious smile.

Fahey was impatient to leave. He had trouble reading this dark and suspicious Levanter. Was it too late to call Rhodes? Burke? Now that he thought of it, he had no idea where Tommy Burke even lived.

ભ

Alesia Noor had dozed through her favorite T-V comedy show. Her dinner of carp in garlic paste, sweet yams and chickpeas rumbled in her soft belly, bringing her awake.

Cullis hadn't come by. Unless somehow she had missed him, which she doubted. She didn't care for this new man, Fah-hay, who talked so fast, and smiled so often, she couldn't understand him most of the time. He reminded her of those quick-tongued traders in the Beirut *souk* before it was bombed into a mountain of rubble.

She kept thinking of the man Fah-hay. Why had he appeared so surprised when she found him behind the couch? He had dropped something on the carpet; she was sure she had seen a bright flash falling from his hand.

The idea of going into the apartment by herself bothered her. That seal on the door, and those yellow tapes crisscrossing the doorway. She had enough trouble with the four- thousand dollars of her money gone, probably lost forever, the amount paid over to Marc Sterne before the girl killed him.

A belch was followed by a lusty sigh. Tomorrow she would call Ferenc Kardas. Hadn't seen him in well over a month.

Chapter Fourteen

Fahey contemplated a party, one of those rip-roaring celebrations he and Rhodes had had in times gone by. Burning with excitement at his discovery, he saw headlines and possibly added retainers from his insurance clients when the word got around that he'd found what the sheriff's detectives had missed like so many blind mice.

He'd tried to call Burke, only to learn the lawyer was still spending his hours with Romaine at the detention center. Pouring his attentions, no doubt. The matter of getting the cocaine into evidence at the trial was beyond him. Concerned him, even. Burke would know; Burke had better know.

Fahey had taken off for Rhodes's house, and now that he was here he'd wrap the whole thing up for Burke, and hand deliver this, his gift. He'd done it again, a masterstroke of investigating. Cullis would scream, but could do nothing. Not with all that cocaine now in play.

"Stroke of luck," Fahey was saying to Rhodes, pacing around but looking downward. "I'll admit the luck part of it, but I hate to. " He admired the shine on a pair of paratrooper boots he'd recently bought at a surplus store. "Jesus, Cliff, break the whole trial open, won't it. Eh?"

"Not so fast. How much you figure is there?" Rhodes asked.

"Bags. You could make a beach with it. A child's beach."

"Half a million? More?"

"Maybe." Fahey shrugged. "Depends on whether it's been cut or not."

"Kardas had his name on a sack of it? And what's the lady's name again?"

"Noor. Alesia Noor. A Levanter, the old bag gargles with fish oil."

"And Karkas, you said? Who's he?"

"Kardas. Burke told me he's an employee of the Sterne's. A domestic of some description. Slave labor, one of those."

"They're both in on it?"

"Name tags are on the bags. Like neon lights. The Brook girl was telling us the truth."

"You put all the bags back, Alonzo?"

146

Fahey shot back a look hot enough to remove paint. "That's not so damn funny."

"I was asking if you put everything back the way you found it."

"The hell you were."

"Don't start anything, okay. A simple question, that's all it was."

"Nothing so simple about the way you said it, boyo." Fahey's voice and facial expression went from sarcasm to a wounded look.

"Sorry."

Rhodes's mind was turning. He had been swimming when Fahey, agitated as a firefly, found him in the pool. But he was glad, very glad that Fahey had come this time.

"While you dry off, I'll see if I can raise Burke, tell him what I found," Fahey was offering.

"No, no, don't do that."

"Why not? He'll want to know."

"Later, maybe. But not now."

Rhodes left to change, leaving Fahey to fume and fuss until he returned a few minutes later.

"Burke is the lawyer here. He's got to know what I know," Fahey told him, still pacing and still upset.

"Fine, Alonzo. Maybe we can also keep Burke from screwing up. Think about that for a moment."

Fahey looked into Rhodes's unblinking eyes, and they seemed cold, almost empty. The small crescent scar on Rhodes's brow seemed to whiten.

"Trying to help Burke a little. I know he's a rookie," Rhodes explained. "He'll need help, all he can get."

"By holding out on information?"

"Which may not be admissible as evidence and probably isn't."

"So why not tell him?"

"Why not loosen your screws a little so we can sort this out," said Rhodes, covering his intentions.

"I don't like this at all." Fahey darkened.

"Let's just see what develops first, Alonzo."

Fahey turned his back. He put his hands on his hips and breathed audibly. "You could be talking about my ticket, my food and drink, Wanda out on the streets to make ends meet." With a spiked voice, he said it, his face reddening as he swung around again.

"I doubt it."

"If Burke finds out I knew about Sterne's stash, that I didn't tell him, he can hang me on a nail."

"I don't think he'll make a fuss."

"'What makes you so sure?'"

"Just a hunch."

"A hunch, is it? On my license? On my living and you want to try hunches?"

"How's he going to know you found that stuff?" Rhodes asked then added, "Don't tell him yet...I'll tell you when, and how, and that'll be best for Burke and for you."

Into Fahey's otherwise very alert senses, a light grew larger. A light with a yellow cast of caution. "What're you up to, Cliff?"

"Nothing. Just trying to make sure we don't start the trial again with another free-for-all. I'm making an exception, just talking to you this way right now. You found what appear to be illicit drugs. You had no search warrant. Knowing you, you probably accessed the premises on some trumped up pretense. How can you possibly think that's admissible evidence?"

Rhodes cinched his belt and then, sockless, slipped his feet into a pair of brown moccasins.

"Don't like it, not at all, and I tell you that for your own good, boyo."

"Look, finding a pile of drugs doesn't do much to hurt the prosecution or help the defense. And I don't want another ruckus."

"Hell, it might help the girl."

"Not if I disallow it as evidence," said Rhodes, greatly relieved the more he thought about it.

"I shouldn't have told you. You've gone and ruined a helluva good day for me."

Rhodes gave Fahey a deep look, one that could mean anything. "And I like to think I know what I'm doing in a courtroom."

He had finished dressing now. He ran one hand though his blondish hair, smoothing it down. He hung the towel he'd been using on a hook, strapped on his wristwatch; and said to Fahey: "Let's go up to the house."

"I've got to get going." Fahey spoke sullenly.

"I need an hour with you. It's important." Rhodes had been thinking of something while be dressed.

Fahey hesitated, then said, "I'll need to make a call or two first."

"Sure thing."

Rhodes had come out of the bathroom carrying a green polo shirt. As be stretched to slip the shirt over his head, a dozen or so worm-like weals showed where shrapnel had sliced into his chest and shoulders. Fahey wondered if the scars still hurt when rubbed or touched. He almost reached out to trace one with his fingertip to find out.

Up in the red library, Fahey made his phone calls and then was handed a yellow legal pad. Rhodes leaned against one wall, talking slowly, giving him a dozen questions for Burke to consider using if and when Romaine Brook went up on the witness stand.

Protesting at first, Fahey asked why couldn't they be typed out? He fairly howled when Rhodes gave him still other queries, depending how the first ones were answered, if at all, by Romaine. Jotting away, cursing, Fahey thought he could see where Rhodes was heading. If she answered the first set of questions one way, Burke should keep right on going; if another way, then use the second line of inquiry.

Fahey scanned his writing during a pause. "I think you lost your sonar, Cliff."

"Not really. As judge, I could ask any of those questions myself. And I probably shall, if Burke doesn't."

"Why, don't you then, instead of breaking my bleeding hand."

"Because I'm not the defense counsel. And I don't care to look like one."

"Weil, you sure as the deuce sound like one. " Fahey looked down at the yellow pad. "And you sure as hell're doing Burke's work for him, aren't you?"

"Judges help beginners all the time. Courtesy of the trade. You're not to tell him I suggested these questions."

Some ten minutes later, Rhodes finished. Fahey shook a cramp from his fingers, then repeated all the questions, complaining that he deserved stenographer's pay. "What're you really up to?" Pestering Rhodes with a piercing look.

"An open story for the jury, the press, and everyone else. And on that lovely prayer, I think I'll have a drink. Like one?" Rhodes moved toward the bar. He took two tumblers off the shelf. That's enough, he told himself, lay off all the suggestions or you'll start tripping the switches so early all the lights will go out.

'You know Burke might wonder where I got all these cute questions," said Fahey as he took his drink.

"I was about to get to that."

"So what do I say to him?"

"That inspiration suddenly arrived and wet your pants for you."

"He may not be in your league, but he's no dummy either."

"Tell him you were talking an idea over with one of your lawyer friends."

"Whoever had one for a friend?" Fahey smirked.

"Funny, fuh-nee, Fahey. That what they call you now, the funny man?"

"Well, boyo, I'm not funning you. So what do I say?"

"Just tell Burke to look them over or he might be missing a bet."

"Really."

Rhodes only shrugged, taking a long sip to hush a jumping nerve in the back of his neck.

"Don't cost me my license, Cliff."

"You're already insured, pal."

"How?"

"Because if you ever told anyone about this little chat we're having, you could cost me a seat on the Supreme Court."

"I still say Burke would love to know what I found in that apartment."

"Tell him, if you like. But be damn sure it's your idea and keep me out of it. And no more discussions like this one, amigo. I've gone as far as I can go."

After another drink, Fahey left.

Rhodes hoped the questions he'd given to Fahey were the same ones Burke would think up by himself anyway. But he couldn't take that chance. Burke had never tried a case on his own, and he'd be standing up there like some farm boy taking his first Latin lesson. It wasn't that Lloyd Pritter was so frighteningly clever, but he'd been around for a long time, knew the ropes, and had the savvy to swamp Burke.

He had his own worries, all running deep. He should've recused himself from the trial no later than the day after learning Romaine Brook was his daughter. Yet he couldn't bring himself to go that far. It wasn't that he owed Romaine Brook anything. Not a dime, not a scintilla. But he owed himself something, didn't he? To ensure that his daughter got her full and fair day in the courtroom.

Drowning in dilemma, he found himself swinging inside a cat's cradle of nearly impossible choices. Help Romaine? Or protect the woman he'd once so loved and probably still did? Or sit back and do the practical, serviceable thing by letting matters travel on fate's road to wherever it led?

If he were there at the table with Burke, leading the defense, he'd rattle Pritter till Pritter thought he was a pair of cubes in a dice cup. But to do it, get the jury going his way, infuse them with doubt over Romaine's guilt, he'd have to fill them with fear and worry that they could end up heaping ruin on a young innocent woman, who, ambitious to succeed, had gotten tangled with a rich fast-living operator, who had paved the way for his own end. To cement the defense, make things murky, he'd have to subtly shift the blame for Marc Sterne's murder…if indeed it was murder…by pointing the finger of suspicion at Audrey. Paint her as the culprit, and lay out the credible suspicion that Julio Sterne had been rigging the deck with the D.A. to implicate Romaine as the best way to protect his wife? Was that what was really happening anyway? Or what about slamming that Kardas character, who might be a drug-operator?

Reasonable doubt, that's all it'd take to sway the jury. How to seed a cloud of reasonable doubt so that it exculpated Romaine? If she went up on the stand, maybe she could do it all by herself? He had bought a DVD copy of *Tonight or Never*, and been bowled over at her skills as an actress. She might be the key to her own victory, if things didn't get too fouled up, like Fahey doing what Fahey always did: crossing the bounds of propriety, nudging up against what the law allowed and the many things it forbade. The man, once let loose, was persistent as a bone-hungry Rottweiler. However, it was he who had urged Fahey to step in to aid the defense, a point never to overlook.

Never stops, he thought.

He went to the bar for another Cuervo, remaining there on the stool for two more of them. Stiff, neat pours: spine-benders. He was afraid, afraid that something was about to go bust. And he'd go bust with it, if he didn't find a way to shake loose of his dilemma.

But he knew he couldn't and he knew he wouldn't. He'd simply have to figure out how to assist Burke by remote control and without the young lawyer suspecting anything.

151

And then the jury; how to deal with them? If Romaine went free, what would the governor do then? Questions flowing into him now like water pouring into a drain, and among them was how to tilt the table to rescue his daughter and do it within legal bounds?

Chapter Fifteen

At Malibu Pointe, Ferenc Kardas sat in the butler's pantry writing up a list of liquor and grocery supplies. On a few items, he increased the size of the order. Those would be ordered but never delivered, yet the full bill would still be settled at month's end, when he dropped by the grocer's for a friendly chat. And his cut.

The phone rang. "Sterne residence," Ferenc answered.

For two endless minutes, he listened as Alesia Noor told of Alonzo Fahey's visit the day before. As she gasped excitedly, he asked, "Have you been up there to see for yourself?"

"Es-sa forbidden."

"Go up and look," Kardas urged.

"No, no. You to go up."

"It might be there. He had to put it somewhere." Kardas fingered his lip.

"I not go up." Noor insisted again.

"I heard you. I'll be by on Saturday. Call me back if they come there again. And you stay with them next time. Watch every move they make."

Hanging up, he cursed. The Noor woman was a nuisance, though useful for the time being. Somehow, he needed to find Marc Sterne's supplier or a new source of top grade Colombian.

Every day in the papers, he had followed the trial. Never once was there any mention of the police finding drugs at Marc's apartment. Another idea, one that alarmed him, causing his eyes to darken: the police might've found it already, saying nothing, and taken the drugs for themselves. It was known to happen, or so he had heard.

CR

One floor up, Audrey was coating the backs of her legs with more tanning lotion. She lay on a chaise on the deck outside her bedroom. The sun was high, the lapis-blue sky clear of any clouds. Below, she could hear ocean slurping lazily against the huge black rocks on this side of the house.

Julio had been giving her the freeze treatment lately. He was worried, she guessed, that a few things might still come out at the trial. Embarrassing moments, or worse. He'd been keeping a distance ever since their rift at the Beverly Wilshire gala.

He knew about Ferenc and didn't really seem to care much either. She'd been maneuvered into being a sexual Tinkertoy, and, realizing it now, she seethed; another of Julio's gambits and she had fallen for it. How naïve. How wounding. Like some paid for slut, she thought.

It was a day for taking inventory of the men in her life, present and past. Lord Robert Huibbard-Hewes, for one—ex-husband, arrogant charmer, who had shown her the world of the theater long before she knew of Romaine's talents. Huibbard-Hewes had swept her off her feet, dazzled her with his brilliant mind and skills, and his circle of fascinating friends in England and on the Continent.

She had needed someone like him in those bleak days after putting up Romaine for adoption, believing Cliff Rhodes was dead. She had never told Robert about the child she had given birth to in California, or, of course, about Rhodes. A woman's secret; one that, if revealed, would ruin her chances for marrying anyone with the standing of a Huibbard-Hewes in the upper rungs of British society. **She** had been tempted to inform Robert of her past facts at the time of their hostile, god-awful divorce. Tell him out of spite, anger, downright malice after she'd been forced to admit to a trumped-up situation of adultery—that never had happened—to secure the divorce in the British courts.

She had never known anyone who could juggle so many sexual affairs at one time as her ex-husband. He tramped after every actress, married or unmarried, who appeared in the many stage plays he produced. She had suffered, in her turn, so many humiliations she had thought she was headed for a nervous breakdown. She ended up hating a man she had once loved, or thought she loved.

To save herself and her young sons from any more anguish, she had taken the fall in the divorce. Ironically, she had almost lost the boys in that so-called bargain, and found out what it was like to go up against England's first families. Standing as stoutly as front-line regulars, they had rallied around Robert Huibbard-Hewes as one of their own, and Audrey became a near outcast. People she had thought of as friends suddenly closed their doors to her, wouldn't return her calls, would not even accept a simple invitation to lunch.

They could say what they wanted to about the decline of the British Empire—it had never declined an iota when it came to the peers of the realm closing their ranks to an outsider. They could burn you alive with one freezing look.

Julio had tagged after her when the divorce was over. She could understand why. He was a first pew player in business circles on the Coast. Socially, however, he wasn't quite seated above the saltshaker in many places. He could go wherever money could go, but that didn't mean everywhere, not by a long shot. There were clubs and homes and get-togethers put on by the Southern California bluebloods, who got along quite well without the Julio Sternes of Hollywood fame and fortune. Or anyone else from Hollywood, for that matter.

Audrey gave Julio what he had so avidly sought: acceptability anywhere. Her family had been prominent in California society for years. Her mother, a McConnico, was heiress to an Idaho silver mine; her father a leading physician: Avery Bartlett of the Brentwood Bartletts, who were well-known and well liked, accepted anywhere they went. The Bartletts could boast, albeit quietly, of supplying medical doctors over three generations to the ill of the Los Angeles Basin.

Though she was Mrs. Julio Sterne now, to many Los Angelinos who mattered she was still Audrey *Bartlett* Sterne.

Cliff Rhodes glided into her thoughts. Somehow, she had to get her hands on those papers at Las Infantas. Bury for good and always any path of discovery by an outsider, no matter how remote the chance.

One romp in bed—no, a good many romps—with Cliff Rhodes and then Romaine Brook had greeted this world. The bewitching stranger—no, the criminal, Audrey thought—and, alarmingly and amazingly, her own flesh and blood. Your own child, a killer? Linking the three of us up, these many years later. She knew she'd never have told Cliff about their daughter's existence had he not ended up as the judge in this red-mess of a trial, with their daughter at its center; and those potentially damning papers at Las Infantas that could unleash a scandal.

Maybe, I shouldn't have told him; but I have, and now what?

Cliff Rhodes had come far, farther than she had ever supposed. Is he as smart, as good as they say he is? Hardly more than a bashful cowboy when she had first met him at a sorority dance. Rough-edged, tall and awkward, and, she was later to learn, hung like a horse who could go all night, whenever they could sneak a night together.

Why she had thought of that, she wondered. Likely, because Kardas was now in her history books. It was making her increasingly uncomfortable that they lived under the same roof. What might he be telling Julio? Indeed, what was there to tell other than piles of sex?

Whenever she was near Kardas, he gave out with one of those expectant looks, waiting, it seemed, for her to return it. She hadn't played his game, and she wouldn't. She wished he would depart, get a position elsewhere. Whatever would happen, if he were called to testify?

What if Rhodes betrayed her? Their secret?

He'd never, would he? *Never!*

Like her thoughts, the sun was beating on her, sheening her oiled skin. Yet Audrey shivered as if an ice cube had just rolled down her spine. She rubbed herself, tensed her muscles, yet couldn't stop the shivering.

✃

Resting one booted foot on top of his paper-piled desk, Tommy Burke slumped in his chair. He was scanning the questions Fahey had taken down from Rhodes, though he had no idea of the source. Reddish curls dangled over his brow. He brushed them aside before finishing with the questions, and put the three-page sheaf on top of a stack of files.

"Got 'em from some lawyer, you said?" Tommy asked Fahey. "Anyone I know'?"

"An out of town guy. We were talking about the trial, and then he threw out some ideas."

"Pretty good stuff, I'd say. Slick."

"He's got a pretty good reputation."

"Does he have a name to go with it?"

"Oh, no," said Fahey. "He's an old pal, he wouldn't want to sound like he's horning in...can you use them?"

"Maybe. I'll have to see," Burke said casually.

"They sounded pretty good to me," Fahey said. "S'why I thought you might like to see them."

"I'll see. I'm not putting Romaine on the stand right away. Something else came up and it's worth a shot, I think. Here, I'll show you."

Fahey came around the desk. Burke opened a folder full of the Malibu sheriff's confidential reports written up the night of Marc Sterne's death. Fahey had perused the folder before. One set of reports dealt with the statements made that night by this Ferenc Kardas, and then another set by Audrey Sterne. Yet another report covered Julio Sterne's statement, taken the day later.

"But the trial transcript reads differently," Tommy Burke told Fahey as they thumbed the pages. "You weren't around at the opening, but Mrs. Sterne testified that her husband went upstairs that night. All broken up. Crushed and whatever..."

"So?"

"So, the sheriff says they took Julio Stern's statement the next day. But look here, Alonzo. See, it's dated the day before, same as the other ones. See it? I never noticed it before yesterday."

Burke pointed at the date-space in the upper right-hand corners of the reports. All three showed the same date.

"A clerical error, maybe."

"And maybe not. I want to pin it down tight...and another thing. I'd like to hear more about are those noises out on the water that night. Boat noises or whatever. You see the way I figure it—"

"What were Wheeler's ideas, his intended tactics?" Fahey broke in.

"He didn't say. I always wondered if he was going to go after Julio Sterne."

"Raye didn't exactly bury you alive with his plans, did he?"

"I was his research department, as I've said. That's all I was, Alonzo. A gofer."

Tommy explained his theory. He wanted to go after the Malibu sheriff, who had appeared as a witness for the state at the onset of the trial. But, as he talked through his thoughts, a new cloud of doubt arose: how had Fahey come up with those clever questions? Whoever thought those up had to be very familiar with the trial.

Across the desk, a green-shaded lamp threw its sickly, yellowish-green light against Fahey's face, showing deep creases over Fahey's nose, moving in unison with his restless eyes.

Tommy wondered why Fahey, usually so easy-going, was so restless today.

About what?

He must call Pritter. Tell him he wanted the state's third witness recalled—the one from the Malibu sheriff's station. A little more grilling on a few open points. The thought of making the call both excited and frightened him.

Frightened him because he wanted terribly to win. To do something big, really immense, big for Romaine and big for his own career that, if anything, barely existed.

He no longer cared whether she ever paid him so much as a bent tin can for all his hard work. All those headaches, all the late and grueling hours. He only wanted her freed. He wanted her around him, her honeyed laughter, that soft look on her face, and those doe-like eyes filling him with waves of yearning, and what he hoped and imagined her touch would feel like.

Would they titter at him? The press and the other onlookers, would they laugh at his awkwardness in the courtroom? His high voice? He'd rather die before making a fool of himself in front of her.

Dialing the Attorney General's office, he knew he'd have to pull it off somehow. Melt down Pritter's iron-sided case. And for Tommy Burke, that meant taking another look at a few people in Malibu Pointe.

CR

Tomorrow it all begins again. Tommy will never pull it off by himself. He's not tough enough. Not been boiled enough. Not schooled enough for this shouting-match. I'll have to do it by myself. Just the Eel and me, chasing each other around with our words. Tommy said he hopes he won't have to put me on the stand. He's nuts. I'm the best thing he's got, and I'm the only thing I've got.

I'm going up on that stand. Rehearsals are over. Been over ever since I set foot in this goblin's hole.

I don't know much about the operations of law, but I'm learning things. How could I not? What I can do is act. And that's what this trial is, an act that takes place in a small theater. Protagonists, antagonists. A very loose script. The jury, the newspaper critics. The judge, he's the director. The

State of California, it's the producer. I'm the quiet ass-kisser trying to get free of it all. Let me up on that witness stand and I'll have this place in tears. Sympathy gushing like Niagara Falls. Turn the Eel on his backside. He gets the vapors whenever he looks at me. Too many times, he's done it and sometimes it's for long moments, like one of those hypocrite priests who want into your knickers.

Tommy thinks the jury is picking up on it; that they can feel the Eel wants me where he's in control of my every breath. Thinks he's so smart and everything. Okay...let's see, Eel...you prick...

PART II

Chapter Sixteen

Oddest week of his life, Rhodes thought, climbing the three steps up to the bench. Calling the courtroom to order, the bailiff bellowed, "All rise." The spectators stood up, more or less in unison, and Rhodes noted a few of them nodding hello and shaking hands. The jurors sat there alertly, stiff-jawed. The press rows turned this way and that way, checking to see if any new notables were present.

Rhodes looked squarely at his *daughter*. She wore green today, a prim apple-green dress with a circular neckline trimmed in white. He wished he could take her out for lunch; tell everyone out there she belonged to him. See what she was like, finally.

"Call your first witness, please," Rhodes said to Burke. And do a good job of it, he silently, fervently hoped.

"May I approach the bench?" Tommy asked.

"Certainly."

He came stiff-legged, as if walking on stilts, his thick-soled boots scuffing the floor. With his mouth half open, he started a weak smile, with his head bobbing loosely.

Christ, thought Rhodes dourly.

"Your Honor, I've been trying to get an earlier witness back on the stand. One of the sheriff's deputies from Malibu."

Rhodes nodded. "What's the problem?"

"He's away for another day or so."

"So?'

"I want to lead off with him."

"The state's witness? What for?"

"A couple of items to clear up, that's all."

"Can't you clear them up when he gets back?'

"It will be more confusing, I think, for the jury, and anyway—"

"What do you have in mind, counselor?"

"A delay. Just a day or so until the deputy—"

162

But Rhodes was already on the second shake of his head. "We've had all the recesses we're going to have for now."

"But, I've got—"

"We're on our way again, Mr. Burke. Today. Anything we find confusing we can straighten out later."

Burke's eyes pleaded. "Just another day—"

"Listen, if we put that jury out one more time, they'll throw us both out of here."

Burke blinked. His mouth shifted into an odd, lopsided shape, and he dragged himself back to the table where Romaine sat, her face uplifted and serene and eager.

"The defense calls Miss Dee-Dee Lessig," Tommy said. The pale petal-color of his face went to beet red as he forced his voice down from a contralto to a quivering tenor.

Journalists seated in the front glanced at him. Burke turned redder. Heads swiveled to watch a woman, thirtyish, with a swinging ponytail, come up the aisle.

When he had her sworn in, Tommy began to identify her: where she was from, lived, her connection to the trial. "Yes, I was Marc Sterne's secretary for about six-months," said Miss Lessig, establishing the reason for her presence.

"And before that?"

"I worked in the costume department at Parthenon Studios."

"For how long?"

"Three years or so."

"And how did you get selected to become Marc Sterne's secretary?"

"I heard there was an opening and asked for an interview."

"And you got the job?"

"Yes, I did." Dee-Dee Lessig beamed.

"Ever go out with Marc? Have a date? Dinner?"

A chair scraped loudly. Pritter was up. "Hold it! Now, your Honor"— trying to keep his eyes on Burke, Miss Lessig and Rhodes at the same time—"I can't see how this is relevant to even one issue in the defense's—"

"Okay." Rhodes held up his hand. He turned to Burke, asking, "Where're we going here?"

"I'm trying to establish the trail of events on the night Marc Sterne died."

"Can you get to it a little more directly?"

Burke lifted his hands, a gesture of resignation, "I'll try." He wheeled around awkwardly, facing his witness again, "You knew him pretty well, Miss Lessig?"

"Quite well, yes."

"Did you ever take messages for Marc Sterne? Messages, for example, from his stepmother? Or from his father?"

"Often from his father, or his father's secretary."

"And from Mrs. Sterne?"

"Sometimes. Yes, a few times."

"How many times does a few times mean? Once a week? A month? How often?"

Dee-Dee Lessig's brow furrowed. Burke let her think on it as he pivoted around to catch a quick glimpse of Pritter and Pritter's two assistants, watching him with intensity, making him more nervous. He only had himself...and then, back about six rows, he saw Fahey waving, and wearing that fire-engine red jacket.

"Once a month, or maybe twice a month," said Miss Lessig in a shallow voice.

"When Marc wasn't there in his office, you always took his calls?"

"Just about."

"Did you keep a record? Incoming and outgoing logs of callers? Or their messages?"

"That was studio practice, all executive secretaries did."

"And you did too?"

"I just said so—"

"Not exactly, Miss Lessig, but you've answered us now."

Tommy had circled back to his table, and then he returned to his witness. "Is this an executive telephone log from Parthenon?" He handed her a light gray sheet of paper.

"Sure is," said Dee-Dee Lessig, looking up. "It's mine. One I kept for Marc Sterne."

"And the one you kept on the day he died?"

"Ye-yes."

"The sixth call down from the top? What's that one say?" His voice slipping on him again, he balled his hands, embarrassed.

"From Mrs. Sterne?"

"Yes. What time? And what's the message?"

"11:14 in the morning. Would he please come for dinner that night at 7:30? Dress informal." Dee-Dee Lessig peered at her writing more closely before she added, "And to thank Marc for doing it on such short notice."

"Good, that's what I thought it said. And you gave the message to Marc sometime later?'

"I gave it to him after lunch, I'm pretty sure."

"That specific message? From his stepmother?"

"I think so."

"Specifically, Miss Lessig. You told Marc Sterne his stepmother invited him for dinner that very same evening at the family home out at Malibu Pointe?"

"That's my memory of it."

"Did he call her back?"

"I don't know."

"You didn't place a call to Mrs. Sterne for him?"

"I don't believe so."

"You're not sure."

A pause.

"Yes, I'm sure I did not," said Dee-Dee Lessig.

"And I'm sure I want to thank you for your time here today, Miss Lessig." Burke smiled a shy smile but one wrapped in appreciation. He stepped back, looked over his shoulder, and said to Pritter. "Your witness."

Romaine was watching Burke shuffle back to his chair. He is the living Tin Man from The Wizard of Oz, she thought. Her facial expression was completely empty, forced empty, from her training and natural capacity to act a role. *I know more about that call than Dee-Dee Lessing ever could. Or anyone else.* Romaine barely noticed Tommy as he sat down. Her attention was glued to the woman on the stand and then to Pritter's wide back that bunched in a thick roll under his arms.

"Miss Lessig," Pritter began, moving even closer, "you continue to work at Parthenon Studios, do you?"

"I'm still there, yes."

"They treat you well there?"

"Wonderfully well."

"And Marc Sterne, how did he treat you?"

"Oh, fine. He was a good boss. Very bright, humorous."

"How about Mr. Sterne, Marc's father?"

"Well, I don't know, I guess so."

"Can you amplify, Miss Lessig?"

"I didn't see him that often. He was on...up on the other floor so I rarely saw him."

"You knew Mrs. Sterne?"

"I never met her."

"A few minutes ago you told us you had."

"I only meant I knew her on the telephone. From her voice, I could tell."

"You never saw her?"

"Not at the studio."

"Anywhere else?"

"Her pictures in the newspapers. She was in the papers quite a lot."

"But you never heard her voice, while talking with her face to face?"

"No."

"How can you say it was her, then, who called on the day you say she did?"

Romaine felt a tremor under her kneecap.

"She had called before," Dee-Dee Lessig answered. "She always said who she was and I got to know her voice. After a few times, you get to know anyone's vice...I mean voice."

"After, let's see, six months as Marc Sterne's secretary...and you testified that Mrs. Sterne might've called a dozen times or thereabouts. Is that right?"

"About, yes. I'd have to look at all the logs to be sure."

"How can you be so sure it was Mrs. Sterne calling?"

"Because of her voice. I told you. If you called, I think I'd know yours."

"But how," Pritter hardened on the witness, "when you couldn't see her talking in plain view? And had never seen her before, in person?"

"I don't know. She has a, well—"

"Yes?"

"Her voice is, well, it's her voice. Distinctive, sort of. Just the way I'll probably remember your voice. Her voice is sort of aristocratic. Like British, almost."

"Sort of. Almost. You're not very sure, are you?"

"I'm sure enough."

Her first ordeal in a court of law, and Dee-Dee Lessig became slightly muddled; why, she wondered, make such a big deal over a phone message? Discomfort set in. Saying the wrong thing, could that cost her her job? Wide as an ox, Pritter was blocking her view of half the courtroom. She looked up at Rhodes, whose face she found attractive, but his attention seemed fixed on the jury.

"Did you know the defendant?" Pritter started again, pointing at Romaine. "Ever meet with her anywhere?"

"A few times. We all knew her by her big film."

"Know her in person?"

"Yes, somewhat."

"You knew, or didn't you, that she was seeing Marc Sterne? Socially?"

"Everyone knew that."

"Did you take any of her messages, meant for Marc Sterne?"

"Sometimes."

"Was there any message from Miss Brook to Marc Sterne on the day he was murdered?"

Tommy Burke's feet hit the floor hard as he stood up. "No, your Honor, the prosecutor can't frame a question that way—he's leading—"

Rhodes swung his gaze to the clerk. "Strike that last question," he said, and then instructed the jury: "Disregard the term murder. The State is here to prove a murder took place...no questions will be allowed that presume an act of homicide as a foregone conclusion." To Pritter, he spoke sharply: "You can rephrase, if you want to. But you'd better do it correctly or sit down."

Pritter shrugged, starting in again. "Did you hear from Miss Brook, over there at the table, did you take a call from her on the same day you say Mrs. Sterne called?"

"I don't remember any calls from Romaine Brook that day."

"Did Marc Sterne ever talk to you about Miss Brook? His relationship with her?"

"Not really. Of course not!"

"Never?"

"Hardly ever. Sometimes I ordered flowers or a limousine for a special night. Things like that."

"And so you knew they were close, or more than close?"

Dee-Dee sighed. She had a sudden urge to go to the bathroom, and was too embarrassed to ask in front of the looming Pritter and all these strange people. She pressed her thighs together.

"I assumed they were close," Dee-Dee said in a pained voice. "Everybody knew, I guess. They were in the newspapers—"

"So you assumed?"

"Yes!" she said crossly.

"Just as you assumed it was Mrs. Sterne herself on the phone that day?" said Pritter, stepping toward the jury, forcibly trying to make his point. He hadn't expected Dee-Dee Lessig this morning. Pritter was aware that she was on a possible witness list made by Raye Wheeler at the pre-trial conferences. No matter, she had done no damage. But for the first time he began to estimate where Burke was headed, and it didn't smell right to his keen nose.

At all costs, Pritter was supposed to keep Julio Sterne either out of the trial or as far from it as possible. That hint, which was hardly a hint, had almost been hand-delivered to him from his newfound friends at Oldes & Farnham.

Was Burke trying to lay groundwork to get at Julio Sterne? The thought nagged Pritter. So did another one, seemingly unrelated, of why the defense counsel wanted another go-round with the Malibu sheriff's deputy. Burke had mentioned on the phone that an item or two didn't seem to tally.

What items, Pritter had pressed. Small ones, Burke had replied at the time.

He took another run again at Ms. Lessig, a wild shot. "Did you feel a sense of envy at Marc Sterne's interest in the defendant?"

"Was I jealous, you mean?"

"All right, yes, jealous?"

"Nope, not at all?"

"Were you ever involved with Marc Sterne?"

"I told you, yes, I was his secretary."

"Indeed, you did, partly. What I'm asking you now is were you romantically involved? Sexually, for example?"

Before Burke sputtered an objection, and Pritter was unable to withdraw his question, an irate Dee-Dee Lessig burst out with, "You're a horrid filthy-minded man. How dare you insinuate a thing like that. I've a mother and father, you annoying idiot…you…you…"

Startled at her outburst, Pritter waved a hand aimlessly, then said to the ceiling, "Nothing further."

"You may step down," Rhodes said to Dee-Dee Lessig. "Next witness."

Tommy Burke sent an urgent look to Romaine. "Look," he whispered, "we'll stall. Just follow me carefully. That guy'll be back tonight and we'll get him tomorrow. You hear me?"

"Sure I do, Tommy. Don't sound so rattled."

"I'm so nervous I can hardly swallow."

"You're great, Tommy. Just great, really."

"Okay, just follow the questions. Nothing else."

"I'm ready."

Romaine stood up. So lithe, proud and resolute, as if she had just alighted from some throne, ready now to grant any favor, even to her captors.

Romaine took her oath, and under Burke's guidance identified herself for the record.

Her belly fluttered as she spotted Pritter again. Did he know the truth about that call? Not possibly, she thought. But all the same he'd come very close. Smoothing her green dress, making sure it covered her knees, she willed her face into a child-like innocence. In the witness chair, she cast her eyes first toward the jury, then paid a sweeping glance at the press rows. A reporter from the Associated Press penciled a quick note to himself: "The look of the Vestal Virgin in a ring of golden ice."

"Will you tell us, Miss Brook," asked Tommy, "how you first met Marc Sterne? And when that event occurred?"

She began, slowly at first, to convey how shocked she was that Marc Sterne was no longer alive. How wonderfully warm he'd been to her. Helping her. Offering the little attentions any woman adores. Building up her confidence, making her feel like the person she had not yet become—a real film star.

Coaxed here and gentled there by Tommy Burke, she revealed previously censored moments of her love affair with Marc Sterne.

Rhodes listened intently. His daughter was speaking, the first time he had ever heard his flesh-and-blood talk. He watched her mouth, the movements of her chin. Her eyelids, how they closed and opened. Her hands changing position. A modulated voice that changed its timbre at times. A faint iridescent glow in her face, the kind seen in Kurlian photography, and

Rhodes wondered if others in the courtroom noticed it. Her lean body was erect and stalwart looking. The barest smile, he noted, perhaps an indication she was pleased that she could finally explain herself. That it was her turn after all these languishing months.

In the courtroom, a pin-drop stillness. The onlookers had come for this—to hear, at long last, her side of events.

The wall clock pointed its hands to 12:38, before the clerk was able to flag Rhodes's attention. He nodded, letting Romaine go on. He was learning her life. Of one thing, Rhodes was certain: she knew who the real audience was, rarely averting her eyes from the jury.

Five minutes later, he recessed for an hour and a half.

ભ

Fahey sat across from Tommy Burke in a booth inside a small restaurant three blocks distant from the courthouse. "Like she read it all from a script," he was saying as he wiped beer foam off his mouth.

"Very good isn't she?"

"And so she may be, for some of us," Fahey agreed somewhat opaquely.

Burke was impervious, though. "God, Alonzo, I've never been through anything like this."

"You're not through it yet, old cock."

"I know!" Tommy said excitedly. "But she's got 'em, Alonzo. Can't you see it?"

"Well, there's Pritter yet to take his swings. That won't be like your auntie's tea party."

"Maybe he won't even try. Juries tend to get upset if you bark at people too hard. Comes a moment in these trials, especially the murder ones, when the psychology shifts...go for the underdog, they do. It happens. From pity. Sympathy. They see themselves up there, and they think of all the times they had reasons to smash the guts out of someone...but she didn't smash anyone. I'd swear she—"

"Easy, Thomas. I belong to your choir, remember."

"You think I'm doing all right?"

"Clarence Darrow in the flesh."

Burke tried more of his salad before pushing it away. On edge, too excited to think clearly, let alone have much of an appetite. "Gotta get that sheriff."

"Slow down. I'll yank that deputy sheriff by his short hairs, if it comes to that."

"Would you?"

"I'm spring-loaded, lad, and at your service. Even got the cuffs ready."

"Alonzo, why ever did you quit trial investigations? You're so very good at it."

Fahey hadn't expected the question. He waited, calculating what to say, even unsure if he should reply. Yet he did, "I dunno. All the fun went out of it when Rhodsey-boy sold out to those mother-hating pols. One day I had to quit when I started puking on my pillow. You see, it all got so serious and all the fun flew out of it."

Tommy weighed the words, unsure if he understood them. It sounded as if something had been stolen from Alonzo Fahey. Something never to be found again, no matter how hard the hunt for it.

Gulping the dregs of a beer, Fahey wiped his mouth on the back of one sleeve. "Stuff is awful," he said wincing. "Tastes like one of Wanda's soups."

"I've got to get back. Are you coming?"

"As far as the door. Got something else on my book this afternoon that won't stand waiting."

"Care to flip for the lunch check?"

"Always, old son. You think because you're a big time mouthpiece now, we suspend the rules?"

Fahey reached into his pocket, feeling around. "Call it," he said flipping a gold Kruger in the air.

"Heads."

Fahey caught his special coin with the tiny notch on the rim of the head's side. He felt the notch, knew that Tommy had won, and deftly reversed the coin with a flick of his fingertip.

"Tails," he reported, showing it to Burke. "You'll do better this afternoon." He slid the Kruger across the table. "Here you are, Tom-Tom, pay with this." But Burke refused the glittery coin.

At the door, Fahey clapped Burke encouragingly on the back. "Hit 'em with those combat kickers you wear. Right in crotch. And that songbird of yours, keep her humming away...and, by the way, are you doing anything about those other questions I gave—"

"We'll see."

"Use them. The Pope's own treasury there." Fahey offered. "Now go at 'em with your sharpest trident."

"Yes," Tommy answered.

"And take it from me, life works like this—it's always third-down and eternity to go. You ever play football?"

"I never even played tiddlywinks."

"Well, we've got our own team. Just us, and that's why Pritter is sweating piss-balls," Fahey teased.

"I hadn't noticed."

"You will, though. Before we're through, he'll be squawking like a gull."

"What makes you say that?"

"I peeked."

"Peeked at what?"

"The sheriff's and the state's investigative reports. They're dross, Tommy. I've seen better gravel pits." Fahey, who never wore any sort of timepiece, and apparently was born with a circadian data center," advised, "Got to get my kickers moving, or I'll be late for my rendezvous with today's destiny."

He arose, aiming himself at other purposes, in other of the world's lesser-known burrows. Fond of Tommy, wishing he had had a younger brother like him, someone to look after, watch out for. He was soft-natured, not enough of life's varnish had hardened on him as yet. And might never. Tommy had the makings of one who should be teaching fifth grade in the elementary school of an upscale neighborhood.

Fahey swallowed a sigh of exasperation. The courtroom wasn't for him today. Too sedentary, the action much too predictable, although he'd yet to settle his feelings about that blonde apparition they were out to lynch.

His mind had traveled afar.

For days now, he had wanted to see the Gypsy, needing her counsel. She'd been too busy to see him last week, when he had had the time for her.

Today they would spend all afternoon together, and he'd press her to engage in one of her spectacular séances.

About the Brook girl.

ભ

Rhodes had returned to his offices taut and tense now that he intended to slip the aces for Romaine. He was putting on his black robe, with Macklin Price helping him so that it hung correctly.

"Two calls from Sacramento," she reminded him.

"Two calls too many."

"What'll I say when they ring us again."

"That I'm busy, in case they've forgotten how to read the newspapers."

"I won't say that. Not to the governor's office—"

"The hell with 'em. Call Fritzi, would you? Ask if she's available for early dinner tonight."

"Sure." Macklin smoothed his hair.

"We'll wrap up today around three-thirty. Get any paperwork together I need to sign or look over...how're we coming on those forms for my confirmation?"

"Everything's done except the financial part."

"Nosy, aren't they?"

He owned some good real estate, a half-interest in several oil and gas leases in Canada, and a hefty list of corporate bonds. In good shape, very good. Eight to ten millions of assets and no debts. It still irritated him that he had to show his finances to outsiders.

He went down his private hallway. Opening the door to the courtroom, he went through it headlong, almost bumping into Romaine as the bailiff led her to the witness chair. She looked at him appraisingly, then deeply, and he thought he saw an amused look invade her face.

The courtroom began to settle. Tommy Burke looked up at the clock. Rhodes is punctual, he reminded himself, yet today he'd need a judge with patience. He led Romaine to the witness box, and, after the usual preliminaries, he stood before Romaine again, briefly pausing as the court reporter fed a new tape into her transcription machine.

"Let's go on," he said to Romaine, "your still under oath. When we

173

recessed, you were talking about how you'd been getting along with Mr. and Mrs. Sterne, I believe." He glanced at the court reporter, asking, "Would you read the last few sentences from this morning's session?"

The reporter droned them.

"Now," said Tommy, "let's proceed from there. You were saying that Marc's father and stepmother welcomed you into their home. Were warm and friendly, at first."

"Yes, quite wonderful really."

"Did they ever talk to you about the film *Tonight or Never* that you made for their studio?"

"All the time, we did. I mean at the beginning it was all the time. It made them a lot of money, I think."

"You won an Oscar, didn't you?"

"Yes," her voice lowering slightly.

"Then what? What came about in your relationship with the Sternes?"

"They cooled off. Became somewhat aloof, if you know what I mean. I didn't know why at first."

"Did they ever say?"

"Mrs. Sterne dropped hints two or three times."

Rhodes leaned forward.

"What did she say or hint to you?"

"Various things. That Marc and I shouldn't be so serious about each other. That we had lots of time. Once she said 'Hollywood marriages are like a wet match in a strong wind' or something like that."

"Anything else?"

"Oh, well yes. One day I mentioned I'd been adopted. We'd been out shopping. She said, 'That's really too bad, isn't it?'"

"Didn't seem to think much of that idea?"

"She mentioned it a couple of times later to Marc. He told me she had."

Pritter bounced to his feet. "Hearsay," he roared.

Rhodes agreed and had Romaine's comment struck.

"All right," Burke went on. Moving to his right now, using Pritter's trick, he blocked the prosecutor's view of the witness. "Can you tell us about your relationship with Mr. Julio Sterne? Did that cool off as well?"

"After I turned down an offer he made me, things sort of went downhill between us."

"What offer?"

174

"He made a terrible suggestion, that if I would stop seeing Marc, he would arrange a two-picture contract for me with another studio."

"Wanting to buy you off? Something along those lines?"

"In so many words, that's what it sounded like. Pretty terrible, I thought."

Tommy Burke let that one sink in. Out of the corner of his eye, he saw the heads of several journalists lower as pens descended to their pads.

"What did you reply to Mr. Sterne?"

"That I was shocked that a man like him would think so little of me. Of us. His own son...we were in love, you know...we had our problems and our arguments. Man and woman things, like, well, like everyone."

Romaine's head turned away from the jury for the first time. Her shoulders sagged, and then she buried her face in both hands. A muffled sob seeped out.

Tommy waited. So did Rhodes, who watched Pritter fume. When Romaine recovered, Tommy asked her quietly, "You all right? Like a break?"

"I'm sorry. I just hate to think of how they were using me."

"We understand...so you refused Mr. Sterne's offer?"

"I had to. Anyone would, wouldn't they?"

"Perhaps not everyone," Burke observed quietly. "So that was the end of it? Did he make the offer again?"

"No. And Marc and I decided afterward that we'd see less of his parents."

"You never saw them again? His parents?"

"Not as much. Things were strained, and I didn't want Marc on their list because of me."

"List?"

'Their shit list, oh sorry." One hand sailed to her mouth.

Guffaws erupted. Romaine looked up at Rhodes as if to ask forgiveness for her gaffe. He smiled at her.

"Did either Mr. or Mrs. Sterne ever indicate to you, in any way, that they thought you were after their money? Anything of that sort?"

Romaine's eyes went glassy. "They say, those people there"—she pointed straight at Pritter "that I killed Marc. Why would I kill someone whose money I wanted?"

"Yes, why would you?" agreed Tommy. "But did either Mr. or Mrs.

175

Sterne ever accuse you of going after Marc for the family money?"

"She did," replied Romaine, barely audible. "Mrs. Stern did."

"Louder, please," Pritter complained. "Your Honor, I can't see the witness when she answers."

Rhodes asked Tommy to stand somewhere else, and for Romaine to repeat her answer.

"Mrs. Sterne took me aside one day and said they were very wise to me. They'd looked into my background. That I might be a good actress and all that, but I wasn't going to marry her stepson, not ever...nor would I ever get a drop of their money. So I'd better give up that notion and vamoose."

"She said that? To you, Miss Brook, directly to you?"

Romaine nodded. "Yes, when she invited me for tea at the Polo Lounge, and let me have it right between the eyes. I was undone, I mean really flabbergasted. Gosh, I'd never said anything about their money. Ever. Marc didn't have a lot of money, I know he didn't. That's why he was dealing drugs."

Pritter roared. "Move to strike. There's been no evidence submitted about drugs. No foundation. Nothing that—"

Rhodes agreed.

Tommy glanced at the courtroom clock. He couldn't figure a reason to ask for a recess, but he didn't want to keep going either. The germ of an attack, forming in his mind for the past several days, was taking shape. He thought he saw a way to go after the Sternes. Yet he needed the sheriff on the stand again before he could shape the scenes he had in mind for the jury. Maximize the impact. Even then, perhaps it was a long shot.

Though Tommy hadn't sent Romaine another question, she had used the break in testimony to make her face become intensely alive, expectant. As if some new thing of crushing importance were suddenly recalled...

"Is it all right to finish," she asked. "Am I allowed to say more?"

"Oh, well, sure, of course," said Tommy, embarrassed, his hands fumbling nervously in his pockets.

"About Mrs. Sterne?" Romaine asked.

"Yes, please proceed."

"She was angry with me for other reasons." Burke waited with no idea of what was coming, letting her have her way. "Yes, other things, too. I think that's what made her so mad at me," Romaine said.

"Other things? Like what other things?"

Romaine brought her breathing under strict control, the trick of a trained actress. Willing a blush to her cheeks, she looked down at her toes as if caught out in some humiliating secret.

"What other things?" Tommy repeated.

"Maybe I shouldn't say," she said looking up, blushing to a beautiful rosy pink under her flaxen hair.

Romaine allowed a loaded moment to pass. She'd had the scent of Audrey Sterne and Ferenc Kardas for some time; seen Kardas's quick glances at Marc's stepmother, knowing looks and then the warning, stay-away looks Audrey Sterne gave Kardas in return. Brief nods, then a turn of her head. Little things a woman always notices about another woman, when a good-looking man is around, but paying attention to only one of them.

"Mrs. Sterne, well, you know—"

"Yes?" urged Burke.

"She had a thing going on with the houseman, and one time I stumbled in on them," said Romaine, rushing out the accusation.

"A what thing? Please be precise as you can."

"An affair. I suppose you could say it was an affair, anyway they were having sex a lot of the time," Romaine said chastely.

Pritter roared something that was lost in the rising gabble racing across the courtroom. Burke jumped with elation. No one saw him or observed Rhodes who, agog, rapped the gavel forcibly. Reporters streamed for the doors.

Two tumultuous minutes elapsed as Rhodes, almost ignored, threatened to clear the courtroom. Banging the gavel again and again, he knew instantly his daughter, sitting wide-eyed below him, had opened a floodgate. Was Burke clever enough to seize his big chance?

He summoned both attorneys to the bench. Pritter was livid, pounding his fist against the meat of his other palm. In the flow of excitement, Tommy Burke kept silent. Agape, however—for, in all their meetings never once had Romaine spoken about this mother lode of damning information.

"Okay," Rhodes said. "We're gonna hear her out."

"You can't!" Pritter insisted.

"I can't?" said Rhodes sharply.

"It's absolutely unsupportable. Where're the other witnesses?"

"Let's find out." If the testimony was off the mark, he could always strike it later.

Pritter's chest heaved. He pivoted quickly and his coat flared around his hips like a matador's cape. Returning to his chair, he sat, one arm suddenly swinging sidewise in fury, accidentally knocking half the wind out of one of his assistants.

No one seemed to take note of the smirk buried under Romaine's innocent-appearing expression. Perfect, she thought. Played it just like a throwaway line of dialogue, one that snaps back fast as a whip.

Burke again stood to the side of the witness box, awaiting the courtroom to quiet.

"I knew I shouldn't have said it," Romaine whispered to Tommy, who had not yet awakened to her change of tone.

"You did and you should."

He then asked her to resume. And with the half-truth that often ruins lives, she spoke fervently, almost prayer-like. However, they heard her all the way down the room, clear to the very last rows.

"I'd gone to the pool house in Malibu early one morning. I'd left a tote bag there when swimming the day before. Some clothes I needed. I was to meet Marc later on and take off for a beach we liked up in Ventura. He liked to surf, you see."

"Marc wasn't there at the pool house?"

"No, I was going to meet him later."

"Then?"

"I had let myself in the back gate. I knew where the key was hidden by the little blue birdhouse...it was early and I didn't want to bother anyone."

"Yes and...?"

"And, well, I went into the pool house and they were there."

"Who exactly?"

"Ferenc. He's their houseman. He testified here. Remember?"

Tommy nodded.

"They were on one of the chaises. The red striped one over by the bar."

"What time was it that morning? Do you remember?"

"Sevenish. I had an acting class at eight-thirty, and I had to hurry to get back for it."

"Seven in the morning?" asked Tommy, nailing the point.

"About then, yes."

"And what did you see?"

"They were lying there on the chaise. He wore nothing, and she...I think she had her bottoms on."

"Bottoms?"

"Panties or something. Maybe it was a bikini bottom...I took off, I just closed the door and ran."

"To where?"

"My car."

"That's all you saw?"

Careful now, Romaine commanded herself to look slightly shocked, not too much, just enough. *Open the mouth,* she instructed herself, *and dilate your eyes.*

"Mostly all."

"What else?"

"She was going down on...oh, you know." Romaine forced her lungs and blushed deeper.

"We'd like it in your words," Tommy said.

"Playing with him, his penis. With her mouth." Romaine closed her eyes, and her breasts rose under a deep breath.

"Fellatio, you mean. Do you know that word?"

"Fellatio, that's the word I was trying to think of."

Two of the women jurors looked at each other, and put the backs of their hands up to their mouths. Mirror images, like feeding flamingos. Someone in the back of the room clapped their hands until a court bailiff found the offender and marched her out.

It was 3:21.

Rhodes, with a thousand-watts of dismay flashing through his head, ordered a recess until the next morning. A besieged daughter in front of him, and a flow of memories about her mother needling him. He felt as if he were in iron clamps, semi-paralyzed: lurid photos of his daughter in evidence; her mother, his love of another time, his love perhaps of the present, having it off with a houseman.

He had expected that Audrey might have to testify again. Nothing unusual about that, but not like this, under a storm of lurid testimony that could rain hard on her for years to come. Make her a gossip target all over Los Angeles. He'd have to cancel dinner with Fritzi tonight. She would howl but it couldn't be helped. What to do next, he wondered; if he could, he'd protect Audrey.

179

ℭ

Fahey, with his jeweler's eye for occult, was wholly content at that moment. It was the Gypsy, who had first shown him newer, more fruitful paths in this life; paths taking him wherever he wanted to go, and whenever the mood struck. His imagination had become his life's fuel; at any instant, he could become like Sinbad on the Third Voyage—a magical world to conjure and behold. Greatest fun, and, more, it buffered him from the crueler realisms of the everyday life, which, in m any ways, repelled him.

His head lay on the Gypsy's bared lap, as he examined her oval-shaped face set off by the long ebony hair braids and golden loops descending from her ears. On each hand, she wore two rings, all of them set with lavender stones. Fahey, with one finger pad, gently traced the drape of her nearest breast, as she once more warned him to be wary of life's joys.

"The addictions of one's soul," she called them. Fahey, as always, did all but genuflect to the mystic insights of his Gypsy woman. Indeed, she was his confessor and soothsayer, all in one.

Adoring her, this, his other wife and his truest conscience. Twice during this visit, he'd pleaded with her to perform a smaller séance. But today, she said, the stars were in a reckless alignment and might bring harm to them both.

"What of the young one, the girl?" he inquired.

"I've never seen her. She's only a vague image."

"Christ, my precious one, she's all over the airwaves."

"But not mine. She is hardly a shape to me."

"Swear to you she's got one of those strange lights about her."

"Then she'll come to no good."

"I need you to tell me all of it. I'm getting somewhat skittish, you see…"

"Another time, perhaps. She is too vague in my sight for now."

"She is quite the beauty."

"So are the skins of snakes and lizards."

"Ah, the slither-ers."

"You must see for yourself, Alonzo," she retorted as another thought invaded her. Did Fahey, her humorist, intend her for the bed today? She might even put another herb poultice on his bad elbow. He always liked that, and then he would stay longer and that would yield a better chance to persuade him into the new partnership she had in mind. A few nights earlier a dream-like vision had suggested the whereabouts of some stolen art Fahey had been stalking for nearly two years. For him, a rare failure. She would gladly share her secret, so long as he split the insurance company's recovery fee. A hundred-thousand, at least. She knew the figure because he'd once told her in a fit of frustration.

Fahey stirred. From his pocket, he drew out the Turkish medal, his good luck charm the Gypsy had given him on his saint's day a year ago. He saved it for occasions that could only occur once, the last time being Raye Wheeler's funeral.

"How do I shine this up? Vinegar? Beeswax?"

"Leave it with me," she offered.

"Can't, my blessed one. What would I put under my pillow?"

"Ancient dreams are always best."

She took the medal from his open palm. With one strong lift of her thighs, she moved him upwards, telling him she was tired. That he must go now. To come back later in the week, Sunday would be best.

But he wanted to stay. He looped his good arm around her, saying he must begin composing her history this very day. Where would they begin? In bed? The best place to talk, always. Get the biology down pat, and the rest of it would skip right into place.

And, by the way, he could find no history of the Turkish army in any important battle during the past century. What sort of gift had she given him anyway?

Herself, she would tell him later.

For now, though, he asked for more tutoring. He wanted to know who wrote the first love song. And why did love always strike without warning? Unfriendly, wasn't it? That it was so easy to be greatest friends with someone till you fell in love with them. Why was that? He divulged his latest theory, that to get along with the women he adored—"you most of all, Gypsy"—it was always much better to have a few strongly nourished faults. Vices, naturally, were best. Else, how could the women correct you, which they so loved doing, then forgive you, and start you over on newer paths of redemption? Women, being born confessors, were infatuated with doling out acts of forgiveness. Forgiveness was an achievement, had its own special graces, had softness to it, and was therefore a female thing. Men, on the other side of it, preferred triggering a bullet instead of forgiving of anything, even a mild insult. Especially this was so when matters of the opposite sex were involved.

"Gypsy love, tell me, why do women recall everything as if it were written on the stones of Moses...whether you praised them or didn't; insufficient praise for their jewels; how their hair looked on a certain night; the dresses they wore. Or if you should've made love to them and somehow forgot to. It is like taking a non-stop test, except school never lets out, not even for one fucking day."

Women, he went on, being such circular creatures with those lovely faces and intense emotions and their hearts so miserable half the time. Those rounded breasts and that other lambent mouth where their thighs met. That inner, silent mouth, so deadly silent, but filled with so much knowledge, that took in your private chemicals and gave back life.

Was that really fair? Would men behave with all that guile, Gypsy, if they'd been given those magic chalices between their thighs? What was he missing, what cryptic code of life was evading him?

With his hand stroking her abundant nest, Fahey's eyes shone brighter now and with a certain peaceable light to them.

Gazing down at his damp face, she widened her knees for him. "You know what I see?" she asked.

"But I never know."

"Behind his back your God holds trouble for you."

"You think?" Fahey sat up abruptly. "That bastard always has trouble waiting in the wings. Floods. Droughts. Hurricanes. Biblical scourges. Got to be an end to Him sometime."

"My crystals tell me you must find yourself a different life and soon."

"Life, you say? Life is a high dive. A quick fuck is what it is, Gypsy. A muscle spasm. You get a few grand moments out of her, then a hot towel and a fast goodbye out the door...and Jesus, look what she charges you even if you don't want her."

"Am I that life, Alonzo?"

"Never, my hallowed one. It's you who keeps me safe from the others. I wish that every day with you had had a hundred hours."

"And no stones of Moses?"

Fahey laughed and his Gypsy laughed with him, as he threw an arm around her great hulk. She wanted him, then, before he engaged her in more talk about the girl at the trial. That girl who the Gypsy could not see vividly, but did not care for, not at all.

"That young one," she said, "who seems to beguile you so much."

She knew her Fahey, and his caressing, exploring hands. He was heading her for bed, for more tutoring in the Romany styles of igniting one's pleasure. And of faraway dreams that were drawing nearer, and of the next day's tragedies she could sometimes sense before they struck.

☙

Returning home at twilight, Audrey found a message written by Kardas on the front hall table.

Please call Mr. Pritter at 736-2400 or 736-1921.

Slipping the note into her purse, she walked across the marble floor toward a study, there to fetch a drink to dilute her worries. She wanted a bath, the longest one ever. She had heard a newsbreak about the trial—her name now linked with Kardas—on her car's radio as she drove up the Pacific Coast Highway. Her heart rate had sped to a level where she was certain her ribs might break. It still beat, not as furiously but wildly enough.

That little witch!

Walking into the study, she saw Julio jerk suddenly at the mention of her name coming over the airwaves. Alerted by an Oldes & Farnham partner, he'd been glued to the 5:30 news on television, and the newscaster, a woman, was summing up the vitals of Romaine's testimony:

> "...*an alleged romance between Mrs. Julio Sterne and a Sterne-employed butler whose name is Ferenc Kardas...it is not known at this point the full relevance of these remarks made by the accused, the actress Romaine Brook...but the trial itself has offered so many twists and turns one expects the unexpected...Romaine Brook seemed to captivate the courtroom as she described the relationship between...*"

At the sight of his wife, freshly coiffed, freshly arrived, Julio Sterne verged on rage. She seemed so mended, so calm and controlled, while he anticipated nothing but smirks, snickers, dirty-talk careening around Los

Angeles's dinner tables, dragging his name through a pigsty of gossip.

His temper about to erupt, he took no note of the fact that it was he who had authorized the dalliance. That the irony of providing surrogate-sex for his wife was, in its way, something of an insurance policy for defending his own reputation. That if he had wrath to direct at someone, then he, by rights, ought to include himself in the fusillade.

Breathing hard, breathing fire, he cried out, "The most famous whore in California arrives. Who was it this time? The hairdresser?" A shabby, contemptuous comment. Still, the words had done their cutting, had sunk into the target, doing the intended damage.

"Julio, oh, this is—"

"Get away! Leave me be and kindly just get the hell out of here!"

"How dare you speak that way. You and Kardas got all this started, you even said as much. Now you want me to be responsible for what that little witch says in court."

"That's right. I hadn't realized you were putting on performances for the neighborhood. Have you no shame?

"Have you no sense, Julio. My God, you know she'll say anything. And don't look at me that way. I feel sorry for you, you soak in your misery, thinking everyone is taking advantage of you. Maybe they are, but I'm not one of them. If you want to call it quits, then call it quits. But how about a little decency? A little of that."

"Leave!"

ೞ

Evening and Tommy Burke stood by the flat black window of Raye Wheeler's office. He could hear nothing of the life ten stories below. Crowds milling about, neon lights blazing, the lingering smells of the taco and burrito vendors, hawkers offering a full cafeteria of wristwatches radios, knickknacks, and hijacked appliances. Street girls, in their finery of pink and purple satins, in the shadowy doorways, impatiently awaiting the night's trade, praying the cops wouldn't roust them.

It was Broadway, the same artery in Los Angeles as in New York, the same as every Broadway of every city that harbors ghettos of the night.

Staring at the one down below, he was tempted to go have a look around, buy a burrito with a side of frijoles.

See, smell, be jostled—pursuing a Muse, and inspiration.

He looked around the office for an enduring moment. It would shut down next month; he had no way, no prospect of keeping the law practice open. To his name, he had but a single client, who was all but broke.

His aching knees had swollen. He'd been on his feet for too many hours that day, so he sat in the swivel chair behind the desk Wheeler had used for nearly forty-five years. After the trial had adjourned that afternoon, he had taken Romaine aside, submitting her to a light tongue-lashing for holding out on him. She had a laid a hand to his cheek, apologizing, while reminding him that he had told her it was all right to continue with her comments when she'd been on the stand; but, he had never thought, never remotely imagined, she would go where she had gone with her incendiary revelations.

Pandora's Box had not only opened, it had exploded, offering a new angle of counter-attack against the prosecution's case.

What now, he wondered?

How to take advantage? None of the stuff Fahey had given him went anywhere near this territory. *Terra incognita,* he thought. Questions had niggled at him ever since he'd left the courthouse four hours earlier. What would Raye Wheeler do with this trove? Tommy needed reliable guidance, now that his client had passed him the magical baton.

If what Romaine had said was true, had actually happened, and he pursued it but failed to corroborate, Pritter would demolish her. Demolish them both.

Where were the witnesses to ratify her story of barging in on Audrey Sterne and Kardas *in flagrante delicto*? All he needed was just one other credible witness but where, where, and who, who? Another of the servants, perhaps? An all-seeing, all-knowing Almighty, that was another perhaps.

A second witness at seven in the morning, observing a scene like the one Romaine had described—a one-in-a-billion chance, Tommy decided. So, forget it. Double forget it.

And where was the redoubtable Fahey? The man of so many notions and disturbing talents. Tommy reached for the phone, fumbling it twice before it dropped on the floor. Why, he wondered, was his hand so shaky? But then, so was everything else.

Chapter Seventeen

Door chimes sounded.

She was here again. Contacted earlier by Macklin Price, who was running a little interference so no one in the Sterne household knew who was really trying to reach Audrey, and asking her to return to Bel Air.

More subterfuges. Things were askance again. Peril afoot.

Consuelo sauntered off as Audrey entered the library. She came in walking a little stiffly, her gray-green eyes glinting after removing her sunglasses.

"Getting to be a real rendezvous, your house."

"Can't think of any place better. Safer is what I mean," Rhodes agreed.

"I heard all that nice juicy ridiculous news from your courtroom," she retorted. "Yesterday on the car radio, then on TV. My husband all but kicked me out of the house."

"Caused quite a rumpus at court, too."

"I'd bet so."

He stood a few feet away, viewing her in detail. " Like a drink?"

"No, thanks. I'm homeward bound, if it isn't barricaded."

"Mind if I have one?"

"Or course, not. Have ten, dammit. What're you having anyway?"

"A double dammit is what I was thinking of," he said, hoping to ease the strain.

"All right, I'll have one, too. Anything-at-all and on the rocks."

It was Saturday, the Sabbath day for some, but not for them. Audrey sat down as he poured two drinks at the bar.

"I can make this quick," he said, handing over her drink.

"Not quick enough. That little wretch! Lying about me in front of all those people."

Still standing, he said nothing.

"Well."

"I don't know of her as a liar."

"You don't know her, then."

"You got that right. Yesterday opened a new jar of trouble. That's why I asked you to meet me...I'm in this too, remember."

"So what is it to be, Cliff?"

Reading from a copy of the court-transcript, Rhodes repeated Romaine's testimony, and the obvious meaning it held for Audrey.

"You really believe that crap? You couldn't, Cliff. It's idiotic."

"It isn't important what I believe, Audrey. It's on the airwaves now. The press, everyone listened...*and how they listened*," he emphasized his words so she would know he was serious. "There's a jury involved, and what matters is what they believe."

"I'll kill that kid, by God if I won't. I'm going to—"

"Slow down."

"I'm damned if I'll let her smear me!"

"They'll probably call you back on the stand. Give you a chance to refute her testimony...probably pull in that fella Kardas, too. You'll have to come back, you know."

Audrey glared over the rim of the tumbler. "Who'll call me back? You?"

"Pritter."

"Pritter wouldn't dare!"

There it is, he thought, the words said so vehemently. A tip-off that the prosecutor was in the Sterne's pocket. That's why all the high-pressure calls from Sacramento. A cabal.

"Would you dare defy the court," he asked, "leave your reputation all over the street that way? That's contempt, Audrey. I'd be forced to go after you."

"Why should I have to say anything at all? I've nothing to hide."

"That's exactly what the jury wants to hear."

"They've heard enough, I should think." Audrey crossed her legs. One foot seesawed in the air, up and down.

"Maybe I can help, Audrey."

"How?"

"By controlling what can be said, and what can't...at least for the record," he added. "I've got to be careful and so do you."

"I'm not doing it. I'm not going back in there again."

"You refuse and you're headed for jail till you come to your senses. The jury might come to all sorts of conclusions, none of them in your favor"— leaning on her, forcing her now—"and all Burke has to do is open the door wider and wider. You'll play right into his hands."

"What do you mean?"

"He'll keep implying that you and Kardas had something going on. And possibly the two of you had your own reasons for getting rid of Marc Sterne."

"That's the most rotten thing anyone ever said. You are some bastard, Cliff, to say—"

"Lots of money. Your husband's an elderly fellow and a handsome Hungarian comes on the scene—"

"Stop it!" Audrey's hands went up to her neck, down to her lap, then up once more.

"I want you to see how it can all go against you," Rhodes pointed out.

"Please stop it."

'You've got to understand how—"

"Into that sewer? I don't have to look down there, thank you."

"No, that's right, you don't. But any lawyer with half a brain can make a jury look there. And they will and you'll be cooked. An argument could be made that the wrong party has been accused of murder. Don't you see?"

"And she'd go free? Is that what you're saying?"

"All the jury needs is reasonable doubt."

"You'd love it, too. That's what you'd love, isn't it? Her to go free?"

"Not if she's proven guilty. But I've never been convinced Romaine is guilty."

"Oh, my God!"

"What?"

"How I wish I'd never met you."

"But you did. And now we're answering for it, for what we at one time meant to each other, and here we are with a very tricky situation on our hands. Not so long ago, you came here asking for help. And that's what I'm trying to do, Audrey. Really, I am."

"Oh, God, Julio will go crazy. He already won't talk to me."

"It's your word against Romaine's. Remember that."

But Audrey had missed his words. A stark image rummaged her thoughts, as she saw Julio smiling contemptuously. She sagged against the back of the couch. "You know what?" she said.

"Tell me."

"You know why we're on earth? It's to watch our dreams crash, it's never to have enough peace, or anything else. Every goddam thing else!"

"We'll get through this. I'll help—"

"You'll get through it, you mean. Wait till your number gets pulled out of the hat someday, then you'll see."

"Oh, it has, it already has, believe me. Now, it's being pulled out all over again. "

"Bushwa. It's me, not you."

"It's both of us. That's while I'll go to bat if I can, Audrey. But I'd like to know one thing."

"And that is?'

"Was there anything between you and this Kardas fellow?"

"Are you crazy? He's the goddam houseman. Butler, whatever. You think I'd shag him!"

Rhodes looked at her dispraisingly. "Okay," he said, standing, "it's all I wanted to hear. I'll walk you out to your car."

"She's a liar, Cliff. Believe me. You have no idea how hard it is to think that about your own child. No idea at all," Audrey said, thinking again of Marc's sprawled body, her missing emerald bracelet, other deceits. "It's so damned unfair. I'm really sorry, Cliff. Sorry I called you a bastard. I'm just so undone. God help us—help us—"

"Just tell the truth. Perjury can go hard, especially in a murder trial."

"What do I do?"

"I just said what you *must* do. Speak truthfully."

She let out a string of curses, as if afflicted by Tourette's syndrome. He led her to the driveway and watched her as she fired up her Maserati and roll down to the road, musing how a woman in mow-down anger was a worthy sight every few years or so.

What Rhodes couldn't muse about, however, was that either Audrey or Romaine was lying. Which one? He heard the misery of choice calling to him again, demanding an answer. That answer could mean anything and everything, especially up in Sacramento. Now for Fahey. He began to feel like Burke's off-stage ventriloquist. He knew, reluctantly knew, that he'd

189

have to get into the fray, ask direct questions from the bench, as he had every right to do.

But not too often. Not too noticeably. Not too carelessly.

CR

She won't even give me a straight answer on the photos, Tommy complained to himself. She evades, says she can't remember. How could she not? Fingers all over her, things sunk inside her, a dog on her.

Pritter will get his opening eventually, and one way or the other mop the floor with her. Even if the courtroom spectators and the media people weren't permitted to see the photos, he'll somehow manage to describe them.

Tommy failed to hear the office nightline until the second ring. He picked it up.

"Wheeler offices."

"Burke's, you mean."

"Alonzo? That you?"

"S'right. All organs accounted for."

"What's the news?"

"Your boyo is in town. I checked. He also got the word from Pritter's office."

"Monday?"

"Up to you."

"That's when we want him. I'll ask the judge to delay Romaine."

"See you later."

"Oh, Alonzo, ah, do you have a number where I can reach Judge Rhodes? He's unlisted."

Fahey rattled it off.

"Terrific, Alonzo. Thanks for everything."

"Go home, it's Saturday. All good Irishers and Jews are supposed to be home."

Hanging up, Tommy let out a whoop that filled the room. He thought out his pitch, then dialed twice before getting it right. Apologizing to Rhodes for bothering him at home, he explained that the Malibu deputy sheriff had returned from his vacation. Could they put him on first thing Monday?

"The sheriff's force is busy," Tommy persuaded, "and I don't know when we can get to him again."

Rhodes heard and agreed.

Tommy thanked him, hung up again and forgot all about what day it was. Saturday was not a day off for him, or Sunday either. If the sheriff's office had made an error on their write-ups of Marc Sterne's death, then they could've made other missteps. He could tantalize the jury with the idea that the investigators had possibly made mistakes, mistakes he would somehow invent if he had to.

What about that syringe, for example, with its telling and curious absence of prints? And that letter written by Romaine that could be read at least two ways?

And that brunette juror, the one wearing the horn-rims, who keeps looking at Rhodes too often? He'd have to keep an eye on her; her body language anyway. Was she signaling something?

Chapter Eighteen

"**Y**ou say you *can't* remember?'' Tommy Burke protested to the deputy sheriff from the Malibu station. "Or that you don't wish to remember? We can wait a moment so you can think it over?"

"I don't have to think it over."

"Then you must remember who it was."

"It was Mrs. Sterne."

"You're sure?"

"Yes, I am now. Very sure."

"But you weren't so sure a moment ago?"

"I had to think. It was several months ago, remember."

"That's right, it was," said Tommy. "Easy to make a mistake of that kind...and you're saying that when you came into the house, the Sternes's home in Malibu, Mrs. Sterne and Ferenc Kardas were there and Mrs. Sterne showed you where Marc's body was?"

"No, Ferenc Kardas did. He discovered the body first."

"You're certain?"

"I'm certain."

"And then did Mrs. Sterne tell you Mr. Sterne was upstairs. Too devastated to talk to anyone?"

"Words to that effect," the deputy agreed. "We decided not to bother him. Wait a day."

"And that all three of them—Mr. and Mrs. Sterne and Ferenc Kardas— had just come in from a boat outing?"

"That's right. It's all there in the report."

"Now, deputy, you testified at the beginning of the trial that several neighbors heard a sound on the water. An engine perhaps...engine noises carry over water very well, don't they, at night...perhaps that was the Sternes's boat coming in?"

"We assumed that."

"Assumed?"

"There's no other explanation."

"Some things never get explained, do they?" Tommy said.

He backed away from the deputy. Slowly because his wobbly knees were still swollen to the size of cantaloupes and pain was shooting up his legs. He picked up copies of the two investigation reports, the first exhibits marked and entered for the record by Pritter at the opening of the trial when this deputy had appeared as one of the state's leadoff witnesses.

Tommy showed the reports to the deputy. "You recognize these?"

"I do."

"You wrote them?"

"And I also signed them."

"You're a trained criminologist, right? You hold a degree in criminology, correct?"

"That's right, I do. From Cal State."

"Can you tell me why the dates on those reports are identical?"

The deputy frowned as he looked again at the reports in his hand. "I— the one here—the other—the other, I think, that's the one for Mr. Sterne-- they shouldn't be—" He stopped, looked again, and flustered, went on with, "A typo, I suppose."

"You dated and signed them, right? That's your signature. Your handwriting. One report describes the statements of Audrey Sterne and then of Ferenc Kardas. The other, for Julio Sterne, is dated the same day. How could that be when Julio Sterne was too undone over his son's death to make a statement when they had made theirs on the night before?"

"A mistake."

"A mistake?"

"Yes."

"Well, that's two mistakes, isn't it?"

The deputy reddened. He looked away from Tommy and away from the jury. Pritter straightened in his chair.

"Isn't it?" Tommy repeated.

"Minor ones."

"How about the syringe, deputy? The one you found by Marc Sterne's body. The one the forensic lab said was used to inject a fatal dosage of drugs into Marc Sterne. Was there a mistake there?"

"What do you mean?"

"You handled it, didn't you? Picked up the syringe and put it in a plastic evidence bag. Could you have made a mistake and wiped away any fingerprints when you did that?"

"No." The deputy wagged his head. "I picked the syringe up by the needle. I used forceps."

"You couldn't have made a mistake?"

"Not on that, I couldn't."

"You remember it so clearly?"

"I sure do."

"Only a few minutes ago, you couldn't remember whether it was Audrey Sterne or Ferenc Kardas who first told you that Julio Sterne was upstairs, indisposed."

"But then I did remember, didn't I?"

"What of the dates of your reports?"

"A typo, as I said."

"Except it's signed and *dated* in your own handwriting, deputy."

"We all make mistakes all the time, don't we?"

"In a murder trial we try to keep them to a minimum. And you, just possibly"—Tommy hesitated—"just possibly might've made one when you picked up the syringe."

"But I didn't."

"You say so, deputy. But anyone in a time of turmoil can do something, and afterward not remember doing it, can't they? I can and you can, and we all can, right? Sometimes we don't even know we've made a mistake until later on, when it's brought to our attention."

"I handled the evidence correctly. By the book," the deputy responded vehemently. His hands balled into fists, resting on his knees.

"You assume the noise on the water was the Sternes's boat? An assumption unproved. You didn't immediately recall whether it was Audrey Sterne or Kardas who told you Julio Sterne was upstairs...you think, and you assume, the identical date on Julio Sternes's statement was due to typographical error, though you took his statement down the following day...and

you dated it the day before in your own handwriting. Right or wrong?"

"Yes, I made an error."

194

Tommy paused again.

"...Yet you're certain as the sun rises about the syringe. That's what you want us to believe?"

"Absolutely," confirmed the deputy.

Burke shook his head. He turned to the jury, a whimsical expression pasted on his face, shook his head again, and said, "I wish we could all be so absolutely sure."

"You seem to be, Mr. Burke."

"Not really. This is the first case I ever tried and I have to say I'm confused...let's go over your statement of a few minutes ago. You said—and please correct me if I'm wrong—that Mrs. Sterne called the Malibu sheriff's station soon after Marc Stern's body was found. Right after that, she apparently called the gate and told the guard you'd be coming through. The guard said, when finding out from Mrs. Sterne that Marc was dead, that Romaine Brook had been there earlier and then she had left. Miss Brook arrived at Malibu Pointe at some time after Marc had already come through the gate...later, Mrs. Sterne told you about Miss Brook, and you checked it out with the same guard. Do you want to alter any part of that statement?"

"No," said the deputy. "That's what I told the court the first time I was here. And so did the gate guard, as I remember."

"Just wanting to be sure, deputy." Tommy Burke looked at Pritter. "Your witness."

"No questions at this time," Pritter announced. He didn't think Burke had done any real damage. But he didn't care to open any new avenues for him, either.

Rhodes had closely followed the exchange between Burke and the deputy. Yet his eyes rarely strayed from Romaine's demure but cheerful-looking face.

Still, experience informed him someone was fiddling with the facts. Burke had failed to shut the lid on the box, when the chance to do it had all but punched him in the nose. As the deputy waited to be excused, Rhodes mulled a moment before asking: "Deputy? One point I'm unclear on. About Mr. Sterne?"

"Yes?" The deputy craned his neck, looking over toward the bench.

"Did you or anyone else from the Malibu station look in on Julio Sterne the night of Marc Sterne's death? Just to see if he was all right?"

"We respected Mrs. Sterne's wishes. We left him alone, sir."

"You're not precisely sure where he was?"

"Upstairs." The deputy shrugged. "His bedroom, I guess."

"You guess? Wouldn't you have verified his presence, his condition, one way or another?"

"It was a pretty rough time for everyone, your Honor, and we had our hands full that night."

"I'm sure. But all the same, wouldn't it be correct procedure to fix the identity and whereabouts of everyone at the scene?"

"Usually, yes."

"Usually or always."

"Well, always. Yes, always."

"But not that time? You didn't follow procedure that time, am I right? "

"I guess we were so busy that...a pretty hectic time and all...I, well, we—" the deputy stumbled again.

"So, the fact is you didn't look in on Mr. Sterne?"

"We didn't."

"An oversight?" Rhodes was pressing the situation, wanting the jury to get it very straight.

"In hindsight, it was."

"You don't know for certain that Mr. Sterne was upstairs or someplace else?"

"We took Mrs. Sterne's word for where he was."

"Well, supposing he wasn't there?"

The question hung there like a gallows' blade. Pritter slumped in his chair. He wanted to raise an objection to the line of questioning, but he knew Rhodes would hardly rule against himself. He was stuck. The one thing he'd been instructed to do—take all steps necessary to keep Julio Sterne out of the trial—and it was rapidly slipping from his control.

"Can you answer me?" Rhodes requested of the deputy.

"We took his statement the next day and that's where he said he was: up in his bedroom in a state of shock."

"That's what your report says?"

"Yes. Mine and the one taken down by the state investigators."

"Why was the state called in so soon? The very next day, weren't they?"

"The Attorney General's office insisted on taking over. Sending their own men in."

"How many men?"

"Four or five."

"Which?"

"Five."

"Quite a few, isn't it? Is it usual for the state to take over on this sort of an investigation?"

"No, not in my experience."

"And were they present when you questioned Julio Sterne the next day?"

"They were, yes, all five of them."

"Who did the questioning?"

"They did."

"But you signed the report as if you'd conducted the questioning. Is that right, deputy?"

The deputy slowly nodded.

"Please answer aloud."

"Yes sir, I did."

"Why didn't they do their own write-up?"

Agitated, Pritter shifted in his chair. Murmuring something to one of his assistants, he sent him out of the courtroom.

"They told me to do it," said the deputy.

"Told you to sign off on their work?"

"This was an unusual situation, your Honor, and we cooperated."

"Other than an alleged case of homicide, how was it so unusual?"

"I guess—well, it was them—the Sternes, you know."

"Know what?"

"They're being so prominent and all and, well, I think you know what I mean."

"Big enough to get you elbowed out of the way, you mean? Make you write reports the way they wanted them written?"

"That's possible, I suppose."

"You have any more guesses, deputy? Did you make a guess that Mrs. Sterne was factually correct when she told you her husband was upstairs?"

"I took her word, as I've already said."

"Because she is Mrs. Sterne?" asked Rhodes, cutting deep, going for the deputy's nerves.

"I didn't think of it that way."

"Never crossed your mind? Not once?"

197

"Yes, I suppose it did, later on."

"Did you mind the state coming in and peeling you off the case?"

"We didn't like it much."

"But you went along?"

"We had to."

"Why?"

"It wasn't my decision."

"Whose was it?"

"The sheriff's."

"And how did he explain that situation to you?" Rhodes asked as he saw Pritter conferring with his other assistant.

"The sheriff said we were out of it. By direct request from the State Bureau of Investigation and the governor's office," the deputy said, putting it as delicately as he could.

"The governor's office?"

"That's what we were told."

"Do you have any idea why?"

The deputy looked confused. Confused and somewhat frightened, as he had been warned to keep his mouth shut about all the griping at the Malibu station when the state had horned in.

"I think your work could've been a lot sharper," Rhodes said to him.

Letting it sink in. A giveaway to Burke, a swipe at Pritter, and a point he was sure the jury would put in their pocket. As he was also sure his ears would soon be blistered by more yelling out of the governor's office. But at least he'd gotten it all out in the open—that political finagling was fully operational behind the scenes.

"Any other questions?" Rhodes asked.

Pritter said no. Tommy shook his head.

Rhodes told the deputy to step down. Halfway down the aisle, a gaggle of reporters arose and followed him out. Rhodes called Burke and Pritter to the bench.

"What now?" He searched Burke's face. "Are you going to continue with Miss Brook?"

"No, we've got to hear from Mr. Sterne."

"You agree?" Rhodes said to Pritter.

"Not for an instant. Why does it make any difference where Julio Sterne was?"

"It might mean everything," offered Tommy. "I've got plenty of reason to believe Marc Sterne was on the outs with his father...Romaine Brook has told me plenty, and we haven't addressed it as yet. We need our opportunity to get the foundation made for what's to come later."

"What're you suggesting?" snapped Pritter.

"Maybe Julio Sterne was involved," Tommy said.

"Did away with his own son?"

"I don't know. Do you?"

Pritter's normally florid face paled. "That's the stupidest thing I ever heard of."

"Aren't we here to find out?" Rhodes said.

Pritter snorted.

"How much more have you got with your client?" Rhodes asked Burke.

"A long way," said Tommy. "But I want to tie this down—the whereabouts of Mr. Sterne—before I go on with her. We have to."

"Am I going to have to subpoena him?" Rhodes said to Pritter. That word again, *subpoena*, he thought.

"Look, the man's been crushed by all this," Pritter replied. "How can you drag him through it again?"

"You've been dragging my client through it for months now...we can knock Sterne off in an hour," Tommy retorted. "Maybe less."

"Knock him off, you say." Pritter's shoulders rose. "You mean the way Brook knocked his son off?"

"Okay, that's enough," Rhodes said to Pritter. "Let's get Mr. Sterne out of the way...do we need a subpoena or not?"

"Won't be necessary. I'll talk to him," Pritter said in disgust.

"Tomorrow?"

"I'll have to see." Pritter looked off, far away, through the walls, across the city, watching his future, his desk at Oldes & Farnham riding off to another planet.

"We'll have to recess...I'm requesting that you," Rhodes said to Pritter, "get him here as quickly as you can. Tell him that comes straight from me. And we'll try to inconvenience him as little as possible."

As Pritter sensed his future catapulting into oblivion, Tommy Burke's world seemed like the light at the end of the pier. Almost floating back to where Romaine sat, he could hardly wait to tell her what was up.

What would Julio Sterne be like, Tommy wondered? Rhodes had swung the gate open. Tripping up the deputy, showing the court how the state Bureau of Investigation had pounced on Romaine; the judge, he thought, had paid out the telling questions. Nice sharp belly-slammers.

Tommy would have sent him a thank you note if that weren't so improper. His knees had stopped hurting.

∞

That evening Rhodes sat with Fritzi on her terrace. They dipped chips in guacamole and drank margaritas in the cool air fanning across Los Angeles's lower hills. Loosening his tie, Rhodes put his feet up on the terrace's railing.

"I love this hour of the day," Fritzi observed.

"The best."

"Are you staying? Say yes."

"Can't. I need to look at some of the trial transcript tonight."

"Do it here. I can be back by ten, maybe earlier."

"The script won't get to my house until eight or so. I need time to go over it before tomorrow."

"Why not have them send it here?"

Rhodes shook his head. "We've walked that track before. That's the way mouths start rumors—"

"Plenty of people know about us, Cliff."

"Let's not add the court system to our fan club."

"That damn trial owns you, doesn't it? I hardly see you anymore."

'It'll be over soon."

"Will we be all over, too, Cliff?" asked Fritzi, her face somber.

"Don't ever say that. This is a big, big trial. And I've got to be damn careful with it."

"Because you got raked so hard over the last one?"

"That's as good a reason as any."

A stillness settled over them.

"You're really hard in the head," Fritzi said eventually. "Sometimes I'd give a lot to fall out of love with you. Just be friends, the sort of friends who only say they care, and not get so worried about the rest of it."

"That's not altogether my idea of a friend, lover-girl."

"Mine either. That's exactly what I mean." She sighed, looking beyond the veranda rail to a sky painted in coral and lilac. All that remained of the sun were those fabulous colors she would love to have woven into fabric for an evening gown.

"You know what?" she said.

"Sometimes."

"Here's one you don't know."

"That makes twenty don't-knows for today."

"I went to my doctor today."

Rhodes was watching a plane descend on an imaginary line in the far distance. At the word "doctor," his attention fastened again on Fritzi.

"Checkup time," she continued. "Told me I'd better get on with having children before I'm forty. My biological clock is in a race with reality."

'They actually charge you for that advice?"

"No, that part is gratis."

"They persuade you to have a kid and then bill you for screaming it into the world."

"You're such a smarty."

"I'm a lawyer, kiddo. Doctors and lawyers all use the same methods to pickpocket their clients."

He tried to find the plane again, but it had dropped out of sight. He sipped at his margarita, betting a hundred-to-one with himself what was coming next.

"And do you know," Fritzi was saying over his thoughts, "he's actually quite right. I don't even have an heir."

"You've got a whole gorgeous head of it."

"Oh, wow, Mr. Clever-Boy." Fritzi smiled half-heartedly. "You can do better, much better."

"You don't have an air. That's what I like about you. Not a lot of bullshitty veneer and posturing—"

"Oh, God!"

"He's the Man you'll need, if you want an heir. From me, anyway."

"Is that so?"

"That's so. Unless you're in line for one of those immaculate conceptions."

"Be pretty hard to prove how immaculate it is in my case."

"I'll vouch for you. Would you think of an adoption...?"

201

"And marriage?"

"It'd sure look better, wouldn't it?"

"Much."

"Would you marry me? I suppose you could always go to one of those artificial insemination banks. Or we could adopt."

Fritzi tossed her heavy dark hair, its lower ends blended perfectly with the black velvet collar of her bottle-green suit, an Austrian get-up, a dirndl, that for some odd reason made her seem smaller. Rhodes thought he could see a flush growing under the pearls around her throat.

"I'm not so sure about having kids," he said. "Or having you sell your insides for one."

"Oh, I don't think I'd have to pay for it," she said, slightly annoyed. She looked at her watch.

"I know you wouldn't...and how did we land on this subject anyway?"

"A child," she said. 'It'd be nice to have one, I've been thinking. I'd be willing to adopt one if—"

"If we paired up legally," he finished for her.

"Correct-o."

"What the hell kind of marriage can we have, if I'm up in Sacramento most of the time?"

"We could manage. Vicarious thrills. Phone sex or something. And we can send each other singing telegrams every Wednesday."

"We manage all right now, don't we?"

"So-so."

"I wasn't talking about the sex part."

"Neither was I, Cliff."

"Marry and adopt a kid? That's what's on the table, is it?"

Fritzi nodded with the pure vigor of a woman who knows her mind with a perfect precision.

"How can I help raise a child? Won't work, Fritzi, and you—"

"We can make work whatever we want to make work. Here I am damn near proposing to you again and you just look for excuses. Thanks a whole bunch."

"I'll—well, let's talk about it later."

"Sure. Later. Like you going to a psychiatrist, it's always later."

"They're quite different things."

"For you, Cliff...I'm not so sure for me."

202

Rhodes's feet dropped to the flagstones, making a sharp sound that served as an exclamation point to his feelings. He was worried. He had trouble, and it was trouble he'd chosen to carry by himself. He didn't care for any more of it, even though he knew she was perfectly right to ask all the questions in the world about their future.

"Think on it," Fritzi said in a voice trembling with complaint. She got up to leave.

"I have, sweetheart—"

"Future tense."

"Christ, I come up here to have a drink with you, get a feel of your sweet ass, and you want to settle the next twenty years on your way out the door."

Fritzi smiled. "Cold steak in the 'fridge if you want," she said brightly.

"Thanks."

"Think on it," she reminded him.

She was gone then, abruptly gone. He could hear her heels tap, tap, tap on the hardwood floors in the hallway.

Habit.

He knew a lot about her thinking habits, and then supposed she knew even more about his. Women always did. They had some very unfair advantages in their radar mechanism.

They hadn't kissed each other goodbye. That bothered him. He couldn't remember the last time, if ever, when they hadn't at least hugged goodbye. He supposed, too, that he deserved it with what he'd been giving her lately. Fritzi had just told him off, but so nicely it had taken him a minute or so to realize it.

Adoption?

He needed an heir, too. An heir other than Uncle Sam of the voracious appetite, who pilfers every centavo you hadn't built a fence around.

Thoughts of Romaine danced on his despairing mood: a lot he would like to do for her. He had money, barrels of it, or enough barrels anyway. There must be some rule somewhere about adopting a child of your own blood, who had already been adopted once. A sort of reverse spin of the family tree, musing, and then taking a slug from a most delicious margarita.

Fritzi would never understand. How could she? How could anyone? Adopt Romaine Brook? Ridiculous on its face, the explanations wholly impossible for such an act. Thinking about it, he felt as if someone had

203

lobbed a hefty rock against his head, making his senses reel, almost the way Audrey got to him. Head and heart, he needed to erase Audrey Sterne from his system. Only two months ago, he had had a happy and mainly sound habit, going with Fritzi, one that was three years young, very uptick, very pleasing and satisfying, and with a promising future.

Until the sight of Audrey again made him come down with a first-degree case of brain confusion. The error had compounded when she let him in, after twenty-two years of silence, on the news of a lifetime.

He ought to send himself out to whomever it was that dished out swift kicks-in-the-canetta. Yet he wanted these women in his life. He loved them, or wanted to love them, and was trying hard to love Fritzi the way she deserved to be loved. He, the inconstant lover.

Enough, he decided...

He went to the living room to look for some matches and found a packet resting in a crystal ashtray on the lowered leaf of a breakfront desk. Lighting a cigar, he looked down through a pillow of smoke at the small Correggio on its brass stand.

A rare and beautifully executed oil of a woman and man on either side of a decaying stone wall; the man offering flowers, the woman, her arms posed in invitation, offering herself. Or so it seemed to him. Fritzi had loved the painting, spotting it one rainy afternoon in a gallery on Bahnhofstrasse in Zurich, where they had been visiting for an address he had given to a group of international trial lawyers.

He had given it to her for a Christmas present and her birthday, and her next birthday. It cost him nearly as much as his own house. But then he didn't often make gifts unless the cost really dug a hole in his bank account. Otherwise, it wasn't a gift but only a token and tokens were for subways.

Down the hallway, he stopped again. He saw another gift, a much smaller one. The two love birds in their gilded cage. They were preening and fluttering their little wings, chirping away, delighted with their small and fearless world.

He was beginning to feel pretty high himself, and not from the margarita either. He didn't know why. Excitement seemed to rush though his every vein and artery. He felt so alive, as if he were not the courtroom referee any longer but was right down there in the trenches slugging it out with Pritter. Hands down, he knew he could take Pritter out with just a few hard moves and quick steps.

Dance-mastering him.

Burke had set the deputy up, and it took hardly half a jab to put him on the canvas. They were a team, he and Burke. Burke just didn't know it yet, and had better not ever know it.

Out the door now, locking it, one matter still bothered him. Why had Audrey called and left a message for Marc Sterne to come for dinner in Malibu? That's how Marc Sterne's secretary had testified. The younger Sterne had complied too, obviously so, but why was no one there to greet and dine with him. So why the call from Audrey, and why the invite?

Except Romaine had come there later on. What gaping dark hole did that little ball of mystery drop into?

None he could see; none he really wanted to see, either

Chapter Nineteen

$\mathbf{A}$ll along the marriage had been one of opportuneness; a combination of needs, the right moment for both, the specter of change and even excitement, security for Audrey, and for Julio a way of preening himself before his peers and underlings. She was a catch, and, in his way, so was he. It hadn't taken long, however, for a lull to set in. And if their union had not been a jet-set love-match at the onset, then neither had it been marked by abiding passion. Indeed, the marriage had dissipated into a sort of indifferent brotherly-sisterly arrangement. Given their age difference, given that Julio's sexual capacities had waned, the marital tentacles could grip for only so long; added to which was the fact that, in Audrey's case, she came from a blue-blood family, while Julio was the product of a Jewish scrap dealer in Compton, a community south of Los Angeles that no one ever, other than its residents, made the slightest effort to visit, unless perhaps you were arrested while passing by for speeding or drunkenness. Their respective upbringings did not exactly clash, but then neither do oil and water.

Then, of course, the Kardas-factor, which, as its ramifications surfaced, had the predictable effect of greasing the skids of a marriage that had never really found its way.

Audrey still smoldered when discovering that her husband and Kardas had been in cahoots about dishing out sexual contentment, as if, like a child, she was being rewarded with treats for good behavior.

The revelation that Julio had gauged her appetites, which he could not answer himself, with a dead-on accuracy had caused her ego to nosedive. She was an open book, well, what in hell did he expect? If he couldn't perform, she *could*. Her humiliation eventually waned, and, as it did, her resentment correspondingly soared.

"Hell Hath No Fury"—had indeed become a daily truism.

With the trial in full swing, his son dead and gone, Julio had convinced himself to cut his losses: Audrey, even with her eye-catching looks, her lively personality, was more trouble than she was worth. The golden-haired trophy had lost its luster. In hindsight, it was what it was—a short-haul mistake and both knew it.

Still, the severing had seemed as sudden as an earthquake. The gloves came off, attitudes hardened, slashing remarks had percolated and had begun to scorch. One day the tension got the better of them; no fisticuffs, of course, but words were exchanged that bruised much harder than any body blows.

"You know what," he had charged, "you're a fucking bore." To which she had sallied," And you, you're a boring fuck. You're not even that, you're like a eunuch."

Pirouetting in a fit of anger, head high and chin extending like a prow, righteously she had marched off. No further talk ensued for three refrigerated days. The had called each other out; and the harpoons had landed on target. It was not a Mr.-and-Mrs. spat; it was a vivid line in the dust.

Of necessity one evening, they had circled their wagons. Julio was due in court again, and the time had arrived to compare notes, if not make amends—plain and simple, reality was gluing them together temporarily.

While Julio deplored the prospect of appearing in court, it offered its own possibilities for setting her up, despoiling her status, as a prelude to dumping her at the least cost possible.

After a lapse in their edgy conversation, she let fly with, "You're not listening to me, are you, Julio?"

"Occasionally I am."

"Well, I'm asking you what're you going to do?"

"Just what I have to do. Go to that goddamn court and speak."

"And say what?"

"The truth, what else?"

"That you weren't here that night? You'd tell them that? You'd say a thing like that?"

"If they ask, I will."

"You wouldn't."

"Don't be idiotic, Audrey. You don't think I'd perjure myself, do you?"

Julio had been calm and remote for as long as he was ever calm and remote. She had expected him to be in a roaring rage. But he had been talking so smoothly, so rationally, she knew he was calculating trouble somewhere in that nimble head.

He wanted something, but what?

Only when the glow of his cigar faintly lit the shallow planes of his face had she any chance of reading his face. "What if they find out everything? Then what about me?" she asked, her voice hollow.

"I don't think they'll be asking me about you."

"They'll know I was on the boat alone with—"

"Ferenc. Yes, I would bet someone will rapidly reach that conclusion."

"Do you care?"

"Do you?"

As Julio inhaled, the night seemed to stop and listen, before readopting its darkness and their darkness.

Neither of them heard nor saw Kardas, who, inside, stood behind the curtains of a sliding door that led to the oceanfront terrace where Julio and Audrey sat. Something was up. Kardas could sense it, even more so when hearing his name. He suspected it was something to do with the trial, and the recent accounts of it in the paper—that he was romantically linked with Audrey. So far, Sterne had said nothing about it to him.

Julio snubbed out his cigar "No, I don't know if I care or not," he finally said. "I tried to cover for you as any husband should and now it's come out as sooner or later it usually does. Even that girl knew about the two of you."

"She's a liar."

"So you say. We'll we've been over that territory, haven't we?"

"Yes, we have. What a mess. How could you do it? Set me up like that?"

"You need sex. I understand. You need dresses, bracelets, rings, a Maserati, hairdos. Besides, I had a notion you'd like Ferenc. Nice looking chap. Good manners."

"Thanks very much!"

"You seemed to like him well enough."

"And you didn't care at all."

"Audrey, turn on your headlights, for God's sake. I'm a good thirty years older than you are. We've both known that from the beginning. Someday that'll happen to you and you'll see what I mean. I know you need

208

that part of your life...that's plain enough. So, you got it because I saw to it that you got it, like everything else you need. And a lot saner than having you pick out one of my younger men friends. Or going off with some Hollywood jocker."

Audrey was shaken, shaken and flabbergasted. "You're so callous, Julio. Everything and everyone is a number in one of your profit and loss statements."

"Don't think you're hurting my feelings."

"Hardly."

"Well, don't worry overly much, they may leave you alone. Why would they care if you were bouncing Kardas' s balls for him? I figured that out on the day I got back from Seattle to find my son dead...and I knew that what you and Kardas had been up to that night could be uncovered by the police. They're not all that stupid, and they'd add two and two and finally figure you as a possible suspect. A person of interest, they call it. Why the hell do you think I've been calling in my due-bills in Sacramento?"

"Not to save me."

"To save me from public humiliation. My dear darling wife slutting-around wife."

"Only with your consent, it seems."

"Private consent."

They sat in silence for several chilled moments. Audrey supposed she was lucky Julio wasn't giving her the hot steam of the enraged and jealous husband. He'd actually been terribly civilized, almost nice. But then he had known for a long time, and hadn't taken that much umbrage on the night of the charity ball, when she'd denied everything about Kardas and herself.

He'd fooled her so easily, she felt idiotic.

"Julio, that girl is dangerous," Audrey said quietly. "She'll be telling lies about us. It scares the you-know-what out of me. She's liable to say anything."

Julio knew that, too, but wanted to hear her side of it in case he'd missed anything. "What lies are those?"

"I never met her for tea at the Polo Lounge, as she claims."

"I thought you might've. It sounds like something you'd do."

"Well, I didn't."

"Any others?"

"Lies?"

"Yes, that's what we were talking about, I thought."

"She never saw Ferenc and me doing anything?"

"Not even fucking?"

"Must you, Julio. Really, *must* you."

"That fellow Pritter gave me a rundown on Romaine's testimony." Julio laughed quickly. "She caught you down by the pool, she says. In the pool house. My God, I'd think there was enough room in a house this size—"

"Stop this, Julio. I mean it. You're trying to flatten me, aren't you?"

"No, that's Ferenc's job."

"I'm hating you, you bastard."

"I can feel it. I did a damn fool thing when I covered for you with the police. I suppose I was covering for myself at the same time...now it'll soon be in the open and they'll play it all to hell and back."

"How are you planning to explain yourself?"

"I'll think of something. I'll have to, won't I?"

"Such as?"

"Such as there may be more than one explanation for how Marc had died."

There. He'd said it. He could almost see his words slapping Audrey's pride. He could barely see her face in the moonlight, but he knew her eyes, sometimes green as spring leaves, would right now be frigid with anger.

"You thought...my God, Julio, how could you think I had anything to do with Marc's death?"

His good ear was his right one, and Julio turned his head slightly. Audrey knew something important was coming.

He said, "I was getting a briefing from the Oldes & Farnham litigators, and they were telling, or reminding me that the truth in a courtroom has so many enemies it's a wonder it ever prevails. One of the younger lawyers said something quite interesting. He said you can tell more about a person from their lies than their truths. He's right, of course. I hadn't thought about it before, but it's a useful thing to be aware of."

"It sounds like you're about to throw me to the wolves."

"Throw you somewhere, anyway."

"And Romaine Brook!"

"Yes, her too."

"Julio, you have—"

"Let me finish," said Julio. "That's why I acted so fast once you caught me up in your lie to the sheriff...that's why I got the governor's people, the state people, involved. So I could keep my hands on developments. I wasn't going to have anyone suspect I killed my son. So when I had to protect myself, then you and Kardas got a free ride on me. I covered but that may result in a boomerang."

"I never dreamed anyone could think up anything this ludicrous. The way you're doing."

"You bet they can, my friend. I've often wondered, Audrey, whether you were actually clever enough to tell them I was here, when I wasn't, so you would force me to cover for you and Kardas."

Audrey's hands rose to her neck. Her face, hidden by the darkness, had turned white as a snowflake. "I'm not that clever. But I suppose I see what you mean."

"Ah, but maybe you are that clever."

"Well, I'm not. I don't manipulate the way you do. I try never to manipulate."

"You manipulated that girl into our lives, didn't you?"

"Believe me, I had no ulterior motives."

"I do believe you because I saw what the Brook girl did to Marc. Slowly, for a year, she got into Marc's brain and blood and made him crazy. Cock-happy. That's what she did, made him cock-happy. She put him back on drugs when she tramped on his—on his heart—"

"You're right. Julio, that's exactly what she did," said Audrey, relieved that he admitted to what she'd known for a very long time.

"A very strange young woman. One of those who kiss you with their fangs. I've known a few others like her. Knock you over with charm and you fall right on their knife."

"Calling her foxy would be—"

"You're all foxy. Everyone who's got one of those furry little gates between their legs is a fox. Women don't get really safe until they're at least seventy."

Audrey smelled the rising tendrils of more discord, and more woe in the offing. Where was it to end? She'd already told Rhodes there was nothing at all between Ferenc and herself. If she admitted the truth in front of him at court, what then? Would he wash his hands?

211

"Let me remind you," Julio was saying, "of how close a thing it was for you. When I came home that morning from Seattle, I drove in through the low road by the golf course only because it was shorter and I was tired...if I'd come the other way through the front gates the guards would have known I probably wasn't here that night. Your story would have been shot to hell, Audrey. That's how lucky you are."

"You've only told me a dozen times, Julio," she said irritably.

"Yes I have. So perhaps you'll let me do the thinking around here until this trial is over."

"I couldn't agree more and—"

They both turned their heads at the sound of a sneeze.

Ferenc Kardas appeared rubbing his nose. "May I bring you anything before I retire?"

"Alone?" asked Julio.

"Julio," warned Audrey.

"Pardon," said Kardas.

"Never mind," Julio said. "I'm going up myself. Need my sleep, don't I? Get in training for the lawyers." He dismissed Kardas with a flipping gesture of one hand, and then raised himself, saying not another word, and he left.

Audrey hugged herself. She'd left her sweater inside. A breeze had stirred and goose flesh dimpled her arms. Julio had gone, but he left enough of himself behind for her to really think about and very hard this time.

What would he do if he ever learned that Romaine Brook really belonged to her? Worry pleated her forehead, and then it knuckled her backbone. Worries and more worries about Romaine, who chewed ceaselessly at her conscience. To have a daughter—or anyone—act the way Romaine had and still did. The girl was a pathological liar, a user, a thief. Was Romaine crazy? Why was she the end result of what had been the long ago love of Audrey's life? And why, oh why, did she kill Marc Sterne? How can anyone take a life like that?

God help me, what if she *didn't* kill Marc, and she's convicted? How am I to bear that?

ભ

Upstairs, Ferenc Kardas shaved as he always did before bed, his dark beard needing two passes every day with an electric razor. He hadn't overheard all that much when eavesdropping, but the tone and the edgy voices, then the mention of his name had sent sure signals of dangerous moments in the offing.

Time to pull out, he told himself. The buzz of the razor kept a rhythm with the feeling in his gut. The Noor woman. He'd have to get over there soon. He had delayed long enough. Pick up the coke, if he could find it, close out his bank accounts, and then ticket himself on the next plane out to somewhere: Yucatan, Costa Rica. Nassau. The name Nassau held a certain appeal; the weather was supposed to be ideal except in summer, and he'd heard there were fabulous women traipsing about for someone to blow them to a good time. He would need to find a woman, maybe two, preferably rich, now that Audrey Sterne had shown him what the good life could be like, American-style.

He switched off the razor but the buzzing in his belly went right on. A soft rap on the door startled him, and he almost dropped the razor.

"Me," said Audrey when she opened the door. She saw the line of ebony hair descending from his naval to his privates. "Put a robe on, get decent. We have to talk, Ferenc, while there's still time."

Kardas saw the determined look on her face. He could pack his possessions in an hour, but would rather stay on for a few more days. He'd listen.

"You're going to have to back me up on something," Audrey told him. "It's for your own good. Sit down and listen, Ferenc, like you've never listened before…"

ભ

Switching on a light, Julio poured a glass of water from a carafe on his bedside table. As he drank, he debated taking a sleeping pill. Wouldn't do, he decided, to be groggy tomorrow.

It's the appearance thing, he thought.

His thoughts swerved to his wife. He had bailed Audrey out of her miseries in London, partly to show others he was still vigorous enough to attract a much younger woman.

This was the second time he'd rescued her, admitting, however, he was the present source of blame for the Kardas revelations.

That first episode in London was when he had agreed to be named as correspondent in a divorce over adultery. Audrey got her divorce and he got her, though, before the divorce he'd never laid a caressing hand on her. Not in that way, he hadn't.

Wanting Audrey, as he had wanted few other people in his life, he had agreed to be a patsy only because her London lawyers had said it was the surest way to get Huibbard-Hewes to agree to an uncontested divorce. It should have been the other way around. He knew all about Huibbard-Hewes, a good showman, an excellent stage-director, and one of the most notorious cocksman he'd ever heard of—in a class with the 15th-century Medici's, it seemed. Or possibly Casanova.

Now that Julio had come to that topic, he recalled he and Audrey had slept together perhaps a dozen times since their wedding in Monte Carlo. He hadn't bargained on her feverish bedroom urges, but knew he could take care of that situation when back in California, finding someone like Kardas and throwing him at her feet: an in-house sex-buddy, no less. Nice and tidy, an insurance policy against a straying wife and wagging tongues.

Still, what else was between them?

Had the two of them plotted to get Marc out of the way so she stood to be first in line for all his millions?

Kardas was a different fish. Cunning, even sly, and someone trained for killing; a former captain of infantry in the Hungarian army. Had they lured Marc to Malibu, planning to sink him? Audrey had never been all that cozy with his son.

Could she engage in that? Getting Kardas to do the dirty work?

The night Marc died, Kardas had been the first to enter the house, while Audrey remained on the boat, straightening up the galley. That was their story anyway.

Lights were on in the house, they had apparently remarked to each other, or so Audrey had said. Yet the house was all but dark when they had departed on the boat. *They* said. When returning from their excursion,

Kardas had spent several minutes up there at the house, alone, with the opportunity to do anything.

Even, perhaps, to Marc when Marc lay there helplessly drugged? Who should take the fall, which of the three? And could a misstep in his testimony exonerate the Brook woman?

When the trial ended, he would turn his attentions to Audrey; getting rid of her on the cheap. An appealing plot had begun to edge its way into his contemplations. He could always cook up ways, when testifying in court, that would target Audrey as a possible suspect. She, too, had had ample opportunity certainly; and, as to motive, he could, at another time, paint her into a corner. Simple enough, for Marc was his only heir. With him in his grave, she'd have a solid claim on an estate that approached a cool billion dollars.

He knew his wife, knew her well; she'd never harm a flea. Still, why pay her any more than he must. Who could blame him for off-loading a promiscuous wife, a wife who possibly had a hand in the killing of his one and only son?

Appearing in court, reluctant as he felt about it, might have its advantages.

Chapter Twenty

"**...I**'ve given you your answer, young man," said Julio Sterne to a nervously impressed Tommy Burke, whose stork-legs were just one tremble short of buckling..

"But if you weren't at your home that night, where were you?"

"Seattle."

"But the sheriff's reports have you in Malibu Pointe. At your own home."

"Somebody got mixed up then. Perhaps me. I had lost a much loved son."

Surprise washed over Rhodes. Seattle? The courtroom stirred. Four jurors hunched over, laying their forearms on the front rail of the jury box; looks of sudden surprise stamped on their alerted faces.

"Would you explain that for us?' Tommy asked.

"I can't. Not very simply anyway."

"Try, Mr. Sterne. We must know the facts. You should want them, too."

"Here's a fact for you. I arrived home very early in the morning. It was just getting light. I knew something was wrong the minute I went through the front door. Those yellow tapes across the entry to the living room and stretched across the bottom of the staircase. Coffee cups, cigarette smell. All those disturbances."

"And then what?"

"My wife told me my son was dead," said Julio. His eyes bore in on Romaine sitting ten yards away.

"The first you knew of it?"

"Yes."

"But then why did Mrs. Sterne say you were upstairs all the time, even the night before? What of that?"

"Ask her."

Audrey lied to us, Rhodes thought. How many times? Gnawing doubts were sprouting, and the pain of betrayal set in. She was using him, manipulating his better nature and feelings.

"Yes, I will be asking her," Tommy said. "But you know you gave that same impression when you made a statement to the sheriff and the state investigators."

"I was sick about it, under strain. Confused too."

"Confused?"

"Yes, confused and broken up about it. I don't know if you've ever lost a son. When you lose one, it breaks you down. Like a truck hit me..."

"I'm sure it must have been awful, Mr. Sterne. I'm sorry. Everyone is sorry about your loss—"

"Not so sorry if you have to call me down here to talk about it forevermore."

"This is a murder trial, Mr. Sterne. We have to know what happened," Tommy claimed. A tremor tugged at his left cheek. Ignoring it, he pressed on, "Mr. Sterne, could you prove, if you had to, that you were in Seattle that night."

"I'm no liar, young fellow."

"I'm not implying you are, sir. But we have to square everything up, you see, and this is vital to Miss Brook's interests."

"Why? She killed him. Don't you know that by now?"

"You can't say that. Not here, you can't. Your honor"—Tommy Burke appealed to Rhodes—"please have that stricken from the record. In no way is Mr. Sterne competent to—"

"Agreed," said Rhodes. He instructed the court reporter to strike and told the jury to disregard the statement, explaining why they should.

Pritter dug at his ear with one fat finger. For over an hour, he'd gotten nothing more than frosty, hard-bitten stares out of Julio Sterne.

Tommy went on. "Mr. Sterne, would you be willing to amend your statement to the sheriff and the state investigators as to your whereabouts that night?"

Sterne agreed.

"Mr. Sterne, how is it the gate guards at Malibu Pointe never mentioned seeing you that morning? I don't believe they listed you as coming through the gate."

"They never saw me."

217

"Never saw you?"

"That's right. I came in by the lower road. The one that goes by the golf, course."

"Why did you do that?"

"It's closer to the Santa Monica airport by nearly a mile. That's why. I use it frequently."

"So the guards never saw you?"

"No, the guards aren't there to keep track of me or the other residents."

"Just to protect your privacy?"

"Essentially."

"How many residents are there at Malibu Pointe?"

"Twenty-one."

"And you, or your property, occupy the tip of Malibu Pointe?"

"Yes."

"How big is your home there, Mr. Sterne?"

"About nine-thousand square feet. Six bedrooms, two ocean decks, eight rooms on the first floor. About that big."

"That's awfully big...would you say it's big enough so that four or five people could be in different parts of your home, and none of them would necessarily know where *all* the others are at one time? At one particular moment."

"I don't understand the question."

Burke repeated it.

I suppose so, yes," replied Sterne. "But I don't think that's—"

Burke interrupted. "We're more interested in what you actually know, and not so much about what you *think*, Mr. Sterne."

"Don't you be flippant with me, young man."

"I'll try not to, but someone else could've been in the house that night. Someone else besides your son and Romaine Brook?"

"Who?"

"It doesn't matter who. Anyone at all. And they could even have come there by way of the golf course road, yes?"

"Not easily. You need one of those electronic clickers to open the gate on that road. Only residents have them."

"I see," said Tommy. "Well, someone could come in by water then? A stranger. Someone meaning harm to your son."

"Probably would've been heard, if they had. I'm sure of it."

"Noises of a boat's motor were heard by neighbors. That's in the investigation reports."

"Could've been our boat."

"How many are on your household staff?"

"Four permanent, and two day-workers."

"Where were they?"

"They have two days off weekly, and that day was one of them?"

"What about some other resident of Malibu Pointe. Supposing one of them entered your home? Or one of their household help had broken in for some reason or other?"

"Without being invited? That's hardly likely."

"But it's possible, isn't it? And in a home your size, others already there might not even know it."

Sterne didn't have to think long about where Burke was headed. "Especially, if you're referring to my wife or Ferenc Kardas."

"Precisely. Or anyone else. But let's say them...supposing, Mr. Sterne, that someone lured your son and Romaine Brook to your—"

"I won't listen to this!" Sterne cut Tommy short. "Those're nothing more than cheap insinuations."

"Maybe so, Mr. Sterne, maybe so. But they are not *cheap* possibilities...you already admitted that others could be in the house at the same time and not be discovered immediately. That goes for Mrs. Sterne and your houseman, who both know the house so well. And others, too, as you said...just so we agree that others may possibly have been present that night. That's all I want to point out."

Sterne pulled a face, saying nothing.

Tommy Burke quizzed him for a time about his son. How did they get on together? Was he aware of Marc's drug habit? Marc had even spent time in a rehabilitation program, hadn't he? Did he know that Marc might have been dealing drugs?

"That's an absolute untruth," stormed Julio Sterne. "By God, I'll have you for slander if you keep on this way."

"You can't slander the dead," Tommy retorted. "I'll take it back for now, but there may be testimony later on that he was a dealer. Then I may have to recall you just to tell us that you know about it. Why not answer now?"

Looking at Romaine, Sterne burst out with, "She's a pretty cute operator. So don't you believe any of it, don't fall for her allegations." Half-rising out of his chair. His lean and solemn face surveyed the room, the press, and the jury to whom he said: "My son was a fine boy. I spoiled him. He had too much, too soon. But I'm a well-to-do man, and my son never had to sell drugs. Don't you believe it and another thing—"

But Rhodes stopped him. Calming Sterne down was no easy task. The man was a presence of power, used to being heard whenever and wherever he wanted to be heard.

"Have you got anything more?" Rhodes asked Burke.

"I'm through, your honor."

No, you're not, Rhodes was thinking. But he could let it ride for the moment. He'd wait, see what turf Pritter would travel over first.

Pritter approached the stand. He started a friendly smile at Julio Sterne, but abruptly it vanished when seeing the look he earned in return. "Romine Brook testified to this court," he began, "that you personally offered to give her a contract for several films, if she would stop seeing your son."

"That's as wrong as it can be. A damn lie," said Sterne.

"A damn lie?" Pritter repeated for the jury.

"That's what I said."

"She imagined it somehow?"

"Don't ask me, I never offered her anything of the kind."

"But you didn't like the idea of her seeing your son?"

"No, I did not. Especially when I found out what she was like."

"What is she like?"

"She's a master at using people. There're ten sides of deceit and trickery to you, young lady," he accused, looking straight at Romaine, whose mouth opened slightly. She pulled at Tommy's sleeve and one soft sob carried across the first rows.

"She's a good actress, you'd say?" Pritter went on.

"First-rate. I'll give her that. She lives in a world of make-believe. A sociopath. I'd say."

"Sir!" Tommy struggled to his feet. "Your honor, no. Wait a minute. The witness can't say that. He's not competent to make a psychological assessment of my client."

"Sustained," ordered Rhodes. "Strike that...Mr. Sterne, you'll have to confine your answers and remarks to—"

"Can't I have my own opinion?" asked Sterne.

"Not unless you're first qualified as an expert witness."

Pritter had made his point though. "All right," he went on. "Let me ask you this, Mr. Sterne. You are chairman of how many companies?"

"Five."

"How large are they? Together?"

"About twenty-two thousand employees."

"How many executives work for you?"

"Several hundred. Perhaps, a thousand."

"And you personally select them?"

"Many of them, yes. Those in the top ranks, I do, all of them."

"So you do know something about forming judgments about people. On managers. Their habits and capacities, ability to operate, how they make decisions, how skilled they are with people?"

"I evaluate executives on an everyday basis, yes."

"You do it often? Assess people?"

"I have to, or I couldn't run the businesses."

"So you're very practiced at judging people for what they are?"

"I think I am, yes."

Pritter smiled. "That's all, Mr. Sterne. Thank you very much for your time," he said it ingratiatingly, thinking again of Oldes & Farnham and the new condo he'd bought on the strength of their offer, which was, indirectly, Sterne's gift. Or was. He went back to his seat, believing he had shown Julio in a favorable light.

Tommy Burke took one more crack, asking, "We know you're a very busy and very successful businessman, Mr. Sterne. A really great reputation for it, I guess...but you're not a trained psychologist; are you?"

"I read up on it."

"You do?"

"Yes, I do."

"But you don't hold a degree?"

"I don't have to. I never had time for much college, young man. My degrees I keep at the bank, all sorts of degrees. Green ones."

Laughter erupted across the room.

"But you're not competent, are you, to make a professional diagnosis of my client?"

"Why not? I hired her or my studio did. Made her famous."

221

"Yes, but that doesn't entitle you, does it, to have an expert's opinion as to her personality makeup? Traits?"

"For me, it does."

"But another psychologist, a trained expert, one with, years of study and practice, might not accept your opinion?"

"And yet they might."

"But not as a professional colleague?"

"Not that way, no."

"Thank you, sir."

About to leave the stand as Tommy Burke headed for his own seat, Sterne still sat, imposingly so, a man used to giving orders, leaving no doubt those orders would be carried out precisely.

Alley rules, Rhodes was thinking. This was ring-time, and you had to keep belting away at every opening. Circle, hit, and hit again until the jury, who were the only judges who counted, began to score their cards your way. Was Burke saving it for Audrey? That might be too late, the last round.

"Mr. Sterne, one moment please," Rhodes said.

Both Burke and Pritter came up fast with their heads.

"What is it?" Sterne asked, turning his head. "Aren't we done here? I'm quite busy, you know."

"I'm sure you are. But we'd prefer not to call you back again, if we can avoid it."

Sterne inspected Rhodes with care. A shrewd look, one of a jeweler searching a stone for its more obvious flaws. He saw the crescent scar over Rhodes's eyebrow, and then noticed that neither eyebrow moved over his eyes. It was as though they'd been painted in place.

Anger dug at Rhodes's feelings. Had Audrey lied to him about everything? No question of it now; she had assuredly lied to the deputy sheriff about her husband's whereabouts on the night of Marc's death. What else?

Was a conspiracy underway to get Romaine convicted, hang her out on a limb and let her swing?

There he was, the husband, old enough to be Audrey's father; why him? Had she been infected by power, money? Blindness?

Rhodes forced himself to speak: "Mr. Sterne, one of the things we must do here is compile a straight record. Testimony is taken, pulled apart, and put together again so we can all see everything as clearly as possible. Time goes by, we forget. Errors of memory are made sometimes. We allow for that, unless it's judged as an intentional omission or commission of an untruth...we may be bordering on some murkiness here...some misconceptions..."

He hesitated, telling himself: that's your daughter—look at her, she *is* you. She smiles at you, needs you.

"I want you, Mr. Sterne, to answer a question of a most personal nature. Someone needs to ask it so that everyone has his or her say. Are you following me?" Now Rhodes's eyebrows did move upwards, forming a double arch.

"I believe I am. What's the question?"

The front row reporters were poised over their pads, two of them whispering to each other. Romaine looked blankly at Rhodes, who saw Pritter rolling up a paper in his hands.

"Four days ago," Rhodes said, "testimony took place here by the defendant. And in part of it she revealed—"

"About my wife? I've already heard about it."

"Would you care to have it read to you?"

"I would not."

"Then I'll ask you. Are you aware, or ever been aware, of some, well, romantic attachment between your wife and the man named Ferenc Kardas?"

Julio Sterne's pause was lengthy. He looked at Burke, over to the jury, then threw another broken-bottle glance at Pritter. No longer was he bored by the proceedings.

"Why not ask them?" he replied coldly.

"Because I'm asking you, Mr. Sterne," said Rhodes, wondering if the floating pause was meant as a tactical slur against Audrey. Had the jury absorbed that nuance?

"Those are matters a man doesn't always know about."

"Agreed. But the question is, *did you?* At any time, were you aware?"

"I'm aware that Miss Brook, there, says anything that runs through her mind."

"Please stick to the question."

"Anything is possible between men and women. Are you asking me to call my wife unfaithful?"

"Not at all, Mr. Sterne," Rhodes went on. "I have no wish to embarrass you or her. However, it's possible the allegation will have a bearing on this trial. You are one person who conceivably might shed light on the situation."

"What bearing is that?" asked Julio. But he already knew and guessed it was bound to come up again.

"The question. Please answer. Directly and now."

"I never saw anything," said Sterne.

"Never?"

"No."

"Even if you didn't see anything, were you at any time aware of anything between them?"

"They're young. Younger than me. Perhaps they had some attraction for one another. Who would know better than they?"

"No one. But you, you yourself, never harbored any suspicion?"

"Let me put it this way," said Julio Sterne bluntly. "I never saw anything, and don't you try to say I have. Suggest that I'm a voyeur or one of those deviants."

"That's your answer."

"It is."

"Thank you very much. And also for your time."

When Sterne stepped down, Rhodes adjourned for the day when Pritter said he had nothing more to ask. With his thoughts partly shattered, Rhodes needed time to weigh matters, then find Fahey before Burke started in on Audrey.

Who to believe, Sterne, Audrey, Romaine? If he was confused, then what of the jury? But then it opened up other avenues, and he felt that burning thrill again: how it used to be when he was dancing juries, in behalf of clients, many of whom belonged in Hell itself.

☙

The jury had assembled in one of the back corridors, ready for their trip back to the hotel. A few talked of Sterne's testimony. A substitute bailiff shot them a warning remark, that talk of the trial was forbidden. By the time they'd taken their seats in the bus, they started gabbing again. They were human, gregarious, curious, wanting to assess events and the testimony connecting to those events.

One leggy juror, the brunette with the horn-rimmed glasses, was thinking that everything really fun in this world violated some rule or other. She liked Julio Sterne. Suave and obviously powerful and rich. What kind of a bitch would cheat on a man like him?

She saw nothing wrong as she worked her way up the aisle to sit next to the bailiff with those baritone vocal cords. Blondish-cute and studdy-looking, with no telltale ring, so quite possibly available for some nocturnal yoga. Sick of this interminable trial, she no longer cared who had put Marc Sterne on his morgue slab; besides, who could keep track of all these goings-on anyway?

The trial was the last thing she wanted to think about, especially if she lassoed the attentions of this muscular male she was headed for. It was time for a man, a new man, which was the sum total of all she wanted to think about just then.

Conveniently, he occupied the double seat immediately behind the driver. One-half of that seat was open, and she dropped into it with the ease of a butterfly on a sunflower's petal.

"Do you take complaints?" she inquired.

"Mam?"

"Complaints. Do you handle those, like the other bailiffs have?"

"Depends. What's your complaint may I ask?"

"I wasn't thinking so much of mine, but yours. You see, I was thinking you wouldn't have any complaints if you were to drop by Room 716 at about…well, say, about eight-thirty. I've got some twenty-year-old Scotch. Famous Grouse, a full fifth begging for company, and I'd bet you the moon you can figure out the rest."

Looking around for any nearby eavesdroppers, he then replied *sotto voce*, "We've got rules, you know?"

"I've got a few of my own. One of them is the rules can go fuck themselves, at least for tonight."

The new bailiff hadn't had enough time to attach fourteen new names to fourteen new faces, so he asked her, "What's your name, my friend?"

"Judy J. Jesus of the Nazarene Jesus's."

"Huh?"

"You heard me. What's yours?"

225

"You'll know by eight-thirty. Order some ice, if you wouldn't mind."

"Let's drink it neat. It slides down the gullet faster and warms those places that need warming."

"Get ice. By the way, I never wear pajamas."

"This isn't a slumber party for twelve-year olds."

"716, you said. Right?"

She smiled. "I love you fast-study types."

The bus neared the Biltmore, less than a mile distant from the courthouse. The bailiff arose, squeezed her knee gently as he edged by, and then went up to the driver, where he pulled a mike off its hook. In seconds, he was droning his spiel, reminding all once more that any discussion of the trial was strictly prohibited, dinner to be served at six-thirty sharp, and drinks must be paid for individually. They'd heard the words a hundred times, and by now were deaf to them.

Six-thirty till eight-thirty allowed plenty of time to get them fed and out of the way. All but one, that is; he had a get-together in the offing with a Jesus-woman, whose legs seemed endless.

Chapter Twenty-one

Today, her turn.

In this courtroom setting, Audrey looked as out of place as a rose garden in Antarctica. It was as if she had lost directions to an outing with the ladies, ending up here by mistake. If that seemed far-fetched, and it was, her stylish appearance dispelled any notion that she was a regular visitor to the Los Angeles's criminal courts. She wore a pink linen suit—Givenchy—over a white silk blouse. A paisley throat-scarf was fastened by a circular gold and diamond pin. Her face struggling for calm, though her moist eyes were quite steady, and occasionally she submitted a sedate smile to the press and the jury. Still, too many looks were streaming her way, as though she were a highly publicized museum piece just this second unveiled for public viewing.

She didn't like the feeling. And her nerves didn't like the feeling one bit.

Barely was it past nine in the morning. Yet it seemed to her it was more like eleven at night, and that she had already run the gamut of moods and sensations that could possibly be absorbed within a full day of one's life. Nonetheless, she felt a sense of reprieve and satisfaction that she'd be able to refute the accusations leveled against her; sad that she must make a spectacle of herself; pissed, too, at her one-time lover, who sat in his black robes a bare ten feet away; and then this gangly young man who was about to tear into her; she'd detected looks of envy on the faces of some of the women, at how she was dressed and the fact that she possessed a magazine-cover face; embarrassed, of course, at what all these gawkers were thinking about her; discomfort, too, that her panty-hose had somehow shrunk in the past hour, at least they seemed a size or two smaller. How had that happened? She had wriggled a few times, furtively, to resettle them but it hadn't helped much.

Fleetingly, she looked over at the jury for the fourth time. Was that a wink from that tall brunette? A hint of a knowing smile on those pouting lips?

Rhodes had shifted his eyes away, so piercing were the remembrances of her. Real ones, imagined ones, every kind, and especially the latest one: that she might've lied to him.

And where had Fahey gone to?

Tommy Burke now entered Audrey's day and her life, reminding her she still remained under oath. He read from her earlier testimony, back to when the trial had first opened; then recited from the damning part of Romaine's testimony; finally repeating Julio's evasive remarks of the day earlier.

"Some of these matters," finished Timmy, "are unclear to us. So if you'll help, we can try to straighten them out."

"I'll be only too glad to straighten anything out."

"Good," said Tommy, stunned once more by her ravishing looks and bearing.

He moved away, getting her into fuller view. Standing by the jury, one hand on the rail, easing the weight from his impaired knees, he began: "Several weeks ago, Mrs. Sterne, you stated Mr. Sterne was upstairs when the Malibu sheriff arrived at your home. That was after you had called the sheriff, and after the body of Marc Sterne was found."

"I thought my husband was there at the time."

"Can you tell us why you thought so?'

"I was confused, I suppose. The whole ordeal was so wretched. A big blur, you might say."

"But your statement, that wasn't so blurred, was it?"

"I was, though."

"What made you believe your husband was upstairs?"

"The lights were on in the house. I thought he'd come home from a trip."

"And they weren't on, as you had also said in your statement, when you had left the premises earlier on the boat with Ferenc Kardas?"

"The dock lights were, but not the upstairs lights in the house."

"So you believed Mr. Sterne had come home and was upstairs."

"Yes."

"You didn't think your husband might've come home while you were out on the boat, and discovered the body?"

"It's a very big house. I thought—well, I wasn't exactly—I don't know. But no one expected Marc to be there that night. I didn't anyway."

"Well, your husband said to this courtroom that he spent the night in Seattle."

"It turns out he had."

"While you went off boating with Mr. Kardas?"

"That's where I was—yes, I was on the boat."

"With Mr. Kardas? No one else other than you and Kardas?"

"Correct."

"During the time interval," Tommy kept going, "when your stepson Marc was supposedly being put to death by Romaine Brook."

"She was there, I heard."

"We all know she was there. But why did you say your husband was there when he was actually in Seattle?"

"I was in terrible shock. My wits weren't about me."

"Must've been terrible," Tommy said sympathetically.

"It was, I assure you it was."

"But you do admit you made a serious mistake thinking your husband was at home?"

"I erred, yes."

"And didn't retract the statement later? With either the sheriff or the state investigators?"

Audrey looked at Rhodes beseechingly. He barely nodded; it was a nod like one might give to a stranger passing by on some deserted stretch of beach.

"Mrs. Sterne?" asked Tommy.

"I didn't retract it, no. I guess I thought my husband straightened it out, when he met with them the next day. It was all so terrible."

"But he hadn't straightened it out, is that right?"

"I suppose not."

"Did you think it was right to suppress vital information?"

"I didn't think about it at all. We were all so flummoxed. A nightmare, don't you get it?."

"What were you covering up?"

"Why do you say that? I'm covering up nothing."

"Mrs. Sterne, have you ever seen this?" Burke waved a piece of paper. "It's one of the sheriff's reports."

"Should I have? I don't think I have. Probably not."

Burke read an excerpt, then said, "It leaves one with the distinct impression that three people were on your boat that night, doesn't it? The third one being your husband, presumably?"

"Well, he wasn't. That's obvious to anyone."

"Not so obvious from this report, though."

"I didn't write it, Mister Burke."

"One wonders who did. And who's covering up for whom, Mrs. Sterne. You signed your statement. This whole business has more holes in than a sink strainer," Tommy added, a line he had borrowed from one of Alonzo Fahey's observations.

"I would've signed anything, I was so undone."

Right there Tommy could've put her to the stake, Rhodes thought, but for Tommy Burke it was all about casting doubt about the actual events of that night. He wanted to be cautious about this woman, who might easily capture the jury's sympathy. He trudged elsewhere. To the other places of her life within the Sterne family. About Marc's relationship with his father?

"So-so, you say? Good, devoted, enviable? Bad?"

The usual, she replied—arguments at times, even fights, but a strong bond had existed between them. An only son, a successor, an heir.

"And what of the narcotics?"

"Yes, Marc had dueled with his demons. As so many young people did nowadays."

"And now, Mrs. Sterne," Tommy said, "Marc's secretary testified here a few days ago. She told us you left her with a message for Marc to come to your home for dinner that night. He came, as we all know, but you had gone out on the boat by then."

"I never left any message that day. Otherwise, if dinner was planned, I would've been there. Why would I ask anyone for dinner, when the chef was off for the night? I don't cook very well. I don't cook, period."

Burke shrugged. "Maybe you wanted Marc there, when no one but you and Mr. Kardas were present."

"I resent that, I really do. You're insinuating something horrible."

"The secretary said you spoke to her. She stated that more than once."

"I did not!" Audrey cried out.

"Who called then?"

"I haven't the foggiest. How could I know anything about calls someone else make? Made, I mean."

Romaine settled back in her chair. Behind her dreamy mask, she kept studying the woman she didn't know was her own mother. Sitting only ten yards apart, they may as well have been separated by the distance from there to Jupiter. All the back-and-forth about that telephone call taken by Dee-Dee Lessing was nerve-wracking. And extremely hazardous.

"Was it some practical joke? Calling him out there for dinner?"

"Not by me. I don't make jokes of that sort."

"But you'd called other times. The secretary said she knew your voice."

"I know when I call and when I don't call."

"On that exact day. Seven months ago, you remember?"

"I wouldn't forget asking Marc for dinner. Not that night or any other."

"Are we to believe the secretary is in error, Mrs. Sterne? She logged your call."

"Not mine, I made no such call."

"You're sure?"

"Of course, I am. You bet I'm sure."

"Just as you were sure your husband was upstairs that night?"

"Anyone, when you're under stress, can make mistakes."

"They often do, yes," Tommy agreed. "And we seem to have taken note of several of them over the past several days."

Burke aimed his remarks squarely at the jury. Leaving the jury box, he passed Pritter's table as he again approached the witness stand. Pritter stared straight ahead, not at Burke or Audrey or even Rhodes. But at the wall clock silently ticking away, a tangible reminder of how the hours and minutes cut away at the state's case. And he was feeling less nervous about his courtroom demeanor.

"Mrs. Sterne," Tommy said respectfully. "The night you came in on the boat to the dock. You told us when you first testified weeks ago that after the boat was tied up, you had stayed behind to clean up."

"That's right. Dishes and things."

"What things?"

"Glasses. Spoons and forks. I can't remember exactly."

231

"Glasses? Had you been drinking?"

"A cocktail or two."

"By yourself?"

A trap, and Audrey knew it. "Yes, by myself."

"Mr. Kardas, he had no alcohol?"

"Not that I saw."

"Would you have seen him, if he had?"

"Most certainly."

"He was steering your boat?"

"Yes. Sometimes I did, though. I like handling the boat."

"While drinking?"

"Possibly."

"Do you often drink with your help?"

"I resent that."

"Do you?"

"Yes, I do. I drink in their presence, but I do not drink *with* them. And no, I don't get overly friendly with the servants."

"Not even that night?"

"That was different. The boat's only thirty-eight feet long. So you're close together sometimes."

"How close?"

"Close enough," Audrey replied testily.

"You got the boat docked and he went up to the house ahead of you?"

"Yes."

Burke referred to some notes from his pocket. "He preceded you by about ten minutes or so. That's how you testified."

"About. Something like that."

"Did he go up to see what those upstairs lights were all about?"

"I asked him to...those weren't on when we left, as I've told you."

"You weren't sure, perhaps, who was up there?"

"No."

"Mister Kardas was gone for ten minutes or thereabouts?"

"Approximately, I guess. Close enough."

"That's a long time. He discovered Marc's body, and he didn't come back to tell you instantly?"

"I don't know why. Later, he told me he was shocked when he found

Marc. And then he'd been looking around."

"Too shocked, I suppose, to look for Mr. Sterne. Who you knew to be grief-stricken, powerless to act or talk. That's what you said in these reports...that your husband was there, and you had first-hand knowledge of the condition he was in. But you couldn't have, could you? Not if Mr. Sterne wasn't there. You couldn't possibly know of his condition, am I right?"

The tips of her fingers alighted on her scarf pin, and she twisted it back and forth.

"I don't know...I can't...Oh, dear Christ! I just don't know..."

"Could it have been, Mrs. Sterne, that you knew all along Mr. Sterne wouldn't be home that night? That Marc would come to Malibu at your invitation...and you and Ferenc Kardas meant to do harm to Marc Sterne?" Unknowingly, Tommy was doing Julio Sterne's smear job on his unsuspecting wife.

A flurry of murmurs as Rhodes rapped for order. Pritter scrambled up, bellowing an objection.

Rhodes heard him out, then allowed Burke to proceed with his questioning. He saw the freeze gathering in Audrey's eyes. Her chin extended, her face now looking hard as a rock formation.

"And while Kardas was up there something happened!" In high voice, Burke nearly shouted at Audrey.

"And you seem to forget and keep forgetting that Romaine Brook was there first...that's been proven!" said Audrey.

"But what's not proven is that she contributed in any way to Marc's death. There was opportunity for at least one or two others to slay him, wasn't there?" returned Tommy. "And why did you lie about where your husband was?"

"That's stupid. Marc had everything in this world to live for," said Audrey, evading the query.

"One would surely think so. But the fact is, and it is a fact, Mrs. Sterne, that none of us really knows what happened. Just a bunch of unfounded accusations, isn't it?"

"You're overlooking something else," said Audrey with a triumphant gleam. "We...I never knew Marc was even there, not until I was told he was dead."

"So you say. His secretary says differently. She is misleading us, are you saying that?"

"A nice way of putting it, I'd say."

Tommy turned again to the jury. He met them with a hands-up, hands-open expression. "Well, we have a good jury here. The best, and they've heard quite a lot already. They can do the deciding for all of us," he said before wheeling around again, nearly stumbling over himself, to face Audrey.

"Mrs. Sterne, are you now, or have you ever been, intimately involved with Ferenc Kardas?"

"That's insulting. You're trying to throw dirt around." Looking up again at Rhodes, who was thinking: there she is, a mother in front of *their* daughter, getting scalped. He looked briefly at Romaine who seemed steady enough. Mother versus daughter, and it began to remind him of a grim Greek tragedy.

"You'll have to answer," Rhodes told Audrey quietly.

"He's offending me. Why must I answer insults?"

Because, as Rhodes advised her, a statement under oath had been made as to her involvement with a servant. Other circumstances, now coming to light, required a reply.

"You mean things she's said?" Audrey glared again at Romaine, who had suddenly turned pale as flour.

"Yes, Mrs. Sterne, by *our* defendant here," Tommy confirmed.

"She's the beggarly liar, then! Not me!"

Romaine shrugged. Rhodes thought he saw tears glistening just below her eyes. She wiped them once, and the jury saw her gesture.

"But did you have an intimate relationship with Kardas? That's my question," Burke hammered.

"You're just being mean-minded and ugly."

"We're not all blessed with your beauty, that's true, Mrs. Sterne...but what we're waiting for now is a straight, full answer."

"*Never* is your answer."

"Never?"

"I just said *never*."

Her hands flew up to the scarf pin once more, worrying it with her jittery fingers. The women jurors, more than the men, were rapt while observing her reactions under Burke's oral assassination of her testimony.

"And so," Tommy continued, "you're asking us all to believe that Marc's secretary, and now Romaine Brook, that neither one of them are telling us the truth. But you and the deputy sheriff and your husband never made a misstep? Never got anything wrong? Everything on the up and up? And never, in your case, have you looked at another man or taken up with one?"

Rhodes wanted to stop it but couldn't, surprised Burke could swing so hard.

"I said I hadn't!" snapped Audrey.

"But you had been divorced, is that not so?"

"I was, yes."

"In England?"

"That's where it was, in England."

"On grounds of adultery?"

Audrey gasped, then groaned softly.

Having fished deep, Tommy let up, saying, "You've been a real help to us. Thank you, Mrs. Sterne."

Pritter then glided her through a few questions. He let her go after a few attempts to show her as a woman who had it all: many more years ahead of her; and a marriage to one of the most prominent men in the west; a golden life, a respected position in society. Why would she risk everything, her reputation, on a servant, Pritter asked not just the jury but the entire courtroom, especially the press.

ଓ

And why would she hide the existence of my daughter from me, Rhodes was thinking, later, in his chambers, and failing to come up with a clear answer. What else was in hiding?

Macklin Price strode in, as he wrestled with his qualms. "Sacramento is on the line. It's the governor himself, Cliff…"

Chapter Twenty-two

Raining again.

Rhodes swept the wet off his sleeves as the door opened, and he glimpsed the willowy Wanda Fahey, then felt the length of her as she gathered him with a lasting hug.

Tall, slow moving, with gray-flecked eyes and thick ebony hair showing its first signs of graying. High cheekbones. The flattish breasts of high-fashion models. A former child of Georgia, she still expressed herself in the rich molasses-like drawl of her beginnings. A deep woman, and Rhodes, who had known her for years, held her in a solid respect. Not overly pious, he wouldn't say that about her, but nonetheless a real kneeler, attending her parish twice weekly.

They gabbed a few minutes. Where had he been, she wanted to know? "How time disappears. We're all getting older, and Alonzo's become hopeless. Wanting a regiment of all things. He's offered me a job to look after the camp-followers. Do you think we can get him committed for a time?"

What of Sacramento? Wanda insisting he was wasting himself, that he ought to marry and never mind Alonzo's attacks against it. Admiring him then, standing quite closely; admiration of a sort known to a suffering woman, who is at last, she thinks, absorbing a man who walks straight, talks straight, acts straight.

"He's wearing my scarves these days, like some flighty Tinkerdoddle, and he used my old garter belt for a sling-shot," Wanda said without rancor. "Never know what to make of him anymore. He's bedding a Gypsy woman, he says, as if I'm not enough. It may be time to get him committed, Cliff, but it's the right thing to do."

She has become Fahey, he thought, a clone as if that were conceivable. Even talks the same way.

"Your scarves?"

"My silk scarves. Uses them for belts. Ascots too."

"We'll have to take him shopping. Is he here? He said he would be."

"He's up there in that hole of his over the garage," she said. "Doing arts for that regiment, he says. Trying on my bras is more likely."

"I'll find him."

'Tea? I'll make some for us."

"Wonderful, Wanda. That'd hit the spot."

"Come for dinner soon? Or we could go out for a change," she said dejectedly. "Say you will, Cliff. It's been ages and ages."

"Yes and yes. Has he been away lately?"

"I gave him your messages." Wanda sighed. "He's having those moods again or something." She tapped her head. "Doesn't even give me a good morning most days."

"Maybe I can gas him up."

"Would you?"

"I'll try."

"He's such a child at times. Takes mothering, he does. Well, you know the way," said Wanda, suddenly thumbing the air, a benevolent smile brightening her face.

Up the flight of stairs, Rhodes turned left, went through a crawlway, and knocked on a Dutch door. Entering, he saw Fahey sprawled in a leather chair beside a desk made from a long plywood plank resting on two sawhorses. Art books were scattered everywhere, some open, and others nested in stacks.

Fahey didn't rise when Rhodes entered. He was practicing an aerial maneuver, like a drum majorette, as he twirled an ivory-tipped walking stick. "Going to the opera soon. Getting my duds cleaned up. Look at this stick, a real beauty. The mayor of Dublin had one, and now I do. Mine's better, got more patina. I rubbed it on the Gypsy's derriere for a straight hour to get it shined like this. I'm leaving it to the museum when I part company with this fucking earth of ours."

"Didn't think we had opera in Los Angeles."

"They're mounting a new company soon. Specializing in Balkan works, so I've heard. The city needs a fleck or two of culture...take that chair over there, the one I spent my life making."

The chair, a wobbly wooden stool, had one leg two inches shorter than the others. Rhodes sat anyway. "Wanda's putting tea on."

"Is she now? Next thing we know she'll be serving us those nature grains she eats. Sickening stuff, makes holes in your bones, and looks like canary droppings. I had it for breakfast yesterday and I almost had to get my gut pumped out. A fuckin' hazard that girl."

"You ought to take her out, buy her a good steak somewhere."

"Won't eat one. Loves the cows too much. She's gone Buddhist on me."

"Make her an offer."

"Ahh! Then she wants the dress, and the hairdo. Be Tiffany diamonds next."

"Nice woman, Alonzo, you're a lucky lad."

Fahey looked away. He rolled the treasured walking stick across the plywood desktop, and it rattled to a stop when hitting the wall. He tightened the collar of the robe he wore: silk, a dark Chinese maroon, thread bare at the elbows, and the back was crocheted with two facing dragons.

"How's my lad Burke circusing these days? Keeping the gallery entertained, is he?"

"All right, not so bad at all."

"And his glowworm? Our little enchantress?"

"Romaine Brook?"

Fahey yessed with his head. He dropped his hands, and at the same time a curl of black hair descended across his brow.

"She's holding up, I guess," Rhodes told him. "I came to see you about her."

"Not out for your evening stroll then?"

"Not on this night anyway."

"Let's talk about the lady Sterne. A real looker, is she? The right geometry, eh? Start a riot or two with her?"

"Pretty nice, Alonzo."

"Here she's been, all this time, rubbing skin with the butler in the belfry. Got that tidbit from our he-man Burke late this very day."

Rhodes tried not to wince. "That's not a certainty, not by any means."

"The rich ones, you have to chain 'em up. Get ideas, go guilty over the poor. Have to fuck their way across their moats, try the lower muscles of the peasants for a change."

"Alonzo..."

238

"They all do it, mind you. Had a few myself. Have to wiggle their booty now and then with the lower ranks."

"What's aching you anyway?"

"On the wagon for a week now and it's shattering my soul. Blood went yellow overnight. Piss it out four times a day. So weak now I have to stay home and listen to Wanda do her prayer-wheel."

Rhodes laughed. "You? On the wagon?"

"The Gypsy went and hung me on the peg. Going to whip me into shape, ready me for the opera season and the regimental drills."

"What Gypsy?" Rhodes had a disturbing recollection of what Wanda had said, but wasn't sure.

"A woman I know, a real thrasher, Cliff. Solves all the sins you ever heard of, and she does it with my head in her lap. Does it all, sees a great century ahead of us. Ought to have her on one of your juries. Clean things up in no time, she would."

"I'll have to meet her one day," Rhodes said, unsure if Fahey's imagination was about to burst its pipes again. He was amazed at Fahey's capacities for life, the man's ever-changing prism for seeing the world so differently than others, and with, it seemed, an ever widening bandwidth for receiving human signals that no one else seemed to hear or see—or not in quite the same way. It was what made him such a good, though devious shamus.

On they went, and, though old friends, it was as if they had just met and were sorting each other out. After a little time flew by, Rhodes bored in: "We've got some work to do, Alonzo, and you'll have to do it. I can't and neither can Burke..."

છ

In the kitchen, Wanda puttered about, making tea. She was enamored of Cliff Rhodes, even making a thinly veiled pass at him once, after a Mr. and Mrs. knock-down with Alonzo over one of his blasphemies. Over the eggs that morning, Alonzo, greatly provoked at some imagined incident, had uttered: "You know, love of my every day, for quite a time now I've had a bone or two to pick with that God of yours. One day it'll happen, and I like my chances. Let Him know about my complaints next time you're chatting about things with Him. Tell 'em ol' Fahey is getting very irked, and it had better be brought to a halt and fast."

She'd been appalled. She was not as devout as Mother Theresa but was as long-suffering. Utterings against the Almighty…*well*…

No perfect man was ever born, made or nurtured. But Alonzo—well, her never-ending task. Uproarious to live with, also exhausting. No beginning to him, nor any end, and never any days of ease. At dawn of every day, he became her ardent lover; then, arising, the day's inventions would begin, popping out of all sides of his head. The unrealized actor in him rehearsing for events so mighty, so impracticable and dream-ridden, they could only happen in the mind of a conjurer who knew nothing about himself. Righting the world's wrongs, or the wrongs as he saw them. His human harmonics often wildly askew. Never *never* knowing what to expect of him, because, of course, neither did he. What kind of man swept you off your toes, taking you to the Galapagos, there to be married by a priest so inebriated he forgot half the words for the exchanging of the vows? She still didn't know if she were lawfully married or a common-law wife. Possibly, neither one. Possibly, a kept woman. Possibly, his live-in tart.

So, there he was and here she was—a void waiting to be filled. Still, she adored him. He always had put his heart around her, when she needed him most; only wishing that she, too, could live inside those dreams and fantasies. Likely, he could've been an incredible filmmaker; that is, if a studio existed that could afford a billion dollars for a single production, taking ten years to get it filmed and in the can. He'd do fifty takes for every scene, then do them all over again the following week, seeking something that could never be captured. Perhaps in that bounding, excitable mind the story would be neatly depicted, however un-writable it may be, and thus never so much as a single frame of film would ever make it to the screen.

Her *amuseur,* yet enough was enough. She had found she had to live three, four, five roles to process her husband, day-to-day.

Up the stairs, carrying the tray of teacups, she edged her way closer to Alonzo's hideaway. Notching up her sonar now, intent with curiosity, intrigued as to why Rhodes was visiting.

The door swung wide as Wanda came in. She slid the tray onto Fahey's plank-desk, then poured from a silver-bellied pot that was heavily dented on one side. She handed Rhodes a white mug and another to Alonzo, whose hair she then combed twice with her spread fingers.

"Thank you, mermaid," said Fahey to his wife, leaning forward to wrap a hand around her thigh, pulling her against his chest "Isn't she the whole bolt of satin? I tell you the best, a gift of the Khalil...look at her, will you? Get a whole castle for her on the Saudi slave market."

Wanda whirled away, laughing, her lithe body arching like a dancer's as she closed the door.

Rhodes burned his mouth on the steaming tea. The rain of the wet night drummed at the window behind Fahey.

"It's time to find Cullis, is that his name?" Rhodes said. "Get him and take him back to the apartment. Show him what you found. But keep the cocaine there, and if there's any trouble on that one, call me immediately."

"Why now?" Fahey asked wearily.

"The trial is swinging everywhere. I want all the possible evidence out in the open."

"Maybe it's not connected. You told me that once, as I think you'll easily remember."

"But what if it is relevant?"

"Let it go, Christ—"

"That's the jury's choice. Always."

Fahey pondered again, then said: "Not for me. I'm out of it. Got a smell to it dirty as the Vatican High Command."

"You did everything I asked of you. I thank you, I really do."

Fahey blanched. "You're over the ledge, aren't you? Way over the mark...why're you doing all this?"

"Everything in this trial is finally about to get put on the laundry line. I want it *all* out there. I don't want this case reversed on appeal."

"For her?" asked Fahey, not knowing which *her.*

"For me," Rhodes evaded. "A problem either way if she's convicted and it goes up on appeal." A weak excuse but all he could offer as a reason, and he'd already used it once before.

They crisscrossed excuses on how Fahey could ask for another opportunity to re-enter Marc Sterne's apartment. Rhodes made a suggestion but Fahey had a better one. More talk, endless talk, enough for a U.N. treaty.

"Send me Tommy boy. I'll tell the louter where it is. He's a tall one, isn't he?"

241

"Sending him, that's too chancy," Rhodes reasoned. "Do it for me, Alonzo...you're really doing it for your client," said Rhodes, grasping at a straw, but ready to grasp at anything that sounded even slightly workable.

"Ah, but the client is still in the dark...our glowworm looking about for pennies. Listen, Cliff, the Gypsy told me about her."

"I don't care about your damn gyp—"

"She's real, real as the night, has dark stars for her eyes," Fahey informed him. "Don't you slur on her."

"Sorry. But you must listen to me now."

Rhodes explained what was transpiring in court. Suspicions were loose. Ferenc Kardas would be on the stand soon, and this was the time to get everything out in the open. Expose other motives, raise doubts if there were doubts to be had.

"I've got myself some work. A fat old mogul up in San Francisco has hired the good Fahey to find art his wife walked out with. A pair of Monets...can't ever trust the bitches, can you?"

"Can you get to Cullis?"

"Will I?"

"Yes, will you?" Rhodes pled.

"Have more tea. Cheer up. This'll take pondering, and I've still my license to think about, boyo."

Though Fahey, gourmand of the unseen, had said neither yes or no to Rhodes's request, sensing it meant nothing but trouble. Cullis, the Noor woman, an odd pair for the drug-peddling game. "There are other rules need looking at," Fahey opined, arising, hobbling toward the door on his walking stick, feigning a gimp leg to go with his gimp arm.

Onto to his women thing again, Fahey spelled out an ultra-sheer theory for marveling at how he was in striking range of explaining women for all of posterity, now that the Gypsy was putting him wise.

"Fantastic, she is, Cliff, and with such elegant sentiments."

"Your mentor, Alonzo?"

"Don't patronize me, I'm serious as sin."

"I'm not meaning to. What's her main pitch?" Playing along, and said with all the patience he could muster at that moment.

"A man, any man, reaches the highest level of sanctity, of earthly heaven, when he learns women were sent here to keep us out of God's busy way...that's why they have all those round and gorgeous ornaments on them.

To distract us from the real sins. Sodomy and treachery of any kind, those are the real soul-peelers. Christ, if I don't despise treachery...that's for honest. Don't you see, Cliff, the women are given to us as great gifts. Treat them like Goddesses and they're ours forever. They are Him, aren't they? Except they're a Her. Have His eggs inside them too, and that's why we can't kick them around as much as we ought to. Give them the old Arab treatment, a few stones to the backside every Saturday. Take Burke. Good solid Irish stock. Wears those mountain boots. Now, there's one who ought to be able to do some real shit-kicking, I'd say, except he's made out of matchsticks...listen to that goddamn rain, will you? We'll be sending for Noah in another hour. I need my friends nearby. Are you agreeing with me today?"

"Yes," Rhodes said tolerantly, recognizing Fahey was on one of his celestial flights.

He could do no less than listen, humor him, well aware that three women were now front and center in his own life. Well aware, also, that he was greatly in need of Fahey now. More, he was laying down a marker, if only he could persuade Alonzo to make another stab, find something to divert the jury to a new plane of thinking and doubt. Fahey was generally familiar with criminal law, not all of its intricacies, but he knew enough of the basics. And would guess, if not knowing for certain, that Rhodes had come tonight to find an ally to put in the fix—well, a slanting of the proceeding anyway. He needed a foothold, a new tack: a gift he intended to present indirectly to Burke, without Burke being aware. Or, if he became aware, he'd shut up and take whatever bows might come of it.

Rhodes awaited Fahey's reaction, knew he had no business asking what he was asking. Slinking around behind the scenes, plowing ground for a very tricky, very risky favor.

About juries, Rhodes knew plenty.

How fluid they could be. Twelve people, and two alternates, none of whom had never met before the operations of law had convened them; now, suddenly thrown together into a sort of makeshift family. Different walks of life, very different upbringings, therefore different outlooks, all of them shifting their feelings one way on this day, another way the next. A slow and hidden thing like the rotation of the earth. Hour by hour, you think you can sense them, but you never really know, not till it's show-time and the verdict is rendered.

You saved your best shot till the end, then slammed them with the haymaker that put their lights out. Just like it happened in the ring, with two fighters going at each other, and here the fighters were two lawyers, and the ring his courtroom. And he the referee. He'd done it to juries before, many times, dancing them to one tune and making them think it was one thing they were hearing, when it wasn't. Never, though, had he used these talents as a judge. Never, of course, with a daughter's life at stake. Never, not even once, had he crossed the sacred line of judicial conduct and fairness.

But now? Was he? Or was he still within bounds? Wasn't it all about truth? Justice?

Well, goddammit, whoever really knew the truth?

Chapter Twenty-three

Once again, the jury was led deep into a bewildering jungle of happenings. Kardas had returned and foiled most of Tommy Burke's questions that morning. Denying everything, his answers laced with undertones of hostility, though always speaking in politely accented English.

The attendees all remembered Ferenc Kardas. His well-knit soldierly stance was hard to ignore; an ex-Hungarian army captain, of honor, as he asserted again and again. A gentleman, always, and now a gentleman's gentleman in the employ of Julio Sterne.

Pritter stood in front of him, all two hundred and sixty pounds shielding Kardas from any doubting looks by jurors or others. Heads in the press rows weaved back and forth trying for a better view.

"You're certain, now," Pritter asked, "that there was never anything between you and Mrs. Sterne?"

"How could there be? As I said to Mr. Burke, him over there, I am only the houseman. She is imp—important lady. I know my place. I am trying for American citizenship."

"She never encouraged you?"

"Encour—" Kardas halted, baffled.

"Made you think she was interested in you?"

"She is very correct, Mrs. Sterne. Always very proper and very good to work for."

"You never touched her?"

"Sometimes I did that—when I serve the dinner or some drinks. Maybe I brush her—" Kardas made a tentative, quick motion with one hand.

"In no other way?"

"But you embarrass me, sir."

A few more questions as Pritter attempted to refute Romaine's earlier claims of a love affair between Audrey Sterne and Kardas. Rhodes digested it all minutely. Neither Burke nor Pritter knew anything about the cocaine in Sterne's apartment. Only Fahey and he knew, and Julio Sterne had strenuously denied his son dealt in drugs. A user perhaps but never a pusher. Rhodes decided to gamble. He had been watching Romaine closely for days, and he began to think he might be getting a little too obvious.

"Mr. Kardas, before you leave us, just a little more on one or two points," Rhodes interjected.

Kardas swung around in his seat. His face showed surprise, then composed itself into a steady look, straight as the blade of a saber.

"Please, sir," he said formally.

"You knew Marc Sterne quite well? Saw him frequently?"

"Quite well sir."

"Remind me, if you will. For how long?"

"Almost two years before he died."

"Did you ever go anywhere with him? Go out to a ballgame? A bar, for example? Any place at all?"

"I saw him at the house. We joke sometimes. Tell men stories. Those things."

"Nothing else?"

"No, sir. Nothing else."

The lie. Perjury. Rhodes wanted it on record so that he could come back to Kardas's denial later. How much later he could only wonder. It depended on Fahey. And was Kardas also perjuring himself about an affair with Audrey?

"You never had any business dealings with him, good or bad?" Rhodes inquired.

"Certainly not, I'm not in the movies."

"Thank you very much. You may step down now."

Rhodes smiled. He wished he could get Romaine alone for a few hours and ask, and keep asking, till he had a feel for what was really going on here. Lies upon more lies seemed to be the invisible graffiti written on his courtroom walls.

Were they all covering up something deeper? Or just those lesser sins of the flesh they didn't want the world to know about? And Audrey's affair, if indeed there had been one, really had no real relevance to the trial. But lying about it, if she had, had plenty of relevance.

Or did it?

He was thinking loosely, blindly, readying himself before he tipped the weight of the proceedings, if he could, in favor of Romaine. Why were they gunning so hard for her, when the weight of evidence was so circumstantial? He was fairly sure he could spring her, acutely aware now that he was on the brink of meddling with the trial, bending its outcome, or trying to. In the past, he had used his brain, training and mouth to free others—some of them guilty as charged—and now he was persuaded to try again. His daughter, a rookie lawyer, lies, questionable investigative tactics, politics; his kid deserved a fair shot, didn't she?

Didn't she?

Of course, she did. She was perched on the high-wire, a frayed and swaying wire. The trial was already tainted with a political fix. He could prove it, but no chance that he'd even attempt to. That'd axe his high court hopes.

A cottony taste had coated his throat. If Romaine knew the truth of her parentage, indeed, if anyone knew other than himself and Audrey, the trial would end up on a pyre of flames. A mistrial for certain. A publicity nightmare. In fairness, why should his daughter victimized by hidden facts, hidden anything?

Trapped in a Hobson's choice, he was damned if he did and damned if he didn't. In that black void, where nothing seemed right and nothing seemed wrong, he had now forfeited his impartiality as a judge at law.

CR

Macklin Price interrupted his fruit salad lunch, taken at his desk, with news that Lloyd Pritter was on the phone. Rhodes took the call to hear about another request by the defense for permission to return to Marc Sterne's apartment. Burke's legman, apparently, wanted another look-see.

"Uncalled for," insisted Pritter with a bark for shattering a chandelier. "They've had their turn. The Hollywood sheriff's station isn't a courier service."

Rhodes settled it swiftly. "Let them give you the key, Lloyd. You can do the courier work."

CR

As the court went into afternoon session, Fahey, miles away in the Hollywood hills, tramped up the steps, just behind Cullis. The lieutenant took them two at a time. Fahey lagged, envious of the man's nimble marching feats. Cullis would make a good drill-sergeant for the new regiment.

"My ass is heavy with work today, so let's make it snappy," Cullis complained. "Where'd you go?" He looked around for Fahey. "This's got to come and go in half an hour. No more, you hear me?"

Fahey tapped on a step with his walking stick. "Slow it, will you? Bad traction today. Can't get the right foot-grip on the world."

"You got yourself a broken ass, too, if we don't hurry it up."

"Mind your manners, Cullis. I've been an invalid all this month."

"In the head, too."

"You don't sound so good today. Been kissing your frog again?"

"What's that?" Cullis swung around, putting a hand against Fahey, who jerked back as if a red hot coal had landed on him.

"You're getting a bad habit with that hand, Cully-boy. Looks like your loving hand to me, and I'd hate for it to go home all bent and crippled."

"Watch your mouth, mister."

"The hand. Remove it."

"I oughta throw you down them stairs."

"I wouldn't. You geniuses have enough trouble as it is."

"I got no troubles."

"No? What about all those fancy reports you filed with the state? Sounds to me like they were written on confetti."

"That's Malibu's worry."

"But this is your hand." Fahey peered down at the splayed fingers on his chest. "You making a pass at me, lover?"

Cullis mumbled as they went into the apartment, still rife with the smell of the decaying plants. He flipped on the lights. The place still made Fahey think of a bordello, the only industry he knew of that he could never improve upon.

"What'cha looking for now? More of them porno photos?" Cullis asked.

"Something I remembered or didn't remember...it clicked later on in my head after we were here the last time."

"Like what?"

"Something the girl told her lawyer and me one day in her dungeon. Christ! Never go near one of those lady's schools for the chosen...steal your whiskey, the Sodders."

"Let's get moving."

"Sure, lover. Help me with this couch."

They yanked the long white couch away from the dull lavender wall. The steel table knife Fahey had used on his earlier secretive visit gleamed its presence, lying there very noticeably on the shag rug. Picking it up, Fahey twirled it a few times.

"Where'd that come from?" said Cullis.

"Search me."

"I just might...I just might..."

Cullis eyed the knife suspiciously. Stepping back, he opened the drawer in the side table. Only a spoon lay there, but he remembered a similar knife from his previous visit with Fahey.

"There was one here, remember?"

"Sure do, boy-o."

"Don't call me boyo."

"Sho-nuff massa."

"Get on with what you came for." Cullis glared at him.

Fahey put his walking stick down. Then, on his knees, he began to inspect the wall plates again. The fake ones and the real ones. He swayed on his knees a few times, humming a Dublin lyric learned from his days when crawling the lesser pubs there.

"What're you lookin' for?"

"A way to save your world, Cullis. Now stand the fuck away, will you?"

Fahey pried a plate loose, the middle one. It came right out easily to reveal the bags again. One for Alesia Noor, the other dangling a tag with Kardas's name. He smiled into his ruffled yellow shirt.

"Lemme see. What's that?" Cullis was almost on Fahey's shoulder.

"Guess. First ten don't count, handsome."

"Give it here."

"Uh-uh."

Fahey opened one bag. He dipped a finger in, as he had when first finding the stash, and then tasted the dust. Looking up be said: "That's not

Aunt Fanny's ice cream...hand me the spoon and we'll take a ride together, Cullis. Have you flying over Baghdad in no time at all."

"Gimme that, you hear me!"

Cullis took the offered bag, sniffed into its opening, then tasted a tiny amount. "Shit-sake! I'm damned. How'd you know—? There more there?"

Fahey moved over, worked on the next wall socket plate, and retrieved the larger bag. This one he gave directly to an astonished Cullis.

"Marc Sterne's by the weight of it," Fahey said. "Got a tag on it," as he already was well aware.

"You're gonna tell me how you knew about this?"

"Only if you tell me first how you Einsteins ever missed it. You've been sitting on this place for months."

"I gotta call the station." A harried frown creased Cullis's black face.

"Not from here, you won't. The line's been canceled."

"Then, Mrs. Noor's place."

"So she can hear you? Her name's on one of those happy bags. Tip her off, will you? Do yet another Einstein for us?" Fahey smirked.

Cullis thought it over, deciding Fahey had the better argument. "Okay, I'll talk from the car."

"Not so fast. *We'll* talk from the car...let's put the merchandise back."

"You crazy?"

"You want to run off with the evidence for a murder trial? Possible evidence? You want to look idiotic again. Better bring in your evidence people, right?" Enjoying himself, Fahey's grin spread in four directions.

"I'm not leaving it here with you."

"So we'll put it back. We can repair to your car, boyo. Make calls up to highest authority and listen to how they'll fuck everything up again. Let's go right at it, I need a good laugh, Cullis. In about three days you'll have your tail in a sling and me, well, old Fahey's gonna get himself a ringside seat at your crucifixion."

In the police sedan, the call was put through to the senior duty officer at the Hollywood sheriff's station. Fahey sat back, his game arm resting a foot away from the muzzle of a shotgun locked in a metal brace fixed to the dashboard.

Chatter rose over a faint hum of static. Cullis explained everything. Fahey whistled another ditty, then asked for the mike.

"Whoever this is, here is the Fahey talking. For the defense...I know how to raise the temperature of the water you're in, if you tamper with this evidence...stay on the wireless here and patch this call in to Judge Rhodes's chambers...we'll wait for you. Savvy?"

After giving Fahey an earful, the Hollywood side of the conversation agreed to a truce, and then he and Cullis waited. Waited more as Fahey whistled a tune to a stone-faced Cullis who shoved Fahey's arm away from the shotgun.

CЯ

Macklin Price had taken the call from the Hollywood sheriff's station. Sixty fast steps later, panting, she delivered a brief message to Rhodes. He recessed the court for twenty minutes, making no explanation to anyone.

In chambers, immersed in the three-way crosstalk, Rhodes's heart leaped. He wanted to kiss Fahey. Two live witnesses, one of them a law officer, vouched for the presence of the cocaine stash.

"Sheriff," he said, "leave it right where it is. We'll have to see if it's evidence in this trial or not. I instruct you not to touch it again."

The senior sheriff's officer in Hollywood started a tirade, began to bitch, and almost yelled.

Rhodes broke him off. "You want a restraining order, you got one...and you listen to me. The news will be out in no time once your station hears of it. That means newspapers, that means the attorneys will know, and that means it'll be brought up in my court. Maybe it shouldn't be, but it will be. Do you get it? You want that sort of trouble on your backs by all this loose talk?"

No, came the reply.

Rhodes replaced the phone. The mosaic was nearly complete, he was thinking, as Macklin appeared once more. "Time to go," she told him.

The sudden image of Romaine filled the corridor, as he walked back to her. Fahey, he thought, must say nothing. A great risk in that wish; Fahey, once underway, was a magpie.

CR

"We'll put a guard up there. Twenty-four hours," Cullis said after telling Fahey to get out of the sedan.

"That's your worst idea today. You can tip off that old sexpot Noor and maybe she'll tell Kardas for you."

"Shit."

"You already have, lieutenant. Don't do it again, not in those nice gabardines you've donned." Fahey peeled himself out of the car. "Have a swell evening," he said, giving Cullis his practiced drum majorette's twirl with the walking stick.

CR

At Malibu Pointe.

Audrey sat before her dressing table mirror finishing the seventieth stroke. Her hair shone like a dew-laden daffodil. A cat with her fur up now, Audrey was thinking of him! Rhodes had betrayed her. Had allowed her to be scorched in public though he had promised to help her.

She'd had had another squabble with Julio again that morning. Hardly listening, he had calmly read his paper, munched on his grapefruit sections, and kept right on with the financial page. She had blistered Rhodes. He wasn't a judge, he was an enemy, letting them flay her alive in that damn courtroom.

"Why don't you do something? Put down that idiotic newspaper and listen to me...he's not fit to walk a dog. Let alone go to the Supreme Court. A disgrace! You'd better let the governor know before it's too late."

Julio had only folded the paper in half, stared and blinked across the table as if she were a child talking out of turn. He had flicked lint off his sleeve, then got up and walked out without uttering a single word.

In less than a minute, he returned. "I want a straight answer," he demanded. "About what?"

"About why you invited Marc out here that night for dinner?"

"I'm telling you I did no such thing. Why would I? I was going out on the boat, and don't you say another damn word about trysting and so on."

"Why was it, then, that Marc's secretary says otherwise? I've had her checked. She's a reliable, loyal employee. Excellent record. So?"

"I can't explain. I've already said so to that kid lawyer."

"Are you saying someone impersonated you? Is that it?"

"I don't know. But I do know someone who probably could, and so do you."

A curt nod and Julio left her again.

She retreated upstairs to be by herself, and spent the day in her bedroom suite. Looking in the mirror again at her eyes, then searching avidly for new worry wrinkles, she couldn't find any. Her skin was still almost perfect. Satisfied, Audrey sipped from her first scotch of the day. Outside, the sky began to darken, yet, so wrapped was she in her predicament, she hardly noticed. She felt the slight burning sensation of the liquor, but it failed to dampen her soaring anger and despair over Rhodes. Rhodes knew. Somehow, he knew she'd been involved with Kardas.

Knew it, knew it, knew it.

Burke's questions, then his own questions. How could he not suspect something or other? If he thought she had been lying to him, he would never believe one thing she'd told him about Romaine. A galling thought, then: Romaine might go free. She herself might even become a suspect herself, with Kardas joining her.

More torment.

Had Julio passed the word to the lawyers to inform Burke, even Rhodes, about Kardas? Her bought and paid for lover. She shivered uncontrollably. Those goddamn conniving lawyers. She put nothing past them.

Nothing.

She was becoming obsessed, paranoid—and knew it. She couldn't help herself. Who could she talk with? No one. A lawyer, perhaps. But as matters stood, as her feelings and emotions mauled her, she despised every lawyer who had ever passed the bar exam.

The hairbrush dropped from her hand. She didn't even hear its rattling noise against the floor. She heard nothing but the noiseless piercing sounds of womanly fear.

ೞ

"Yesterday, they come. Two men, same men," Ferenc heard from an excited Alesia Noor on the phone.

"How long?"

"Long time."

"Were you with them?"

"No. They not let me go up. You better come..."

"I'll come tomorrow. In the afternoon."

"You better. That tall one with the stick, he-sa the one to watch."

Ferenc had no idea who she meant. But he sensed an end to the luxurious world of Malibu Pointe. Thinking recklessly, and at speed now, he could empty his three bank accounts in the morning. Was the cocaine still findable? He didn't know, but certainly it was worth a look. Noor saw something, she had said, the last time the police were poking around there.

He blew a kiss toward the ceiling, aimed at Audrey's room. Goodbye, baby, things are getting too hot. Not as hot as you, but too hot to stick around.

◌঵

Like hell they weren't screwing! It was no dainty handshake, for sure.

She's still a looker at forty-two, maybe it's forty-three or four. She doesn't say her age. She's a ripe one, all right. Has her own personal trainer. And she's got chops, I'll say that for her; and especially messing with that houseman, Kardas, when Julio Sterne was away. Which was more often than not, so she and Kardas went at it like honeymooners. One night, from Marc's bedroom, we saw them doing their horizontal yoga down by the pool house. On a chaise. It wasn't as if they were trying to hide anything. Marc had one of those fancy Hasselblad cameras with a Senko lens. The pictures he took at night are as vivid as if he'd shot them at high noon. He took about twenty of Audrey and Kardas, really going at it.

I knew Marc would make her pay for them somehow. He didn't like her and she barely tolerated him.

That Kardas, what a lout he is. A Hunkie from Pest. Pest is across the river from Buda. That's Kardas, too, a Pest. He did a number on me once. Walked right into the women's dressing room down at the Sterne's pool. I'd just exited the shower and there he was, sitting on a wicker chair, gawking. He got up as soon as I came through the shower curtain, a big-ass grin plastered on his face. He reached for me. I'd taken judo lessons at a Korean studio over in North Hollywood, and am pretty sure of my aim. I let him have it square in the huevos with a swift crotch-kick, and down he went like

254

a shot bird. Gagged and threw up and made a mess. The last time he ever came after me.

Marc thought he was another Ansel Adams. One day, he picked me up after a ten hour shoot at Parthenon. Fagged. I was beat. He'd been snorting and he let me have a look at the photos he'd taken in the desert that time. He said I could have the originals, if I'd forgive his debt to me. Practically, my life savings. Otherwise, he'd let the photos circulate on the web, and get his father to have me blackballed in the industry. Three or four phone calls and I'll be in the dust. A fallen star. Marc had another jar of Beluga with him; he wanted to go to his apartment, smear me with those b-b sized black eggs, suck me all over and have a romp.

In my life, I've had three men between my legs, not including that bastard of a priest, whom I don't count. Only lovers.

*Marc, easily the Romeo of all. A real Sampson. A shitheel, too, but a useful one. He was using me for sex and because I was getting a lot of ink in the papers before this shambles. I was hot, hot, hot. **Variety** said I had received more news space last year than any other, except one, actor. Not bad. If you want to survive, or get to the top or anywhere near the top in this racket, your connections and what's between your legs are your best buddies.*

One really oddball thing about Marc is that he was really weird sometimes about sex. He liked to smear me with caviar and lick it off. "Lunch," he'd say. Or we'd have sex two or three times and then he'd want to read the Bible to me. I did a lot of my growing up in a Catholic situation where nuns ruled my every hour. By the time I was sixteen I had so much Bible infused in me, casting out my devils, I began to think I wrote every verse and gospel.

For Marc, I think it was all a sham, attempting to impress me with his moral character. Fuck your brains out and then pray over yourself. He had the morals of a shark. No, a snake. An extremely hungry snake.

He's a Jew, I'm Catholic, or was. Too many guilt trips for me. I'm a nothing now, I suppose. And I'll be less than nothing if the Eel has his way. Time to double down.

Do it by myself. Tommy, he's so lovable but he's a bumbler. He's dime store. And if I don't do my thing, I'm going to get sent up. A year ago, I was riding on top of the world. Now I wonder if I'll ever get a film again.

I see the judge looking at me, a lot more than he did before. Probably got a lot of natural flavor in him. Right off, he lit my candle and I'd do it for him. He must have twenty-years on me, but so what? I'll find out about his action, if ever I get my butt out of here.

What's in his head?

Well, do it mister, whatever it is. I'll make it up to you.

Tommy says it's the State's burden to prove every allegation. But that Eel is always on the prowl. I wonder what would happen if I had him for a night in the kip. An attitude adjustment, perhaps, and then maybe he wouldn't say such horrid things about me. Pritter almost did me in, or he could've. That call that Dee-Dee took from Audrey Sterne inviting Marc to dinner the night he was killed, the same night she was doing Kardas on the boat—had taken me hours of rehearsing. That call was what got Marc out to Malibu Pointe that night...

Tommy said Dee-Dee wouldn't be recalled. One hole is now closed, and forever closed, let's hope.

Chapter Twenty-four

Alesia Noor watched without a blink as Ferenc Kardas doled out the contents of the largest sack into two glass bowls, dividing the white crystals evenly. They sat in her kitchen on either side of a small table covered with a red-checkered oilcloth.

She had taken him up to Marc Sterne's apartment an hour earlier, showing him where Fahey had stood behind the couch the night when he'd come back alone. Kardas knelt, searching about. It took a little time before he noticed the scratch-marks on the baseboard and the switch plates. One plate was slightly ajar.

The rest was easy. Fahey and Cullis in their haste had left an easy trail to follow; one that led to more treasure than Alesia Noor ever imagined would shine so invitingly into her widening eyes.

"You have a scale here?" Ferenc asked. "For weighing this?"

"Not any good one."

"I do my best then."

The pouring of the sugary crystals titillated her senses. All that white money, embalming her with joy, as it piled up by the inch.

Kardas asked her to come around the table. In two bowls, he had smoothed off the grains with a metal spatula retrieved from the kitchen. He examined his work with an approving grunt. Knowing she would insist on an equal cut, he had favored her bowl with slightly more than his own, certain she would take notice. A few grams difference was worth hundreds of dollars; or thousands if the cocaine was pure, which Kardas doubted.

"Is okay," she said after examining the bowls carefully.

"You certain?"

She nodded approvingly, happily. But that was just before she became a dead weight in his arms and collapsed to the floor with a loud thud. A short hard clip to the carotid artery had driven a quick shock to her brain. Her eyes had rolled back involuntarily on the trip into his waiting arms.

Dragging her out of the kitchen, he propped her in a chair facing the television set. Her breath came evenly. To make sure, he loosened a few buttons at the top of her dress, knowing it wouldn't help her, but the gesture made him feel better after chopping her that solidly.

He finished off his burglary in the kitchen, taking only a moment to pour both bowls into a large Zip-loc bag.

On the way out, checking the woman again, he set the lock, closed the door, and sauntered off. Next stop: Las Vegas, where he'd unload the coke. From there, Nassau. Sun, yachts, a tax haven, and rich divorcees.

Still, California had been the most stupefying path of promises he'd ever known. Golden girls, sun swept beaches, gilded dreams, the heaven-sent Valhalla for every mother-fucking hustler with half a brain.

He threw the car into gear. He'd already added up his score—all that white honey was practically under his very nose, right there in the back of the car. So easy, he thought, rounding the corner and heading for the freeway.

Easily, two-hundred thousand, maybe two-and-a-half. The American dream wasn't dead, not by a long-shot.

Chapter Twenty-five

A hush settled over the courtroom. About as much sound as a hummingbird makes; everyone in their own limbo, eyes fastened on her, as, for the second time, she occupied the witness chair. Her face, was it the face of a truth-teller, or would it seem shifty, evasive? And that voice, would it falter, quiver—or be full and resolute, as Pritter slugged away.

Romaine wore a crisp blue dress, with a box-shaped neckline. A modest necklace of small white seashells looped around her throat that sometimes moved as she uttered small gasps of disbelief. Her tawny hair swept across the full width of her shoulders when shaking her head. Then other looks, looks that were full of sudden surprise, or sometimes simply sympathetic as she shaped her face in an endearing repose.

She could do them all, even the more intense ones of anger and shock. She was on her stage today; she was everything she had ever studied to be, when she wanted to appear a certain way.

Tommy Burke surveyed the ranks of impatient onlookers. They wanted more. More of Romaine's hide or more about her romance with Marc Sterne, he wasn't sure which. Action, that's what they'd come for. He hated Mare Sterne, loathed him. That coroner's report was sure to be on today's menu of trouble.

Only a short hour ago, he had raised nervous giggles from the faces staring at him, tying his nerves in knots. Trying to re-stage events on the night of Marc Sterne's death, Tommy had stripped his jacket off, unbuttoned his shirt, and bared his knobby ribcage.

He'd done it for her.

They had performed a small playlet together, with Tommy lying on an old camp cot as a prop. A crude model of the bed to show how and where Marc was lying the night he emptied his last cocaine cocktail into his artery.

Around his own arm, Tommy had wound a length of surgical hose, tightening it until a vein swelled blue with blood.

He pricked his vein with a hypodermic syringe bought only a few days before in a drug store. Blood had flooded the syringe, and he had asked Romaine to put her thumb on the plunger.

And push it down, so everyone in the jury could see.

Exactly as he had rehearsed her to push it down, she had, so that everyone in front could see the blood emptying out of the syringe, back into his arm. He came off the cot then, a little shaky but smiling.

Lunging at Romaine, she had fended him off, his shirt tails flying. They were close, close as a mother's hug. In the flurry of their arms, Tommy had slithered an edge of his shirt over the syringe still sticking out of his arm; then, close as they were, he surreptitiously wiped the plunger's top very quickly.

He had worked on that trick for over a week. Had he gotten away with it? Had the jury seen him do what he'd done? Showing them another way things might've happened that night in Malibu Pointe.

"Was it like that? That sort of a rush at you by Marc Sterne?" Tommy had asked her. He turned so the jury could see him, the syringe still in his arm, filling again with blood pumping out from the vein.

"Something like that, yes, I think so." Romaine agreed. "Oh, be careful of that thing."

"Would you say he was hopped up? Drugged?"

"Yes. Speeding his brains...Oh! Poor Marc, he'd just lost himself all over again."

Everyone's eyes had been riveted to the red flow filling the syringe.

"He was going for you? Meant to harm you?"

"I was petrified. His eyes were devil-black. That's what I remember most of all."

"But meaning to harm you? Was that your impression?"

"It was so fast. He wouldn't, though, not really...I mean that's what I hoped anyway. He was so hurt, way down deep. Beautiful Marc, but still...oh, I don't know. How can you know what another person is thinking when they're on a trip like that?"

When their act was over, Burke had come before Rhodes and raised his eyes up to the bench. "Would you have someone remove this syringe?" he asked. "Just so they don't touch the plunger's top. I want someone else to remove it. The last person to touch the top was Romaine Burke." And he had looked meaningfully at the jury again. They got the message, hadn't they? No doubts were there? Reasonable doubts anyway?

Rhodes had also eyed the blood-filled syringe, wondering how Burke could spare the loss of a single drop.

"A doctor perhaps…wait—" he said, glancing over at the jury. "Aren't one of you ladies a nurse?"

The brunette with the horn-rims raised her hand. Rhodes asked her to come forward. Tommy pulled a clean handkerchief along with a thin white box from one pocket. Untying the surgical tubing from Tommy's arm, the nurse carefully removed the syringe, dabbed Tommy's arm, then placed the hypodermic in a small white plastic box. They were no more than ten feet from the jury, when she gave the blood-spotted handkerchief back to Tommy.

"Your Honor," Tommy had said, holding out the box, "this will be our only exhibit for the defense. I ask that it be marked for evidence and sent immediately to the police department's forensic lab so they can check it for fingerprints. Romaine Brook's prints especially. No one has touched the plunger top since the defendant…you all saw that, didn't you?" Riding his eyes point-blank into the eyes of the jurors once more.

Rhodes had ordered a bailiff over, giving him a very precise set of instructions. His respect for Burke was mounting, and he had shown it with a deferential look at the younger man.

CR

All this had happened two hours ago. The hypodermic was being checked, and, meanwhile, the trial had resumed.

Tommy put his water glass down, and turned to see Romaine floating a baffled look his way—what was taking so long? He would skirt around the issue of those photos and see how and if Pritter clawed her on that one.

"I want to know only one more thing, Miss Brook," he said to her, up by the witness stand now.

"Yes," she said eagerly.

"This morning you and I re-enacted, as best we could, how you described the events of the last night you were with Marc Sterne."

"Yes…so sad and everything."

261

"You remember how you pressed your thumb on the plunger, running my blood back in."

"But I didn't touch the syringe that night."

"This morning you did."

"I know."

"So your fingerprints should be on it, shouldn't they?"

"I guess so, I—"

"Unless in our little scuffle they somehow got wiped away," said Tommy, leaving the thought hanging.

Pritter's jowls puffed out and in. He jostled an assistant with one elbow, saying something.

"I don't know," Romaine said. "I couldn't say, for sure. You were all over me..."

Knowing laughs from the first row.

"Now tell the jury, in your words—did you kill Marc Sterne?"

Her face lit up and seemed a size bigger as her lips parted slightly. A vacant day-dreamy look appeared for only a fleeting moment. Going pale, as if suddenly blessed to see what went on at the fiery core of earth, Romaine's eyes shone with stark amazement.

"We are all of us, are in God's hands, and I know that," she offered. "Some people, whoever they are, forget how I loved Marc Sterne. He did everything for me, don't you know...oh, please, don't you know," she said, gift-wrapping her sentiments for the jury again.

She misted up before loaning out a few wet sobs to the hushed onlookers. No one there could remember her coming apart so visibly. Not even once, in all those months of observing her so closely. Her words: Tommy already knew them and had known they were coming, but still they ripped at him.

"Your witness," he mumbled to Pritter.

Pritter began easily. He took Romaine back to the beginning, back to the coroner's report, back to the traces of drugs found in Marc Sterne's body. "Acute poisoning from cocaine; heroin and Meperdine," intoned Pritter, adding, "Do you know those drugs?"

"Not very well."

"How well?"

"I've heard of them. Everyone has, I suppose."

"Meperdine? You know what that is?"

"Like Demerol, isn't it? A painkiller?"

"Yes it is," agreed Pritter, surprised but pleased she knew. He handed her a page he'd been holding. "Recognize this?"

"The letter, isn't it, the one I wrote Marc?"

"You tell us."

"A copy, yes, it's a copy of my letter."

"Your handwriting, too?"

"Mine, yes, most certainly mine."

"Care to read that letter out loud so we can all hear how you threatened Marc Sterne?"

Burke moaned. He labored to his feet, sounding an objection—the jury had already seen the letter. No purpose was served by spilling it out to the press. A few reporters shot unfriendly looks at him.

"Sustained," Rhodes ruled. "I'll let you go at it another way, counselor."

"How would you characterize the letter?" Pritter asked Romaine.

"Sort of angry, which I was."

"Angry? How about threatening?"

"No."

"No?" Pritter wagged his head. "You explicitly said in it that you were going to talk to his parents. Tell the newspapers certain things. Expose him as a thief, a criminal."

"I was upset, Mr. Pritter. Really boiling."

"Upset? The letter sounded to some of us as if you wrote it with sulfuric acid."

"I shouldn't have been so mad. I was wrong." Pritter, trying to stop Romaine right there, though failed. "He owed me money I needed, and I believe Marc took my share to finance his drugs. The ones he used on himself and the others that he was dealing."

Rhodes breathed a prayer of thanks. She'd gotten the issue of drugs back into the record.

"Perhaps, Miss Brook, you'll favor us with answers to the questions we're asking you," Pritter said.

"Oh, excuse me. I thought that's what you wanted to know."

"Not precisely. And how can you say that Marc Sterne sold drugs. Did you buy from him?"

"No, never. I don't take drugs, Mr. Pritter."

"Never?"

"Oh, no. Gosh, how could you say a thing like that?"

"But you say you saw him negotiate drug sales?"

"Many times."

"Where?"

"Parties and places."

She told him of strings of parties she had attended with Marc Sterne. Often he would leave her by herself when he drifted out to his car for his stash.

"Could you name names?"

"I wouldn't. That would be a terrible thing to do to others."

"Convenient, too. Making it so we can't verify your statement that Marc sold drugs?"

"I'm not saying who those buyers were. Anyway, it was done in privacy, so I couldn't say about actual money passing hands. But he always had rolls of it, when we left those parties and sometimes asked me to put some of the money in my handbag."

"You were an accomplice, weren't you?"

"I didn't sell drugs to anyone, Mr. Pritter."

Prodding her, he stated, "No, not you. You were the money-mule," and then pressed her with, "Why didn't you report it to the authorities?"

Romaine gave the jury a look of astonishment. "I wouldn't ever do that to Marc. I loved him."

"When you don't report violations of the narcotics laws, Miss Brook, it's the same as if you conspired in the sale yourself."

"But I loved Marc. How could I...besides, Mr. Pritter, you'd have to report on half the people in Hollywood."

Rhodes joined in the laughter flooding the room.

Plugging onward, Pritter asked, "You said he owed you money. From the sale of drugs?"

"Please don't accuse me of that anymore. I never sold drugs in my life to anyone."

"Or used them either?"

"No, of course not."

"Never."

"Right, never."

"Why did Marc Sterne owe you money? He earned a good salary, didn't he?"

"Yes, but money to him was like water to me. He really spent. And he said his father underpaid him."

"But why borrow from you?"

"He didn't exactly borrow. He took my share."

"Share of what?"

We did a treatment of a screenplay together. A story I dreamed up. We wrote a treatment of it in thirty-two pages and Parthenon Studios bought the rights to it. But he kept my share."

"Which was how much?"

Romaine told him.

"Wouldn't the usual thing be for Parthenon, when they bought story rights, to pay each author separately?"

"I think so. But Marc went funny on me. He submitted the story under his own name."

"Not yours?"

"No, you see that's why I sent the letter. I was hopping mad, I tell you, because I was the one who created the idea for the story...and really I needed money then."

"Can you prove you were legitimately a co-author?"

"I know the story by heart."

"Doesn't make you a co-author, though, does it?"

"But I was. Yes, I was too. You weren't there, Mr. Pritter. You really don't know a thing about it."

Pritter scratched his round chin, pursing his mouth in the shape of a horseshoe.

"You trusted Marc Sterne? A man you say was a drug dealer and a thief. Who you say took your money. Money you say was yours but we have only your word for it. The same, isn't it, for those people who supposedly bought drugs from Marc? No names, just your word?"

"It's all I have," replied Romaine, sheepishly. "And my word wouldn't be worth much if I started telling on people."

"But you have."

"On who?"

"On Marc Sterne. Just now."

"That's not the same," said Romaine defensively. "Marc's gone."

"How about Mrs. Sterne? And Ferenc Kardas? Didn't you tell us slanderous things about them, trying to kick innocent reputations apart?"

"I didn't lie. I saw them."

"They deny it."

Pritter had been facing the rows of reporters, but now he wheeled and walked to where she sat in the witness stand. He loomed so close that Romaine could part his hair with a fingernail. Oily black hair, she thought, slick as eel skin.

"That's the third time now where you've said something we can't verify as truth. The money. The drugs. Mrs. Sterne's alleged behavior. Except in her case, she claims that you're lying blatantly."

"God will punish her one day. He'll have to..."

"You're getting very hard to believe, Miss Brook. Even Mr. Sterne denies he ever offered you a picture deal with any studio—his studio or anyone else's—so that's the fourth example of your lies to us."

"I'm not lying to anyone. You just say I am. It's very unfair of you."

"You want us to think everyone else is lying to us except you. Four liars to one truth-teller."

"I'll admit, Mr. Pritter, it may seem strange—"

"Strange!" exclaimed Pritter, firing back at her. "Not so strange for you, is it? You're not in the same world as the rest of us. Everyone's a cheat and a deceiver, everyone, that is, but Romaine Brook. The poor little innocent put-upon actress."

"I'm proud to be an actress and of my work."

"So you are. So why not act the part of truth for a change."

They went on, Pritter snarling, fencing, cornering her. Painting Romaine as a female Lucifer, a cheap temptress, the Eve of all Eves. A few jurors nodded in agreement.

Burke, starting to sweat, became nervous. He watched for an hour as Pritter hounded her, setting one burning match after the other to her papery claims of innocence.

Rhodes, taking it all in line by line, word by word, wondered what would the lab report show. Would her fingerprints show up?

Pritter lowered his gunsights. "You've seen these?' He held out a packet of 3 x 5 color prints, copies of the originals that had already been offered into evidence. The photos were now so notorious they had become settled images in everyone's imagination.

"I've seen them, yes."

"Tell us where they were taken."

"In Palm Springs. I was there with Marc. And the other hands in the pictures, I'm pretty sure I know who they belong to."

"And who would they be?"

"A Mexican couple."

"Their names?"

"I don't know. Valdez, I think, it might be Valdez."

"You don't know again. You don't know the names of people who you let roam your body?"

"That's not very nice of you, Mr. Pritter," said Romaine quietly. "You shouldn't ever say a thing like that to anyone."

Pritter stepped back from the witness stand. She'd caught him off guard with her slight rebuke. "Miss Brook," he said, "these photos have been withheld from the public and the press. Do you know why?"

"They're awful. Pornographic, I suppose."

"And therefore they might unjustly influence people. Is that right? Or cause undue harm to your reputation, the way you've been causing it to others."

"I think they would harm anyone, Mr. Pritter. Not just me."

"Yes, I would imagine so," Pritter said, softly for a change. He held the fan of photos out at arm's length, studying them, knowing he was mortifying Romaine. "How are you dressed in these photos?"

"You can see."

Tommy Burke sputtered an objection. Any way you looked at it, he complained, Pritter was defying an earlier ruling that the photos would be restricted to the jury, the court, and the attorneys.

Rhodes overruled him, a ploy on his part.

"What were you wearing?" Pritter repeated.

"I was quite bare."

"You certainly were." He shuffled the stack of pictures, showing Romaine another one. Pritter's jowls went pink, and then he mocked her in a conspiratorial tone: "You were—sort of wearing something here, weren't you? What do you call that?" Pointing at one photo.

"A dildo."

"Where is it exactly in this picture—?"

"Okay," Rhodes said to Pritter. "That's enough. You made your point and the jury's seen the photos."

Pritter protested. "I want to find out the circumstances under which the photos were taken. And I—"

"Then ask the defendant," Rhodes said.

"I am," Pritter replied.

Rhodes gave him a look, and Pritter shrugged. He sidestepped a few paces until he faced Romaine again.

"Miss Brook," he said, "those of us who've seen these, um, photos are aware that other people were present when the pictures were taken...hands other than your own show up. In one picture a large dog—were you posing here or what?"

She did not answer Pritter face to face, but spoke to the air in a louder voice, clear as an opera singer's. "I would never do that." Her head shook. Golden hair swirled back and forth across her shoulders as she rubbed her eyes. She looked at the jury, her face expressing shock.

"But you did!"

"Not knowingly, no sir."

"Tell us, we wait your latest version."

Romaine, in sonorous tones, told the entire courtroom once again how she and Marc had gone to Palm Springs for a long weekend. While there the first day, swimming, he'd made her a cool drink at the outside bar. A short time later, she felt dizzy and faint, then faded away into a dream-like wild journey.

"I was drugged-out, as I said," she told the jury. "I said I don't take drugs and I don't. I was tricked that time. I don't think I really woke up for hours, came out of it. When I was unconscious, that must've been when they did those things to me...took those awful pictures."

"What sort of a drink did he make for you?" asked Pritter.

"A spritzer. A white wine spritzer."

"You drink alcohol often?"

"Rarely."

"That day you did."

"I asked for some iced tea. But it was all gone by then. So he made me a spritzer."

"And you say you were drugged."

"I was. I'm sure of it."

"And yet you said earlier, Miss Brook, that you don't take narcotics. Remember?"

"Not by habit."

"You didn't say by habit, you said—"

"Mr. Pritter, I don't take them by choice," Romaine retorted sternly, "and I don't sell them either...please stop badgering me that way. I'm asking you, please to stop..."

"You don't take drugs. You don't drink alcohol."

She shook her head again.

"Perhaps you just engage in orgies," Pritter rapped at Romaine, not waiting for an answer.

"I dizzied out. Everything became yellow and red and—oh! I don't know. Freakish."

"And we're to believe Marc Sterne drugged you?"

"Who else could have?"

"Didn't you say there was some Mexican couple there with you?"

"I did, yes. The doctor and his wife."

"A doctor? You said a doctor?"

"A Mexican doctor from Tijuana, or one of those border towns. Tijuana, yes, it was Tijuana. A friend of Marc's."

"And you don't know their names?"

"Valdez, I think it was. I just told you."

"That's all?"

Romaine nodded, then said very solemnly, "I think Marc was trying to make it easy on me. That's why he drugged me."

"Make what easy—"and Pritter tried to stop his own question, and Romaine grabbed her chance. "The abortion." She hurried. "We'd gone there because I needed an abortion and—"

"I'm not asking you that," Pritter scolded her.

"Oh. I thought—"Romaine patted her mouth as if to apologize.

Once again Rhodes spoke. "You go right on ahead," he told Romaine.

"That's not my question, your Honor," Pritter grumbled.

"It is now. You began it. You told the court earlier you wanted us to learn the circumstances of the pictures. Get to it please."

Pritter sighed deeply. "You were having an abortion in Palm Springs. To be performed, I suppose, by some half-named Mexican doctor?"

"Yes, you know all about it then?" Romaine asked innocently.

"No, Miss Brook, I don't know anything about it," said an exasperated Pritter. "And neither does anyone else."

"Well, Marc, he wanted to relax me, I guess. I was very upset and he was being so nice and caring."

"He cared so much he drugged you?"

"He knew I was so terribly upset. I think that's why. He could be very unpredictable."

Tommy Burke was staggered, furious, too. Romaine had never really explained the photos and had never uttered so much as a comma about any abortion.

"Are you saying," Pritter was asking, "that Marc Sterne drugged you prior to an abortion procedure? Drugged you when there was a doctor, supposedly, present?"

"Marc liked doing things his way. You can ask anyone who knew him."

Pritter already had. She was right.

"And this abortion. Was he the father of the fetus?"

"Yes, naturally, Mr. Pritter...ohhh, you're being awful again. You're implying it was someone besides Marc."

Pritter didn't know how to break down the front Romaine was putting up. She was either too coy or she gushed in pained surprise, whenever he closed in on her. Twenty-odd years in California courtrooms had given him a healthy sixth-sense, signaling him when witnesses were gaming him. This one was a pro, a trained and talented actress who knew stagecraft better than he ever would.

On another tack, he asked, "Miss Brook, have you ever posed nude for what some call 'men's' magazines' or 'girlie magazines'. *Playboy* or *Penthouse?* One of those, any others?"

"Anyone who knows me knows I wouldn't."

"Uh-huh. Just in Palm Springs?"

"When I was put asleep with drugs."

"Having an abortion?"

"Yes."

"Why didn't you go to a clinic? A hospital?"

"Marc wanted it done very privately. So did I."

"Why?"

"People talk."

"Doctors?"

"Their nurses or secretaries or someone. They can, Mr. Pritter...and they have, as you must know they have."

"What were you afraid of?"

"Mr. Sterne. Marc was afraid his father would raise all get-out, even kick him out of the studio."

"Over an abortion?"

"Oh, no, not that. Supposing I'd decided to have the baby. That would've made it a Sterne heir to all that money. Marc told me his father would wring his neck. And then mine. Mr. Sterne is so powerful. He might've made me *non grata,* ruining my chances with every Hollywood studio...that's why I agreed to the abortion. And now I wish I hadn't."

"Did you say *non grata?*"

"I did."

"Know what it means?"

"It's a Latin phrase. I think it's really *persona non grata.* Means when you're not welcomed."

Wishing he hadn't asked her, Pritter swore under his breath. She was too cunning. Spinning one account after another, and all of them so intricate he couldn't unwind any of them. He had to shake her somehow. Quake her was more like it, he thought.

"Why would Marc Sterne—the father of your unborn child—and the man you say you loved, and who presumably loved you, take those pictures of you?"

"Maybe he didn't take them, Mr. Pritter."

"Who then? The Mexican doctor and his wife?"

"Possibly."

"Why?"

"I don't know. What if they had some...some scheme?"

"Such as?"

"Blackmail maybe...I don't know."

"The pictures were found in Marc Sterne's apartment. If he didn't take them, how would he have them in his possession?"

"Maybe he bought them to protect me. I simply don't know. Possibly your state investigators could find out."

The courtroom burst into titters. Pritter flushed. "We have no names to go by, Miss Brook. No place to start. Only Mexicans, with uncertain names, from Tijuana."

"You started easily enough with me...and look what you've done to my life. And I've never done anything against you or anyone here in this courtroom. I'm a decent person, and I resent you trying to injure me this way."

The wall clock showed 12:40. Some of the reporters covering the trial for the European news services had already left to wire their stories.

An abortion? Rhodes had nearly become a grandfather, even before he knew he was a father.

He recessed.

OB

A technician slid a set of print images into a small tray on the side of a square gray machine, a little larger than a standard desktop computer. Under a pale green light, the images magnified. Side by side, she saw a picture taken of the plunger-top of the syringe brought over by a bailiff, with the picture's image showing a fragment of a fingerprint. She matched it with a set of prints belonging to Romaine Brook, taken when she had been booked for homicide.

Adjusting a knob, the technician peered intently at a backlit screen. Romaine's prints stood out in sharp relief, magnified by a power of three. With a tiny chrome pointer, the technician traced the loops, whorls and arches on the thumbprint that had been lifted from the chrome plunger-top of the syringe; she did the same to other prints left on the syringe's finger grips.

She compared, compared again.

Swiveling in her chair, she stood up and went to a bench, bending to the eyepieces, confirming the earlier observations, she saw the red and white fibers also found on the plunger top.

Only twenty minutes had passed since the bailiff brought the syringe to the forensic lab, telling the Latent Prints Section of L.A.P.D. of an urgent request for a speedy identification. Pretty simple, thought the technician, sitting down and tapping away on a keyboard.

ROMAINE BROOK, she typed on the second line, then remembered how much she enjoyed seeing *Tonight or Never*. One film actress down the pipe, the technician thought. How could people screw up like that, when they had it all?

By 1:45, the jurors were in their seats again. Three of them had skipped lunch, using the time to make calls to their families, who hadn't seen them for over three months.

Romaine was still on the witness stand. She tried a weak smile on the jurors, getting small reward for the effort. As she smoothed the pleats of her dress, she wet the inside of her mouth as Pritter approached.

A little more, she told herself, *be the character you have to be or he'll grind you into red hash. Be Joan of Arc or anyone who ever went through an inquisition. Smile more. Show him* you're *not frightened.*

For the next half-hour, Pritter hacked away, ripping the weaker seams of her story.

Romaine stuck to her guns. Occasionally, her slim hand would touch the little shells of her necklace, reminding Rhodes of Audrey's nervous habit.

By mid-afternoon, Pritter was nearly through. He stood near the jury, his wide face in a rumpus of contempt. His vest was partly unbuttoned over his deep belly that seemed to grow when he rammed his hands deep into his pockets. Rocking on his feet, he was distracted as a bailiff handed a paper to Tommy Burke.

"Miss Brook," Pritter started in, "you remember well the night you last saw Marc Sterne? The night he died in your presence?"

"But he didn't die in my presence. He was still alive, when I left."

"Was he really?"

"Yes."

"You knew he was in trouble? Injected with a fatal drug dosage?"

"I knew he'd taken something...I didn't know what drugs exactly. Or if they'd be fatal. How could I know that?"

"You knew earlier in your testimony. You knew about Meperdine, you said."

"I knew what they said Marc had died from. But I know very little about actual drugs. Or dosages. I suppose you can die from too much iodine. I'd have to ask a pharmacist."

"How did you know how he died to begin with?"

"Reading in the newspapers. And Mr. Wheeler showed me the coroner's report once."

Pritter rocked on his heels again. "Why didn't you seek help for him? Call a doctor? Do something. Wasn't this man dying before your eyes, the man you supposedly loved?"

"But I didn't know." Romaine gulped visibly. "I was so frightened when he went after me. Sort of crazed and everything. I didn't know he would OD and die. He hadn't dies at other times."

"OD?"

"Overdose."

"You know that term?"

"Doesn't everyone? You hear it enough."

"So you let him die on you. Your love, your lover?"

"I said I didn't know he would die. I'm not a doctor. I couldn't tell anything. Diagnose him. I can't do that, couldn't even start to…"

"You wouldn't take even the simplest precautions to save a life? Come now, Miss Brook."

"I keep saying I had no way of knowing he was going to die. And I was so scared when he tried to seize me. You're not me, you can't know how I felt. I was worried, very worried."

"Worried?"

"Well, you see, if I called a doctor or the paramedics and Marc was all right, there could have been a lot of bad publicity. I don't think Mr. and Mrs. Sterne would've forgiven me."

"For saving their son?" asked Pritter.

"But I didn't know! I just didn't know. Would you?"

"When you made a statement to the state investigators, you said"— Pritter read from a sheet—'*I came to the Malibu house when Marc called me that day. Inviting me to have dinner there.*' Like to see this?" Pritter offered her the report.

"I remember that, thank you. I don't need the report."

The other call to Marc's secretary. Does he really know? Suspect? Romaine felt her breath shorten.

Pritter dropped the report in front of an assistant. "But there was no dinner planned at the Sterne house that night," he said. "Mrs. Sterne has already testified to that effect. You were present here, when she did."

"I didn't find that out till I arrived at their home."

"But you were willing to have dinner with him anyway?"

"Of course."

"With Marc Sterne, whom you hadn't seen for a while. Who had drugged you in Palm Springs? Who perhaps had those photos taken of you. Had even stolen your interest, you say, in some film story rights."

"Yes."

"That's implausible."

"Everything about this trial is implausible. It all happened just as I'm saying. Photos. Money. Everything. You weren't there, Mr. Pritter, but I was, and so I know," Romaine answered indignantly.

"How long had you been split up by then? A month?"

"We hadn't split up. We'd been physically apart for six weeks."

"Why so long, Miss Brook?"

"I was recovering from that abortion. I had classes to attend. And for two weeks of that time, he was on location doing principal photography for a film. In Oregon. Up there."

"Did you ever talk? By phone?"

"Once a week, sometimes twice."

"Hardly very often, was it, for two young lovers?"

"I don't know. Enough for us anyway."

"That's why you agreed to go for dinner with him in Malibu? For a patch-up?"

"We weren't patching up. We were in love. I was going to give up my acting career. Make a home for us. I could do it for Marc, give him a destiny, a family."

"A destiny in love?" he parried.

"Yes, Mr. Pritter. And another thing was that Marc said he'd pay me the money he owed me."

"Oh, he did, did he?"

"I really needed it, too. I was late on my tuition. The rent was overdue. Had a pile of other bills."

"He could've sent you a check."

Eyes sparkling, Romaine folded her hands. "I went for the biggest reason of my life," she said.

"Tell us."

"We'd decided, Marc and I, to tell his parents of our decision to marry. We couldn't stand being apart any longer."

Tommy Burke thought his head was coming loose. Never had Romaine mentioned any marriage. Ever. And Pritter looked like someone had knocked out his molars. Stillness blanketed the courtroom. Rhodes sat back. Rows of elated faces whispered to each other, trying to absorb this latest swerve of news.

"How touching," said Pritter. "Isn't it too bad Marc isn't here to tell us what he thought about marrying you?"

"You've no idea what that would have meant to me. Plea—oh! please— I'm sorry." Romaine's head dropped to her hands; her voice broke into muffled sobs.

A moment later Rhodes asked if she wanted a recess. Wiping the tears away, Romaine shook her head.

Eleven times, Pritter had openly refused to believe her. Eleven. At about the ninth round in their sparring match, he had shaken his head like some punch-drunk fighter. His eyes roved the courtroom—the reporters, the spectators, to Burke, up to Rhodes, over to the jury. His arms rose, then flopped to his egg-shaped sides.

In a heavy blast, he raked Romaine: "Here I've been twenty-three years in courthouses. Never yet have I seen the likes of you. You're an actress. For my buck, you're the greatest actress alive. No, not an actress, Miss Brook, you're a symphony of deceit. Of tricks and moods and prevarications and in a voice that can call in birds from the mountains...you've evaded everything, haven't you? You won't name persons Marc Sterne allegedly sold drugs to... he took your money, you say, for a film idea but the studio has no record of your co-authorship...Mrs. Sterne is, according to you, a faithless wife and, naturally she denies it...Mr. Sterne say he never offered you some picture deal. Then there's some mysterious Mexican doctor who performed an abortion..." Pritter halted, looking around the room before lashing out again. "And those photos, no one knows who took them. Nor do we know if Marc Sterne was father to your aborted child."

Romaine closed her eyes. Her lips moved as if she were engaged in silent prayer.

"Then you say," Pritter went on, "Marc Sterne drugged you before the photos were taken. But Marc's no longer here to confirm or deny anything, is he? You tell us he invited you for dinner at the family residence. You say you were going to tell his parents that you were to marry...and at the end, you want us to share your convictions that he was alive when you left the Sterne house...your word, Miss Brook, against everyone else's. Or your many allegations which we can't check. The roads to those facts are all so much lost dust. Isn't that so?"

"But why is that my fault?"

"No, we can all see you're faultless. You've had months to figure out how to get away with a capital crime. By lying and lying, and lying more"—Pritter pounded a wooden rail until it actually wiggled—"and you do expect to get away with it, don't you?"

"But Mr. Pritter, it's you who's doing all this to me," Romaine cried out. "You're the one who's saying all these horrible falsehoods. Making me look so bad...oh, Mister Pritter. I know you're a very important lawyer. But why do you want to...well, oh...torment me. I don't know who killed Marc. I guess no one does, do they? I think he killed himself, so why do you keep blaming me? Don't you think it's possible he killed himself? People do that to themselves, don't they? Sometimes?"

He ignored her. Patches of sweat had begun to appear under his arms on his suit coat. A thin sharp ferret-like gleam entered his eyes.

"Maybe you'll tell us something else," Pritter pounced again. "Have you ever had medical treatment for gynecological disorders?"

"The abortion."

"Yes. Do you know what a D-and-C is?"

"I do."

"Have you ever had a D-and- C other than at the time of your alleged abortion, the one done by the Mexican doctor who lives God-knows-where?"

"No."

"Then, Miss Brook, so that we might ascertain whether you might've had an abortion, would you submit to an examination by a competent doctor?"

Tommy Burke hadn't expected this looper. He shook his head, praying that Romaine would see him.

"What doctor?" she asked.

"Why, yours."

"I don't have one."

"You don't have one? A woman your age?"

"I don't believe in them. Besides, I'm very healthy."

277

"A healthy enough liar, I'd agree," said Pritter, seeing Tommy's face contort as he fumbled out of his chair.

"All right, all right, counselor. I'll save you the trouble...statement withdrawn," Pritter said to him and to Rhodes. Sighing, he continued, "Then by a doctor appointed by the court, Miss Brook. How would that suit you?"

Romaine was perplexed. "I'm sorry—you know I wouldn't let just any doctor examine me!"

"We'll get the best in the city. I'll even ask the state of California to pay the bill."

"No, thank you."

"Why not?"

"It's against my religion."

"Oh?"

"I'm a Christian Scientist and we don't believe in it."

"I see. Where do you practice this religion of yours?"

"In private. My readings. I do them before I meditate."

"Meditate on how you're going to beat the—" Pritter halted. He knew Burke would collapse to his feet again if he continued along that line. "Never mind," he added.

"So that's thirteen times," Pritter went on, "we can't get to your side of things. An unlucky number." He looked up at Rhodes, complaining, "We've got a defendant, the last person to see Marc Sterne alive, therefore a prime witness, and she refuses to cooperate in a trial about murder, your honor. Yes, murder...will the court rule, kindly rule, taking notice of the logjam here, that the defendant must undergo a medical examination?"

"On what grounds?" Rhodes replied.

"To get to the truth about this purported abortion. Those are the best grounds I can think of."

"I'll take it under advisement."

Pritter argued harder, bullishly, his cheeks scarlet.

"I'll make a ruling after I check the law," Rhodes continued, "but I can tell you this: the defendant is not required to do or say anything that might tend to incriminate herself. The state brought the case and the state's now asking the questions. And it's up to the state to disprove any answers it doesn't like...that's well-settled law, as you surely know, counselor," Rhodes finished. He wasn't worried, though. He already knew it was medically impossible to tell whether a woman had ever gone through an abortion.

"She's evading," Pritter protested.

"If she really is, then it's up to you to find out what she's evading and why it's relevant to this trial."

"Can we bring in a minister to find out if she knows anything about the tenets of Christian Science?"

Rhodes knew his answer before Pritter was halfway through the question. "I'd have to check that point, too."

Like someone ready to spit, Pritter stood with his lips and chin twisting. He turned away from the bench. "Thirteen lashes," he said to the jury. "Thirteen lies flailing the unsuspecting heart of Justice." Whirling, he faced Burke. "Take her. She's worse than trying to nail a cloud to the wall. A modern Judas…" paying off Romaine with cold scorn, "No wonder that she won the Academy Award."

4:14. Rhodes recessed for the day.

ଓ

In chambers, Rhodes's own beating heart fought with his muddy conscience. No time to reconsider the risks now. He must do what he must do in exactly the right way. When facing the heat, she'd been superb. Yet Pritter had scored on her high, low, higher again. A pro in what was mostly a man's game, he had slammed away with everything he could muster. And Rhodes suspected some key points, as to Romaine's veracity had been stacked up with the jury.

Photos, abortions, a marriage?

What if Marc Sterne, tired of life, so burned out and drugged up, had taken his own life? That Romaine was being truthful, all along? That human scarecrow Burke was doing all right, not spectacular, but passable or better, still he kept missing opportunities to go for the jugular, opportunities that weren't an everyday thing by any means.

Pritter had two assistants; Burke none—a whopping difference right there.

Rhodes leaned backward, measuring, contemplating. He lit a cigar, shrouding his desk in blue smoke, thinking of Audrey. How livid she must be, and that thought led him into more barbed wire.

279

Tease fate again?

Go through with it as planned or almost planned? A gamble he must win, and a gamble he must make. Were Audrey ever to confess—tell anyone she was the mother and he the father—the lights in his world would extinguish for good. As he knew, as he had known ever since Audrey's stunning revelation. Audrey was now the greatest risk of any and all. If Romaine walked free, would Audrey someday reveal the truth of her parenthood, doing it out of out of spite or anger? That, if she went down, he would be dragged down with her— a Damocles Sword swinging over his head for all his life. Wishing now she was gone; not dead but gone to a very far place.

Rhodes wanted that jury badly. He had been devising subtle ways to influence them, if he could, when he could. Plenty of judges had been fixed before, but he was the only one doing any fixing now, and it was to himself.

Yet was that really so? He was charged with getting the truth out, all of it; wasn't that what he was doing?

He rang for Macklin. When she came in, he had her sit as he told her, "In the morning, stop by the Clerk's Office and tell her to hustle up a couple or researchers. Have 'em plow through the trial dockets for the past three years or so. Get copies of any that had any connection to narcotics charges taking place on or near Malibu Pointe. The dates, the circumstances, the parties involved. Convictions, too, if any."

"That it?"

"Get a count. How many instances? Shouldn't take more than an hour or so of computer searching."

"You want them sent here?"

"Yes, one copy here, then a copy each to Pritter and Burke. There was that big bust out there a couple years back. Names, you know. That cartel king from Columbia was named, I think…"

"Right, I'll be sure to have them check on that one."

When she left, he brooded for a time. Burke would have to be the klutz-head of the century, if failing to catch the clue.

It was before noon when the answer arrived from research: eight trials, three convictions. Two or three well-known names, one a neurosurgeon, another a baseball team owner, yet another who was the top honcho at a big-name record company. Enough, in all events, to suggest plenty of illicit action went on at Malibu Pointe. Who did the dealing?

Chapter Twenty-six

"Now if you'll please follow me," Tommy Burke suggested to the jurors. "Remember all those sheriff's reports? Perhaps they were accurate for once when telling us Marc Stone had his shirt open when they found him. Like mine was yesterday, when Miss Brook and I attempted to reenact the scene on that night he died. Marc had lunged at her, that's precisely what she told us. The syringe was still in his arm...the needle buried in his flesh. Just as this one was yesterday in my arm"—he held up the syringe, waving it back and forth—"and then in the scuffle, with Miss Brook trying to defend herself, the syringe perhaps gets caught up in one person's clothes. The prints might get obliterated if fabric is wiped against the syringe...Marc's prints?" Tommy pointed out. "Were they his prints? Listen to this..."

He read from the lab technician's reports, explaining briefly what loops, arches and whorls meant. "Those are those tiny lines and oval squiggles on the pads of everyone's fingers."

Romaine's fingerprints had shown up on the chrome grips of the syringe they had used the day before in their little skit before the jury. "Her forefinger and middle finger"—Tommy held his own up so the jury could see how her prints had impressed on the wings of the grips—"you see, like that. But then we scuffled a little, the way she did that night with Marc Sterne, and my shirt happened to wipe away most of her thumbprint from the plunger top. What was left was just the edge of her print. You remember, don't you, how she had her whole thumb down on the top when she squirted the blood back into my arm...and here's what else the lab came up with."

He read more, then looked up.

"Yesterday I wore a red and white striped shirt. I have it over there." He went over to his table, picked up his shirt and dangled it in front of the jury. "The same one. And in the lab report here, the part I just read you, they found red and white cotton fibers on the plunger top...so, you see, my shirt, when we scuffled, rubbed part of her thumbprint off. Just like that night with

282

Marc...but you see, it could've been Marc's print and only his print that was erased. But, on the other hand, what if it was someone else's. We've heard plenty of testimony that others could've been inside that huge Sterne house, unbeknownst to anyone else. Who knows who they might've been? Or perhaps it was no one else other than Marc Sterne himself. See how easy it is for the prosecution to get you thinking one way, even when they have no hard proof. But now you can see circumstances in a different light? That's what we mean by reasonable doubt..."

Jurors glanced sideways at one another.

"...the state says, Mr. Pritter over there, he says there had to be prints on the syringe that was used to kill Marc Sterne. But it really isn't so, is it? Oh, no, nothing about any of this is as cut and dried as Lloyd Pritter wants you to believe. I hope you follow me. He must prove and prove and prove, and he can't...see...reasonable doubt, that's the bar the state can't climb over..."

As Tommy moved away from the jury, Rhodes asked him to come up to the bench. Pritter as well. They discussed if either side had any more witnesses.

Tommy shook his head.

Pritter said he still wanted a medical examination of Romaine. Or at least a test of her knowledge of Christian Science. "It's all too pat," he grumbled.

Rhodes refused him. His court wasn't about to tangle itself in anyone's religious beliefs. Pritter ought to know better.

"I plan to take a crack at this new syringe," Pritter said. He looked at the small white box Tommy Burke was holding.

"Of course," said Rhodes. "After you do, can you keep right on with your closing arguments?"

"I certainly can," he said.

"No more witnesses then?" asked Rhodes of both, needing to know their plans so he could begin to put his own in motion.

Standing below the bench, facing Romaine, Pritter started in on her again. His deep voice bounced off the farthest walls. He was right where he wanted to be, center ring, where he could scorn Romaine and Tommy, and be most visible to the media.

They're quite a pair, aren't they?" asked Lloyd Pritter of the whole courtroom. "Don't see many like them. They just sit there and dig a hole we can all fall into. They're not interested in bruising justice...they want to massacre it. Allow me to show you."

He singled out how the charade they had witnessed yesterday was an insult to everyone's good sense. Burke had shown them a second syringe, claiming that in a scuffle most of Romaine's prints were smudged.

But not all of them were, were they? On the finger grips, part of one fingerprint was clearly identified. The lab report emphasized that fact.

Yet on the syringe found next to Marc Sterne's body, *all* the prints were missing. Where had they gone? Who stole them? "Romaine Brook, that's who," said Pritter, crashing his words against the ceiling. "There's no other logical explanation." Pritter argued, "you're being puppeted. They don't pull wool over your eyes. Instead, they use silk. The silk of deceit and of blatant trickery...who else could've done it? Some phantom or other? Her motive? Passionate jealous rage. Marc Sterne wanted nothing more to do with her...Romaine Brook is a sociopath. Someone who knows the difference between right and wrong, but doesn't care..."

When Tommy Burke's turn came to sum up, he confined his remarks to a narrow target. "The state's case is circumstantial," he insisted. "Romaine Brook was there that night and everyone knows it. But supposing one night I was in your neighborhood," he spoke directly to the brunette with the horn-rims, "and I was at your door, lost, trying to get directions. So I push the bell and your next-door neighbor sees me in the same way the gate guard saw Romaine Brook enter and then depart Malibu Pointe. Um...um...ah...there's no answer when I push your doorbell but why not? Because you're not at home, that's why. And certainly no answer comes from the burglar who is upstairs, busy robbing you...so I simply go away. You come home and find you've been robbed...I was there, yes. Yet no one knows exactly who robbed you. Still, I was seen on or near the premises. Am I the suspect? The robber? I took nothing. And Romaine Brook didn't take Marc Sterne's life either, and no one can prove to you that she did."

Tommy stopped. Limping across the room for more water, he knew he was an odd sight—his jerky movements like those of the Tin Man. Stammering. Yet he felt surer of himself. Stronger. After gulping from a glass of water laced with Gatorade, he smiled at Romaine, his Adam's apple jumping a full inch in that scrawny neck.

"You've heard her," he said as he turned to face the jury again. "Has Romaine Brook given you any reason to doubt her? Any at all? The

284

slightest? Yes, she was there while Marc Sterne hopped himself up. And because no fingerprints were found on the syringe, the state wants you to think she killed him with narcotics. We've been all through it, haven't we? The state's case doesn't hang together, any more than a falsified allegation I was the one who supposedly robbed your house," he said once more, aiming directly on Miss Horn Rims. "What we have, in the end, is Mr. Pritter's antics and obfuscations against *her* word. That's it, nothing else. Not a thing except for hot, hot air…

"Ladies, gentlemen," he said, "the Romaine Brook you're looking at is an intelligent woman. An acclaimed actress, a very warm and loving person...does anyone here really think she'd go through the Malibu Pointe gates, sign in and out, in an attempt to kill the man she planned to spend her life with? That's the only question you need to ask yourselves…and then he pounded in his last nail into the memory of Marc Sterne, using the anonymously provided outcomes of other drug-related crimes levied against Malibu Pointe residents. "They answered for what they did and he might've been next on the list, but let us not make Romaine Brook pay for his wanton behavior."

Above all, he reemphasized the catechism of *reasonable doubt.* That handy tool of the law giving everyone a hook to hang their vote on while feeling they had just gotten the inside word from Moses or God Himself.

He engraved it so deftly that for the rest of their lives the jurors would never see black and white again in the same way as before. They needn't soak their consciences, he told them, in the elixir of purest justice, for it didn't exist except in one's flowery dreams.

"I thank you… and know you'll do the right thing by acquitting her. She's been through enough…and…well, so have you." And then he sat, finished, utterly drained.

○

In his chambers, Rhodes mulled.

Should he do it, or should he let events travel their course without any interference. Burke had been persuasive, but persuasive enough? If the jury went against her, would she ever find the resources to mount an appeal?

Cost a million dollars, maybe more. He'd put up the money himself, but that was obviously impossible. Hell, he could resign the bench and defend her for free. Yet another impossibility.

What was missing? Had he been defending her, what would he have done that hadn't already been done?

If Marc Sterne hid narcotics at his apartment, as Fahey had assured him, and Romaine had been truthful in her statements about all the drug dealing, then the jury, if they were to inspect the scene, first-hand, might well be persuaded other of her statements could be depended upon.

Something big, something crucial, something that was the first cousin to reasonable doubt.

Chapter Twenty-seven

"Whatever...what're you saying?" Tommy Burke exploded into the phone.

"Ease it down, boyo. You're stinging my ear. Bad for hearing the opera."

"You found what?"

"Bags of little white emeralds...one hefty one for ol' Marco he'll never get a sniff of. Two more, and one of those for that old skirt-chaser Kardas."

"When d'you find it?"

Fahey told him.

"God, Alonzo. Oh, my God! The jury's out, they're deliberating right now...why didn't you tell me?"

"Listen, if Cullis hadn't been there, I'd have lammed off with the stuff myself. Financed the opera and the regiment, both. I was sorely tempted."

"What a stupid shithead you are."

"Tut-tut"

"It could have meant everything."

"Not too late, is it? Tell old Cliff-boy what's up. He's very imaginative sometimes. Not in the Fahey's league, but he can rise to surprising heights if you blow the right bugle."

"How can I go to him? Now? Oh, God!"

"Lace up those storm trooper's kickers you wear and be off. Be sure to tell him Fahey wants a medal."

"Oh, shuddup, Alonzo. Let me think..."

"Time is wasting, lad."

"Why the—oh, hell!—why'd you sit on this? Why did the sheriff? Cullis, he's one of theirs."

"Yes, and it's the sheriff who *is* sitting on it. Know all about it, they do."

"For how long?"

"A few days. Let's see—"

"If Romaine gets convicted because this was never known—"

"She might if you don't saddle your goofy ass up and move fast. I've got errands for the Almighty today. Bye."

Tommy punched the numbers three times before getting them right. He asked to be put through to Judge Rhodes. A God-sent thing had happened. The record could now show it was Burke who had opened the door, letting more light in on the trial.

Minutes later, Rhodes sent a message by bailiff to the jury. They were to suspend their deliberations, pending a new development.

It had worked. Fahey had connected, thought Rhodes. Would the jury bite?

☙

An hour later, Rhodes heard from both attorneys in his chambers, "Call it my mistake, Lloyd," he was saying, and I certainly want to rectify it, if it is a mistake. I wasn't sure that finding supplies of cocaine meant as much as it now seems to. In fact, I didn't know any supplies existed that belonged to Marc Sterne. Apparently, the sheriff knew or knows now. If they've been withholding evidence, and you knew anything about it, then you're all in some hell of a fix. Flat out, Brook would win on appeal, and you surely know it."

"The sheriff never said anything to me," Pritter replied.

Tommy said, "You accused my client of lying, when she told us that Sterne was a dealer."

"Narcotics aren't at the heart of this trial," Pritter replied hotly, evasively. "Marc Sterne, he's not on trial here. She is."

"Oh, no!" Tommy said. "Narcotics are all over the trial. That's what killed him, for God's sake."

"You can't reopen now," Pritter argued with Rhodes. "The jury's reaching a verdict—"

"No, they're not, Lloyd. I suspended—"

"You what!" With effort, Pritter heaved himself off the couch. "How can you do that? They'll be confused as all hell."

"We may have to reopen," Rhodes suggested.

"But then—you see what you're doing? You're tainting the record," Pritter said.

"What's better, Lloyd, a tainted record or an incomplete one that could lead to a faulty conviction?"

"Please, Judge Rhodes...you gotta, Judge," Tommy urged. "Romaine's whole life is on the line here."

"That's why we're meeting. I think it's got to come in, don't you, Lloyd? Really? Mr. Burke here has a strong point. You've accused Miss Brook of wholesale deception and serial lies. Maybe she isn't lying. If there's evidence that confirms she's been telling us the truth, then the jury has the right to know..."

Rubbing the back of his neck, Pritter seemed to swell up like a balloon about to burst. "Where's the precedent for this sort of nonsense and—"

"Here's one," Rhodes said. He opened a book, finding a place he'd marked a week earlier. "I looked it up after Burke called me. The Sassounian trial before Judge Richard I. Nelson,"—and he read the relevant case history—then added, "Seems they reopened the trial twice. It was a murder-one trial, Lloyd."

Pritter exhaled audibly.

"Look, Mr. Pritter," said Tommy. "If the jury goes against us, we have to appeal. For that reason alone, this evidence will come out at that time. You can't possibly keep it out."

"The Appeals Court might not even consider it," Pritter said.

"They'd almost have to, Lloyd," Rhodes offered.

"Appeal why don't you, and we'll find out."

"In the end, maybe an appeal will be necessary," Rhodes said. "But we'll complete the record at this level first."

Pritter countered, "Even if Marc Sterne was a dealer, and I'm not agreeing he was, how does that change anything?"

"If Sterne wasn't a dealer, why did he have a one-kilo bag of white with his name on it? Kardas did, as well. Smaller, but there with Marc Sterne's just the same. If your theory of a murder is anything but a theory, then how do we really know if the right person is on trial? We've got other motives in play now. Get real!"

Rhodes looked at Burke, who looked at Pritter.

And is Audrey in it, too—thought Rhodes. Can't be, can it?

Chapter Twenty-eight

A pagan moon glowed upon the night. Breezes swished the tree-leaves, separating them so that streaks of an odd orange-ish light shone through.

A night for the Druids to be dancing among their standing stones. Fahey loved it, captivated by the night, captivated by his discovery of the stash, and with a regular platoon of scandal-seekers on their way to gander at the scene, which might spring Romaine Brook form the clutches of the law. A night for new things, newer revelations, and he wished the Gypsy were at his side to patiently, successfully guide him. He felt in need of an African goatskin drum to tap out some sinister beats. Wiggle the spine of this night. His own was wiggling, as it was, and it would wiggle almost beyond his belief, later on.

He had arrived shortly after Cullis, who had come with two of his superiors by the look of them. Together, they watched as the bewildered jurors filed though the door into Sterne's apartment, with Burke, Pritter, then Rhodes following. Barely able to contain his eagerness, Fahey begged for a comet to blaze across the sky, a dazzling signal, and if it appeared, he'd name it after the Gypsy.

Alesia Noor lurked in the shadows of the entry door. She had raised up on tiptoes to see better.

Fahey sported his walking stick. Edging his way around the room, he chatted idly with the nurse who wore the horn-rims. Learning of her profession, Fahey suddenly complained of a bad back. "From alcoholic abstinence. Most likely you could aid me," he murmured. "Front and back, hard rubbing. After dinner. Know just the place for us. Best couscous in town."

She sniggered pleasantly, letting her hip jostle his.

Rhodes quieted the room, telling the jurors why they'd been summoned from their deliberations. They would, he said, certainly recall how the defendant's credibility had been challenged on the stand. Many of her statements, as the prosecution had stated, couldn't be proven, one way or another. Yet, throughout, the state had insisted Romaine Burke was lying. Here was possible evidence she had been truthful. That the jury, if they so chose, could weigh this evidence when deliberating.

With speculating minds, the jury looked around, some of them dumb-eyed at the lavender-hued walls. Rhodes spoke again. "The sheriff here will show us what was found recently...I was told about it, several days ago, but I wasn't sure the evidence fit in with this trial. I didn't want you, who're the real judges here, to be prejudiced. But then I felt it only fair to change my mind and let you see for yourselves."

"But why?" asked one juror.

"As I said, the defendant's truthfulness is at stake. That's an issue the state put right square in front of you. The state asked the defendant for proof she wasn't lying to us...perhaps we have it now. Or some proof, at least. You'll have to consider everything."

This was the first time in months the jurors had been in a home. They were eager to see why they'd been called out, and to feel their way around in a world they had, in some part, forgotten.

Fahey stood in the back, still at the side of the brunette with the horn-rims. Just over his breath, he conveyed how this night was so right for a moon bath. Had she ever partaken? After the couscous dinner, he knew of a place—a spa—high in the Hollywood hills.

When Rhodes shot him a look, Fahey moved off.

Cullis and one of the other sheriffs wrestled the couch away from the wall. They shoved the sections to one side so everyone could easily view the baseboard.

With a screwdriver in his hand, kneeling, Cullis pried out the wall plates. The jurors, all but one of them, strained forward. Cullis's two superiors, a few feet behind him, watched intently as first one metal drawer, then the other, were pulled out.

"It's gone," Cullis said, straightening up. "Was here, I swear I saw it, but it's traveled off somewhere."

Fahey roared with laughter. He stepped forward, moving through the jurors, who parted to make way. "Now, how could that be? Trying to fund your new haberdashery store, is that it?

"You know something we aren't privy to?" Cullis asked Fahey.

"Lot of things, Admiral."

"You were here, weren't you, with Lieutenant Cullis?" asked one of Cullis's superiors of Fahey.

"I most surely was."

"Where're those bags?"

"Beats me. You boys come back and get them, did you? Probably out on the street by now. What about a decent split? A finder's fee."

"Listen, Fahey, you're on a real quick skid here—"

"I'll take care of this, sheriff," said Rhodes barging through the circle of jurors. He asked the officer to step aside, then asked Fahey, "You know anything at all about this?"

"Just that it was here. Cullis saw it, too."

"That's it?"

"All of it I know about."

Rhodes inhaled a woeful breath. His ace in the hole was still stuck somewhere up his sleeve, and he'd wagered plenty on this one. Turning to Cullis, he asked: "What about it, lieutenant? You have any thoughts or guesses?"

"No, sir."

"Okay then, tell the jury in detail what you found here with Mr. Fahey."

Cullis went through the whole finding, step by step. Of how he was there twice with Fahey by request of the defense. What they'd seen on the most recent visit, and how they'd left it. "All written down on a confidential report down at the station," ending his dissertation.

The jurors wore mixed expressions. Pritter leaned back against the iron railing near the steps down to the living room, relishing the despair on Tommy Burke's face.

Fahey searched the room for Alesia Noor. She looked as baffled as everyone there, while standing near Pritter, plucking nervously at her ivory hair combs.

Fahey hadn't seen Cullis work his way into the group of jurors, but he immediately sensed the brunette melting away.

"You sure got yourself a fat mouth, don't you?"

"You should hear my lungs, Cullis. Really, you should. Going to sing the lead soon in Madame Butterfly...might even offer you a discount ticket, old sod..."

"Goin' to sing you something, too. You're comin' down to the station, buddy-boy."

"Next month maybe…listen," Fahey lowered his voice, "you'd better get onto the Noor woman. She might know something. Her name was tagged to one of the bags, remember."

"I will." Cullis motioned to Alesia Noor, calling her over. Rhodes, standing near the jurors, threw a glance at Tommy Burke, who looked away.

"You been in this apartment since I was here last?" Cullis asked her.

"Never."

"Where'd you get that bruise on your neck there?'

"Cleaning up, mopping. I slip."

"Anyone else been here?"

"That man." She pointed at Fahey.

"No one else?"

"You tell me apartment is sealed up. No one come here," she said. "Him, he come."

"I know about Fahey. He was here with me."

Narrowing his eyes, Fahey attempted to warn her. He even tried a smile, the sort made only for a first meeting with God.

"But he come other time, when you not come."

"When was that?" Cullis asked Fahey.

Fahey explained how he had come back to pick up his misplaced notebook, having mistakenly left it there when visiting the apartment for the first time with Cullis. Only for a few minutes. It had been latish, he needed his notebook, and Cullis had already gone off duty. The jurors moved a little closer to Cullis, as if taking sides, as Fahey told the room: "Needed my notes, had to advise Mister Burke."

"Why did you let him in?" Cullis demanded of Alesia Noor. "You were told not to allow anyone to—"

"But he with you," she protested.

"With me? No, I'm a sheriff—"

"But he show me the…hees-a badge."

Cullis looked at Fahey. "What badge?"

"Nothing," Fahey said. A gift from the wife, as I remember."

"You been impersonatin' a law officer?"

Alesia Noor moved forward. Still furious that Kardas had taken her share of the cocaine, she was determined to take a swipe at anyone. "He show me. He have it in hees-a wallet." She patted her rump in a gesture of where she had seen Fahey remove his wallet.

293

The situation was one spark away from exploding, and Rhodes feared it would as he saw Cullis and the two other sheriffs leaning all over Fahey, finally forcing him to display the honorary badge, embossed with a bogus number by his jeweler friend.

"A technicality," claimed Fahey, who glanced at Rhodes, adding, "Isn't that right, Judge?"

"Not exactly," Rhodes answered. "But the main thing is that you and Cullis found the drugs here a few days ago."

"We did," Cullis agreed. "But Fahey shouldn'ta come back here without an escort. That's a violation."

Alesia Noor sidled around to Cullis. "That man no good"—again she pointed at Fahey—"he come here and stay a long time. I find him there by that wall. He dropping something there. He say you come later. But you never come."

Cullis's mind blazed. Dropped something? The table knife that was behind the couch when they both had returned the second time?

"You told her I would be here?" he asked Fahey.

"Was trying to reach you—"

"Cat crap. You're coming with me, Fahey. We're about to have a long, long talk."

Before Fahey could protest, get his quick brain and quicker mouth in action, Rhodes stopped him.

"We'll sort this out later," he said. Turning to the sheriff, he asked, "You're going to make a report on this?"

"It's a must," was the reply.

"You have another report? From when Lieutenant Cullis and Mr. Fahey found the drugs?" Rhodes asked.

The sheriff nodded.

"Have copies of both in my court tomorrow morning by nine o'clock."

"Including one on Fahey for breaking and entering?" asked the sheriff. "And tampering with evidence? Impersonating a law officer? I can think of three or four more and I haven't even started."

"Whatever you think best. But if you intend filing charges, don't bring them to my court."

"But you'll be a witness to Fahey's violations?"

"Now wait a goddamn minute everyone," Fahey interrupted, his voice storming. "You're getting this all wrong." A flush crept up his ruddy face filled now with ferocity. He rapped on Cullis's shoulder with the ebony, Gypsy-blessed walking stick. "Noor knows more than she's letting on...she says she saw me here. She could've come back and looked and found everything. All the goods. And you, Cullis, you saw that bag with Kardas's name on it. What about him? You and I phoned in all the findings, so there'll be a record, a recording. Burn it up, did you? "

"At the station, Fahey," Cullis retorted. "We're gonna spend some time near the floor on all of this."

"With your arse going down first."

"Want to try on the cuffs? Here they are, fat-mouth." Cullis pulled out his handcuffs, but Rhodes intervened with a few temperate remarks. Still, an untidy, touch-and-go situation and Rhodes dampened it, then asked that the jury be escorted to their van, before they saw more of this awkward, perplexing turn of events.

CR

Outside, Rhodes walked up the sloping street of the cul-de-sac. Fahey, panting, caught up with him. "What're you going to do?" he demanded.

"Finish up this trial, if I ever can."

"About your friend Fahey, that's what I meant."

"I'll have a talk with the sheriff."

"You got me into this. Get me out."

"Later."

"Now, Cliff, right now. What if they charge me, and pull my license? Christ, man! It'd be the graveyard, the one with no crosses."

"Lower your voice, dammit, and move off."

"Son of a bitch!" Fahey cursed, pounding the pavement several times with his stick. The sounds echoed like pistol shots. "You're all the son of a bitch there ever was, ever."

Rhodes walked ahead. His shoulders pulled forward as he made the climb to the next street. The moon had begun to change its arc, the light shallower, as the night slipped into its own shadows. He thought he heard Cullis calling to the enraged, wounded Fahey. But so had Romaine been dealt her wounds, and she was all he cared about at present. The trial was costing too much in human payment. Audrey. Now Fahey. Even himself, and his wayward conscience. And, he suspected, all the losses had yet to be tallied.

Trudging up the road to where he'd parked the Bentley, Rhodes was working his brain at flank speed. He had come here to sell the jury on one idea: that if drugs were linked to Marc Sterne, then Romaine was worth believing; besides, her testimony about Marc Sterne's involvement with drugs and drug trafficking, there was the porous testimony of Audrey, the botched investigations of the sheriff and the state investigators. Other flaws, other cross-ups, other contradictions. Burke ought to be ecstatic, ought to be on a flight to Jupiter or somewhere as exotic.

Still, key and possibly persuasive evidence for the defense had gone missing. How, though? By whom?

Rhodes was anxious about the media. What would they have to say about pulling the jury out of its deliberations? The next morning, he found out—the papers called it judicial stunt. Courtroom quackery, said one account. Another blatantly stated: "Possible wrongdoing…"

Chapter Twenty-nine

The trial had re-convened

Burke and Pritter jousted over the value and relevance of the missing evidence. Burke won out. He used the copy of the sheriff's report that Cullis had filed, confirming the presence of the heroin bags concealed at the apartment. "Obviously they're missing, but that was another matter for another day. My client said Marc Sterne was a dealer, and so he was...do we need anything more...hasn't she been telling you the truth all along...?

On he went, the law's newest gladiator, a force-field on the loose pounding away as he drove his arguments deep and deeper.

For almost three full days, the jury deliberated. On the afternoon of the third day, the foreman polled jurors for the second time.

Then, a collective sigh of satisfaction. It was finally done with...no more squabbling, no more tantrums, no more lover's spats that began at the Biltmore and ended up in unsaid rages that bore, in their very defined way, on other person's lives. Twelve people, along with two alternates, had met and met again and yet again to decide. Yet how could they decide anything, when cooped up for months seeming like years.

They wanted one thing: *to get out, go home*. War was over. Peace was sought.

The foreman finished marking a document, checked several boxes, penned a long sentence at the bottom, then signed her name. The jury had pronounced its finding. Across the table, looks were exchanged, a few nods. Chairs scraped—the sound of metal legs against a wooden floor—and, one by one, a file of humans passed through a door for their final time.

In the courtroom, the foreman glanced at the clock: 4:23.

The foreman handed the folded form to a bailiff, who gave it up to Rhodes. He read it as if he were seeing his own life exposed, then passed the paper down to the court clerk who stood inspecting the press and hundreds of intent faces behind the press.

"...find the defendant not guilty," was all anyone seemed to hear amidst the tumultuous shouts.

Joy crowded Rhodes's throat. But he was exhausted and somehow it seemed to him he'd been standing in one exact same spot for the past year. His eyes shifted to his daughter as she hugged Tommy Burke, tears streaming down her face; tears wet and heavy and yet somehow seeming as golden as her hair.

Burke whipped out a long arm to fend off some reporters pushing in, clamoring until the commotion rose to total chaos. Other reporters, their questions set on rapid-fire, peppered away at the jurors.

People thronged around Romaine, Rhodes saw, and he supposed that's how it must be at a splashy film opening. He stopped for only a moment, watching a rank of bailiffs surround Romaine and Tommy. The human ring began to move, creating its own channel among the throng of well-wishers and shouters.

Rhodes thought: now she's in a human cage that may prove more alarming than the one with the iron bars.

In the corridor, lights were set up for two portable video cameras. Pritter stood before an interviewer from the local NBC station, his eyes about as friendly as two gun muzzles.

"...And what did you think of your opponent?"

"Which one? If you mean Burke, I can't really say," Pritter told the interviewer. "He has a pretty good mouth game, but you have to listen closely."

What're your feelings about the trial?"

"We lost. She got away with it. That happens, unfortunately."

"How about the jury?"

"Ask them."

"Care to comment about Judge Rhodes's handling of the trial?"

Pritter bristled. "He was a pretty swift lawyer before he came to the court...he's done some odd things here. So odd that I'd have to call it a screw-up. I'll be entering a complaint soon."

"About what?"

"You'll see." He moved then, all two-hundred and forty-six pounds at once, like half of a bull let loose. "I've got to shove off."

"One more question, just one." A burly reporter tagged along, furiously waving the cameraman back so the shot would still show both Pritter and himself in frame.

"Will the state open an investigation against Mrs. Sterne or Kardas?"

Pritter stopped, merely shaking his head. "No comment. No, hold on. I can sum it up for you in two words: *stay tuned.*"

Off he went. What good did it do to yell about the outcome? It was over, but then it would never be over, not for some. Lives had been torn up. Who would mend them?

Pritter wouldn't. He meant to get to his office and find the nearest hatchet. He would offer himself as an unnamed source to two well-known reporters he was friendly with; he had things to tell them. Things they could use for lurid news accounts, the kind they liked best.

◌

In an anteroom screened off by two bailiffs standing guard outside its door, Romaine sat across from Tommy Burke. She practically pranced with uncontainable exuberance. She was up on her feet one moment, then sitting next to him moments later, alive and eager and he had her all to himself.

Outside, reporters had gathered, ready to open up with a fresh barrage of questions. Bashful around any spotlight, Tommy didn't cherish the prospect of mixing it up with them. Besides, he'd fought with everything he had in him for this moment, and didn't plan to share it with any outsiders.

"You do all the talking, Tommy. You got me out of this hell."

He grinned crookedly. "It's you, they'll be after."

"You do it," she countered. "I hate those people."

"You're the big news."

"Oh, Tommy!" she burst out. "Isn't it glorious...and I owe you everything. Everything! That reminds me. I can't pay your bill for a while. But I'll do it soon as I get work again."

"There're just the expenses. A few thousand. But there's no bill for me."

"Oh, yes there is."

"Nope. I did something I never thought I could do"—though a flicker of doubt swept his face—"and you made that possible. I'll get all sorts of cases after this."

"I'm paying. You'll have to let me pay."

"We'll talk about it some other time."

"You just remember everything, Tommy. Add it all up."

"Sure." Saying it absently, more interested in something else. "Can you have dinner with me tonight? At my mother's? Or we'll find some quiet spot."

"I couldn't."

"You have to eat. Something to celebrate on after all the prison food."

"I can't, Tommy. My agent, Max Shapin, is picking me up. He's out there somewhere...and I have to be alone for a while."

"Tomorrow then. Take the day off, and we'll go somewhere."

Her hair danced around her shoulders, "No, Tommy. I'm sorry. You've been the biggest saint, but I'm putting all this shit behind me. Everything and everyone."

"Me?"

"Everyone. I've got to get myself cooled out."

Elation instantly was swallowed up by misery. "I thought maybe we could be friends. We could have a laugh with Fahey. He can be fun."

"I don't like him at all. He's a destroyer."

"He's quite funny, actually."

"You're so naive, Tommy. So sweet but terribly naive."

"Yes, maybe. But let's do something. We can go up to San Francisco next week."

"You don't get it, do you?"

"About what?" he said.

"Nothing, oh, nothing at all. Let's go play fuck-ball with the press, Tommy, and get that over with," she said, standing up. "I've got places to get to."

"Without me, you mean?"

"You'll be okay. But it's better if you stay away from me." An insolent smile rocketed up to shrill laughter, bounding from one wall to the other. "I'm free," she cried. "Eight months, Tommy, that's how long I've been behind that fucking iron gate. We beat them!"

"I know," he said, recoiling inwardly at her language.

"You could never know. My mind, Tommy, it's all blued out. I have to—"

"I want to help."

"You did, and so marvelously."

"I'll help more."

"I need someone different, Tommy."

"I could be—could try to be—"

"You never could be, not for me."

"Try me, Romaine."

"I have."

"Romaine?"

"Yes."

'The press is going to ask you a raft of things."

"I suppose they will. But who cares. We won, Tommy."

"There are some matters you testified to that you never told me about. Marrying Marc and the abortion, to name two."

"So?"

"Why didn't you let me know?"

"Oh, Tommy, there are some things you can't tell anyone. Not ever, unless they force you to." She smiled radiantly.

"But you did tell. You told the whole courtroom."

"I had to see how things were going first."

He waited before asking, "You didn't trust me to handle it for you. Is that it, Romaine?"

She looked down at her feet. Then her head came up with a face replete with rapture. "Tommy, trusting other people has cost me everything I ever had. I trust only myself. "

"You told the truth, didn't you?"

"No one will ever *catch* me lying, Tommy. The truth is bigger than all of life with me. I have to go. My agent's waiting. We'll catch up one day. Somehow. Bye Tommy. Have a good life and I'll pay you soon as I can."

As the door closed behind her, it seemed to him as if his heart had stopped beating. She would have to fight her way through the reporters, and he didn't have it in him to join her. He wondered if his knees would ever stop swelling. Or his heart. Nothing fit right, not at that moment, especially those yearning hopes he had nursed for so many weeks now. Most dreams, daydreams especially, are made of fluff; and he knew he'd live with the fluff of Romaine Brook for the rest of his days.

He would've given anything, anything at all to have Romaine for even a week; indeed, he had already given her his all but was yet to realize it, and was yet to clear his vision of who she really was. He had had his moment in the sun, had hit for the winning run in the bottom of the ninth...and all he stood to get from it was the fleeting applause and cheering heard by everyone but himself.

Chapter Thirty

Rhodes was writing a letter at his library desk, when the phone rang. Moments later, Consuelo came in just as he was sealing the envelope.

"The señora," she said, sounding cheerful, for he was home with regularity now and she could fuss over him, and say womanly things that were really her subtle instructions, yet he could not think of them that way.

"Which señora? Put this with the other mail, please." Handing over the letter.

Consuelo told him which señora, and he squinted for a few seconds. "How're you, Audrey?" he said into the phone.

"How the hell do you think I am?"

He said nothing.

"Are you there?"

"Right here."

"Well, you really did it at your ef-fing trial…"

It's over, Audrey."

"Hell, if it is."

"You'll be all right."

"Says you! The sheriff's been out here asking more questions…" and she burned his ear with how her life was still in torment. And Kardas had disappeared, making matters worse. Her newest persecutors want to know where he was, and, when saying she didn't know, they threatened her with obstruction of justice.

"I'd guess they'll go after him," Rhodes said.

"And me?"

"Any good lawyer can handle your end."

"I despise lawyers."

"Don't despise them too much. At least, for the next few months."

"And you should be ashamed of what you let them do to me in your court," Audrey said.

"I wouldn't have stopped that, Audrey, even if I could. Which I couldn't."

"Thanks millions. And now she's off scot-free."

"She is, isn't she?"

"A disaster. You mark my words, Cliff Rhodes. You let her go and—"

"If anyone let her go, it was the jury. That's how it still works...and I'm a little busy right now, Audrey."

"I've something to tell you, though I don't know why I should."

"Shoot." He changed the phone to his other ear.

"I'm not taking any more chances, Cliff."

"On what?"

"I want those adoption papers back, and I'm going to get them."

"That'd be a mistake, Audrey. Just leave things be."

"No, it isn't. What if other people were to find out?"

"Leave it alone, Audrey. And why tell me anyway?"

"Because I don't know if you're planning to tell that girl who her parents—"

"I haven't decided anything yet."

"I know you and—"

"Here's some free lawyerly advice. Stay out of it, or you're likely to find cleat marks all over your—"

"I'll do the worrying about me, Cliff."

"Suit yourself. But I'm warning you, Audrey, those papers could turn out to be a blowtorch for everyone."

A click, then the phone died ominously.

◌◈

Next day, Rhodes's mood had brightened, his worries easing. Having a good healthy attack of happiness, as he thought of it, when he heard tires flying the gravel off his driveway. He'd been loading a couple of bags into the Bentley.

Fahey got out of his Buick convertible, walked up to the garage. Unshaven, his black beret tilted over bloodshot eyes, he stopped a few feet away. "Off to somewhere?" he asked.

Rhodes told him.

"I'm not invited?"

"Not on this one. Fritzi wants to get away. Hardly seen her for a month." Rhodes could smell Fahey's whiskey-heavy breath.

"But you saw some of me, didn't you? On the run, aren't you, when my ass is on the cooker?"

"Take any guestroom upstairs. Sleep it off—"

"You got me into this, old cock, now help get me out. You know what those chummers will do? Suspend my license, that's what. Even got a preliminary hearing set up."

"I'll try to figure something out, Alonzo."

"Do it one better than *try*."

"Meaning?"

Suddenly, Fahey went a shade darker under the black stubble on his face. "Tell them what came down. What really happened. Don't ask me to fall on the sword for you. You're standing on my feet, man, and you've got to do something. Savvy?"

"I can't get into it. Not straight out, I can't. You know that."

"Then, boyo, I will. This is friend Fahey you're calling upon to cover your bloody ass—"

"Alonzo, I've got to go. We'll talk about it after I have a chance to think. I promise you I'll take care of it for you. We've got to let things calm down."

Fahey stepped closer. "Cullis is frying me. They're gonna pull on me, Cliff. Know how that feels?"

"I think so."

"Do you, now? And supposing they find out all Fahey knows? You'll not be getting the Good Housekeeping Award."

"Don't force me to deny it, Alonzo. I'd have to, you know."

"What a sweet one you are. You used to be a fighter—"

"I said I'll think of something." Said curtly, said with a finality.

"That's not good enough, laddie-boy. Not by fucking half, it isn't…"

Rhodes bent over to load the last bag. Looking up again, he met Fahey's sullen face, those luminous eyes, slits, as dangerous as stars about to explode.

"A black one, you are. Black as a bloody coal digger's ass."

"Keep your nerve. We'll get by it. Sorry to run off, but I'm late to pick up Fritzi."

His face contorted, Fahey roared, "You need a reference sometime? Have 'em call me. I'll give you a reference, you grubby bastard—"

305

How could he ever tell Fahey the wholeness of the story? About Romaine? Or Audrey? Of why he'd done what he had done; that he had been trying to protect his own daughter. Fahey, the unintended casualty, but Fahey had himself to blame, in part, when using bogus law enforcement credentials and then entering an off-limits site without permission. Police became abruptly peeved over deeds of that ilk. Getting them to overlook it would take tricky mouth-work. The media, already criticizing his decision to have the jury visit Marc Sterne's apartment, would go into frenzy if ever learning he, as the sitting judge, had had a hand in bringing Fahey into the case.

If ever forced to explain himself, he could only say he had been honoring a request of Raye Wheeler, the lead lawyer for the defense and a man on his deathbed. Rhodes, so far, had not lifted so much as an ounce of help on the state's behalf; the aid, for whatever it was worth, had been completely one-sided.

Hardly impartial, but then neither was blood. Neither was love, and neither were war, politics, religion or much of anything else. Impartiality was an ideal reserved for those yet to be born.

The media had been sharpening their razors on his hide, as if he were an old-fashioned leather strop. They'd been hounding him ever since he had represented a rich Argentinian leftist accused of gunning down two reporters of the *Los Angeles Times*. The man, though fully guilty, was freed when Rhodes got him off on a technicality.

Thinking about it, his innards tightened. More slashing was bound to come from the media.

About to back the car down the driveway, he glanced at Fahey: still very present, still very rancorous, vigorously fisting the Bentley's hood. Whiskey-defiant, shouting curses. Spittle bubbling at the corners of his mouth; his forehead beaded with a sheen of wetness; eyes war-like, still so enraged he was kicking gravel against the Bentley's front fenders.

Time to get out of here, and he did.

Chapter Thirty-one

After dinner at the Montecito Lodge, they had repaired to the terrace for music and dancing. She had had him to herself for four days running, and tonight, as they had listened to the slow beats of the orchestra, danced, had drinks, she was in bloom. Gay, laughing, affectionate, huggy.

They were out on the floor, dancing again.

Fritzi glided along in a mellow haze. She pressed her tilted cheek against the silk of Rhodes's soft white jacket.

I've been thinking," she said, when the music trailed off. "I don't ever want to quit this place."

"Open up another Masquers, you mean?"

"I meant just stay a little lost and crazy here for a while, like you made me so crazy this afternoon."

"Lucky we didn't get thrown out," Rhodes said. They'd made love for the first time in over a month.

"Any old time," Fritzi hummed.

"There's the other thing." Holding her closer, his arm pressing hard against her lower back. "We could do it, Fritzi, if you really want to." He'd never said it before, not to anyone, and the words tumbled out slowly.

"Do what? More sex? Let's go, let's just get lost for a while."

"I was thinking of something else, actually."

"Such as?"

"Marry."

She stopped, dead still. Her arms dropped to her sides, as if she had lost control of them.

"Marry?" she said. "You mean—" Fritzi didn't finish. She gripped him around the neck with both arms. Her weight hung on him until he felt his neck start to give out. "Cliff, darling Cliff, I'll make you love marriage. You'll see..."

"I'm seeing right now. But I'm about to black out."

He kissed her as she stood up straight, easing her weight away. A long kiss and they were deafened to the music floating on the night,

'When?" Fritzi asked as they returned to their table. "Oh, Cliff!"

"A month or so. After they confirm me." He held her hands.

"Are you going to have any trouble? The newspapers and all that?

Rhodes tugged. "Shouldn't think so. Why?"

"I don't know. The publicity...ragging you again." Fritzi said, almost raving to herself. "They're getting the best in the world. A supreme for the Supreme." She suddenly went serious. "My God, there's so much to work out, isn't there?"

"I'll say."

"We'll have the best life together. We'll be the talk, Cliff, you wait and see."

He grinned. "I don't have to. We're the talk right here in case you want to look over your shoulder."

"I love you. Forever, I love you," said Fritzi, waving excitedly and cheerfully at two couples sharing a nearby table.

ଔ

Back in their casita, Rhodes had poured himself a José Cuervo. He was sitting on the edge of the bed, feasting on Fritzi's deep breasts, rounded belly, the smooth flanks and wide hips and thighs; a born breeder, he thought. He sipped, smiled at her, and said, "I have to ask you something. A favor."

"Anything. Name it." Fritzi sat up.

He asked if Romaine could stay with her for a week or two until things settled down and some sort of a life could be planned for the girl. Get her out of the public eye, away from all the glare.

Explaining himself, then, saying though he was not obligated in any real sense, he had found out Romaine Brook was the blood daughter of someone he knew very well. A random coincidence. He had become aware of the situation halfway through the trial. The parents, her real parents, want to see that she's helped"—how weak, he was thinking—"and I said I'd see what I could do." Knowing he was being evasive, Rhodes was playing directly to Fritzi's generous nature.

308

"They can't help or they won't help?"

"Can't admit they're the parents, no."

"Well, well—"

"I'd put her up myself," said Rhodes, but that wouldn't go over at all."

Fritzi gave him a look. "I agree...sure, she can stay for a while. Be a little strange, I'll say that."

"Strange, how?"

"Taking in a murderess. Imagine?"

"But she's not. She was let go."

"That won't make much difference to some people," Fritzi offered.

"A jury's a jury," he said, though knowing she was right.

"I guess so...anyway doesn't she have any friends she can stay with?" asked Fritzi, having second thoughts.

"Probably does, sweetheart. But maybe she needs time to adjust. She's been a prisoner for months, you know."

"Who're the parents anyway?"

"I'm sworn on that, darling. I'm sorry, but I can't tell you."

"Not even me?"

"No one. I can't."

"Important people? With names?"

"Yes."

"I'll be damned." Though whetted by curiosity, Fritzi sighed wistfully,.

"They couldn't have been more astonished. Or helpless, as it turned out."

"Do I know them?"

"I'm pretty sure you do and that's all I can really say about it."

"I hope she doesn't expect to entertain or be entertained or anything. At my house, I mean."

"I'm sure she doesn't, and I don't know if she'd even stay or not. A gesture, that's all it is."

"Your friend or friends, whoever it is, must be *some* friend." They talked on, with Fritzi inquiring whose house they would live in after they married. How big a wedding? Wasn't everything so wonderful? In her joy, she laughed that laugh that was like no other. She was young then, young as you ever get at mid-life. She made love to him again, the length of him, and even where he was shy. She told him she would gladly have made love in the middle of the dance floor, if he had wanted her there.

Maybe not, but then maybe yes, too. A fantasy. So worked up she couldn't sleep that night. She thought earnestly about their life together and what a drag Sacramento would be. By comparison, Romaine Brook would be a lark.

⳹

Past midnight, Romaine sat with her legs tucked under her up in a chair across from Max Shapin; her agent, an old hand in the film industry, with a stable of well-celebrated clients.

They were playing backgammon—nickel a point—and Romaine was beating him four games to two. Very soon, he would score her with a fifth win.

Max's wife, Sarah, had departed earlier that morning for Los Angeles, where she taught speech and breathing and dialogue techniques to actors. On Thursdays, she spent the day at Hollywood Children's Hospital, where she struggled with the speech defects of retarded kids—five, six, seven years of age. She was one of those; a good-hearted, giving woman like Fritzi Jagoda.

It was Sarah Shapin, who had first spotted Romaine one night at a community theater in Santa Monica. At her urging, Max had caught the next performance. Two days later, he had signed her to a contract. Max had handled her budding career expertly, not hurrying anything, giving her time to mature her talents.

The Shapins had picked her up after the trial concluded, and Romaine had spent the night at their Beverly Hills home. The next day, the three of them drove down to La Costa, a resort on the northern rim of San Diego County.

La Costa was a great favorite with some of the film colony: a playground with a spa, a dozen tennis courts, a championship golf course—a place where loud money came to quiet down temporarily. Reputedly, it was backed by two or three Mafia families.

With real privacy assured.

Which is why Max had chosen it. He was known there, a regular. And the onlookers, if hearing Romaine Brook was in residence, wouldn't get in the way, or be allowed to nose around. A brief word with the manager had taken care of that potential nuisance.

Romaine rolled her dice. Double fives, in glee she said, "Snakes and bad breaks. I'm off the board, Maxey."

He grimaced "You're a guest here, kid. You ought to ease up."

"You're letting *me* win, Max. I can tell you are."

"Never threw a game in my life."

"And you never throw anything so far you can't reach it, right? You told me that once."

"S'right. Shapin's first commandment."

Max began to pencil the score. Before he could finish, Romaine's hand shot out and she ripped the score sheet off the pad.

"We'll finish tomorrow, okay?"

"Tomorrow is never. Don't forget that one either," Max said.

"How could I? You tell me every week."

"So's you don't forget," he admonished mildly."

A teddy bear, thought Romaine. Right down to the curly-knit gray hair that capped his head, the paunch, the heavy sloping shoulders; a bear who made wisecracks through ten-thousand dollar teeth. Teeth that chewed money out of the studios so that Shapin clients ate and lived among the best in town. Except for her. Except for the talented, wanting, piqued, Oscar-winning Romaine Brook.

"Quit moping," he said, tossing the pencil aside.

"You weren't even looking at me."

"My peepers are here." Max touched his nose. "You like a drink, a beddy-bye drink?"

"No thanks."

"Smart girl. But I'm needing one to switch off my engine." He ambled over to a small tiled bar in one corner of the room.

"What am I going to do, Max? No one wants me anymore."

"There's nothing else you can do for now. The dust has to settle some."

"I'm really flat, Max, and I owe everyone in the world."

"You can't get work right now, not in this town" Max said over the splash of water from a tap. "Studios, they're like anyone else. Sensitive. They got a helluva lot to protect. Don't take chances with their audiences and why should they? You're too hot. You caught yourself a big dose of controversy. As I say, play it cool. A little time passes and I'll find something for you. First, some nice articles…some p.r. and a couple of heart-grabbers. He came back from the bar, still talking to her. "But you're the best. Never you forget that, beautiful. I know. I handle some of the biggest."

"I've got to get work, Max. I have to."

"But you can't, not here in the States. Not for now. That Julio Sterne, he'll put the voodoo-words out on you. He's got the clout. Next year, that's different. We'll see."

"Next year is the next century. Either you find me some work or I'll take up *Cosmopolitan's* offer. "

"Stay out of those mags. Like I told you, that'll only heat things up again. *Cosmopolitan* we forget. Yesterday, we already forgot it."

"But it's a hundred-thousand, Max. A *hundred-thousand*, so why not?"

"Why not, is that they'll turn you inside out. You got nothin' to say about what they decide to write. Nothin'. When they're through, you'll be looking like a killer, or a possible killer. They write what they can't talk about in the courthouse. They want a piece that sells. Waddia think they talk a hundred-k for? Your next birthday present?"

"What if I were to set rules?"

"Not for ten times that money would I let you."

Romaine's shoulders slumped. She fiddled with the ivory discs on the backgammon board, making a loose triangular design. Where were her friends? Who were her friends? Frustrated, she swept her hand across the board, sending the discs flying across the table.

Max barely noticed. "First, like I say to you, and my Sarah she agrees...get yourself to London. I got friends there. Get you some parts, I'm sure, on the stage. You work hard, knock 'em flat, like you can do"—Max snapped his fingers—"and whammo, you're back in Hollywood and with their checkbooks open wide."

"London's rainy, isn't it?"

"Rainy-shmainy. Who should care? You start yourself again, but there and not here. On this, I give you Max Shapin's word."

"I already started once, Max. I had it all going for me. Everything."

Max skipped a palm off the side of his head. "The moment you're born, you start. It's who finishes and where they finish, it's all that counts. Don't make me suffer."

Romaine stood up, yawning. No more advice tonight, not even from her darling Max. "I'm tired."

"Sleep good. Tomorrow I gotta head back. Some tennis in the morning, bubee?"

"Sure, what time?"

"Whenever we wake up. Eight, let's try for eight."

Romaine didn't sleep a wink. She lay restlessly for an hour caught in the murk of depression, the rails of her young life twisting off into a shapeless future. The trial wasn't over yet, not for her; she might even be on the unwritten blacklist by now. The studios had one, even if they denied it, and the Sternes could make sure she occupied slot number-one in the "to be avoided" group.

She contemplated Max's advice about London. She didn't know anyone there. A wet and lonely place, and she'd be starting all over. Max would help her, he'd said so. She remembered how Audrey Sterne had once discussed her first marriage—to a Lord Huibbard-Hewes, a famous producer there. Maybe him...

But Max Shapin turned and turned again in her anxiety-ridden thoughts. Grizzly Max, so affectionate, so kind. He knew her ego, her sensitivities, how to nourish and protect them. Occasionally he would even grab a friendly fondle of her breasts, always with a small joke to distract her.

Any man right now, Romaine thought.

She slipped out of bed, padded down the dimly lit hallway and opened his door. She could barely make out the loose hump of him under the sheets, but heard his snoring.

"Whaz-whoz'at?"

Her hands were on him fondling, and her leg was draped across his thick middle.

"Me, Maxie, just me for you," she said in a sweet low voice.

"You crazy? Sarah'll kill us."

"She won't, Max, because you'll never tell her, will you?"

"Stop it, kid...oh, Jehu, sto—"

"It's been ever so long for me, Max. I can feel how strong you are. Hard, Max, really nice and hard. Shall I stop? Just tell me to stop, Max."

He groaned from somewhere in his soul.

About the only way Max could have stopped would have been with a straitjacket wrapped around him. They rolled and tossed, and afterward, chuffing for breath, Max clamped one hand against her smooth bottom, the other over his heart. He lay there, doomed and fallen, yet filled with ecstasy.

313

No tennis the next morning; only room service with steak, eggs, a pot of coffee and two champagne mimosas for Max, who was strangely quiet. He had called his office. "Be here another day," he told them. "Coming down with a cold or something." Later he'd figure out something more original to tell Sarah.

Max wrote Romaine a check for five-thousand dollars that afternoon.

"Shopping money, that's all," he said to her, figuring that he'd reap it back dozens of times. His hunches about talent rarely failed. Romaine, she was spectacular—in bed, too, he thought as his eyes rolled—and she was yet to truly find her range and depth as an actress. Another Garbo, maybe, Max thought, as he had signed the check.

He always trusted his instincts. The kid had the right fire in her to become a top, top actress. She would just have to take it, bear up, till he could get her re-packaged and in front of the camera again. Jesus, if she wasn't something else in the kip. She had a future somewhere; of that he was dead sure.

Chapter Thirty-two

Audrey, all ears today, listened closely.

She was gauging her chances with Sister Marius. The first time they'd met seemed ages ago, though it was, at best, only two years since Audrey had sought help in finding her daughter. She had begged then and paid then—with annual donations to Las Infantas mean to ingratiate herself with the good sisters.

And there had been that call from Sister Marius, a few weeks before, telling Audrey a detective had come looking for precisely what she was now after. The call that had started an avalanche—*that call...that unbelievably troublesome* call—thought Audrey, afraid she might scream at Sister Marius about it, but wisely deciding to let a sleeping dog keep on sleeping.

Better to be patient, but then she'd been extremely patient for the last half-hour. Time to cut up the butter, pay off, and be gone. But only please, please, please let me have those papers.

So she listened.

"...Quite a problem for everyone it seems," Sister Matins was saying over her upturned palms.

Though her sentiments were in cold storage, Audrey forced a polite smile. "*Quite* is a very wide word, wouldn't you say?"

"Forgive me, Mrs. Sterne, but no, I don't agree. For us, it is still quite a problem."

"But why? Why this big problem? It's so simple."

"Not necessarily. Please remember that detective was here to make inquiries."

"What was his name again, Sister?"

"Fahey. Quite a charmer. Or rascal, I should say," said Sister Marius pleasantly, recalling the roses he had brought her.

"His name, you said his name was what?"

"A Mr. Fahey. F-A-H-E-Y."

"But you told me you didn't tell him anything."

"That's absolutely correct, I didn't. He only knows Romaine was adopted from here. Nothing more."

"You're sure?"

"Quite sure."

That word again. *Quite* this and *quite* that, said so pertly and with such finality. Mr. Fahey, whoever he was, sounded as though he might be a shakedown artist. Who was he, and how had he gotten wind or any connection between Las Infantas and Romaine?

"I suppose," Audrey said, "you know why I'm here again."

"But you surely understand we're a religious order. We have our obligations to others and those papers are part of our most confidential records." Said so nicely this time and through a beatific smile that would do the Mona Lisa proudly.

"And it's a record of part of my life, as well, Sister Marius."

"Yes, when you put it that way. And your daughter's."

Sizing each other up, they traded the quizzical look of two strangers who sensed an opportunity, but were sure whose turn it was to begin the bargaining.

"We were very sorry about your son, Mrs. Sterne," said Sister Marius a moment later.

"Stepson."

"Stepson, yes. May God rest his soul."

"Well, I'd like a little rest for mine right now."

Audrey reached into her green alligator Hermès handbag, drawing out a cashier's check. She placed it on the desk blotter in front of Sister Marius. "I'm prepared to rest that much of my soul on Las

Infantas in return for the file. We can even destroy it together if you'd like that better."

Sister Marius's eyes widened. She'd never beheld a gift of this size: a hundred-thousand dollars, sent straight from her Savior. A sum that would solve her worries for months to come. Unpaid bills galore were stacked in the drawer next to her fidgeting knee.

She handed the check back to Audrey. "I'm afraid you misunderstand us," she said, nearly weeping inside. "We could never accept your generosity this way."

"But I want to be generous, and I'd like you to be generous with me."

"The material aspects of this world are of little con—"

"Sister Marius, let's not kid each other," Audrey broke in. "This place'll be condemned if you don't do something. I'd like to help...but I want some help, too. What do you care about those papers? They're twenty-odd years old for goodness sakes, and they've done far more damage than good."

"And the young woman?"

"Naturally, I want to protect her. She's been through a hell of...excuse me, an extremely difficult time." Audrey placed the check on the blotter again before continuing, "My husband doesn't know anything about this— that I'm the mother. I'm in a terrible bind, you see. That was his only son, and we've all been through..." Audrey stopped, afraid she might say *hell* again.

"You needn't go on, Mrs. Sterne. I had a pretty fair idea why you came here today."

As if in search of guidance from above, Sister Marius steepled her hands, glancing again at the cream-colored check on the blotter. The devil's work or God's? Temptation teased at her unmercifully.

"The check is a gift," Audrey said. "Think of it as the start of more gifts."

"A gift with strings."

"Yes. Strings around my neck if you wish, Sister. More like a rope, I'd say."

"I wasn't suggesting—"

"But I am."

Silence again. Suddenly, Sister Marius alighted, swooping out of her chair. Her blue habit flew about and lifted up to expose her high-laced shoes. Audrey was reminded of a greater heron rising in a sudden frighted flight as the nun disappeared from her office. Waiting, Audrey was no longer so sure of herself. Would Sister Marius call someone for advice? Take a community vote? What?

Curtains thin as a negligee fluttered next to the open window; laundered a thousand times, Audrey supposed. Ceiling paint hung in scabs, threatening to come down in a gentle snowfall. The floor carpeting, once a shade of plum, had faded to a sickly brown. When assessing her surroundings, Audrey could've kicked herself: she likely could have secured the goods for a fifty-thousand or a measly twenty-five. This place was only a rung or two above those lopsided decaying edifices littering the Mexican border towns. She dueled with her impressions long enough to realize she'd better banish them somehow or she'd be in a mood of deep regret for the rest of the day over the money she was shelling out.

A bell pealed, and then again, somewhere out in the hall.

The brass door latch clicked a few minutes later. Another swirl of blue-serge cloth as Sister Marius returned, with Audrey blinking and an anxious smile rearranging her face. Anxious, because she didn't know how tough she needed to be. The stakes were rising, and she had had to hustle to raise the money she was offering.

Sitting down, Sister Marius clasped a file to the starched circular bib shielding her ample bosom. Then she placed the file on the center of the blotter, untying a mothy black ribbon that bound the covers together. She opened pages, yellowed with age, and pushed the file toward Audrey.

"I'm due at the noon Angelus soon. Read this if you wish. I'll be gone a while."

When Sister Marius left, Audrey thumbed the brittle pages. A drop in the bucket of the ever-long history of eggs and sperm uniting. Less than a drop, and all because she had let a man enter her body at the wrong time. The wrong monthly time and the wrong any other time.

All the brutal grief that sometimes comes from the crazed flight of what you go through when you're in love. Or when thinking you are; as if no other love in all history compared to the nerve-twisting sickness assaulting you at an unwieldy moment.

She wondered what the high-and-mighty Cliff Rhodes would say, or think, were he here now and could see his name on the yellowish form affixed to the second page. There it was, the record, the indelible history of a few illicit days on the Monterrey Peninsula, where they had, in their ecstatic thrashings, broken a bed one night.

Somehow, he'd gotten Romaine off.

Or perhaps he hadn't, but he had been there presiding over that dismal, bone-bending, Christ-awful trial. And he had definitely been there when

Romaine stated she had seen Audrey with Ferenc at the pool house one morning. That was possible actually, or faintly possible, and Audrey resented Rhodes for not stopping Romaine flat in her tracks from speaking so openly to a courtroom full of strangers and all those newshawkers.

And the worst of it now was that the Malibu sheriff wanted Kardas for more questioning about Marc Sterne's death. Audrey, too, had been interrogated three times already, quite politely but with enough innuendo to let her know she was under suspicion. She'd been stained. She could tell by the way some people looked at her. By their indifferent greetings. By what they *didn't* say to her.

She read on, flipping the file's pages. She came across a tabbed section about the adoptive parents: Chatham Brook, the father, a theatrical musician, though without the devilish talents of his adoptive daughter, Audrey would wager.

Hearing the ding of the clock, Audrey noticed twenty-minutes had traveled somewhere. She shut the file. Her eyes strayed to the desktop. The check was missing.

An unspoken signal? A deal sealed with an invisible handshake? A little subtlety employed by the good sister?

Audrey smiled at no one, other than perhaps at her good fortune, as she slowly bent the file covers, squashing the file into her handbag. The clasp wouldn't fasten. She tried again, then gave up and headed for the door. She looked both ways down the corridor. Nothing there, only silent walls that knew little of laughter, walls that never had sheltered a lover's embrace—of the heterosexual variety—of that she was certain.

Walking quietly, with the steps of a burglar, she hugged her handbag tight. Reaching the wide front door, she inched it open, restraining an urge to break into an all-out sprint for her Maserati.

On the drive back to Malibu, she eyed her handbag several times. Inside was that papery dynamite-stick and it belonged to her and her alone, as of an hour ago. What to do with it? She could always pull over and lay on a little beach party celebration, complete with a fire. She especially liked the idea of a fire. Maybe, before destroying anything, a lawyer should be sought to give some of that four-hundred dollar per hour advice. What was four-hundred at this point?

Maybe Rhodes, after picking himself off the floor, would give any needed advice for free…that shitheel…

❦

At noon, it was still dark in the deeper crevices of Fahey's spirits. He avoided lunch and instead was testing a low-calorie whiskey he'd recently seen advertised on a billboard.

Fahey smacked his lips twice, then wiped them on a napkin. He sat in a booth across from Tommy Burke in the small Mexican restaurant Tommy liked, the one near the courthouse.

"We better get out of here if you have to talk this way," Tommy told him. He put his coffee cup down, trembling slightly.

"Who can hear us? Hi! Ho! And fuck 'em anyway."

"Anyone can hear you. Quiet your voice, will you?"

"This voice," said Fahey, "has only begun to shout. Telling you right now, Tommy boy, never fucking ever trust your friends...save your kisses for your enemies."

"I'm leaving, if you don't quiet down." Tommy leaned forward. "And I have to tell you, Alonzo, I can't help you either."

"Someone has to. That filthy bugger Rhodes doesn't know us anymore."

"He can't help you with—"

"Time to get out the fighting sticks. You'll be my second, I trust."

"Alonzo, you did a no-no when you entered sealed premises without permission. Maybe they'll only suspend your license. Sixty days or something."

Fahey glowered. His black, caterpillar-like eyebrows spliced together over his nose. He whistled a few dry-lipped notes at Burke. "Who are you people? Fair-weather farters, the whole lot of you. I'll tell you this for nothing. Enemies are behind every tree. My wife tells me to forgive my enemies, and I do, but I always make sure to remember the bastards' names."

"You'd better be careful, Alonzo. You can't prove anything on Rhodes. Those are serious charges you're making."

"He danced me about. Told me—"

"Even if he did, so what? You can't prove anything. He's a big name, besides."

"The wife was there when he came over. Christ, she never lies...and never marry that sort of woman, I tell you. Ruins everything when they're too honest."

"Still won't make any difference. God, why didn't you tell me about those narcotics when you first—"

"Told me to save it, sit on it. Rhodes did," Fahey said, pleading. "And those were his questions I gave you. He gave them to me."

"You told me they came from a lawyer friend of yours."

"He *is* a lawyer. He *was* a friend."

"I can't believe it," Tommy said, but then he did.

Tommy's forearm, lying idly on the table, was suddenly seized in a grip so powerful his eyes watered. "Believe me, he did." Fahey had growled so intensely a passing waiter stopped to watch.

"I'm just astonished...and you're breaking my arm." Fahey's fingers relaxed. "Why? Why would he do it?" Tommy asked.

"Fair trial and that sort of toilet talk. I think he wanted to try the damn thing himself."

"From the bench. Don't be silly."

"He's a cute one, Thomas. Could kick a hole in a Rembrandt and you'd never even notice."

"What you're saying, Alonzo, I just can't buy it. Not any of it. Zero."

"We can talk to the papers. Fuel things up a touch. They're already on to him."

"You're nuts, all the way nuts."

"Listen, hey, of course I'm nuts. How do you think I survive all the treachery around me?" Fahey, almost in form again, smiled gallantly.

"Alonzo." Burke leaned forward again, desperate for some calm, some quieter talk. "I think you're great. Really something. But I can't represent you. If all this comes out, you'll wish you were a manure pile. And that's how I'll look, too, if they think I was involved. And I wasn't. They'll fry us both. I've got the Bar Association to think about..."

"But he was—Rhodes was dotting all the i's twice," Fahey reminded. "He jitterbugged on us. On me anyway."

"Thanks all the same, but I don't think I'll tangle with him. Even if you *could* prove it."

Across the coarsely woven tablecloth, they looked dejectedly at each other: Burke grim-faced and Fahey with his teeth grinding in disgust.

Tommy wanted to do anything for Fahey, who had been so helpful; then again, he had no proof of Rhodes's maneuvers because Fahey had none either. And what could be done about it anyway? After all, he wasn't the county bar association; he was nothing but a no-account lawyer who had had his fifteen minutes in the sunlight of massive publicity. Hollywood's kind of publicity, with all the stops pulled.

He was swept by an urge to tell Fahey how Romaine had behaved after her acquittal. Such elation. Then, out of nowhere, she had become so iron-minded, so diffident and off-putting. Didn't want to see any of them again, ever. Had actually called Fahey a destroyer. He would never repeat her insult to Fahey. He loved Fahey, loved the loose swinging gate of Fahey's many ways that knew no season, and were always so full of fun.

"Alonzo, let's go."

"Not till I finish pissing on your shoe."

"Take a walk with me." Tommy started to slide out of the booth.

"A walk? Take you straight to the Gypsy, Tom-Tom. She'll walk us to Bulgaria. Has her own camel brigade, I think. We'll go see her, the drinks and fucks are on me."

Tommy stood up, a frown galloping across his thin face "I can't drink like you can, thank God."

A distant look passed across Fahey. He bit his lip and his eyes shimmered up to a brilliant blue. "Maybe a church," he murmured. "If you find me here tomorrow, get me to a tall holy church. Nearest one you can find."

"A church?"

"Right. Time for a little small talk with the Big Crusader. Wanda's other boyfriend."

"That's tremendous, Alonzo. But I'm on my way out the door." Fahey sent him a sullen, dismissive wave. "Alonzo, I can't help you," Tommy repeated. "It's not that I don't want to. It's just—". Shrugging, he didn't finish. He couldn't.

"Panty-ass lawyer, aren't you? Can't expect more. The hell with it all. Let's have that fräulein over here," Fahey suggested, pointing at a Mexican waitress. "Guzzle ourselves a Corona. Sonofabitch I'm thirsty. Haven't talked long enough, eh?"

Fahey looked straight ahead, unhearing and unseeing, as Tommy shoved his hands in his pockets and moved off. Halfway out of the restaurant, he turned to see if Fahey had changed his mind and would come along.

All he saw was Fahey's back slanting out of the booth. An errant hand was groping for the bouncing frontage of a Mexican waitress. He had her giggling. How did that lunk-headed Irishman do it? He would give anything to be another Fahey. Be that good-looking, that crazy and sentimental, a man who stamped his name on every day he lived.

Tinged with friendly envy, Tommy Burke went through the door to the street, his thoughts skipping again to Romaine. Where was she? Would he ever see her again? How would it feel to touch her, just once, the way Fahey jollied with the waitress, and with such casual abandonment. No matter if he were in the throes of profound drunkenness, could he ever imagine himself doing that with Romaine—wishing with all his bones and his being she was thinking, even for a few seconds, about him.

And with that wish done, he wiped his blurred eyes against the sleeve of his jacket.

PART III

Chapter Thirty-three

"**M**iss Brook is on the phone. Finally got her at her landlady's," Macklin Price told Rhodes.

Rhodes was sifting through papers for the packing boxes, and, when pausing, Macklin detected an excited gleam in his eye. His thoughts were colliding. Some were akin to the alarms of a boy calling a girl for a first date—the hand-on-the-knee thoughts of a sixteen year old. The papers, stacks of them, signaled a change in life—a new life, up in Sacramento, a welcomed distance from Los Angeles murder trials.

When Macklin left, he picked up the phone. They talked for a solid ten minutes. How she was getting along? Was the press bothering her? He had resigned from the court; a small and flat joke, when telling her, "She'd been too much for him." Would she care to stop by his house for a chat?

When he hung up, Rhodes sat with his elbows on the desk, his head anchored to his hands. Fritzi had agreed to have her as a guest for a couple of weeks. At least, it would be a beginning.

The next day at four o'clock, he saw Romaine again for perhaps the hundred and-fifteenth time. But this would be only the second time he had directly talked with her. Still strangers, still anxious, acting somewhat uneasily toward each other.

They sat on the terrace of Rhodes's home, while he talked about the hurdles faced by the accused; who, even though freed, had been scarred by their prison days, contending with ongoing trauma, suffering barbs or worse in the press and the wagging tongues of skeptics. "They call it," he said, "the criminally innocent syndrome". Big words. Sort of like having social flu for a time." Implying he could help, if she allowed it.

"I know," said Romaine, with a hint of a smile but her eyes glum as tar. "They asked me to leave my acting classes. Said it's too distracting for the others."

"Give it some time."

"I don't have time, and you sound just like my agent."

"Who's that?"

"Max Shapin, with William Morris Agency. Do you know him?"

"I don't, no, but I've heard of him."

"Do you know London?"

"Slightly."

"Fuck it anyway," Romaine bristled. "I want to live now, instead of being a leper."

Jolted slightly at the expletive, though he let it pass. She reached to the far end of table separating them, pouring herself another cup of tea. As she stretched, he could see her legs perfectly defined by skintight dungarees. Audrey's legs, he thought, consciously dividing Romaine in half; so much belonging to her mother, so much to him. Becoming aware of what he was doing, he brushed aside his thoughts.

"Why're you so interested in me? Isn't that a problem for you?" Romaine asked.

"A problem?"

"You being my judge and everything."

"I resigned from the court, as I mentioned yesterday. I expect to be appointed to another, but meanwhile I'm an ordinary citizen. I should tell you something. My interest is more than the usual here."

"Like how? What's *that* mean?"

He steadied himself. "I know your parents, Romaine. They live in this city and I think they'd like to know you're getting along all right."

"My parents. That's a laugher. My parents are dead and more dead. My mother is anyway, and my father might as well be. He hit the road years ago. Goodbye and good riddance."

"I meant your real parents," he said, tensing for her reply.

"Real? What's so real about them?" Romaine stopped and thought again. "Oh, I get it. You must know, then, that I'm adopted."

Rhodes nodded. "They'd like to help you. Your real parents, I mean, and maybe they can."

"Who are they?"

"They're not in a position to come forward right now," feeling idiotic as soon as he had said it.

"That's certainly courageous of them. Real live heroes, huh?"

"It's a complicated situation."

"Are they rich?"

"Enough to help, I'd say."

"Where were they when the bombs were dropping on me?" Romaine smoothed her hair back, and the sun's light gave it the color of a canary's. "No, I don't need them at all. They never needed me, did they?"

"Maybe more than it would seem."

"Are they in the industry?"

"Films, you mean? I couldn't really say."

"Or won't?"

"Not now, I won't."

"Missing parents are baggage that I don't really need. So don't go rousing them on my behalf. I got by without them. I've been alone before, most of my life I never had anyone, not really...not until Marc came along. But then, well, you know...you heard...the step-mother, she was nice for a while but then she...she went south on me...I guess I'll never have anyone, will I?"

She went on for a time, even mentioning the sexual mauling by that priest. That one of the matrons at the detention center had taken a shot at her. Everyone wanted something of her, it seemed; but, for her, she lived in a state of rejection now, and with no end to it she could see.

Rhodes lit a cigar, watching Romaine grimace at the sight, then he got up, went over to lean against the stone balustrade a few feet away. Not going to be easy, he could see that, hiding his regret behind a fan of smoke.

"Everyone needs help at times," he said to her, "someone to look out for us, someone we can trust"—and he thought of Fahey, then Audrey. "You've been through a rough patch, but I've seen a helluva lot worse."

People, he said, might help but not if she kicked away the offered hands. Her acting career, where had it led her? "A hard game at best. You get used, you get thrown aside. One day the phone stops ringing. Build your own life, so you can control it better—not completely, just better."

Rhodes mentioned Fritzi. Who she was, her droves of friends, how much everyone liked her. Romaine could stay there for a while. A lovely house, a place to ease off and work out the next steps.

"Why her?" asked Romaine. "She owes me zip. Less than zip."

"She's close to me. We're getting married soon."

327

"All because you know my parents? She'll help me because of something like that?"

"She's willing to do us a favor, let's say. About the most favor-doing woman, I've ever met. You'll like her, believe me."

"I sort of know who she is. I went to Masquers once or twice...I like the restaurant St. Germain the best of all."

"What do you say, then? I'll see you as much as I can, and in a few weeks, who knows, you might be up on your wave again."

"I need a job. I've got some money but not enough with all my bills—"

"That, too. Make a list. We'll see what can be done."

"Mind if I ask you a question, Judge?"

"Go right ahead."

Romaine's throaty voice suddenly took on a different tone. "Have you got a thing for me? Are you into some sort of weird trip over me, because you think I'm flat on my ass? Want yourself a young girlfriend on the side?"

So steeped in trying to establish some sort of a connection with her, he'd never thought about her side of it. "It's all on the level," he returned somewhat stiffly, "all of it. You'll have to see for yourself. It's totally your call, but you don't sound to me as if you've got all that many options."

She had seen him as many times as he'd seen her over the months. Nice looking, she thought, tanned, trim and hard, with good shoulders and arms. She had even known him in fantasy, in the loneliness of her cell, when wanting a man. There were times—the more vicious ones at the trial—when he had seemed to help her and help Tommy, especially toward the end. He was well off, that much was easy to see, and probably well connected too. She could handle him—what man couldn't be handled if you came right down to it.

"Please don't think I don't appreciate this," Romaine said after a moment, "You're very nice. *Very*."

"So are you."

"Tell me who my parents are."

"Maybe I can someday."

"That's not a good way to begin trusting each other."

"That's how it has to be," he said with an easy smile. "For now, anyway."

"Are you pretty tough?"

"Never."

"You always smoke-cigars?"

"Two a day. Sometimes three. Bother you?"

"I don't think anything you'd do would bother me, judge."

"Are you doing anything special tonight?" he asked, avoiding her eyes. "Care to have dinner here?"

"I'd like that very much."

"Wonderful. Afterward, I'll see if we can get you introduced to Fritzi."

"Is there any chance I could stay here?"

"No chance whatsoever. Sorry, but that is absolutely out."

"I see. Not a good idea, eh? Can I call you something besides judge? I don't like to think about being in court and—"

"Sure, of course. Call me Cliff."

"You're pretty smooth, aren't you?"

"I'm about to smooth my way into a five-thirty drink. Want some more tea? Anything else?"

Romaine got up, stretching again. With her arms raised over her head, the sky-blue pullover she wore became carpet-tight against her breasts. Though shifting her gaze away, she had an unerring instinct of where he was looking. Exactly where she intended him to, pleasing her.

"I rarely drink, judge…Cliff, I mean. Maybe a little one."

"Don't start on my account."

"You really are very nice. You're different than other men, aren't you?"

"Not a bit."

"I think you are."

She drank like a small bird, as if lapping nectar from a dew-misted flower. Chatting along, they came to a necessary understanding—to never discuss the trial again. Every so often she would slide in an inquiry about his past life. He kept strictly to the rule of letting her find her own way with him. The ice, if not all the way broken, was at least melting somewhat. He wanted it that way, a gradual thing, steady, like the rising of the sun. And, for his part, hoping earnestly for the a little spreading brightness.

A beginning. Small enough but what could either of them expect? She was bound to be somewhat on guard, wary of him and his motives. So slow up, he decided. Many days lay ahead. Days for overcoming the misbegotten past, yet a past that had given him her.

CR

Audrey was too far away to hear what was going on at Julio's end of the dinner table. He was talking with two executives and their wives, the men employed by the Seattle chemical company where he was board chairman. All were laughing at something, and she would ordinarily want to be included, but an apathy had set in.

The view from the dining room carried out to miles after other miles of the Pacific, a vista that usually held her rapt.

Not tonight, though. The dinner bored her. Seated at her end of the twenty-foot long glass table were the head of production at Parthenon and a major film distributor from Italy. Neither had their wives with them. She had variously tuned out-and-in to their trade talk, smiling and nodding, while pretending interest.

But she was still recoiling from Julio's blunt warning before the dinner guests arrived. "Better find yourself a decent lawyer," be had instructed. "If you know where Kardas is, that might make it easier for everyone. For you, most of all."

Putting a distance between them as fast as he could now. At bullet speed, it seemed to her, adding to her daily pressures ever since the sheriffs came snooping around every few days.

An active, almost raging dislike for Julio was building in her.

Trying to blot out the implications of Julio's remark about finding a lawyer, she renewed her efforts to pay a little more attention to the Italian from Rome, who, when talking, waved his hands around as if rehearsing an orchestra.

She was headed for the Italian, but started obliquely with the Parthenon production chief saying: "Do you think Julio is getting senile?" No ordinary question from a wife about a husband sitting twenty-feet away.

"Why?" he asked, startled.

"Because," Audrey said earnestly, "he's talking of firing you soon. I heard him on the phone. Wouldn't that be absurd"—then looking quizzically at the Italian, leveled him with—"as is his idea for cutting you out of the distribution rights for Italy."

"You are not serious, signora," the Italian said, jerking his head as if it he had been slapped.

"There's a mistake. You probably misunderstood him," the production chief broke in, his face suddenly pale and stiff with anxiety.

Audrey smiled. "Have it your own way...Julio always does, doesn't he?"

The two men stared speechlessly at each other. Audrey finally caught Julio's eye. Smiling lavishly, she waved with feigned affection, well aware it would unnerve him.

Oh, you wretched-wretched bastard, she thought. Smiling again as if she were just about to have her picture taken for being elected as Mother-of-the-Year. Or even Wife-of-the-Year.

She couldn't decide which, as she focused again on the Italian. Italians were fun. They liked women, particularly women married to film chieftains, and if they were led to believe that chieftain was thinking of giving them the heave-ho. She knew she shouldn't have misled him in the way she had, but her cold anger had gotten the best of her.

Chapter Thirty-four

The day he announced his resignation, was also the day Rhodes decided to refuse all calls from the media. Politely, he told them no go, or had Macklin Price do the declining for him. The trial was over, the verdict delivered. The state attorney general's office could complain all they liked, but he had resigned, and that was all the story there was, or ever would be, at least from his office.

Retaliation soon reared. Echoing the cry of Pritter, one local paper printed an editorial headed: THE WRONG MAN.

"...Rhodes may have done nothing illegal," it stated, "but his actions at the ending phase of the trial clearly influenced the jury to return a verdict of not guilty. In the end, it was as though the deceased Marc Sterne had gone on trial himself for the unproven crime of dope trafficking. A blind spot remains in this long and often ugly contest that cost the taxpayers well over two-million dollars. Yet Rhodes is now in line for an appointment to the highest court in our state. In our view, he has disqualified himself. The judiciary acts as our referees in legal disputes, not as puppeted string-pullers. Californians deserve better..."

The third hatchet job of that week. As yet, no word from the governor's office. A silent hint, was it?

For the record, and to satisfy a committee of senior peer judges he had already answered their questions with a memo of his own. No two trials are the same, he had responded, and in this one, hounded by publicity, it was also enmeshed with politics, and forced into a sort of uncertainty when Raye Wheeler passed away. And it was the specter of narcotics lent some credence to other motives, and perhaps, even to other persons involved in the still unresolved circumstances of Marc Sterne's death. Perhaps, he had stated, it was suicide. And if a homicide of one degree or another, the elements of proof were either absent, or sorely lacking. One dense paragraph dealt with the shoddy investigative work by both the state and the sheriff's offices. Posing this: *Was it someone else who had perpetrated the crime?* To help resolve that issue and other vagaries of the proceedings, he had intervened. If there, in retrospect, were other guilty parties who were involved in Marc Sterne's death, than the remedies were quite apparent. Let the police look into the matter, and if suspects are found, then refer their findings to the district attorney.

And there, as far as he was concerned, the matter rested.

Set aside, for the time being, was a far more interesting task, that of completing the draft of his ideas for improved criminal justice statutes, he had promised the governor: a revisiting of what constituted admissible evidence in capital crimes trials, ways of speeding up trials, better methods of securing legal representation for the indigent.

He wanted to put the finishing touches on the monograph before going up to Sacramento.

There was his own estate to square away, and his will and last testament to go over. He would change that, too. Over the past several days, he'd been thinking about what to do with his money.

How would Audrey react? Well, he didn't really give a damn. He intended to set up a trust, with Fritzi as one trustee, with Romaine as principal beneficiary. He had millions. He'd provide for taxes, list several charities for gifts, set up a scholarship at his law school alma mater, and let the rest of it run to Romaine.

Romaine had been at Fritzi's for several days now. Getting along well together, it seemed, yet he must soon devise a better solution.

For the previous four nights, he had dined privately with Romaine, while Fritzi attended to business at Masquers. Delirious fun for him, as they explored some of the lesser known haunts in the beach towns south of the city. Romaine had worn dark wigs and blue-tinted eyeglasses. Using a makeup trick, she even changed the shape of her lower face by inserting small dental sponges around her upper gums, removing them when eating.

Romaine had comported herself like any young woman out on a dinner date. Her humor had improved. He could see, and with pride, why men found her attractive. She owned a natural charm, often giving the impression she could do anything, and would, and do it only for you alone. Bright, too. More than once, she surprised him with her satirical comments on politics or religion, or devastating insights about the theatrical world.

Sometimes she made the same mistake he had at her age—of thinking she knew more than she really did or could. A few times, she had tried to impress him with people she had met and known, and places she had traveled. Somehow, he doubted she could have crowded all of those people and places into her young life. Never once, though, had he tried to trip her up. He knew he was living an illusion, but she was a precious find and he was building bridges to her, sturdy ones, and wouldn't chance wounding her confidence.

She was an actress, he told himself, and they had their own prisms: not how life actually happened, but of how it should be and was always meant to be. They did roles, even when not before a camera.

Like Fahey would see it—life as a mirage: a mirage meant hope, and sometimes the stilling of pain and privation.

CR

At Masquers, Fahey, in a dove gray suit, black shirt, and matching black tie, worked harder on Fritzi. They sat in her office, with Fahey downtrodden one moment and fighting mad the next.

"I'm sure he'll help," said Fritzi, who was finishing a Cobb salad at her desk.

"Don't go deaf on me, love. Crank his ear, will you?"

"I already have once."

"Again then. Near the well-known pillow. Before the act of entry."

"He says he can't now, Alonzo. It's not an opportune time."

"Opportune. Christ! Opportune, did he say that? What the hell about Fahey's opportune?"

"What can I do?" she implored. "It's all legal heebie-jeebies, Alonzo."

"Cut the bastard off. Turn him out on the streets."

"We're getting married."

"He called to tell me. My heartiest to you, that's one reason I came. You're getting a dog."

"Alonzo..." Fritzi gave him a baleful look.

"All right, then, a blind, ungrateful dog. Needs a whipping."

"Alonzo, I don't know what the heck is really between you two, but he loves you. You know he does."

334

"Love!" Fahey's chin shot out. "Listen, that was my friend. *Was.* I am what I give, and I always gave him everything of myself. Former friend, if he ever was…"

"Cliff told me you hung up when he called you about us. That's a no-nice, Alonzo."

"Forgive me, love, but your great fan Fahey's got his prime troubles these days."

"I'll talk to him again, I promise."

"Do, love. Till he sees the lighted path." Fahey brightened at a fresh thought. "Found a church for you, Fritzi. Just the place for the marry-up. Great stained glass all painted up with high-minded virgins and the Magi…run you by it soon as you're ready."

With a light knock at the door, Ginty Jellicoe stepped in. "Health inspectors, Fritzi," he said. "They wanna talk about the kitchen. We need new stoves. Somethin' like that."

"Oh, no they don't," she said. Those stoves are only, what…three or four years—"

Fahey came to his feet. "Let me. I know the type. Have them in for a jar and we'll thrash it all out in the bar."

"Stay right where you are, Alonzo," said Fritzi, and then to Ginty, "I'll be right along."

Ginty departed.

"Pay them off," Fahey advised her. "Get some brandy, lower quality stuff. Works every time."

Fritzi stood, laughing at him. "You stay right here. I'll send in some lunch." Nearing the door, she turned to face him. "Alonzo."

"Yes?"

"How would you like to give me away? At our wedding?"

Fahey's face became a celebration. "You mean it?"

"Sure do, will you?

"You're a hug, the whole win, you are…carriages, get that Budweiser team with those white chargers. I'll drive—"

"And I'll be right back. Have your lunch. We'll figure something out," she added hopefully.

"Right as a diamond-filled rain, Fritzi. And kick those Healthers to hell out of here. Tell them we're planning a ducal wedding, a misery of dry tears, you tell 'em so and then—"

335

She skipped through the door. Fahey was left alone, newly enthused yet mired in his own worry. She is the best, he thought. God, why hadn't he landed her a thousand months ago? Free drink, set the place to rights, poison every last son-of-a-bitching lawyer in town, and, after them, the health inspectors.

He would have his lunch, wait for her return and then lend counsel to Fritzi on the more fatiguing aspects of marriage.

Ԕ

Rhodes was turning out to be more fun than Romaine had expected. Still, why all the attention? Disarming. There were flighty moments when she imagined him as a lover. Why not? Only twenty-two years apart in age, and she'd seen others of her generation go out with older men. Making the moo-eyes, hanging on every word and jaded joke. New cars. Walk-around money. Furs, clothes, whatever.

Actually, Rhodes had already staked her to some lovely clothes. Wouldn't go with her to Giorgio's and Niemen-Marcus, but gave her permission to charge up to four-thousand dollars of frills. A few of the boxes were delivered a short while ago; others had arrived the day before.

She had shown the ones from Niemen's to Fritzi, who gushed over them until Romaine told her who footed the bill. Fritzi's jovial face instantly turned to a jack-hammer look that could shatter a sidewalk. Romaine had easily caught Fritzi's unmistakable reaction.

Gathering up the boxes, Romaine decided to go back to her bedroom to try on her latest outfits. She passed by Fritzi's room. On a sudden whim, she stopped, rested the boxes against a wall and went in.

She sat down at the mirror-topped dressing table, whiffing one bottle, then two others. Fritzi was a three-perfume woman.

A nice enough person and popular by the count of silver-framed autographed photographs scattered about the living room: film personalities, diplomats, business tycoons, five astronauts. Pretty enough with her smile and rosy skin and blue-black hair, but haunchy and with the legs of a country girl. Romaine couldn't fully grasp what Rhodes saw in her.

They'd talked, giggled, run the gamut of chatty women-talk during Romaine's first days at Fritzi's home. Gossiped, too, about local notables

336

and the talk about them making the rounds at Masquers. Items one would never hear while living in a detention cell.

Always though—Romaine had noticed—Fritzi steered clear of the trial, or of what jail was like and how she'd been treated there.

Admiring herself in the mirror, Romaine posed herself in different moods and faces, liking the one of the ingénue best. Her hand wandered idly to a small leather-bound address book lying on one corner of the table.

She mimicked Fritzi's mouth, how it curled up in laughter. She tried Fritzi's voice, aloud, by lowering her own natural pitch. Tried again. Better this time. Again, for several minutes, and putting more inflection on the vowels.

Romaine leafed through the address book. Who would know Fritzi's voice but not intimately? She put one end of an eyebrow pencil in her mouth, then dialed the Borendo Salon.

"H'lo, Barendo's" came the answer.

"Hi, there! Fritzi Jagoda here." Romaine moved the pencil to one side of her mouth.

"Yes, Miss Jagoda...good morning..."

"I have to cancel...oops, sorry, I'm eating an apple," said Romaine, slurring, attempting Fritzi's laugh.

"You wish to cancel on Thursday?"

"Cancel me, would you? I'll be away," said Romaine, shifting the pencil again.

"Shall I re-book you?"

"Monday. What do you have that's open?"

"10:30, all right? I'll mark it in."

"And a manicure."

"We have you down."

"Bye, thanks so much."

Romaine dialed again, this time to a tree service. Would they send someone to cut the oleander hedges in front of the house? Take them down to two feet or so. Thanks awfully.

Smiling into the mirror again, Romaine thought how easy it was to act, portray another. Reasonable looks, photogenic bones, the changeable voices of a choir, buttressed by imagination. Either you were born with the desires to move people's emotions, or you could never understand what it was really like: that power to control other's feeling.

Where was he taking her tonight? Dante's, he'd said. Some jazz place in North Hollywood. She'd make herself look older, sag her boobs somehow. Thirtyish at least, ugh!

If they were so much in love, why didn't Cliff and Fritzi sleep together?

Getting up from the dressing table, it crossed her mind how much Rhodes amused her. He could probably open the palace doors for her, so why waste it? Protect her, too. A big-ass judge. Besides, she needed him more than Fritzi Jagoda ever would.

Her hand reached out to a peg at the side of the mirror that held twists of glittering gold chains. From one of them swung an enameled gold pendant, a lion with tiny ruby eyes. Fritzi had worn it one afternoon over a light gray sweater, the lion lost somewhere in the crease between those dairy-like udders.

Untangling the chain from the others, Romaine twirled it around in her fingers. On her way out of the bedroom, Romaine overhauled a plan she'd been conjuring: edge Fritzi out of the scene, drive her nuts. Fritzi would be worth studying, closely enough so she could clone Fritzi's physical reactions whenever she chose. Doing her voice was snap. *Be every woman you have to be, and be a few more while you're at it.* Fritzi might be good for a chuckle, but everyone has things to learn. Castles crumble. Her own certainly had, so you build another. Isn't that, more or less, what Cliff had told-her? Max Shapin, too?

At the back of the house, in the kitchen, the garbage disposal hiccupped as she fed the chain and gold lion into its perfectly round throat, and with it went any chance of a friendship might've found its feet, might've eventually even blossomed.

CR

The air had turned wintry in Julio Sterne's office at Parthenon Studios. At a round table in the far corner sat Julio, the two Oldes & Farnham lawyers who had rendered advice on prosecution tactics to Pritter, who sat there nervously fiddling with the lower buttons on his vest.

"Bungled," Sterne railed. "Screwed up investigations. The trial made to look like I don't know what was going on in my own home." He glared at

Pritter with the sort of look one sends a relative who has owed money for too long.

"We did everything to keep you out of it," Pritter said. "Everything we could think of."

"Not enough," Sterne replied.

"Couldn't be helped. Rhodes decides who testifies—"

"All over that damn Malibu sheriff's report," Sterne interrupted. "Can't even"—his jowls shook—"one of our janitors could do a better job of it."

Pritter clamped his teeth tight. Two errors had been made: Sterne pressuring the governor to bring in the state investigators too early; and Sterne stupidly implying, by not coming clean for a time, that he'd been at home when he was in Seattle the night his son died.

"Has Kardas been tracked down?" Julio Sterne wanted to know.

"We're working on it," Pritter said.

"Drop it."

"What?"

"Drop it, I said."

"I don't understand—" Pritter's eyes bolted to the other two lawyers. Calmly, they returned his baffled gaze.

One of them, the elder, said: "Lloyd, what Mr. Sterne is suggesting is that someone else may be responsible for his son's death."

"And that's just the way we want it handled," said Sterne.

"Why now?" asked Pritter. "We've got the FBI alerted about Kardas. All-points bulletins were sent to every state police headquarters. Immigration was notified and—"

"You're not to press it," said the second lawyer.

"Mind telling me why?" asked Pritter.

"You'll be too busy with us, Lloyd, for one thing," said the elder lawyer. "Clean this business up. Your new office is two doors down from mine."

He didn't have to say more. Oldes and Farnham still wanted him, even after the trial had gone off its rails. Pritter was sufficiently overwhelmed not to ask why. But he knew a hitch lay somewhere in the arrangement. Kardas had had the time, when alone, that night, to put Marc Sterne away. And Audrey Sterne, she was another possi—and then it clarified. They were going to wring her by the neck, wanting him to cooperate.

"Mr. Sterne," said Pritter, his senses still askew, "let me get this straight. You want us to let Kardas get away without any further effort to find and question him?"

"You figure it out," said Julio Sterne. "Be sure you figure it out the right way this time...by the way, can Rhodes give us any more trouble?"

"He resigned," said Pritter. "He's completely out of it."

"You're keeping up the pressure with the newspapers?" Sterne pressed him.

"As much as we can. We can't make it overly obvious."

"Good," Sterne rose. "No mistakes this time," he reminded Pritter, who remained wary of this sudden yet fruitful turn of events. Sterne ushered all three lawyers to the door.

A short and crisp meeting, just the way he liked them.

Back at his desk, he examined the monthly budget overruns on films in production. Three films currently in the works were well over their estimated costs; three properties in pre-production were in abeyance until the right actors were found; another film was being readied for release next month and its publicity outlays were prodigiously disheartening.

He'd been hearing howls from his company directors, the same from the banks. Parthenon hadn't sent a film into the winner's circle since *Tonight or Never,* which still racked up steady revenues all over Europe.

Studio profits were slumping, and, predictably, furtive grumblings made the rounds: "Sterne's too old, out of touch, has his fingers in too many companies, spreading himself too thin and losing his touch". Comments of that nature.

He had been overly busy, he supposed, figuring how to save himself eight to ten million dollars in settlement costs with Audrey. Keep her thinking she was under suspicion by the sheriff's office, helped. Pressure her. Scare her, then fix everything for her, and settle with her for a sand pile.

No, he hadn't lost his touch. If anything, he was, like good wine, improving with age. Julio Sterne, mogul, and that was that.

He buzzed for his secretary. Time to nudge the governor into action again, and he planned to stop off in Sacramento on the way to San Francisco the day after tomorrow. Rhodes ought to be slam-dunked. The newspapers were dogging him nicely. He would show the doubters, whoever they were, how Julio Sterne could still draw breath and exhale fire.

☙

In the studio parking lot, Pritter conferred quietly and quickly with the Oldes & Farnham lawyers. He wanted assurances he had heard Julio Sterne correctly.

He had.

In his office an hour later, he called the Malibu sheriff. They were to press the investigation further, adroitly and with finesse this time. Keep leaning on Audrey Sterne. "Work the money motive," he told the sheriff. "Keep her guessing but squeeze her till she's a prune...if Kardas turns up, I'm to be notified immediately."

☙

In the half-dark interior at Dante's in North Hollywood, Romaine listened to Rhodes play his trombone. He was up on the small stage, there by the piano, leaning his head into his muted golden horn. Romaine had no idea he would be sitting in with the small quartet appearing at Dante's that week. She hadn't even known he played the trombone, finding herself pleasantly surprised.

Two men, seeing she was by herself, dropped by the table. They were probably as old as Rhodes, older perhaps; in the dark she couldn't really tell. Offering to buy her drinks, one of them even asked if she'd like to take off for a discotheque.

She shooed them off, nicely though. Her disguise of this night was working, she decided; it made her look thirtyish. She was done up in black mid-length skirt cut full, black lizard-skin boots, a black wig, with bangs. A red velvet ribbon was threaded through the high collar of her laundry-fresh white blouse. She had even gone so far as to flatten her breasts with an Ace bandage. Makeup tricks did the rest. With her newfound stealth, she convinced herself she could get away with anything, even do a Virgin Mary act if she must.

341

Loud applause when the set was over, and Rhodes thanked the quartet's leader as the stage emptied for a break. He lingered there, putting the trombone back in its case, then handing it to a waiter.

"Attracting the barflies. Class always tells, eh?" Smiling at her.

"Don't leave me, then."

"I need to blow some sounds once in a while."

"You're neat up there. Really terrific."

He sat down across from her. She clasped his hand with her left one.

"Like some wine?"

"No thanks. I had another glass while you were playing."

"I've awakened a great thirst." Rhodes motioned a waiter over.

"Cliff? Would you take me to church on Sunday?"

"We're chancing it as it is, don't you think? Frankly, my nerves are getting squashed...too many people looking at us. At you..."

"A small church."

"Only takes one person to see us."

"Fun, isn't it?"

"Be a helluva lot more fun in Bali or somewhere."

"Are you sorry? About me?"

"Nope, of course not. Never think like that."

Romaine breathed audibly. "Are you going to kiss me ever?"

"I have."

"Only on the cheek."

"That's where most kisses start."

"And in my case, finish?"

"I'm your—" stopping himself, then, before saying but thinking anyway: *"I'm twice your age, Romaine, and twice a lot of other things, too."*

He set the glass on the table close to Romaine's left hand. Rhodes had been looking at her face as they talked. Reaching for the tequila, his hand came to an abrupt halt. She was wearing a bracelet he had never noticed before. Green emerald stones framed by pavé diamonds caught the light from a flickering candle.

"That's a knockout," said Rhodes, touching the bracelet with a fingertip.

"Looks real, doesn't it?"

"As the moon." He pulled her hand closer, an intent look furrowing his brow.

"They're only paste, unfortunately."

"Certainly looks like the real article."

"Do I ever wish."

A round dime-sized clasp appeared as Rhodes turned the bracelet on her wrist. Small markings stared back at him, tiny empty eyes that formed the letter A, and then something else that scraped his heart. The missing bracelet—Audrey's. Instantly, he knew; instantly, he recoiled inside. *Christ!*

"Quite beautiful," he said. "Paste or not".

"A charity bazaar. When I saw it. I had to have it. Only eighty bucks."

"A charity bazaar?"

"Oh, one of those they put on all the time." Romaine pulled her hand away. "Saint John's Hospital in Santa Monica, I think. Last year sometime, I forget when."

You are tearing me to bits, lovely one of a hundred disguises, and you don't know what you're saying. Or do you? I hope by God you don't. Not after all that's been done to give you your life back—at least some kind of life. Rhodes thought he would get sick, and knocked back the rest of the drink in one swallow.

"Let's shove off," he said, getting up.

"Are you all right?"

"Nope, I'm not."

"Let's stay," Romaine protested, tuning in to the quick shift in his manner. "It's not all that late."

"The older you get, the faster dawn comes...c'mon. We're skedaddling."

On the way out with Romaine walking behind him, he picked up his trombone case. He walked too fast for her, not even turning when she yelped at his pace. On the twenty-minute ride to Fritzi's, he kept to himself, leaving her bewildered and huddled against the door. Twice she tried breaking through his crusty silence, only to meet with the higher wall of his unspoken fury at himself.

His thoughts fled to Audrey. Had she been telling the truth all along? Romaine was most certainly wearing the missing Bulgari bracelet. Was he sitting next to a felon? And a murderess?

Unable to think straight, he nearly swiped a parked car as he sped the Bentley up the winding road to Fritzi's.

343

She was home. Her car was parked in the circular driveway. He'd stay with her tonight. To hell with trying to play it so sacredly in front of a daughter who didn't know she was, and might never.

"Let's have a nightcap with Fritzi," he said, turning off the ignition.

"Are you upset? So quiet and everything?"

"Lots to think about."

"Me?"

"Yes, and how much I'll miss you," he said, trying not to raise any alarm.

"Why? I'm right here."

"I meant when I move up to Sacramento."

"Cliff, we'd be so great together." Her hand grazed his knee, settling on his thigh. He barely heard her or felt her hand as he opened the Bentley's door. He was halfway to stupor, making weak explanations to himself, yet the hammer of truth had come down with a resounding thump.

Chapter Thirty-five

Trying to get a better fix, trying to understand, trying to figure out what to do, and beginning to think he had made a mistake he could never make right.

At the shallow end of his pool Romaine turned, flipping over and free-styling her way back to the other end. Sleekly built, lithe as an otter, and he recalled how Audrey had weakened him in other days with her body. Watching her swim, thinking hard as he thought about her; Romaine had lied flatly to him. Nothing she could say about it would persuade him differently.

He dozed off, but awoke to a cool liquid stroke moving up and down his thigh. Romaine was rubbing him. She held a bottle of suntan oil in one hand, had slipped off her top. The rounds of her breasts, pale and firm, wavered as she oiled his skin. Her nipples, ruby bullets, stared at him.

"Didn't want you to burn away," Romaine murmured. Unabashed, she kept rubbing. "Kiss me, bubba-man."

"Absolutely not."

He moved her fingers away, but she strained to keep them near to where he had begun to bulge. He opened both eyes, seeing that she noticed his rise, smiling at him now.

"If you ask nicely, I'll let you take a tour of my carburetor...where all the combustion happens." Attempting to fondle him again.

On his second and more forcible effort, he bent her wrist slightly, holding her hand away.

"That hurts...stop..."

"Then back off."

"Let me."

"No," he said.

"For un souzand pesos I show you my see-ster but I geeve you me," she mimicked.

"Cut it out." Yet he smiled.

"Fiva hon-dred. Ees better, no?"

Rhodes laughed.

"Zen nossing. You good man, so I fuck you for nos-sing. Am vair-y clean, señor."

"That's not funny."

"Ah, but I make you laugh, no?"

"Not any more, you won't."

"I might surprise you," she said in her real voice.

"Don't talk that way. I don't like it."

"Take me. You'll never again want anyone else, I promise you."

"Go put your top back on." He sat up, a savage scowl on his face.

Romaine stood next to the chaise. Bright as a triggered flash bulb, the sun shone on her and he could see the downy fluff on her upper legs. For a long moment, she was Audrey again, a thought he wished he could assassinate, for he could not ever think of his daughter in that way.

"Why don't you want me? You've been so nice. Let me *do* you."

"I'm out of season, kiddo. And so are you. Scram, right now, and I mean it."

"I know you're not gay," Romaine teased, watching how his eyes passed across her breasts. "Fritzi told me."

"Fritzi would tell you plenty more, if she caught you like this."

Romaine leaned over, very close. "If Fritzi were here, she might kiss you like this."

The kiss missed his face completely, going lower as intended, much lower.

He pushed her away, forcibly. She merely smiled again at him.

"You're behaving badly."

"And you're being stubborn...Fritzi isn't the one for you. Don't you know that?"

"No, I don't. And thank you, I'll be the judge of that."

"That's what you just resigned, I thought. Being a judge."

"Not in that department," Rhodes said, alarmed now as he looked into her very knowing eyes.

"But I really could be so much better for you."

Standing over him, lusciously perverse, she wiggled her fingers into her skimpy bikini bottoms.

"You do that," Rhodes said, "and I'll slap your ass till it's purple."

"How exciting. I'm ready."

"Get going." Hot and angry, the muscles in his shoulders bunched up. He pointed to the pool house.

Romaine pouted. Before, her face was relaxed, almost softly inquisitive as she pleaded with him. It changed suddenly, all of its lines and planes and shapes becoming a stone frieze; the visage of a marble statue.

"You don't have any feelings. Who are you anyway? I could hate you, I really could." Tossing the bottle of oil off onto the grass, she sauntered away. "You *are* a fag. I just bet you are." He heard her taunt, and then what sounded like shrill laugh.

As she vanished into the pool house, Rhodes balled his hands, whether in anger or frustration he couldn't tell. He wanted to love her, fend for her, create some kind of a life together. It was becoming impossible, an act of reckless folly.

Could he tell Fritzi?

Tonight they were supposed to review wedding plans. She had already informed him that Fahey would be giving her away. "A surprise," she'd said, before landing on him for failing to help his old friend. If she knew enough to parse his situation, she'd probably go catatonic—what to tell her?

But he couldn't. Not all of it. He had to reserve an airplane seat for Sacramento, deciding to tell Fritzi part of the situation after he returned.

の

In the pool house, Romaine unpeeled before a full-length mirror in one of the dressing rooms. Studying herself, posing, lifting her hair over her head, shaping it into a different style; and her face with it.

The face could be better, but the body has all the right scenery in all the right places. Why doesn't he want me? Is he for real? Knowing my real parents, and wanting to help me—is that some sort of a trick? In bed, I bet I

347

could find out. Men talk in bed. Jagoda must go! she thought as she fastened her hair with a purplish ribbon.

Chapter Thirty-six

A closely held dream was kissed goodbye after two years of waiting for it to circle and land. His chance at what he hoped to do for the rest of his life went down in imaginary crash right in front of his nose. Rhodes stared out a window, barely listening to the governor's pious ramblings.

"...This state's, any state's Supreme Court must be above this sort of controversy...Cliff, are you hearing me?"

"Not too well, Harry."

"You've got the newspapers on your neck again. The legislature is growling about your appointment...I've got a letter here from a senior judge on the Supreme Court who's bitching. Surely you can see the wisdom—"

"Out on my ass," said Rhodes, swinging around. "Is that it?"

"Not necessarily. Let's let things die down. You can have the next vacancy."

Die down, he thought; the same advice he'd given his daughter. "Which could be ten years away," he said, a little too loudly, before he could catch himself.

"Yes, it could," the governor agreed. "But two of those fellows over there practically need crutches."

"All over the damn trial, isn't it, Harry? Your boys lost one, and it was one of the most fouled up investigations I've ever read or seen."

"You didn't have to rub their noses in it."

"Harry, they had a kid up there on...on a bum murder rap," said Rhodes, a little weakly.

"Some people don't think so."

"Then the hell with them."

"Easy for you to say, Cliff. But I have an election coming up and it's no time to upset anyone."

"You seem to forget pretty fast, Harry. I helped you stump this state, and gathered up a lot of money for your campaign. I don't say I made the difference, but I sure as hell helped you."

"And I'll never forget it."

"Right this minute, you are."

"It's all very regrettable. Very embarrassing for me. But there it is." The governor opened his hands, outwardly, in a fan-shape, as if to protect himself from more heated words.

"Is Sterne in on this?" Rhodes asked. "The two of you setting up an ambush?"

"A terrible thing to say," the governor said. "Terrible." He laced hands together, cracking the knuckles nervously.

"The *terrible* truth, you mean."

"Don't talk so foolishly—"

He was tempted to relay what Audrey had told him about her husband's kibitzing, but thought it advisable to steer clear. Audrey Sterne and the governor's wife, Ella, were close friends, and, if she complained, Ella would likely hear of it. Instead, Rhodes said, "I wonder what people would think, Harry, if they knew how many times I got phoned by this office during the trial."

"What're you suggesting?"

"That Sterne wanted pressure put on me...and you know it, Harry, so don't look so goddamn innocent."

"Begging your pardon, Cliff, but all I ever called you about was the court appointment."

"Your ninny of an aide did it for you. How do you think the newspapers would play that one?"

"Well, he shouldn't have."

"Sterne never met with you about the trial? Are you really saying that, Harry?"

"We're old friends. A shocking thing, the son's death," the governor soothed, "we could hardly avoid talking about it at times."

"I'll just bet." Rhodes didn't believe what he was about to say, but it wouldn't hurt to troll a few doubts before his host. "Your pal Sterne damn near perjured himself in my court. He wasn't even there on the night he insinuated that he was...think about that one, Harry. Think about whether he was covering for his wife, Harry, and then, Harry, you can think about whether she and her boyfriend did away with Sterne's son... and they needed a patsy to take the gaff and the girl was unlucky enough to be around..."

"I'd say that's preposterous."

"But you weren't there and you weren't on the jury, were you, Harry?"

"You're reaching for straws."

"You'll never know. Neither will I, but such things do happen. Even in films they happen, as Sterne would know."

"Perhaps so. But you obviously don't know Audrey Sterne at all. She'd never in a thousand years—"

The governor's voice trailed off.

Rhodes was tempted to set the governor straight, and watch him fall off his sanctimonious throne. Instead, he said: "The jury rejected Audrey Sterne's story. So you might want to think that over before mentioning things about Audrey Sterne. I can tell you this, she didn't make the proceedings any easier."

"You know, Cliff, there's such a thing as a man being too good at what he does. Gets folks upset sometimes. Maybe you ought to go back to lawyering again. You were the best in California and maybe that's where you still belong. Where you'll be happiest..."

Rhodes knew he had forced the governor to deny any tampering with the trial. One look at that craggy evasive face told him it was time to leave before a war party started up. Circles of deceit. Top to bottom, everyone sidestepping the hard truth. Himself, too. Strange, he thought, how the trial had touched lives not even remotely connected to an act of murder.

Rhodes started for the door. The governor made an effort to rise but Rhodes stopped him with: "Don't bother, Harry. I know the way home."

"Cliff—"

"Harry, we've got one chance left to stay on speaking terms. And that's only if we both say not another damn thing right now."

Reaching the street, yanking his tie and unbuttoning his shirt collar, as he strode into the gritty hot afternoon. He moved along almost aimlessly, barely aware of others on the street.

A year of life frittered away. Save the daughter, lose the dream.

Romaine was getting to be the most expensive kid in history. His history, at least. Had it been justice? Justice: not always ethical, often a fine grind, was a fairly easy thing to reach, and a fairly easy thing for most to accept. A sort of balancing act that worked most of the time. Doing the right thing, however, was more complicated; fraught with all sorts of twists, turns and blowbacks.

It cost, always it cost plenty.

Blocks later, his shirt damp and clinging, Rhodes shoved open the door to Frank Fats, a saloon that was a home for some of the sharpest political hucksters in the country. He waded through the guzzlers, two or three deep at the bar even at this hour. The biggest bar in California, long and oval shaped, built of a mahogany that shined gratefully from the hundreds of elbows rubbing on it every day,

Near to three o'clock in the afternoon.

Rhodes looked around at the rows of faces up and down the bar. Without knowing their names or where they slept, he knew those faces belonged to lobbyists, hangers-on, legislators and whoever else had a deal to cut in Sacramento. Favors to exchange. Laws passed. A place where sooner or later white bribery takes over, and green cash starts to move like a river after a heavy rain.

He ordered a Corona beer. He shook hands with two bartenders he knew from days when he used to come to Sacramento to appeal cases to the court he would never be seated upon.

Well, fuck the court, fuck everything.

He drank his beer, feeling cooler, a little cooler anyway. The rejection by the governor still stung, still threw him. He drank, he moped. Unaccountably, he began adding up his life, the part of it he could remember and weigh. The part of it he could still bring himself to remember.

Marriage was about to say hello. Step right this way, hold your breath— one of those moments stepped on his head. Out of work, though far from broke. How nice. He would rather be broke, do what he really wanted to do—so few ever having that opportunity.

The girl he had wanted to marry an eternity ago, when he was young and slightly dumber, was already hip-by-hip with the sonofabitch who had the guv on a leash.

He could always go lawyering again. Always plenty of crooks to defend. Some of them, he bet to himself, could be found within two feet of where he was draining his beer. He was too numb now to get his thinking in touch with his clearer senses.

Rhodes glanced at his watch. Three hours before his plane departed, so he asked one of the bartenders if he could borrow a phone. Calling Fritzi, he could easily explain to her that their honeymoon might last for the next ten or twenty years. He had nothing else to do that seemed to matter anymore. Or, if Fahey ever talked, let loose, he might even qualify for rent-free quarters at San Quentin.

"It's me," he said when she answered.

"Are you back?"

"I'm just about to leave for the airport. I'll be there by seven-thirty or eight."

"Come straight to the house," Fritzi told him in a shaky voice. "Soon as you can--"

"What's the matter?"

"I don't have time to go into it," said Fritzi hurriedly. "But she's crazy. She's a fiend."

She hung up before he could tell her how the governor had cashiered him. She'd probably celebrate, he thought, throw a big dinner party and send old Harry a campaign donation in ever-lasting gratitude.

∞

The plane circled Los Angeles for almost an hour before it was cleared to land. By the time he reached Fritzi's, he was tired and hungry, and still coming apart inside. But those things were forgotten when he saw the sizzling fret she was in.

He threw his own arms around her as she spoke into his shoulder, looked up occasionally with her filmy eyes, seeing if he was getting it all.

"One thing of...after...th...the other. Hexi-hexing me," Fritzi sobbed. "Sc-creamed at me like as I was the one who was wrong."

"You have to calm down, darling," he told her quietly. "I still don't know what's going on here."

Fritzi moaned. She gripped his forearms and he felt her strength shooting right up to his shoulders. "Goddamn her, she's really—"

"Okay. C'mon, let's go sit down. You can tell me whatever. Where is she?"

"Drove off in her car to who cares where." Fritzi rubbed her eyes, and Rhodes passed her his hanky. I'm sorry," she said, sniffling.

"You don't have to be sorry about anything."

"I just hate to disappoint you."

"About what?"

"You wanted her to stay here. But she's got to go. Tonight, I mean!"

Fritzi clasped his hand, and led him off toward the living room. "Look at this." She pointed to the small Correggio displayed on a stand inside the breakfront. Rhodes bent down. The faces of two lovers had been blotted out with blue ink.

"Does she know where the painting came from?"

"I told her."

"Why, Fritzi?"

She shrugged. "We talked about you a lot. Romaine was curious, I guess...she tried to wreck the painting, and those precious little lovebirds you gave me are gone—"

Fritzi told him how she had found the cage door open, the birds missing. Romaine said she watered them, and must have forgotten to close the cage. Fritzi had asked her how they'd flown out of the house. Romaine said she was mystified—maybe up the chimney. Then the damage to the Correggio was noticed when Fritzi saw it was skewed slightly on its ivory stand.

"Did you see the oleander shrubs out front?"

"No, it's too dark."

"It's all knocked down in half, practically. They say—the gardening service—said I called and told them to cut it."

"And you didn't?"

Fritzi shook her head. "I certainly didn't, but they insist it was me. The same as my hairdresser. He called yesterday, wondering why I failed to show up."

He thought about Audrey's bracelet, and then, adding things up, he thought about the phone call Audrey denied ever making to Marc Sterne's office. He thought, too, about nights he'd taken Romaine out, in disguise, and she had at times altered her voice to fit the person she was imagining herself to be. He'd been amused. He was anything but amused now.

"She's going tonight, Cliff. I won't have her around here. I don't care who her parents are..."

"She say when she'd be coming back?"

"I didn't hear and I don't care. I gave her unshirted hell and she swore at me. Then took off in a snit."

"Are you going to Masquers?"

"Not till this is settled."

"Let's go pack her up then."

"What're you going to do with her? I felt sorry for that kid. Now I think they ought to put a fence around her."

Rhodes shut his eyes, counting the blows to his heart that no one could see and only he could feel. "Yeah. Something's wrong, Fritzi. I don't know what, but I'll find out."

"What is she to you anyway? Get rid of her."

"I can't. Not now, I can't."

"Why not for God's sake? You're behaving like an idiot."

"Someday"—he exhaled—"not now, but I'll tell you one day."

"Who're her parents? Why do you have to get into it?"

"Long long story. Some other time."

"You must owe them the damn world, Cliff." Her eyes questioning, awaiting a reply.

He thought before he said: "They owe her something. I've a feeling life torpedoed Romaine once too often. I just don't know, I honestly don't."

"So what're you going to do with her?"

"Put her up at my place, I suppose."

"Jolly. Isn't that the silliest thing I ever heard you say? And what about those damn disguises she wears?"

Rhodes put his hand on Fritzi's shoulder. "Let's just pack her up."

"Fine. That's fine. I can't wait, I really cannot wait even another second."

"I'll start on it. How about if you do me up an omelet or a sandwich?"

She saw how haggard and punched out he looked. "Sure. Let's have a drink first. We can pack her up later."

He needed to be alone for a moment. "You go ahead, I'll make the drinks."

Waiting until Fritzi headed for the kitchen, Rhodes went out to the hallway leading to the bedrooms. He passed by Fritzi's, then by a linen closet, then by the door of another bedroom, before going into the one at the end of the hallway. A gay bright room all colored up with flowery chintzes against powder-blue walls. The furniture was country French, and two side-by-side windows overlooked a rose garden full of early spring blooms.

355

Rhodes opened the outer doors of an armoire and slid out the drawers full of panties, bras, some sweaters, silk hosiery and several flesh-colored garter belts he thought had gone out of fashion years ago. He opened another drawer. Cotton shirts. In the lowest drawer, he found a jewelry box of green leather embossed with gilt scrolls at its corners.

Inside the box, along with several pairs of earrings, gold bangles, and a signet ring was Audrey's emerald and diamond bracelet. He dropped it into his pocket just as Fritzi poked her head through the doorway.

"I thought you were going to pop the gin," she said, then saw the pained look on his face. "What's bothering you, Cliff?"

"Bad day, I guess."

"How was Sacramento? I forgot to ask."

"Where's Sacramento?" he said glumly.

"What happened?"

"Harry dumped me on my canetta."

"Oh, no!"

"Oh, but yes. Rolled me into a doughnut, the kind with no hole."

"You poor thing." She was near him in three quick strides, holding his face between her hands. "Tell me...tell me..."

He did. In four clipped sentences, he painted the portrait of his afternoon in Sacramento.

"I can't say I'm really sorry. I know you wanted it, but I'm so glad you'll be here. Very glad," Fritzi whispered to him, her eyes filling again.

"I'll get your drink."

"God, I'm sorry I bothered you with all this."

"I'm not, honey. I had to know."

"Cliff?"

"Yes."

"Do you think she's whacked out? Disturbed? Officially disturbed?"

"Something's wrong. Has to be something, doesn't it?"

"Is she safe to be around? I don't like her being at your house. If anyone finds out, it'll look funny. They'll talk and—"

"I can't lose track of her. Not just now, anyway."

"Well, when then? What's going on?"

"Soon as I can get her squared away. I have to do that, somehow. Please be patient."

Fritzi asked, "Why did you buy her all those clothes?"

"Her father paid for them," he said, again feeling like a damn fool as he said it.

They left the room. He joined Fritzi in the kitchen where, drinks in hand, they talked as she made ranchero omelets with ham and chili peppers. As they ate, Fritzi worked him over about the wedding, then about Fahey, and his own plans now that Sacramento was in the past tense.

He nodded to almost everything, or shrugged, sometimes answering her with an exhausted silence. Woman questions, get to the bottom of everything; check out all the new compass bearings, all in one fell swoop. He loved her, but he was washed out and needed a century of quiet.

They packed up Romaine in three suitcases, a dress bag and a duffel. The new dresses were folded back into the boxes they found on the closet shelves.

"This is a pain for you," said Fritzi as she zipped the duffel.

"I don't mind."

"Doesn't she have friends who can put her up?"

"I'll find out."

"Don't take her out places anymore, all right?"

"I'll see."

"No, look at me. I want you to promise me."

He looked at her.

"Promise?"

"How can I? How would you feel if you'd been through that she has?"

"Like I was lucky to be alive. That I might even wiggle myself before the judge who may have saved my neck. And when miraculously he comes to my rescue again, I might really get ideas—"

"That's nutty and you—"

"She is nutty for sure." Fritzi latched the last of the suitcases.

"I'll take this stuff out to the car."

"Why not let her...I'm almost sure she can brush her own teeth. Or will you do that too?"

"You're beginning to sound very married."

Fritzi huffed. He gripped two of the suitcases and lugged them out of the bedroom door. She wasn't there when he came back. He made two more trips. On the last one, he heard her on the phone. A few minutes later, she appeared in the living room, wearing a black chiffon dress and a strand of pearls around her neck.

"I'm going over to the restaurant. Want to come along?"

"Thanks, no. I'll wait for her."

"Don't be ridiculous, Cliff. We've both had a rotten day, and somehow, when you think about it, she caused it. Let's get out of here."

"That's why I'm waiting. I want to be sure we don't have another rotten one."

"Well, I don't want to be here if she comes back here tonight. I don't trust myself."

Rhodes went to her. He held and kissed her, but Fritzi was as wooden as some child's toy. When she left, he sat and waited. Nothing else to do but wait and he went out into the breathless night, and, sitting on the terrace, lit a cigar.

If Romaine was sick, all the more reason to help. Maybe she was high-strung, flighty, full of the fragile emotions of the talented actress she apparently was, and somehow some lunar force was shaking her. Shaking him, too. He knew now he had blinded himself by the instinctive, irrepressible need to protect his own; and he was paying for it, paying in the coin of major distress backed up by the whip of desperation.

In his pocket, he felt for Audrey's bracelet, and then he tossed it lightly in his hand a few times. Tossed jewels. Was that what Romaine was—a tossed jewel?

Fahey, for the tenth time that week, came to mind. A nagging item that had to be dealt with. As he started to pick the lock of that problem, he heard the front door open. He waited and then heard footsteps. Finally, she showed up at the terrace door. She wore no disguise tonight. Her hair was pulled back, and she had on white slacks, red sandals, and a blue pullover. She looked like one of those five-dollar souvenir posters of a California beach girl, blond as a daffodil and just as fresh.

"I saw your car," said Romaine. "Are you alone?"

"Have a seat."

"What're you drinking?"

"White blood. My own. Like some?"

Romaine's mouth tightened.

"I guess it's time for you to move on," he said. "We packed up your gear. We didn't know when you'd be home to take care of it yourself."

"I can't wait to get out of here."

Looking dispraisingly at her, saying, "How wonderfully ungrateful of you."

"She told you? About getting mad and everything?"

"I'll say she did."

"Fritzi has everything mixed up. She's realty got the wildest imagination when she's not humming the right way."

"We all do."

"Not like her. She was so nasty. God, and how nice I thought she was."

And still is, he thought. "Let's skedaddle. You can stay at my place."

"Really? Can I?"

"Where else? It's getting on. The time. Let's march."

"You don't sound so enthusiastic."

"It's been a long wait, Romaine. Longest one I ever made. Twenty years or more, and then you show up—"

She laughed. "No one waits that long."

Romaine went to check her room and returned quickly. "I suppose I should leave a note...I guess I should. She was really very nice sometimes."

"Call her and tell her."

"I'd never do that. She isn't worth all that, you know."

"Right you are. She was only your hostess for almost two weeks."

"You don't have to be sarcastic."

"It's the sarcastic truth and you'd do well to remember it. We're going now before my head cuts out."

Neither of them looked back: Romaine because she didn't care to, and Rhodes because he didn't have to, knowing the house and grounds as if they were his own. Wanting, also, to erase the slightest recollection of this day and this night, neither of which would ever forget him, nor would he soon be forgetting them.

He knew now he was sitting side-by-side with a liar. A killer, too? That's what Audrey had claimed. His thoughts were awry as the hay in a haystack. Still, snaking through the traffic, having nothing to say to her at this moment, he forced himself into a different lane of thinking now.

Or was it simply the justifying of guilt?

Had this been a father-daughter scam, and in his courtroom? Was that what they had pulled off? For her part, playing to the jurors, subliminally asking: *Who do you like better?* Me, with my only weapon being a stork-legged lawyer who could barely walk a straight line? Or that door-wide Pritter? And the hell with the truth. Because, she was the only one who possessed the truth of that night in Malibu. And she did not ever have to incriminate herself.

He had abetted her. He had been a father protecting his own. He had made a wrong move, a stupid choice, going all out to side with his ambition of being on the Supreme Court, a very estimable honor.

He could tell himself all he wanted to, a thousand times, that it was up to the jury to convict or make free . It was for them to decide and decide they had. But how might they have decided if hadn't put a thumb on the scales of justice? Telling himself it was all about fairness, about being fair-minded enough to help the fledgling lawyer, Burke. He had helped others. He had helped scores of students, sometimes by showing them why to steer clear of becoming a criminal practitioner.

That, too, was abetting, wasn't it?

She needed help. She might even need a new soul, but he was the wrong man for it—he was no soul-maker. Nor had he ever met one. So, what now?

Chapter Thirty-seven

Audrey read the enclosed card for the second time. She had just opened the small box from Cartier, unwrapped the tissue paper, and then, eyes staring in disbelief, she read:.

> *Lost and Found.*
> *Cliff*

A medley of elation raced through her, as she draped the emeralds around her wrist. Curious, she called Cartier and was referred to the service department; there, they told her the diamonds on the clasp had been missing, and had been replaced three days earlier, when the bracelet, as requested, was given urgent priority by the repair department.

"Is anything amiss, mam?"

"More than you can imagine, but not with the bracelet. Thanks very much," Audrey said, still surprised by it all. "Is the bill coming separately?"

Already paid, she was advised.

She tore Rhodes's handwritten card into pieces, tossing them into a wastebasket. Better that way, she thought. How he'd ever come across her bracelet? Audrey's mind turned the point over and over; obviously, it had been retrieved from Romaine, but exactly how had that come about?

Her curiosity raced, yet she decided not to call him after all. Perhaps later or with a letter. But that didn't seem such a good idea, either. Yet if he paid for the repair, decency said she ought to do something. Then again, maybe he owed her that much and more.

Four blocks from the Gypsy's house, Fahey dropped to his knees. Massively serious, he settled into a pew in the unfamiliar haven of a small church.

This is me checking in from Your forgotten planet. I sing of my friend and my friend is Alonzo Fahey...We are again under siege down here. Many feet are stepping on me. So for God's sake...I mean for Your sake, listen...

You still need me.

Sinners are everywhere. It's so much fun, You know. Rhodes, I'm sorry to say, can no longer be counted on; Cullis, whose heart is black as his face, has red teeth getting even redder on my bones; and about Burke, he of the wounded walking. You must also dismiss him as another disloyal. He's a lawyer, so we cannot expect more...

By the by, the whiskey swear-off doesn't work so well. You could've told me, or passed the word to Your ever-disciple. Besides, what's a soldier without his jug?

I know what You're about to say. The ladies, right? But You who have known me for these thirty-seven years, also know it's always been the married ones for me. Much safer. So neglected they are; spiritually too, of course. Can't have them running around with their straps loose, can we? Or out on the streets peddling their hips? Why have You made them so soft breasted and hardheaded?

At Your signal, I shall ignore them all. A very, very clear signal. Nothing half-hearted this time.

I'm off to see my Gypsy. Shan't lay so much as a fingernail on her this time. Perhaps, a kissing of her mad eyes, and I swear to You that shall be my limit. She's a true gift You've sent my way, and it shall not go forgotten. Not like some, we know. Fahey, this Fahey, never forsakes his friends.

Uncanny abilities there in the Gypsy, have You noticed? I think of her as one of Your closest cousins. I'll take her off to Las Vegas one day, clean up at the tables, and tithe You for the usual ten-percent. Make it fifteen.

I'm off now. Remember that friend Fahey is Your first soldier and he will suffer a mortal blow if his ticket is lifted. It's my calling, just as You have Yours. Otherwise, who'll stop the art thieves at the Vatican, or go after those Cardinals You and I already know about...

Is heaven crowded these days?

Come see us sometime. Do wonders for our spirits. Be delighted to make the announcement for You.

Bless You, Meister. I need my ticket, so don't go fucking with me. Till next time, cheers...

Outside the church, Fahey walked at a quickened clip, his face loaded with mountain-hard resolution. He seemed in less of a coma, his mood lightening now that he had made a tentative peace with his Maker.

Over his shoulder, he glanced back at the church, then up to its belfry. They ought to be ringing church bells more often, he reflected, or what was the point of having them at all?

Bells were meant for ringing. Vigorous ringing, at that, to commemorate every golden-plated sinner, he thought. All those mellifluous gorgeous clanging sounds for summoning the living, telling of the dead, that the hour had arrived for opening up the saloons, and, after the saloons, come the schools for the childies. And what of the biggest bell of all, the one that tolled midnight? So whoever kept the Book of Hours would know another day had croaked, and all of us remaining behind were to fall to our knees and mourn its passage.

Who had had the impudence to shut off the bells? Cursing now at whomever they were, because they stood against his newest friend, God.

He'd look into it: another non-paying investigation, and they always meant trouble, and not only in the wallet.

But first, his Gypsy-girl; his alter-conscience. He would confess to her how he had so recently sanctified himself on his knees. Recite a psalm to her, perhaps; a psalm no doubt swiped from the Hindus or Jainists. He give her the one having to do with the lads in the Dark Valley, or that other wild myth, about those rogues in Sodom who had been having such a lovely time for themselves before bring converted into salt statues.

How had that been managed? A trick worth knowing and he'd put it on his list for asking the Gypsy, thinking also he ought to know more about her genome. There might be parallels with his own. Commonality, that was the order of his day, and he hardened his jaw as he footed deeper into his day.

Chapter Thirty-eight

Rhodes spent most of a day—one appointment in the morning, the other in early afternoon—with two UCLA psychiatrists, both top men in their fields; he had wanting separate opinions. In his lawyering years, he had engaged both as expert witnesses.

He recited everything he could think of about Romaine, without mentioning her name. Making casual inquiries, he said, though neither doctor was prepared to offer much of an opinion without a professional examination of the patient.

Impossible, he told them.

With caution, one of the doctors made a conceivable, theoretical prognosis and referred Rhodes to several textbooks. When Rhodes asked about offshore treatment, one of the doctors offered to contact a highly regarded clinic in France.

In the medical library, he requested the reference texts, and then slid into a chair at a long table, where bleary-eyed students moped over books, some having nodded off. He read, read more, making notes on a yellow pad, losing his way sometimes in the arcane vocabulary of psychiatry.

Pathological Narcissism. A new one for him.

How it was that certain people could behave acceptably most of the time. Can work, even excel, to fulfill great ambition. Earn the admiration of others but nonetheless possess a constant need for praise and are quickly bored when others fail to heap it on them. Exploit you without any feelings of guilt. Manipulate the feelings of others. Charm and engage you, play you as if you were a harp. Scruples—those are for others, not for them. Love of self: never apologize, always brush off any insult...and if one doesn't submit to a narcissist's basic desires, then one must expect a reaction, even harm.

Emptiness swept him. He stared off into space, thinking of her again. Was she that way? Really?

ଓ

At the pool house, he fixed them both soft drinks. Romaine played with the ice cubes in hers; indifferent, impatient too, as if he were a nuisance for barging in on her.

"I put some money in your account today," he said, leaning against the wet bar.

"How much?"

"Enough to carry you for a while. Several months."

"From *my* parents, I suppose."

"That's right, Romaine. Have you a passport, by the way?"

"I do," she lied. "Are we going somewhere?"

"How would you like to see Paris, and then the south of France? Cap Ferrat or Monte Carlo?"

"I'd love it. Sure. When do we go? "

"Next week. I'll get reservations. We'll have to fly separately."

"Whatever. Can we go somewhere tonight?"

"I'm seeing Fritzi."

"Pooh! What the hell am I supposed to do? And you can tell her something for me."

"You tell her."

"She'd deny it."

"I doubt it."

"She takes things."

"She took you in as a guest. Is that what you mean?"

"No, it isn't what I mean at all."

"Well, then what?"

"Oh, nothing." Romaine pouted.

He would bet half of what he owned that she was thinking of the bracelet. He intended to wait her out on that one until she told him straight, if she ever dared. He would go on as if he knew nothing about it. Otherwise, he would have to reveal why he sent it back, and Romaine would deduce that he knew Audrey Sterne on more than casual terms.

"Is France to be our fling? Bathtubs of champagne, violins, a tree of candles in a gorgeous black bathroom—"

"You sound like Fahey."

She winced. "You know him? He's crazy."

"Not really," Rhodes said. A mistake, using Fahey's name, and he knew it the moment he'd opened his mouth.

"What about Fahey?"

"What about him?"

"What's he to you?" Romaine scowled, her eyes intent.

Rhode shrugged. "Known him for years. Lots of people know him."

"He's a scuzz, the sneaky kind. Thinks he's so funny, and all the time he's a snake charmer, if I ever saw one."

Right on, thought Rhodes, and he may well have saved your sweet backside in a bargain still clamoring to be paid off.

"Maybe I'll go back to my old apartment and stay there, if you're going to see *her* again."

"Stay wherever you like, of course."

"Cliff?"

"Yes?"

He'd been going for the door. He turned around now to see Romaine with both arms stretched out behind her, as she leaned against the counter of the bar. Her long legs were apart, and the place above her legs had arched, inviting him to her again.

"Why're you doing all this? Europe, the clothes, money?"

"I thought I told you."

"Not really."

"There'll come a time when I'll tell you everything."

"Futt to you."

He smiled. "Glad to see your language is improving."

"You swear sometimes."

"I don't know any better...see you later."

When he left, she went back to a journal she'd been keeping. She wrote some lines and then drew a sketch of Rhodes. The drawing, quite good, showed him blowing on a trombone, adrift in a cloud of blackened musical notes.

CR

Ah, Cliff, what's the use—it was the tag end of Fritzi's thought as she listened to him over dinner. They were at Ma Maison, because it was impossible to be alone with her at Masquers.

She had listened to him, hating it. France, why France and with that scamp?

Are you so dumb stupid, she wanted to say, that you don't know you are killing me over this silly-ass business with your little actress? Are you trying to get even with me for something? Do you know what you mean to me? What we can have together, if you don't wreck it?

Rhodes stopped talking so he could eat his steak before it got any colder. He knew she wasn't taking it any better than he expected her to take it.

"But why Europe?" Fritzi asked.

"Because I want to get her out of this town. Off this acting kick, at least for a while. She needs help. And I don't want her all screwed up with more Hollywood fantasies, which is all that'll happen if she keeps hanging around here."

"But why you? It's like you're on some romp with that girl."

"The hell of it is I don't think you'd believe me, Fritzi. I hardly believe it myself sometimes."

"Try me, why don't you? Just try!"

He hardly knew where to begin because it had all become such a great maze; and he had to keep Audrey out of it, though he wasn't sure why. But he did begin, in a low voice, telling Fritzi the barest essentials—the broken ribs of the past and the un-mended ribs of now.

Stumbling out the words, Rhodes saw Fritzi change from her usual rose color to a fish-belly white. As her color changed so did the shape of her face, a face now filled with shock, as if someone, naked, had just dropped by for a friendly chat.

"I can't believe this," Fritzi said when he finished.

"Neither can I. But there it is."

"You're not making this up?"

"I wish to hell I were."

Fritzi looked off, then back again. "Aren't you in trouble then? I mean couldn't they do something to you?"

"I am if you ever let on what I should never have told you, but had to."

"Oh, my dear Christ-*sakes!*" Fritzi cried out loudly before she rushed a hand to her mouth. A woman sitting at a nearby table glanced over, her wide-eyed face full of sudden interest.

"You can't say anything. You realize that."

"I almost wish you hadn't told me, Cliff."

"You asked and have been asking me now for weeks."

"I should never have pried. I'm sorry."

"You had to know sooner or later."

"You had me so worried and now it's even worse."

"I know it looked crazy," he said. "Running around with her, especially with all those disguises. But I needed to learn about her. Get to know her somehow, on some way."

Still poised on the teeter-totter of disbelief, Fritzi was bothered by all the very real trouble that might chase after him. The newspapers had already ridden him hard. The governor had swung the worst punch of all. A real blow to his pride, that one; and she decided then and there never to mention again his situation with Romaine.

"And she doesn't know who you really are?" she asked when he flagged the waiter for coffee.

"I don't know how to tell her."

"And if you did, she'd have you right by the neck."

"And a few other places."

"Who's the mother, or shouldn't I ask."

"You can ask, babe, but I'm not saying. Not now, I'm not. You wouldn't want to know."

"Someone I know, isn't it?"

"Yes, you do."

"Can I ask you something else? Did you actually get her off? Is that really why Alonzo Fahey is in trouble?"

"Something like that...yes, I suppose I did help get Romaine off. I've been getting a lot of people off for the past twenty years. And she's my daughter and I couldn't help myself. So I did everything possible and now Alonzo is taking it square in his chops. I'm sick over it, but I'm damned if I know what to do about that, either."

"What a—it's catastrophic. What'll you do?"

About his future, he didn't know precisely, and said so. At forty-four, there was still plenty of road ahead. But his life had changed so swiftly be hadn't the time yet to draw up a new map. And, no, he would not go back into criminal law. Maybe teach. Or hold up one end of the bar at Masquers, how would that be? He could always ramble around Europe, thinking about what the future portended. As soon as he said it, Fritzi reminded him: "No, you don't. We've got a date, remember?"

"I damn sure do. But you better think on that one for a while."

"I have."

"Well, think some more, Fritzi, because I honestly don't know what'll happen if the milk ever gets spilled."

"You mean Alonzo?"

"For one, yes."

"Who else?"

"Romaine's mother."

"Does Alonzo know all this?"

"No, and he never can either."

"You can't leave him hanging, Cliff. He's your great friend."

"Or was…"

"Can't you help him?"

"I don't know how to, as I said. I'm swinging in the wind myself as it is."

Serving their coffee, seeing their bleak expressions, the waiter eased out a joke. They laughed when the punch line was forgotten.

"How long will you be in Europe?" Fritzi asked a moment later.

"A week, maybe two. A clinic in southern France, in a town called Gorbio, was recommended to me. I don't know how she'll take it. Probably not very well, so I'll have to persuade her somehow."

"Well, it's for her own good certainly."

"Maybe I'll check in myself and let 'em change my light bulbs, while they work on hers."

"That isn't exactly a ha-ha."

"What is? I can always say I went crazy and had to hole up for a while."

"Don't, Cliff. Don't say that sort of thing."

"It's been a helluva strange time. I'm boxed forever. But I want to get behind her and help. I'm going to…still it hurts, you know, it really does. I can't tell her who I am. That's too dicey. And I can't have her in my life or

369

someone's going to suspect something. I think of it by the hour. Hours, plural. And then I think about what you said not so long ago, Fritzi. About having kids. Adopting one. I'd like a family. You. Romaine. But that won't work either. Maybe we should adopt. We'll have any kind of family you want, if you want. A promise. But as I said, sweetheart, you'd better think over this marriage again, because I don't know what'll happen if it gets out that I'm her old man."

"Don't ever tell Romaine anything," Fritzi said, reacting to her own growing fears.

"You're overlooking her mother. Someday she might yap and then what'll you do? Or I do?"

"Deny it."

"How? After I've taken Romaine to a clinic and all the rest of it...and the more I do, the worse it gets. Besides, DNA tests would confirm everything."

"I meant deny you knew about her during the trial."

"Perjure myself?"

"Oh, yes, there's that. Old friend perjury. I should never have sent her away."

"Yes, you should've. And that's about the hour I woke up and to no music, either."

"Do you think she killed him?"

"I can't think about it."

"You have to, don't you?"

"I don't because I can't...they never had anything like an open-and-shut case on her anyway," he told Jaggy—and himself and for the fiftieth time.

"Which is beside the point," Fritzi made herself say.

"You're so very right. But they were up to all sorts of tricks including sloppy work and plenty of political heat on yours truly."

"You never told me that," Fritzi said.

"It happens sometimes. It shouldn't but it does and it made me mad as hell, Romaine or no Romaine."

"Can't the mother do something? Take her to France possibly? How about that?"

"Not a chance," said Rhodes.

"Shall I come with you? To Europe?"

"I'd love it, but I need time alone with her. I'm going to get as close to Romaine as she'll let me. Try to sell her on what's best for her life, if I can. Better, I think, if it's one on one. A guess but there it is." It wouldn't do anyway, not with Romaine's mistaken, one-sided, angry thoughts about Jaggy.

"I suppose. I don't like the sound of any of it. It's so, well, it's weird. Really weird."

"She thinks I'm odd anyway. She's put the moves on me twice already, and gets all fired up when I rain on her."

"You bring her around me and I'll—"

"Fritzi, she only knows me as a judge. Another guy, older, but not fifty years older. She's bound to be confused and don't forget she's got her problems. And it's always possible she isn't aware she has them. That's what I've been told, or professionally been told."

"That doesn't give her any right to—"

"I know. But nothing is happening so please don't get shipwrecked about it. Let's drop it and drop our way out of here, too. I'm damn sorry to put you through all this, but you had to know."

On the street, Fritzi said she was exhausted and wanted to go straight home. Would he come with her? He kissed her till she struggled for breath. "I better not," he said when they broke apart. "I don't know if she's still at the house or not, but I think I'd better find out before she pulls off another Caravaggio."

"Oh, I forgot to say. The Caravaggio is being restored."

"I could use some restoration myself."

Fritzi held him tight, pressing all of herself against him again, thigh to thigh, belly against belly. She never wanted to let him go and almost suggested that she go home with him. But if Romaine were there, a bitter flare-up might ensue; Fritzi wasn't up to that, and knew it would only make for more woe.

Chapter Thirty-nine

"**D**on't you ever listen, godammit?" said Rhodes, seriously provoked.

"This was more fun. Surprised you, didn't I?"

"You've got strange ideas about what's fun."

"Oh, don't be so stuffy, Cliff. I thought you'd at least laugh."

"Hardy har-har. Good God!"

Turbulent air bounced the Air France 787 and, as Romaine grabbed the armrests, he caught his drink as it slid across the tray table.

"Goblins are slapping us tonight." she said. "Please don't look at me that way." Her mouth taut.

"What way?"

"Like you're about to bite me." Romaine giggled. "I wish you would though. Tenderly, up by my ear."

"You'd better get back to your own seat."

"Not until this plane quits jumping around. I might lose my wig. Do you like it?"

"Swell, Romaine. Just really great."

"Well, you never knew until I sat down and started talking. So how could anyone else tell it's me?"

"How'd you ever get through the check-in anyway, looking that way?" And then it dawned on him. "Are you using someone else's—"

"A friend's. Edy Pachmayer. She's in one of my drama classes."

"And now you're Edy. God, Romaine, do you realize what you're doing?" he asked, another worry to contend with.

"Of course, I do. But how can we be together, if I use my own passport and have to keep looking like myself?"

"It's France we're headed for. Not Beverly Hills."

"That's just what I mean."

Leaving Los Angeles somewhat hastily, he hadn't taken the time to think much about the excursion to Europe. *Tonight or Never* had played to wide audiences throughout Europe, and, because of the film's popularity, photos of Romaine in Europe's news outlets were commonplace during the trial. Certainly she would be recognized, if she weren't camouflaged somehow. And yet that would be a pointless act, if she kept to her real name and had to deal with customs and hotel check-ins? Word would get out. Concierges made a slice of their living when passing tidbits to the news hawkers and paparazzi.

"You're probably right," he said, after reconsidering.

"I am right. It's so much better this way. Think of the fun we'll have fooling everyone," Romaine replied "Anyway, lots of people travel incognito. It's cool."

"More people don't travel under someone else's passport. It's illegal."

"I don't even own a passport. And who's to know anyway?"

"One sharp customs official is all it would take."

"Here, let me show you."

Romaine rummaged in a leather tote bag. As she bent over, he saw the swing of her heavy reddish hair and the small beauty mark near her chin. He swore he could see faint freckles on her cheeks. But then it might've been a trick of light in the dimly lit cabin.

She handed him the passport. The inside photo bore a close resemblance to Romaine, as disguised. At least, what he'd seen of her as she swept into the vacant seat next to him, out of nowhere. Same approximate age, he saw.

He handed back the passport.

"Super girl, Edy," Romaine said. She leaned over, nuzzling his shoulder. "I'll be so good. All behaved and very upright and say my bed prayers every night."

She rested her hand on his thigh. He tried not to notice, which was the same as trying to ignore she was female. A woman half his age, perfumed, with a slim and youthful neck and her breast pressing against his upper arm. She was that unnoticeable, and he made her straighten up before something in him did. He blushed some, glad the cabin was dark.

"Is your ticket in your friend's name?" he asked.

"Hein. Jawohl, Die Samen," Romaine aped. "The Prussian Pachmayers, famous for their pretzels and the finest of fornicators."

"Stop it, damn it. I only wanted to find out if—"

"I'm at least that bright. I turned in the ticket you gave me."

"Someone'll know then."

"Umm-hh. I say fuck-all to them. I've been in a goddamn jailhouse for months. Newspapers all over my ass. Can't do this, can't do that. My career in the toilet. Road kill, that's what I am. You asked me to France and all I want is have some plain ordinary privacy. What the hell do you expect anyway? I've got a round-trip ticket, if you want me to use it when we land in Paris."

"Okay…okay…"

"Want some champagne, it's free in first-class?"

"No thanks. I'm for some shuteye. And you, you're for your own seat."

"Cliff, I hate traveling alone. I'll stay here. You sleep and I'll count the sheep for you...gosh, Paris! Won't it be grand?"

She unbuckled her seatbelt and hurried up the aisle. A few moments later she was back, leading a flight attendant who carried two pillows. Romaine edged into her seat again, her hands busy with two snifters of cognac.

"One for me, one for thee," she said brightly, passing him a snifter, then taking the pillows from the blue-smocked attendant. She stuffed one behind Rhodes's head, then passed her cognac under his nose. "Sniff, isn't that how they do it?" She laughed. "Like that old white evil-dust." She tasted hers. "Whoo-eee. Yuck, that's awful stuff."

Later, he leaned against the window and tried for sleep again. He'd been halfway there an hour ago, when the first voice broke in, warning everyone to buckle up, the air was going to roughen. A nice voice, very French and soft, awakening him at that time. Then Romaine had plopped herself into the adjoining seat. A woman, as far as he could tell in the shallow cabin light, who was dressed in a loose dark skirt, white cowl-neck sweater and black leather boots that crackled slightly when she crossed her legs. Around the slim waist glittered a silver Concho-belt.

"H'lo, handsome," she had said, "you look so lonely. I'm from Traveler's Aid. Like a back rub or possibly a front rub...compliments of Air France-Chance. We always do our level best to please our customers." All of it said in perfectly spoken, French-accented English. She had fooled him completely, until saying, *sotto voce:* "Gotcha' didn't I?" she had said triumphantly.

Rhodes had been speechless. How in hell had she gotten here, he had wondered at that moment? They were to fly separately, he on Air France and she on a later Delta Airlines flight. Out of the blue, or the black of night, she had appeared like an unwanted apparition, severing his nerves once again.

As he tried to sleep, he heard her breathing. Nice and even breathing, the breathing of someone with nothing to worry about except for the entire outside world.

❦

Fahey read the letter he had dreaded now for weeks. A notice to appear for a preliminary hearing to answer a complaint filed by the Hollywood division of the sheriff's department.

Cullis was on him.

Fahey scorched his wife's ears with a string of oaths. Crumbling the letter into a paper ball, he lofted it into a wastebasket several feet away.

"Leave it be," he told Wanda as she went to retrieve it.

"So you won't forget the date, Alonzo."

"I'm not going."

"You have to, don't you?"'

"Fuck their dirty filthy minds."

"Please don't, Alonzo...being foul-mouthed doesn't help anyone."

"Christ, you too, now...tell me a better word. Fuck is a transitive verb blessed with its own creative forces. What's a more imaginative thing than fucking? Can't even talk about the rumble of the flesh, can we?"

Roused in anger now. They were sitting in his makeshift study over the garage, the same place where Rhodes had come to open up Pandora's box on that dark rainy night, when Fahey's woes had begun to circle ominously before their crash-landing.

"Alonzo," his wife broke into his sunken spirits. "Let's go to Saint Bridget's tomorrow. We'll talk with Father Malley. Maybe he can help."

"Already been to a church this year. Spoke right to the Big Boyo. Haven't heard a word back, either."

"You went to see Father Malley?" asked Wanda. "You never told me."

"No, not that old fraud," Fahey griped. "Went to the soldiers' church...didn't even ring the damn bells when I came for a little chat."

Bells? Wanda had no idea what he meant, electing not to ask, not when he was like this, in a surly unpredictable mood. His churlish face, those eyes as wary as a cat of the forest, warned her off. She would try another idea,

375

though nothing in the way of her other suggestions had earned even the slightest rise lately.

"I've been thinking, Alonzo…" She paused to see if he listened.

No reply.

"Alonzo, I could always go back to work. I know I could. That would make it easier"—Wanda saw those eyes lift—"and I wouldn't mind at all"— and she saw his hand began to rise—"and when all this blows over, and it will, Alonzo, yes, you know it will—" the raised hand thundered down like a drop hammer. The crash of a toppling table filled the room.

"Are you telling me, woman, you're to go hustling money for *me*? Can you suppose how that looks to everyone? Especially me."

Wanda flushed. "We have to do something...you never ever saved a dime in your life. Look where we are now."

"Money" Fahey shouted. "Money is an infectious disease. Who saves up diseases, for Jesus sake? Green as gangrene, it is. You want to be like everyone else? A serf? Owned by the Philistines, Wanda, woman"—he leaned forward as if ready to pounce—"all I want is to fucking do what I damn please in this dog-forgotten world. Have you the faintest idea what it costs me to keep us free. Sing the song of life that only I seem to hear, and that's all I ever need to save for. All this silence in my life is what's killing me. Not money."

Springing to his feet, Fahey kicked the toppled table out of his way.

"Where're you going?" Wanda asked.

"To burn, that's where. Burn down Rhodes." Fahey smiled suddenly. "Then I'll find that black bastard Cullis and swing him on one of those unused bell ropes. Tell that to your priest and tell him to ring the bells, if he knows what's good for him this year."

"Alonzo, please stay. Please, oh darling—"

But the door had slammed on her plea, leaving her in fear of what was to come next. She had suffered him for years, his escapades, his women, the drinking. The whims and rages, and the other ways about him that only the Lord and she had any chance of understanding.

A heavy, heavy pain at times. Yet she craved him, was thrilled and charmed at how he could move her deepest currents. She had no name for those feelings he instilled in her. A long time ago, she had stopped wondering how he could make her half-crazy so much of the time. It was easier, she had learned, just to let his currents keep electrocuting her. She had learned how to suffer from him and for him. An outlandish force, courageous to fault, and mad-capping fun. Wanda murmured prayers. One for herself, and two long ones for her beloved stranger on this earth.

Chapter Forty

Paristown—The Ritz. *Wunderbar*!

Hoping a change of scenery might prime her spirits, warm her to his suggestion about a stay at a private clinic, he had opted for a few days in Paris. She had never been, and he, only twice.

They had footed their way around the city for three days and nights, with Rhodes having his best time in years; and Romaine, her spirits flying, thrilled by the sights. Rigged up in her Edy Pachmayer disguise, she had eluded recognition and kept him forever surprised at how she could imitate accents to pass herself off as a Brit, a Swede who spoke only a slightly accented English, even a New Zealander, and then his favorite—an expatriate from Barcelona, with a Castilian lisp, who was in Paris studying at the Sorbonne while also modeling for Dior.

And the lawyer in him recollected that phone call to Marc Sterne's office, allegedly made by Audrey, that had joined young Sterne and Romaine at Malibu Pointe on that fate-making night.

Absorbing her, hoping for her and for himself, he was content for now in his role as the father unknown.

They lunched at the Eiffel, dined at Lasserre, another time at Tour d'Argent, gawked at the soaring grace of Notre Dame by twilight, cruised Montmartre, boated the Seine, and popped into the garish cabarets of Pigalle, sometimes scouting elsewhere for the lesser known Gallic temples.

Everywhere she wanted to go, they went, their every hour supplying the work of two. He was printing her in his memory, not sure when he'd see her again after they got south to Monte Carlo.

One afternoon they passed a cinema where *Tonight or Never* was playing. Romaine saw he pretended not to notice—neither the look she gave him, nor her name up on the marquee.

Sometimes, in moments like these, she turned stiff-lipped, obdurate, and even churlish. He ignored the swings in her temperament, not knowing what else he could do.

So he could be by himself, he told her of an errand he had to run. One more ruse. Wandering the Left Bank, feeling older, feeling at odds with himself, he passed an hour under the crimson awning of a small bistro. He jotted postcards to Fritzi, Consuelo, Macklin Price, other friends including the Faheys. In between jottings, he observed the everyday life of Parisians passing by, gauging what little he could of their lives, making guesses as to who was a shop clerk, who the plumber, a nurse perhaps, a housewife, a bank employee, a messenger: a stupid pastime, he gave it up after a while and drank another Fischer lager.

In mid-afternoon back at the hotel, he called the clinic in Gorbio, alerting them of his arrival date. That he'd come by, personally, to finalize arrangements. Hanging up, beset by doubt, that perhaps it was the wrong thing to do: the thought of making another grave mistake loitered in his mind for the balance of that day.

Chapter Forty-one

At the Hermitage, Rhodes leaned against the balcony railing, craning his neck head as he gazed down at the gardens and their sprays of mimosa, roses and hyacinth, then looked out to the harbor. A navy of luxury yachts were settled in their berths. Beyond, he could see the huge blue mouth of the bay spreading out before Monte Carlo to where bluer water touched the sky on the wavering horizon. A gusting wind from the south pushed its way across the water, kicking up a swath of whitecaps.

Unlike Paris, where they had shared a two-bedroom suite, here he had reserved two smaller suites. Paris was a big place. Even an Edy could go to ground for a few days in Paris and go unnoticed, for no one knew or cared about Edy Pachmayer. Monte Carlo, in acreage, was the size of New York's Central Park. You never knew who you'd run into. Celebrities came from all corners, including Hollywood, especially Hollywood and New York and London. Glitterati abounded and so did the stringers for Europe's gossip rags; and the stringers dished out hefty tips to the concierges who, in turn, provided info as to who was in town and trying to keep it quiet. It was said that more illicit trysts took place over a given weekend in Monte Carlo than in all of France. Not likely, but it made the point.

Given their obvious age differences, it was best, he had thought, to draw as little attention as possible. Separate abodes were thus called for, and he welcomed the time when he could be alone and think of what he must say to her, and when.

The clinic asked if he could be there by nine-thirty the day after they had arrived; otherwise, the clinic became so busy it was hard to spend much time with visitors. He had left a message on Romaine's phone that he'd be among the missing for most of the morning, unaware she wouldn't be getting the message timely since she hadn't spent the night in her rooms.

Calling down to the hotel's front door, he asked for the red Mercedes he had rented two days before at the airport in Nice. He tidied his tie, went down, and the car was already curbside. Rhodes slipped a Michelin map out of the glove compartment, then paid strict attention as the doorman used his stubby finger to trace the road to Gorbio, a town nestled in the hills above the Corniche.

Passing through villages tucked in valleys or set into mountainsides, he noted the way of life in semi-rural France. Many small gray stone houses, some washed stark white or painted in pastels. Close together, ascending with the rise of the land, the homes seemed to be standing on each other's shoulders.

He felt slightly sick. He knew it wasn't from food—he'd barely eaten for almost a day.

Twenty miles north of Monte Carlo, he rolled into the town of Gorbio, circled the tree lined square, and drove out a road favored by the morning sun. A mile later, he saw the sign fixed to a stone pillar almost hidden by a stand of pines. He had almost missed it.

LE RESERVE, it read, the letters done in gilt-scroll, a warning perhaps of the bills yet to be rendered.

It took a good part of his self to drive onward. He spun the wheel and backed up.

Up the road, he drove by a dipping meadow, and, further on, by a pond with swans gliding across its dark surface. Across the pond, he saw a slate-roofed chateau-sized building—her next home. He wanted to look the clinic over at least once, make the money arrangements, meet the doctors, tell them he would be delivering Romaine a day late.

Or even two days late, he suddenly decided, as he braked the Mercedes to a crunching, sliding stop on the gravel driveway. What was another day or two out of a lifetime? Level with her, he could do that much, act cleanly and straight with her, quit trying to dodge, the way he had dodged marriage to Fritzi for so long.

And he drove off, in search of a delay. In search of himself, also, still at bay over what to do about the family he wanted. Could she ever be part of it, now that he planned to leave her here, in Gorbio, a place that might as well have been as unknown to him as a moon crater had it not been for the recommendations of a psychiatrist in Los Angeles. With no assurance she could be cured; with no assurance, either, she was a disturbed narcissist, or that she wasn't.

Nor any assurance, for that matter, or anything whatsoever.

CR

Unexpectedly, he saw her standing by the newspaper stall on the street fronting the hotel. About to pull into the driveway, instead he eased the Mercedes over to the curb and rolled down the window.

She came over, smiling, looking daisy-fresh in white dungarees, a blue shirt and a white sweater draped casually over her shoulders. Her mouth was painted with an iridescent berry shade of lipstick, a color that clashed with her hair.

Leaning through the window, a few curls of her red wig spilling across her cheeks, she asked: "Where'd you go?"

"Had a little task to take care of. Tell you about it later. How're the picnic arrangements?"

"Ready any time."

"You hungry at all?"

"So-so."

"I skipped breakfast, so I'm half starved."

"You didn't eat last night, either." She hopped in. "Can we go to the Casino again tonight? I'm on a lucky roll. I can feel it."

"How'd you fare last night?"

"Twenty-one hundred Euros on roulette and almost another thousand at the baccarat table. Beginner's luck, but I found it exciting. So are the people. Never saw such a display of jewels. I wonder if they're fake. I saw one old blue-hair there with rubies the size of pigeon eggs. I'd really like to go back tonight, if that's okay with you?"

"That's quite a lot to win in a single night," he said.

Rhodes had stayed at the bar when Romaine went into the gaming area to try her luck. A poker player, he didn't care for casino games; in none of them could you bluff, so you gave away too big of an edge to the house. Tiring of the scene, somewhat sleepy, he had been about to find her and tell her he was heading back to the Hermitage, a short walk away.

He had seen her laughing with a handsome younger man wearing a tuxedo. He had watched for a long moment. He'd been raised on a ranch, had never known what it was like to be this young, and particularly this kind of young in a place like a world-famous casino; deciding not to barge in, he slipped away.

"I looked around for you last night," she was saying. "You'd vanished."

"I got sleepy. Sea air does then to me. I saw you with some fella, and you looked like you were having a nice enough time. So, I went my way. Nice looking guy. European?"

"Dutch, yes. I guess he's part of that Amstel beer family. He says he is. I stayed the night with him at Hotel de Paris. A great fuck-fest was had by all; all two of us, that is—"

"Romaine, don't, just *don't*. Okay?"

"Oh, you! You're such a prissy-ass prude. You're so…so *yesterday* at times."

"You don't have to go around talking like some street slut."

"Glub, glub. Cha, cha, cha! I'm all shook up. Mercy me."

"Or be a smart-aleck."

"Here's a little text message for your iPhone, if you own one—the message is that I talk the way I want to talk. Here's a good example: Fuck, fuck, fuck. Besides, I haven't been laid in almost a year. Well, once. Try that sometime. I did and last night I put things in first gear. Like I might tonight. You getting jealous yet?"

He made no reply.

Pulling up to the front door, he asked the doorman to send in for the picnic hamper. Romaine wanted to drive as far as Cannes to see the Carlton Hotel, the main celebrity watering-hole whenever the famed international film festival was underway. And, then, perhaps a gander at those topless beaches she'd heard so much about.

After the door attendant loaded the hamper into the Mercedes's back seat, Rhodes swung the around the driveway and cut into a side street.

They weren't going far. Nothing in all of Monaco was very far from wherever you sat or stood or slept. Two miles distant was all, up the Boulevard Du Larvotto, a turn toward the beach route, and then head out for Cap de la Vielle, a narrow finger of land jutting into the sea. From its upper slope, all three harbors can be seen and miles of the bending rocky coastline. He had made a quick survey the day before, after asking the Hermitage's concierge where to find a not-too-busy spot for a picnic.

℞

A blowy day. Heavy clouds swam across a gray sky, the sun having little luck breaking through. He parked the Mercedes near a small building and, following the signs, they made their way up a tree-lined footpath. Rhodes lugged the wicker hamper. A gust of wind, then another, swiped at them as they emerged from a copse of pines. Romaine ducked as the wind tossed the sweater knotted around her neck, then kicked her way through the palm fronds tumbling across the grass as they emerged from the trees.

"Too windy, you think?"

"I like it, it feels so fresh."

"Down there," Rhodes said, pointing to the lee side of a stonewall latticed with climbing ropes of scarlet flowers. "Run on ahead."

"You need help?" she shouted against another gust of wind.

"Thanks, I can handle it."

Reaching the lee of the garden wall, still with a generous view of the tossing sea, he set the hamper down, and spread the blanket. Busying herself, Romaine lifted out a metal tin of sandwiches, a sack of fruit, a wedge of cheese, olives, and checkered blue and white napkins. Rhodes opened a bottle of Sancerre, and dug out plastic cups.

He sat on one side of the blanket, eating a chicken sandwich as Romaine lay down across from him, nibbling on salted black olives. Her face was turned down and away, and be wanted to see her as he talked, hoping she could somehow make it easier for him.

"Romaine?"

"Ummm-hh." She then turned his way.

"Been fun, hasn't it?"

"The greatest, Cliff. I could hang around here forever."

"How 'bout a few months instead."

"With you? I'd love it."

"I've got to go back. But there's a place, a very nice place, you can stay. I saw it this morning."

"By myself? I don't know anyone here. I mean the Dutch stud but he's here for only a few days. What're you saying? Are you dumping me?"

"You know I've got to get back," he said. "You can stay on, though."

"At the Hermitage? You crazy? It's a fortune there."

"No, I'm referring to another place and they might be able to do a few things to help."

"Help who?"

"You. Me. It's not the Hermitage, it's a clinic but quite attractive, more like a country club and—"

"I don't need any clinic. A clinic for what?"

"You've been under enormous stress. Months of it. Anyone would need some help coming off all that." Rhodes looked at her, imploringly. "We've talked about this before."

"I feel fine. Just fine, thank you. If anyone needs a clinic, it's you and your hang-ups."

Going to be a tough sell, he thought. "I assume you know what you did at Fritzi's was pretty punk."

"She's been lying to you. She's all dizzy about getting married. You're making a really dumb mistake, you know."

"That's my worry. She did you a favor, when not that many others seemed to care."

"Others? Like the family I'm supposed to have, and you never tell me about?"

"Those and others," he said blandly.

"I've plenty of friends."

"Who are they? Where were they?"

"They're private...Tommy Burke, he's one."

Rhodes drank some wine and chewed on his sandwich. Damn, he thought. But then what could he expect?

"There are people who can help you," he tried again. "Right here in France. They're top-notch, I'm told."

Her eyes stabbed at him, before she averted her face again. "You're sounding pretty shitty. We've had such a perfect time, and now you want to spoil everything. A fucking clinic, you must be nuts yourself."

"I want to remember our time here, Romaine. And mostly I want to help you. Believe me."

"Oh, fuck off."

"I don't like that kind of talk, I've told you." He could feel it coming out, unable to stop himself. "Then there's the bracelet. I took it the night Fritzi and I packed you up," Rhodes said. "It was the genuine thing, wasn't it? And it never belonged to you."

Her head shot up as the wind swept her hair back; the taut line of her jaw and chin gave her a threatening appearance; the look of someone aiming a pistol, ready to fire.

"You can damn well give it back to me. It's mine! Marc gave it to me!" screaming at him. "I just didn't want to say anything about it before."

"No, I don't think he did give it to you. Nothing like that, in fact."

"Well, you don't know! You just don't know, mister, do you? "

"I know you didn't pick it up at some charity bazaar, as you said to me."

"You're a real bastard! A thief, too. God, how I'm starting to hate you." Her face hard as the craggy rocks a few feet away. "You're not even a man, you just look like one."

"At any rate, I'm not *your* man. And you better quit talking like a spoiled little bitch."

"Or what? I want my emeralds back, goddamn you. I'll sue you."

"You won't be suing anyone. You could end up back in jail for a thing like that. You stole the bracelet from Audrey Sterne, and they've been returned where they belong."

"How'd you ever get that notion?" Then the revelation blazed in her. "I don't remember anything like that coming out at the trial. It didn't...how do you know anything about her? Her jewelry, things like that? How do you...she's a liar, too. The biggest. Audrey Sterne is the worst liar I ever met..."

"But the bracelet is hers, Romaine," he said as softly as he could over the wind.

"Mine! It's mine! How do you know anyway?"

"I heard, let's say." He felt like a fool again, like a collector's edition of a genuine jerk.

"So smart, aren't you? You make me sick. You're just like the rest. You want to control me, own me, stop me from my career—"

"Not at all. Nothing like that."

"You're in with the Sterne's. I know you are. You're all out to stop me one way or the other."

Wind slashed against the other side of the stone wall, setting up a heavy rushing noise. Waiting till it veered off, he said, "I want more than anything for you to get on with your life. Get a fresh start. For that, you'll need help. Try to understand what I'm saying."

He kept reasoning and pleading, trying to conceive some way whereby she might acquiesce, see what he was trying to do; at least, be willing to discuss the possibilities. It was, he supposed, something akin to the act of intervention when a family member was being persuaded to seek treatment for an addiction.

386

Resistance, denial: all of it coated with anger. It was, after all, an assault to anyone's ego.

She started in again. "I know what you're trying to do, you're trying to get me to admit I did it, aren't you? One of your slimy legal tricks, right? They couldn't get at me in that courtroom, so now you're trying this way, aren't you? You shit, you!"

"Admit to what? Taking the bracelet?"

"No, you ninny, that I killed him."

"Marc Sterne?"

Her eyes held a detached cold look, as if she were piecing together some dangerous image; he began to recall some of the passages he had read at the UCLA medical library.

"Well, did you?"

"What if I did?"

"Then you have a helluva lot to answer for. Do you want to tell me about it?"

"Why should I? So you can take me to court again?"

"No, Romaine. You can't be tried twice on the same charge."

"On some other charge, I'm sure you can dream something up."

"I have no idea. But if you had anything to do with his death, you might feel better getting it off your chest. If not with me, then at the clinic."

"Yes, my chest. Want to see my tits? You do, don't you?"

"I have."

"Yes, you already seen them once and I could tell you were about to jump me."

"Maybe you were fantasizing."

"Men go crazy for me."

"Marc Sterne did, it seems."

"What a nothing he turned out to be."

"He turned out dead, that's how he turned out."

"Deserved it, too, the bastard."

"How can anyone deserve something like that?"

"You killed people. Jagoda told me you were...you fought in the Middle-east."

"I did."

"Killing."

"I did that, too."

387

"Well, bully for us. I killed to, had to kill him."

"Why?"

"Why should I tell you?"

"Don't then…"

"I can't be accused again?"

He shrugged. "Accusations are a dime a ton. What I said was they cannot take you to court again on murder charges for having done in Marc Sterne. You've been found innocent as you surely know. You're free as free ever is."

Her eyes kept changing, this time softening as if some pleasant interruption of thought were about to unfold. Yet just moments ago they were agate-hard. Standing, she faced the sea as though it were an audience, talking to no one and yet to everyone. And slowly but openly she spilled it.

"Marc had pushed me too far, you know. I was about to go over the edge, and so I took it all into my own hands. No one else that I could turn to…no one…those photos did it. I saw them in my dreams, in the bathroom mirror when I washed, on the pages of scripts I memorized. I could see them passed around with all the snide jokes and my reputation falling to pieces…just as that nude calendar pose had nearly ruined Marilyn Monroe…I was going to go right to Julio Sterne. Beg him to get those pictures for me or I would threaten to tell the police about his bastard of a son dealing those drugs. I knew plenty. A fair trade. If I went down, they would all fall with me, including that bitch-headed Audrey, loving herself so much in the social columns. I set them up. Even when they didn't want to see me anymore, I arranged it anyway. Called the house, faked it as if I was a shop girl at the florist, and Kardas took the call: 'Would the Sternes be home that evening to receive a large horse-shoe arrangement of roses, a surprise from an admirer? Very perishable. I used a different voice. 'Yes,' he said, 'Mrs. Sterne would be home.' Then the other call I made to Marc's office, using Audrey Sterne's way of talking, which is easy. I can do anyone's voice…any woman's I can. That's when I left the dinner invitation for him with his secretary to come out to Malibu that night and to bring me along…sure as there's a Hell, I thought that that Eel Pritter had got that one figured out…I was scared shitless he had, but I guess not…see, we'd all be there in Malibu, and we'd have it out…let everyone choke on it…but when I got there and only Marc was there, and that's when I begged him again for the photos and my money…he laughed in my face. All juiced up, and I could see he'd gone off to bongo-land again. He wanted sex. 'I told him okay, sure, lets'…he fixed up a speed-ball; laughing and taunting me. He opened his fly, dangling his noodle. He was crazed, I played along, getting him ready, and the next thing I knew he was fixing the syringe…I calmed him, playing with him, undressing. Then undressing him all the way. I helped with the syringe, so pissed, so wound up that I doubled the doses…dosages. He kept touching me while I got his arm ready, twisting the hose, watching the vein go blue and putting that needle in him ever so gently. Pushing the plunger; wiping it off, telling him to feed in the rest for himself, and he did. Then I pushed again, but with my thumb on top of his.

"After I left, with him babbling on the floor, he must've known he was done for. I wiped his print off the plunger…I should've taken the syringe but that would've been a dead giveaway, right? No syringe and they'd know someone had to be involved and my name was at the gate. So there he went, the rotten fucker. He killed himself…I just helped him get what he deserved. I rid the world of an evil, evil shitheel…"

She sat on the grass, apparently finished, and Rhodes drew a deep breath; his heart racing on him, his soul in shreds.

"Want to hear me do Audrey Sterne?"

"Sure."

"Turn around I'll show you." When he did, she waited a few moments, readying herself. Then she spoke. The inflections, the intonations, even the little pauses were a perfection of Audrey's voice. He couldn't believe what he was hearing, couldn't believe it wasn't Audrey herself. But then he recalled her antics in Paris, impersonating others.

"Very impressive," he told her. He would never come close to feeling like this again.

"I won a prize for impersonations in my acting class. Practicing dialogue."

"Practicing something."

"It fooled Kardas and Kardas knew Audrey like she was his full-time whore, which she was."

Rhodes blanched, saying, "You can have everything you need to heal, Romaine," he told her. "All the help in the world. But you have to want it first."

"Why should I trust you?"

"You have to trust someone. Otherwise, it'll get awful lonely out there," he replied, still recoiling.

"I trust only what I can see, smell, or put in the bank."

Jesus! he thought. What was the point? She still seemed lost in a forlorn dream. He was practically crying dry, trying to get through to her, trying to get through to himself. He had paid with his high court appointment, and with Fahey, and now with guilt that no soap ever invented would wash away. He had helped to free a killer.

Romaine's suddenly body went rigid and then she leaped to her feet, shouting at him, her eyes glassy.

"If you'd told the jury the straight story, I think they'd have let you off," Rhodes told her. "Or maybe only a light sentence."

"You might take that chance with someone else's life. But not with mine, Mr. Ding-dong."

"And now you're screwing it up something fierce."

"Uh-uh. You're not as sharp as you think...if I had told everything and still got off, I'd be known as a murderess."

"But you are a murderess. An accessory anyway. Probably more than an accessory."

"Even if I am, only you and I know that. Right? Are you going to rat on me?"

"I'm not. I'm going to try helping you. That's why the clinic. If you undergo treatment, it'll always be in your favor."

"With my parents paying?"

"Probably."

"Maybe I should. It's sort of therapy, right? Counseling for your head?"

"They'll tell you all about it. We'll go tomorrow and you can ask whatever you want."

"You set this up and you didn't say anything."

"I was of two minds about it."

"What about my mind?"

"I don't know about your mind, and I'm not so sure you do either."

"What shit, really. You're really full of it."

"Why not have a look, see for yourself?"

"You'll go with me?"

"I'll drive you there. I don't think they'll want me involved in any discussion, however."

She went silent for a time, then said, "Okay, Cliff. Okay, as long as it's you…it's okay, I guess…"

"Wonderful." Leery now that she had reversed course so quickly; even doubting they were through with the dispute, but right now he'd take what he could get.

"Have some more wine?" she asked, her smile ripening.

"Sure."

She poured to the brim of his plastic glass. He drank most of it in three swallows, relieved at reaching an understanding, tentative as it might be. He drank fast, coping with the roil inside himself.

"He was out to use me," she barked suddenly. "Nobody uses me." She glared at Rhodes.

"Who?"

"Marc, who else?"

"I'll remember, Romaine."

"You'd better. Never, ever use me. You're all the same, that's why. Out to get me. Now it's the booby farm."

"And you believe everything you just said?"

"Believe? Of course, I *believe*. I know. I was there, you ninny."

Her eyes suddenly gone flat, dead of expression. Leaning against the stonewall, Romaine laughed till a blood-flush came to her face. Short, sharp peals of laughter, and her hair whipping at her cheeks.

Somehow he had to keep her in Europe or she would destroy herself and maybe others, including himself. He'd had enough by now, much too much to negotiate for one day.

Getting up, he began to dump the plates, cups, food tins and jars into the wicker hamper. Folding the blanket, he noticed Romaine had left the vicinity. Done with his tasks, he looked for her and saw her standing on a concrete ledge that overlooked the Mediterranean Sea.

&

She was shaking a little, scolding herself as damp sea air mopped her drained face. *Catching me off guard, how stupid of me to tell him everything churning in my guts. Gone too far, gone way too far. Something happened, I'd become someone else…channeling everything…now he knows and he's a fucking judge…what if he talks? He's a weirdo, wouldn't even take a ride between my legs. He's the one needing help. Seemed so nice, but it was a hoax...he wants me in a cage! I just got out of a cage...*

Her head in flux now; wiliness running amuck in her.

Staring fixedly at the nervous, slashing sea, froth and spray cascading everywhere, she noted something bobbing to the surface, then fading away, then reappearing. A darkish cylindrical-shaped object: was it a log or was it perhaps a body?

Exactly, exactly, exactly—everything now sharp, so abundantly clear. A little happier now, a little more certain of how to restore control, rid the threat.

She braced her thighs against a rusted rail guard anchored to the cement apron of the ledge. The wind sharpened, whipping at her, and, turning away, she held her wig so it wouldn't blow away. Her face had lighted up with elation. No one else was there but him, thirty yards away, waving to her. He'd never guess, she thought, never have a clue.

Screaming suddenly, a rising yodel-like sound. Throwing one hand to her forehead, covering her eyes with the other, she shouted and pointed over the rail.

Rhodes, seeing her in chaos, trotted to where she stood. "What is it?" he yelled into the teeth of the wind.

"Down there." She pointed and then pointed again. "A body. Look there!"

He leaned over the low railing rattling in the thrashing wind. "Where? I only see—"

"Straight down. Floating."

Rhodes leaned out again. She had moved, squatting behind him, her hands poised and aimed at his rear. In a mighty upward shove, pushing with all her strength, hollering: "It's *your* body...don't you see it, ding-dong...you will, yes, you will...you'll see it down there in Hell where Marc Sterne is waiting for you..."

His arms flailed wildly. Rushing air forced open his mouth, and bent him backwards till it pained. Twirling about, he tried to cry out, but his throat had paralyzed. He spun toward the rocks that looked reddish under a breakthrough sunray, but the real red was the explosion in his head seconds later.

ભ

She ran, bolting through the pines, down the path to the parking area, racing onward to a building near to the Mercedes. With every leaping step, she breathlessly invented explanations. Bounding up the steps, flinging open a door, she heaved out a banshee's wail, startling a woman who was busy stacking tourist brochures in a rack.

"Oh, help! Help me, oh God please!" Romaine cried, a wide-eyed look of shock stretching and whitening her face. "A man—m-my friend w-went over. The wind took him...help me. Oh-hh ..."

She tumbled to the floor, slapping at it hysterically with two weakened hands. Going motionless suddenly, feigning a fainting spell.

Chapter Forty-two

$\mathbf{A}$ rescue team from the Monaco police had sacked Rhodes's broken body in a dark canvas bag. It lay in a heap next to the port gunwale of a harbormaster's launch.

A distasteful job, thought Paul Matin, who watched the churn of the wake from the stern, as the launch sped back toward the harbor. A deputy inspector, he had been assigned the task of tidying up after the accident, interviewing, doing up the necessary reports. He would sign the remains into the morgue, bringing that matter to a close on this grisly morning. By no means would it be the end, but perhaps the start of the end. Chagrined now, recalling that Monaco had gone eight straight months without a tourist fatality.

Stopping by the Hermitage earlier, he had inquired about the well-being of the young American woman who had reported the incident. Soon he must take her statement. She'd been asleep, when he first tried contacting her, or at least had refused to answer her phone. The hotel had offered the services of a doctor to the shocked and red-eyed young woman, but she had refused, saying she needed to be alone, that her grief was too overwhelming.

Matin had asked the hotel-reception for both passports—hers and the deceased—a formality.

What struck him as slightly odd was the hotel manager's statement "Mam'selle Pachmayer has asked the concierge to call Air France to arrange a seat for London."

"Nothing else, no other calls?" Matin had asked, almost absently.

"She requested a disconnect on all the phones to the suite," said the manager.

"Has she a cell phone?"

"I am not aware, one way or the other."

"I see."

Strange, he thought—why hadn't she notified someone in the States? Family members? Friends? Someone to help with returning the body to America, and for all the other depressing details of a sudden death. Well, that was the job of the U.S. Consul and not the police.

An illicit romance, perhaps. Stolen moments in Monte Carlo, so famous as a lover's oasis. Maybe that's why she hadn't called anyone, unless she had used a cell phone. He intended to find out, at the latest by tomorrow.

Matin hoped the dead man strapped to the gunwale was a nobody. A casual tourist, nothing more. No wife, no special honors or prestige that would whet the appetite of the media or bring a sortie of prying questions from the American consulate in Nice. Years and years of police business had inured him; he knew the tricks and acceptable dodges, the many ins-and-outs of the policeman's trade. Ways existed to blanket the smaller indiscretions of foreign paramours; occasionally some fancy footwork was called for, though hoping none would be necessary this time.

With *le affaire de coeur,* secrets often abounded—sometimes unpleasant secrets. Sighing, then, as he reflected on the mound of paperwork facing him.

Chapter Forty-three

Next afternoon, Matin knocked twice on the door. In his pocket, he carried Edy Pachmayer's passport, having already copied the vital pages of Rhodes's before sending the original over to the U.S. Consul in Nice.

The door edged open.

"Mam'selle Pachmayer?"

"Yes, I am."

"I am Matin. Paul Matin from the Monaco police prefecture."

"Yes. Hello."

"Would you be good enough to answer a few questions? Small details, then I shall quickly depart."

Romaine sized him up. A florid complexion, rimless glasses, and a six-pack belly. His bristly hair was cut military style.

"I'm very tired," she said.

"I assure you I shall be brief. Only a few minutes, mam'selle." Matin smiled. Romaine saw that be had very good teeth, pearly white, straight.

"All right, I suppose it's necessary. Come in."

Matin followed her into the parlor. A fresh looking room done in pastels, with plushy stuffed chairs and two settees covered with a lime-colored damask fabric. A water stain showed in one corner of the white ceiling, and the blemish immediately caught his observant eyes.

They sat across from each other. Behind Romaine, the curtains billowed from a breeze flowing in from the balcony. For a moment, Matin frowned, noting her honey-hued hair, not the redhead as described in her passport. Yet with women's fads, who could be sure of anything, one day to the next. Difficult to assess her facial reactions with those blue sunglasses. Eyes could reveal much about one's emotions during an interview. Tempted to request that she remove them, he thought better of it, not wanting to put her on her guard.

"May I express deep sorrow," Matin began. "A most lamentable accident."

"I'm sick over—sick from my nerves. A marvelous man. But what is it you want from me?"

"Perhaps you can advise me of what happened. What you saw."

"I saw very little. It happened so quickly."

"Whatever you saw, then. Forgive me, mam'selle, I must make notes." Matin withdrew a small black book from his inside coat pocket, then unscrewed the top of an old-fashioned fountain pen.

Tersely, Romaine described the picnic outing. They were there at Cap de la Vielle for no more than an hour, maybe less. Terribly strong winds but they had elected to stay on. Have their little picnic for two. He'd been drinking most of a bottle of wine and seemed drowsy.

"Did you mean an entire liter?"

"I think so. I had none."

"Proceed, if you please."

She went on, telling Matin that when they were about to leave, Cliff Rhodes had walked around to clear his head. After repacking the picnic basket, she went to look for him. He was out on the parapet, leaning over the rail there, and a terrific burst of wind took him...he might've been sick, she told Matin.

"Sick?"

"He hadn't been feeling well. Or possibly from so much wine." She shrugged indifferently.

"You were nearby?" Matin asked. "When seeing him by that rail?"

"Twenty or thirty yards...oh, it was so awful. He was the most wonderful man." Romaine made her face tremble.

"You'd known him for some time, then?" Matin asked idly.

"Yes, you see we were going to marry. We'd come here to think it over...I'll never get over"—Romaine looked away, her fingers straying to her chin.

"Such a terrible shock for you," Matin said, sympathetically. "We'll do all we can to ease your, uh, grief."

"Oh, yes. Thank you. When can I go, leave Monaco?"

"Very soon, I should think. There is an autopsy underway," Matin explained.

"An autopsy? But why an autopsy?"

"That is our way here in Monaco. Our regulations. We need the facts. Your government will insist on a complete report. We can do no less."

"Even in an accident?"

"Especially then, mam'selle."

"That's ghoulish. He should just be buried in a nice place." Visibly, she whitened now.

"Is something the matter?"

"I get a little ill remembering it, that's all."

"Of course," said Matin with added sympathy. "Will you be accompanying the remains to America? Your U.S. Consul in Nice wishes to know."

Romaine hadn't counted on that one. "I'm unable to." Hesitating, she added, "I'm due in London for rehearsals."

"Rehearsals? Rehearsals of what nature?"

"A tryout for a stage play. It's all very uncertain, but I must be there," she said, deciding yesterday she would follow Max Shapin's suggestion to try her luck in London.

"Ah! Mam'selle is an actress, then?"

"I've been in films," she said suddenly, feeling prickly. She could never fly back with the casket. The questions. Customs or whatever. Supposing they checked her passport? She had to get loose, put everything behind her, once and for all.

"You have not yet called anyone? Relatives or close friends?"

"I couldn't. Just couldn't bring myself—"

Matin nodded, solemnly. "And, Mam'selle Pachmayer, you were born where?"

"California."

"You live there now?"

"I always have."

"I must visit there one day."

"The best of all places. But...well, so many memories. I don't think I want to go back there for now anyway."

Matin closed his notebook. "From your Consul in Nice, I have learned that M'sieu Rhodes was a judge. In California, no?"

Romaine nodded.

"A judge, yes," Matin said. "Too bad. Still a young man."

She didn't care for these questions, where they were headed or the sneaky way the inspector was asking them. First, going in one direction, then to another. She'd already had enough of the police to last three lifetimes.

Worried about her passport, she had discarded the pretense of being Edy Pachmayer. The wig, the fake mole on her cheek, and the makeup that whitened her complexion. She would explain everything, tell Matin, hope for his mercy. Tell him things he could never verify; no more than Pritter, that horrid eel, could check on her story at the trial.

"Inspector?" Romaine leaned forward.

"Yes?"

"There's something I should tell you. I hope you won't blame me too awfully much."

Instantly alert, he replied, "Please, yes."

Calm and slightly sniffy, as she talked now. She had worked it all out, and would make it sound like a love sonnet...of how they had left California on the spur of the moment. There had been no time to apply for a passport, so she borrowed one from a friend.

Noticing Matin's eyebrows coming together, Romaine burrowed for sympathy once more. She gave him her real name, who she really was, said she had been a defendant in a murder trial where Cliff Rhodes had presided as the judge. Many months she had spent in his courtroom, and it was there that their ardor had budded.

"Kindly, the spelling of your name." He wrote, careful to conceal his concerns. "Please, proceed."

Removing her sunglasses, she unloaded her tale. What the hell would some French cop know, anyway, or even care? "After I was declared innocent, he took a deep interest in me. Trying to help. He even told me he knew I hadn't been guilty. We fell in love, unexpectedly and helplessly, and so we came to Europe to be by ourselves, Inspector...and, then, well, I suppose I shouldn't say it, but Cliff Rhodes was trying to escape the clutches of a woman who'd been chasing him for years. A sort of hussy, you know, one of those women with a, well, a history to her...I needed a change myself," adding how the notoriety of the trial had left its scars. An awful time, harrowing, had nearly broken up her life till him, who she had come to love so fervently...so you see, Inspector," Romaine looked at him, careful to show respect, as composed now as some second-story artist in the dark of night, "we had to come over here. We could never marry in California or even live there together...the publicity would be just...well... ruinous."

"You were in love, you say, with the, uh, deceased M'sieu Rhodes?"

"I suppose it sounds ludicrous—"

"Lud—?"

"Crazy, you know. Absurd, him being the judge at the trial and everything...but I've heard of patients falling in love with their doctors. Haven't you?"

"Just so, just so."

Matin was uneasy, his mind clicking away, cataloguing things while evaluating her remarks. What fit, what didn't? That morning a call had come into police headquarters from an administrator at the LE RESERVE clinic in Gorbio. News of the accident had reached them via Radio Monte Carlo— and was this the same Rhodes, they had wanted to know, whom they'd been expecting? An American, they had said, who had been arranging to place a Romaine Brook under their care. Had she, too, been in the accident?

"What about it?" Matin asked Romaine, his voice lowering a notch. "There could not be two Americans with the same name as yours in Monte Carlo, could there? The clinic, they were referring to you, I assume?"

"Oh, yes. That was his idea. He was always so right about everything." Romaine snuffled again.

"Perhaps, you'll elaborate."

"We were going to the clinic together. Before we married, we wanted to be sure. It had all been so sudden, Inspector. I mean we were in love but he was older and everything, you know, and we were to have one of those tests. One of those compatibility exams, I think they're called. I'm not sure. He was taking care of it..." She broke into tears, expertly so, and the world had a small new river today as glycerin-like droplets s dribbled down her cheeks. "Oh dear God, Inspector, look what's happened. He's gone...he'll never be back. And he was so fabulous. The best thing that ever happened to anyone."

Slumping forward in her chair, her shoulders jerked in a cadence with her muffled sobs.

Matin, staring at her, was perplexed.

Before him was this endearing young woman with tragedy stamped all over her. Yet he possessed the cautious mind of a policeman, and hadn't liked the business about the passport. Not at all. She told him she had stood trial for murder, and he didn't much care for that revelation, either. But he was aware of strong winds the day the accident took place. Heavy enough to topple several smaller boats in the marina, and other damage to a number of homes. Power had gone out for an hour or more. And what judge, even an American judge, would be seen openly with a defendant from his own court unless some unique reason existed? It came to him as a little odd, her story, but in his years of police work one heard most everything. Anyway, they were Americans, weren't they? A race of children, liable to do anything.

Yet she had been open, direct, and hadn't weaseled about the false passport matter. Matin credited her on that one.

Going over to where Romaine sat, he stood and waited until she looked up through tear-flooded eyes. He had wanted to touch her shoulder reassuringly, deciding, though, it was much too familiar a gesture.

"Mam'selle?"

"I'm so sorry. I didn't mean to cry on you." Wiping her eyes slowly.

"I quite understand. You've been through a most upsetting time." Matin hesitated a moment, and then, "Still, I must inform you that you must remain in Monte Carlo until this passport irregularity is put right."

"Am I in trouble?"

"We shall have to see. It's against the law what you've done. Much will depend on what the U.S. Consul has to say. At present, you are undocumented and in violation of our immigration laws."

"Will I have to go see the Consul?"

"No. They'll no doubt come to see you...and I shall want your word you won't leave the principality until we clear up matters."

"Naturally, yes. You have my word. I hope you'll help me. I had to get away from California. I had to...you do understand, Inspector?"

"Perhaps, and yet I'm startled an American judge would allow you to travel with him, and you using a false identity. Most unusual, it would seem."

Romaine looked away as she said her first truthful thing that afternoon. Blushing becomingly, she said, "He didn't really know until it was too late. It was my mistake, not his. We were so in love and, oh you know how that is."

Matin nodded dourly. "I'll let myself out, mam'selle. You'll be hearing from me in a day or two."

401

"Do I have to stay in these rooms?"

"You're free to go anywhere in Monaco. I warn you it will go hard on you if you violate your word. You are on your parole. Kindly honor our trust."

"*Naturalament,* Inspector." Her moist eyes became small mirrors of gratitude.

"One more thing. You will be picked up at three and brought to the prefecture. You will be required to make a formal statement and sign it. You will do this?"

"Whatever you ask, sir. I want to cooperate, then leave for London soon as I can."

After the door closed behind Matin, she waited for a long moment, then let out a sigh of relief. A very contented sigh, like the one after good lovemaking. Earlier, she had channeled her Muse, seeking ideas. By openly declaring her bogus use of a friend's passport, she was confident she had persuaded Matin as to her honesty.

Matin was hers. Or would be.

ଔ

Consuelo Ramirez was just finishing up her morning tasks in the kitchen, when interrupted by the phone. This might be the call she expected from her sister, who lived below the border in Aqua Caliente. Smiling then, at the thought of passing some time gabbing together.

Wiping her hands on her apron, she picked up the receiver. Several moments passed before she could untangle the identity of the caller from across the Atlantic. She thought it might be Rhodes, at first. But the voice she heard was strange to her, a voice that kept asking even stranger questions.

Confused, and not knowing what "next of kin" meant, she gave the caller the phone number of Rhodes's former chambers at court. Hanging up, she returned to her work, wondering what a consul was in France. Why the call anyway, and what did kin mean? Or was it the American name—Ken? Who was Ken? The only Ken she knew of were the three Kenmore vacuum cleaners in various closets around the house.

A wrong number, was it?

☙

Twenty-minutes later, Macklin Price, while sealing an envelope at her desk, heard from the same caller. Everything dropped inside her, as she burst into a babble of tears.

From the outer office, others scurried in to see what the howling was all about. They waited as Macklin tried to calm herself, but she could not, and after sharing her shock with the onlookers, she dialed Fritzi.

And sobbed with her till she heard the phone drop to the floor at Fritzi's end.

She was quite certain Rhodes had no next of kin, as the caller had requested. An only son of a ranch foreman and his wife living near Lewiston, Montana, and they had passed away years before, though she couldn't remember exactly when. She called an officer at Brown Brothers Harriman & Co. local office, where his personal financial affairs were handled, to see if they knew anything.

At Brown Brothers, the officer, who fielded Macklin Price's call, did some checking of her own. Calling the vault, she asked for Rhodes's files to be sent up immediately. She remembered how he had made changes to his will only weeks before. Needing details now. She handled many trusts and estates, and amendments to them flurried in with frequency; thus better to check and be accurate.

Within the hour, she had read the file and untied the maroon ribbons that bound up his will, skimming her way through the key provisions. Seeing the name, well, two names, but one in particular, she turned pale; aghast, and scurried to the elevator on her way upstairs to the legal department. The publicity angle worried her; she worked for a very respected, very low-key private bank. Publicity, unless of the gilt-edged variety, was viewed as abhorrent.

☙

Fritzi had lain on her bed for hours. Her heart in smithereens. She remembered Macklin Price calling and remembered almost collapsing to the floor at the news. Hours later, her mind still whited-out, she shut herself off from the world, her only world, her no-more world.

CR

Audrey Sterne had heard nothing at all about Rhodes. She answered the door that morning because the help were off. No more Kardas, either. The doorbell changed everything. She had greeted a nicely dressed woman who had courteously asked Audrey to sign a receipt for an envelope.

From Julio's attorneys, she found. He had filed for a separation. His attorneys would be pleased to hear from hers so that temporary support could be arranged with as little fuss for everyone as possible.

So very goddamn polite, she thought, staring at the neatly margined pages.

Audrey had known it was coming. Even so, a chiller. She had seen precious little of Julio, since the trial had ended. Whenever she succeeded in reaching him by phone, he sounded as if he were on a distant planet. An exceedingly cold planet.

Her attorneys could wait; they were busy enough with the Malibu sheriff who was still sniffing around, wanting quick answers to their idiotic questions. Damn them all, she thought.

The phone rang. Three times it jangled at her before she elected to touch it. Brown Brothers Harriman was on the line.

"Is a Mrs. Sterne there?"

"Speaking."

"Mrs. Sterne"—and the woman introduced herself—"I have something rather urgent to discuss with you."

"Everyone has, it seems. Okay, your turn, I'm listening."

As the bank officer went on, Audrey kept stiffening. "He's dead! Are you positive?"

"I'm afraid so, Mrs. Sterne. Er, I'm calling because you are named as a trustee under the terms of his will and—"

"—you must be very mistaken there, I'm afraid."

"It's very clear, Mrs. Sterne. I checked it with our legal department. Could you possibly come by here tomorrow? There may be a problem, and we'd very much like to take it up with all concerned."

"Who is *all*?"

"Yourself and a Miss Jagoda, at least. She's the —"

"I know who she is, thanks. Why so urgent? Don't these things take months?"

"There's a possible incident in the making, Mrs. Sterne," warned the trust officer. "We don't think Mr. Rhodes's death has been publicly announced yet and this might be the best time—"

"What incident, what do you mean?"

"I don't think we should go into it over the phone. It's too involved."

"I see." Baffled, Audrey's curiosity romped.

"We could send a car out to Malibu for you."

"I'll make it on my own thank you. What time?"

"Is ten all right? We're on the sixth floor of Arco Tower North and you can park in the lower level of our building. Ten, then?"

"Ten it is, I'll be there."

Afterward, she bent her head down, turning it back and forth. My dear God—he's gone.

The image of the returned bracelet entered her mind. Good of him, even gallant. She started to weep softly and didn't know why.

Hours melted away so slowly that Audrey thought time had actually frozen on her. In the wilderness of her huge glass house that was no longer a home, she tried steadying herself against the double smashes of that day.

Darkness fell later and she treated herself to two stiff gins. Julio had nearly disappeared from her thoughts, but she couldn't seem to eject the remembrances of Cliff Rhodes. Another jangle of the phone, about four jangles, she couldn't be sure, lifting her out of her trance.

She heard the urgent voice of Sister Marius. The good shepherdess herself demanding the return of Romaine's file. It seemed the five o'clock newscast, with its mention of Rhodes's death, had pierced the cloistered walls of Las Infantas.

Scold, scold.

"Sister," said Audrey at length, "if you receive any disturbing inquiries, I'll think about returning the papers to you."

"You still have them, don't you? All the trouble they've been—"

"No, Sister," Audrey said very sweetly now that the gin was working on her so adeptly. "The papers weren't the trouble. The trouble began—oh, never mind."

"You'll send them back?"

"When you return the money, I will," Audrey replied stiffly. Fatigue hit her at last. Feeling a yell was about to fly from her throat, she added: "G'night, Sister. I think I hear my plaster angel calling."

Closing one eye, she centered the receiver over its cradle and let it drop. It missed. This entire day had been *amiss*, she decided. Time for a third gin. Who could she call for dinner? She was getting lonely. The house, all of its cold glass, no one to talk with other than the day help, and she was getting herself bombed for no reason other than she was so wretched.

She was as alone now as a falling star.

Chapter Forty-four

"**I** stayed out of it back there," said Fritzi, exhausted and depressed, "and I'm still in a tangle."

"The bank isn't confused, I'm pretty sure of that." Audrey kicked off her shoes, tucking her feet under one hip as she leaned back in a couch. "I suppose that's why they were in such a hurry to read us the will."

"I can understand why Cliff involved me. But why you?"

"That's a story without an end to it," Audrey said. "Maybe it's finally coming to an end somehow."

Fritzi looked at her. "Mind letting me in on it?"

Not everyday friends, they were just two women who were well enough acquainted, then had found themselves suddenly paired up by a tragedy. And did not know, and could not know that the morning just spent together at Brown Brothers Harriman would ally them for a long time to come.

"You wouldn't have a spare martini around the house," she suggested to Fritzi. "I've got a slight hangover today and all that legal rigmarole didn't help any. Try not to spare the gin."

Watching as Fritzi left the room, Audrey thought of a suffering widow; a widow who had never been married. Sympathy grew, helping her to forget her own troubles.

They had come to Fritzi's home after two maddening hours talking with the woman officer, a bank lawyer at her side. The reading of Rhodes's will at the bank had forced her to admit, once more, she couldn't change what was already done. The past clung to her like a barnacle, one never to be scraped away.

Soon, there'd be a public record in the Probate Court. Already, there were too many records. The newspapers would pick up on it: DECEASED JUDGE NAMES MURDER SUSPECT AS TRUSTEE. Just peachy. Just what she needed. The gossip-mill would go into overdrive again. Guesses would morph into rumors, and the rumors soon become suspicions. The worst kind of suspicions. And Julio would become the pest of this and every century.

A hand from the grave, Audrey had thought. The dead making a one-sided bargain with the living. Those dull passages in Rhodes's own writing: to her dismay he had finally made them into a family. Not much of one, but finally accounted for, in the most inopportune of ways and at the most inopportune time.

Miffed that they'd been cut out of the trustee's fees, the bank showed even greater unease at Andrey's role under the will. Why was she, they had asked her, a trustee for Romaine Brook?

Fritzi's very same question of only a moment ago.

Audrey had brushed the bank off, suggesting they mind their own business. She suspected they were far less worried over her than they were about their future relationship with Parthenon Studios.

Cliff Rhodes had pinned her absolutely—and absolutely publicly—to the daughter she had denied for twenty-three years. Fritzi had inherited half, outright, of a considerable estate. The other half was to be held in a ten-year trust for Romaine's benefit, with Fritzi and herself as co-trustees.

There were other bequests, but Audrey had paid little attention. Suffering in fright now that she was shackled to Romaine as surely as if they were Siamese twins. Her thief and Marc's killer, she was sure of it. God, thought Audrey, I've never committed enough sins in my life to keep on paying and paying this way.

She could still hear Rhodes's written words: "*I ask you to help me with Romaine and with her future and well-being. You will know why, both of you, and I am forever confident you will understand why I must turn to you. After longest thought this is the only way, I believe, for Romaine to be looked after. No one but the both of you can help her should I die or become incapacitated.*"

Listening to the request, as read, Fritzi had stared off into space, alternately rocked to her lowest levels, fretting and perplexed. How could this happen? The bank, she demanded knowing, had called her for *this*? She neither needed nor wanted the money. She wanted *him* back. Act as Romaine's guardian? There must be some other way, Fritzi openly appealed to all present.

"The courts could assume the task, or possibly even appoint us," advised the bank officer. "We are only informing you of Judge Rhodes's last wishes."

Hearing these words, and after a little more sparring, Fritzi's resistance had softened. Audrey remembered her looking over and saying: "I'll act as trustee if you will. I hope you've got a good, strong iron-hand. Mine's already cocked and ready to punch."

Bewildered, they had asked about the mysteries of estates and probate matters; how money would be handled; what was the tax catastrophe? What were the other headaches to contend with? Do they need lawyers?

Then they had come here to Fritzi's house for woman-to-woman tête-à-tête, catch their breath, consider what to do next. Or not do, as they dwelled on their private worries or heartaches.

With an early afternoon drink in hand, a desperately needed painkiller, Fritzi was about to have an earlier guess confirmed.

Of how Audrey and Cliff Rhodes, caught up in the slap-happy love of two young adults, had made a daughter. One that Audrey, for a hundred and nine reasons, had once wanted to find and then to help as an anonymous mother.

Fritzi had never before linked Cliff with Audrey Sterne. Casual acquaintances, her appearances in his courtroom, yes, but nothing else. Nothing like this! Audrey, after all, had lived in London for nearly seventeen years before marrying Julio Sterne. A long interlude, and then the past had pounced, wanting its voice heard. A voice now shouting.

"He had said something one night at dinner," Fritzi said, stunned again as Audrey had let her in on the missing half of the story.

"About me?" Audrey asked.

"No, he never mentioned you. Only that he was her father. God, I never heard anything like this. Not ever in my life."

"It's true as it can be. I've the papers to prove it. I had to buy them. Imagine. It's like buying your own history. I was thinking of destroying them."

"You didn't, did you?"

"Not yet."

"Don't."

"Those papers are incendiary. Atomic. I can't have them known about."

"I see what you're saying. Maybe you—oh, well, nothing."

Audrey put her drink down. "It's been worse than you can imagine, believe me. Julio still has no idea I'm the mother. He'd blow his feathers." Audrey told Fritzi what she'd been telling herself all these months. Romaine had been an accident. A love child. What good would it do anyone to spade it up, years and years later? And when Marc Sterne died, it was too late to confide in anyone. "I was petrified," said Audrey, looking wanly at Fritzi. "You just don't know."

"But you told Cliff halfway through the trial—"

"Yes," Audrey broke in. "Because of that subpoena threat to get to the records at Las Infantas...I was afraid for both of us, so I had to tell him. And he decided to stay in the trial anyway."

"I wonder why."

"One reason is all the commotion it would cause...and, well, me. Nice of him. He told me they'd find out somehow I was the mother, if he withdrew from the trial. Then there was the Supreme Court business. "

"I still wonder."

"I don't, Fritzi. It wasn't so hard for me to find Romaine. A wad of money is all it took."

"Was he named as the father?"

"Yes. That was a mistake, adding his name to the records. But my family insisted on it at the time. They damn near broke my neck, as it was."

Thinking now of something else, Fritzi shook her dark curls, saying, "Romaine stayed here for a while."

"You don't mean it?"

"I very sure do."

"She's trouble with wings on. No one seems to believe that but me. Well, Julio, he knows her, knows what she's capable of."

"Now she's trouble who's worth more than five-million bucks."

"It's just outrageous. How could he ever? Godsakes!"

"You suppose she's still in France or Monte Carlo?" asked Fritzi, almost to herself.

"Who? Romaine?"

"Cliff took her last week. To some clinic. This kind of clinic." Fritzi tapped her head with a finger.

"Why didn't you say so?"

"You've been doing all the talking."

"A clinic? For her?" Audrey hesitated. "He knew she was loco then?"

"Troubled, yes. Crazy, truly crazy? I don't think he thought that."

All the time she'd been talking, Fritzi could feel a stream of more pain mixing with her insides. She tried to block it off, but it kept roaring through her anyway. Talking helped, talking, indeed, was like an epiphany. She thought, then, of Fahey. He would have to know. He must be told.

"Tell me something, Audrey. Do you think Romaine actually killed your stepson?"

Audrey nodded. "She beat the rap. People do. They just get away with it sometimes. I think she had a hand in it somehow. I'm not sure, but I went along with Julio, who was certain of it. Julio has his faults, a real bastardo at times, but his instincts about things are usually sharp. Terribly sharp."

Audrey explained the stolen emerald bracelet, and how Rhodes had managed to return it to her.

"But you're still only guessing."

"I'm no lawyer, Fritzi, and I'm no murderer either as some might think...Romaine got Marc to do something that night. She had him twisted around her every finger."

"But no one will ever know, will they?"

"Not technically maybe, but I have a very, very strong feeling." Audrey threw out the words slowly as a frantic light shone in her eyes. "God, they really think I might've done it. They're questioning me still." She looked to see if Fritzi understood.

"If I promise to never breathe a word, will you tell me something?"

"That all depends."

"Here goes anyway—did you have something going with your butler?"

"Fritzi, Jesus! Please!"

"I'll never say."

"Supposing I said nothing, that I didn't answer you. Would you be able to read me?"

"Maybe. But I wish you'd say, one way or the other."

"He was great in the sack," Audrey said suddenly.

They smiled at each other, and Fritzi felt much better. She wasn't judging her. Half the people Fritzi knew were having affairs, or had had them, including herself. But if she were going to be dealing with Audrey for the next ten years over Romaine's trust, it was better to know who she was dealing with.

Fritzi said, "I swear it won't leave this room."

"Supposing I said I hadn't. Would you have believed me?"

"I would now."

"You were testing me?"

Fritzi nodded.

"And if I said I hadn't been with Ferenc Kardas and you didn't believe me, then you might doubt me about Romaine and Marc?"

"Something like that, yes," replied Fritzi. "How is Julio going to take all this, if he learns you're a trustee?"

"He's in Hong Kong buying movies. Yesterday he served me with papers. He wants a divorce. He'll learn. Sooner or later, he hears everything. And, besides, there'll be public record of Cliff's will. Then Julio will add four and four and get ten-thousand, the way he does, and the Great Titan will put my empennage in the well-known sling. It's in one already."

"Well, I'm sorry. Really I am."

"So am I. But the divorce, it's for the best."

"Hope he'll be generous with you."

"Generosity isn't Julio's long suit, when he wants out of something," Audrey said. "Fritzi, do you think we ought to call someone in Monte Carlo? Find out what's going on over there?"

"I've been thinking about it for almost two days." Fritzi's face clouded. "I only went to the bank *not* to think about it and now I'm thinking about it all over again." Her face widened and then part of it dropped from the nose down. "We were going to marry and now it's become a funeral." Her voice faltered. "I-I can't bear to—to bury him."

Audrey sprang to her feet. She went over and sat on the armrest, snugging Fritzi close, feeling Fritzi shudder. Someone had to do something and soon. Romaine had to be located and burial arrangements organized. It was too much, all at once, too enveloping, as if floundering in quicksand.

Fritzi was mopping her swollen eyes.

"If you'll be all right," Audrey said, "I'll start doing some calling to Monte Carlo. What time is it there?"

"Night. Eleven or so."

"Well, I can call the State Department," said Audrey. "They can find things out."

"I know someone who can help, I think."

"Who?"

"Do you know Alonzo Fahey?"

412

Audrey dimly recalled that name from somewhere. "Should I know?" she asked.

Fritzi explained who he was; of how he had once worked for Cliff Rhodes, had even assisted in Romaine's defense.

But now she recalled Fahey as the man Sister Marius had talked about. Cliff Rhodes, too, had dropped his name but she couldn't remember in what context. "I'm not sure I want to know him,"

"He's marvelous. Mostly. Wild-headed but marvelous. He was going to give me way at the wedding—"

"Oh, that's different then. How do I get a hold of him?"

"I'll do it."

"Fritzi, you can't tell him one word about me. That I'm Romaine's mother."

"I wouldn't."

"Won't he want to know why I'm here?"

"I'll think of something."

"You promise me?"

"Absolutely, I do."

Fritzi went down the hall to her bedroom. Sitting at her dressing table, she dialed, and then spoke in hushed tones to Wanda Fahey.

Idly, she stroked the strands of the thin gold chains on a peg next to the mirror. One that Cliff Rhodes had given her, her favorite one with the enameled lion pendant, was gone. Recalling Audrey's story about the emerald bracelet, Fritzi's emotions shot from wet despair to dry anger.

Two hours later, Fahey turned up.

He looked as if he had come in from a climb through the hills somewhere, wearing his faded dungarees, a navy blue and often- patched sweater, and a vivid red bandanna tied around his sturdy neck. Tousled dark hair fell everywhere across his forehead and a perfect line of beard shadowed his face.

"I meant to call when I heard," he said to Fritzi. "Never even said goodbye to him. Thought you'd be sore at me...and now look at you with all the sand in your eyes." Fahey came forward and swung his one good arm around her.

Audrey stood away, watching them embrace. She tried to catalogue Fahey, and instinctively smelled a lean healthy male around, who was looking back at her now over Fritzi's bowed head. Deep warm eyes, Audrey saw, blue as a Swedish lake, and with thick lashes. An arm stiff as a toy soldier's. At last, the Las Infantas interloper.

They broke apart, and Fritzi fluffed her hair. "Alonzo, this is Audrey Sterne. A friend of mine."

"You who I think you are?" Fahey said to Audrey. He came over, barely a foot away, surprising her.

'Probably."

"A looker, eh? You've a lovely pair there, too. A real set of twins, I'd say."

"Alonzo, stop," Fritzi reproached him. "God, do you never know when to behave?"

"But they're nice, aren't they, and she looks so gorgeous. Like the Magdalene in a painting I saw once in…hell, I forget where. Probably San Salvador," he said, and then to Audrey: "Hurt the feelings, did we?"

"Not at all," said Audrey, rubbing her neck slightly to cover a rising blush.

"Alonzo, we need some help," Fritzi said. "There's some things you ought to know. They absolutely must stay in this room. Not a word to anyone."

Fahey nodded.

It was to be his last nod for some time, as he fell by degrees into a sump of disbelief. Fritzi gave him the bare bones at first, and then astounded him by revealing that Cliff Rhodes was Romaine's true father. "Imagine the iron box Cliff had found himself in…and why at the end of the trial he could not lift so much as a finger to help you. Everything teetered on the edge: one misstep, one stray word, and disaster would mow him down for good. Losing out on his appointment to the Supreme Court, he had taken Romaine to France for help and to get her out of Hollywood…he loved you, Alonzo, you know that," Fritzi went on. "And he worried so about you. I know, because I saw him go through it."

Fahey wondered why all this news in front of a stranger like Audrey Sterne. All of it was so cockeyed. With both ears ready for more, he loaded his glass again. Halfway up to his mouth, he was thinking: how neat, Rhodesy-boy, you the old Dance-Master, pulled off a real courtroom heist. The idea held a peculiar shape to it that appealed to Fahey's sense of irony.

He began to assess his part in the tragedy. It was he, after all, who had gone out to Las Infantas one fine day to help Tommy Burke find the real parents. The nun had run him off as surely as if he'd come to steal her praying virgins. To make shorter work of it, he'd thrown down the idle bluff of a subpoena.

And now he could see, starkly see, that if he'd just shut up, Rhodes would probably never have known about Romaine. Who she really was, to him. If he had never known, and never cared, he wouldn't have gone to Europe to die. Still be here, and Fritz-girl would still be dishing out her good-natured laughs, a dozen at a time. Fahey knew he would be shadowboxing with his jumpy feelings for a long time to come.

He thought of himself as a sort of curator of this world's foibles, keeping a loose catalogue in his head about them; something to draw upon in puzzled moments. Or to reassure himself that, Bible or not, democracy or benevolent dictatorship, nothing was likely to make the world fight. It wasn't so much that it was doomed, but clearly it was lacking in the fundamentals of order and sanity. He could see, right here on these premises, woe and suffering was in the air. He'd have to worm it out of them, he knew, but that was, after all, his life's work. That and the care of neglected women. That and getting rid of people like Cullis. And watching out for his friends; friends like Cliff Rhodes.

He was hungry, saying so, wanting to know if they should head off to Masquers. Check out the action, see how much Ginty was filching from the cash register. To maintain him, Fritzi left to make sandwiches. He turned his attention to Audrey who gazed back steadily. Why was she here, he asked through a smile that came at her like a thrown bouquet. "How is it you're here?" he asked her. "You from the sugar industry? You look to me like you probably invented it. On sugar, the, uh, of the female genus, I'm something of a connoisseur..."

"Really, how nice. Connoisseur? Wow! Is there a school one goes to?"

"Indeed so. The Fahey School for the Propagation of Dreams and Other Sexual Advancement. I'm headmaster. Last time I checked, I was. Care for a scholarship? We've actually a real live gypsy heading up the faculty. A powerhouse, a genuine floodlight. Makes the eyes water much of time. Shines like that smile of yours you keep suppressing. You can infect your tonsils that way...you're doctor'll tell you but not for free, of course..."

She shook her head, partly to say no to the scholarship, partly because she'd never run across anyone like this man. She hove to a new tack, saying: "To answer your earlier question, I came by to see Fritzi. See how she was

415

holding up," Audrey replied blithely, still held, nonetheless, in a semi-coma of fascination with this...this whatever...

No mention of the bank meeting that morning, nor that she was Romaine's mother, of course. Audrey wondered if the handsome lug sitting so near to her would guess there was more to it?

"I guess you knew the girl pretty well?" Audrey heard Fahey ask, as if reading her thoughts.

"For a while I did. Or thought I did," Audrey answered. "What did you think of Romaine?"

"A lovely but unfinished toy. In need of a bridle, I'd say."

"That's all?"

"Only met with her twice," he said. "An actress, of course, so an invention. We invent them so they can invent other worlds for us...I adore them for it. They blot out our so any of our miseries."

Audrey mused on his comments. "Maybe, but did you like her? The *actual* her?"

"In which way?"

"I don't know." Hesitating. "Was she, did she sound right to you? Or start pulling some of her cute numbers?"

Fahey thought, then replied, "Flames of ice."

"Nice?"

"I-c-e. Ice-like. Cold orgasms probably. That type."

"That's a peculiar thing to say," said Audrey.

"Have you read Cyrano?"

"deBergerac? That Cyrano?"

"Hercule-Savinien de Cyrano de Bergerac. Yes, he's my patron. Like a saint or an iconic figure who one is given to emulate."

"I saw the movie a long time ago. Twice or maybe it was three times. It was so long ago. How did we get on this?"

"You remind me of Roxanne. The same effervescent beauty. Honey in the vocal cords. A perfection of the nose bone. Quite rare, you know, finding both qualities inside one shell."

"I can't say as I do know anything like that, Mr. Fahey. But I suppose I should thank you all the same."

"No need to. Your presence, ah, actually it was your body that has thanked me, and even before we'd passed a single word. I couldn't anyway pass words, for you'd taken all the breath from me...I'm thinking of several songs that were probably written about you...or someone very much like you. Shall I croon them, while we wait for drinks?"

"Please, no. That's entirely unnece—no, no." Her hands fluttered, nervously, so that she had to clasp them, hoping he hadn't noticed.

"Well, I'll croon them anyway to you the first time we shower together. Crooning, you see, bends the sound waves in the steam and that's what enlarges the soap bubbles. Really strains them. Strains any number of things—"

"Shower? What do you mean by that?"

"Shower, surely you shower? Or do you prefer the bathtub. We can do that if you—"

"Are you in your right mind today?"

Conversation abruptly lulled when Fritzi returned, balancing a tray on one raised hand, a trick-of-the-profession she had learned from one of the waiters at Masquers. Grateful that she had been saved by Fritzi's reappearance, Audrey nonetheless was unnerved by Fahey's ramblings. Unsure of what to say, especially about the inestimable idea of taking a shower with an utter stranger; she had not yet succeeded in getting a real bead on this handsome sapphire-eyed so-called investigator, who had caused such a ruckus at Las Infantas. Mister Subpoena, in the flesh. She battled with a strong craving to give him a piece of her mind, but that risked the raising of questions she could not conceivably answer.

Still, a hundred-thousand dollar buy-back was no light matter to her. She'd had had to scrape deep to amass the sum so quickly.

Wonderment mounted—*a shower, he had actually mentioned a shower, for the love of Nellie! Whoever did he think he was anyway?*—and with an awesome effort she painted her face with a lavish smile while Fritzi doled out drinks and appetizers.

When Fritzi sat, eyeing him carefully, she said, "Alonzo, I want to bury him over there. I can't think of him here, so close by and in the ground. Will you come and be with me...he loved you, Alonzo. Everything Cliff did he did for reasons of his own. He only told me the main one and I guess he felt he couldn't tell you even that much. You or anyone else, and it's not so hard to figure out why. Not anymore, it isn't."

"How can you ask me to forget what happened? Like a bullet to both kneecaps and one in the neck."

"You must try"—she hurried on anxiously, encouragingly—"bygones are bygones. He wanted the Supreme Court and he lost it all over that damn trial. He's lost his life now. But he shouldn't lose you or me, should he?" Pausing, then, to catch her breath. "Please come, you will...please..."

She sat only a few feet away, near Audrey, as Fahey soaked himself in newer thoughts. He easily could grasp why Rhodes had maneuvered at the end to help show how Marc Sterne might have died in other ways. He looked over at Audrey again. He knew she was under suspicion, though he thought it rather absurd of the sheriff, who was likely trying to deflect attention from the earlier botched investigation.

Audrey Sterne entranced him. He felt an urge to explore her mouth, lay the edge of a fingertip on those Arabian-like lips. She's orchid, he thought: an intelligent orchid.

"I'm on short rations these days," he said to no one and to everyone, including himself. "The larder has gone bare on me."

"I'll take care of everything," Fritzi answered. "Leave it all to me."

"Never borrow from women. Bad form, that's what I always say."

"You would know, you certainly know a ton of them," Fritzi shot back.

"A plate collection, you think? Pass the hat for old dog Fahey...on the curb there with his dented beggar's cup extended to all passersby." Fahey frowned. He held to a fast rule, never to discuss money with women—they had so much of it these days. Should all be sent out to weed the fields for a month-long training exercise of every year. Better if it were two months. Great for slimming the thighs and keeping all other parts limbered up for the nights ahead.

"What about me?" Audrey said. "I'm still on the outs with the sheriff, and I'd like to know what happened over there."

"You really want to come?" Fritzi asked.

"You mind?"

"Not at all." Fritzi gave her a knowing look. "That settles it...Alonzo, are you in?"

Fahey stood, his decision made. "You'll have to bail me out with a few thousand, if I'm to go."

"No problem—"

"I can lend it to you," Audrey quickly offered, somewhat happier now that a man was in tow. An offbeat man, but likely a useful addition.

"Jesus," said Fahey, enthused now. "Let's all get together more often, if you're handing out the shekels so readily."

"Thanks, Alonzo," Fritzi told him. "I mean it. Really."

"I'll need your phone," he said. "What time is it? Fourish?" Fahey had the others of this world tracking the time for him, never carrying a watch himself. He despised them; he was no time-robot. Clocks of any kind interfered with his freedoms.

"About 4:20," Audrey noted, glancing at her wrist.

"Midnight or so in Monaco. Good hour to raise them out of their bedding," said Fahey. "I might be a while. Slow of hearing over there. No telling what were up against. "

"Use the one out in the kitchen. It's on the counter by the bulletin board."

Waiting till he left, Fritzi suggested, "Those papers you mentioned?"

"Yes, what about them?"

"Bring them along, in case we need them. Just in case."

"I'll think about it, okay. I'll see...I worry..."

❧

It took some digging before he acquired the number of the Monaco police prefecture. When connected, he worked his way up to the night watch-commander, and then initiated his *parlez* in rapid-fire, clipped, no nonsense tones. "Listen, Rhodes was a brother," he said to the invisible presence manning the far-off phone. "And me, here, with my hands full of wailing women...and what about all the boggling inefficiency? Why did I have to be notified through the fucking newscasts? You Monacans are bad as the French...you *are* French...or is it Italian? Schizoids, the lot of you...like to hear the bawling of these women in the next room, would you...I'd hand them the phone but I'm feeling gracious today. A*mi,* these women feed on broken beer bottles and eat ears for dessert. Deafen you for life, eh?"

The police officer politely agreed to call Matin early in the morning, making mention that the inspector was undoubtedly asleep at this hour.

"*Nein,*" Fahey contended. "Not good enough. We've been sorrowing like the Madonna for days. Well, hours. Hard hours. *Verstehen Sie.*"

"Are you German, m'sieu?"

419

"I've the right genes for it. My grandfather was Gestapo. Attached to the Eiserplatz office in Berlin, I believe. That's where they kept all the filthy-minded ass-kickers, and he was the worst of them."

"*Moment,* m'sieu."

Fahey waited. His need for action had been sparking and was now fully alive. He had started something back there at Las Infantas. He thought of Cliff Rhodes. A debt to pay there perhaps, but how do you pay off the dead?

Back on the line again, the police officer gave a home number for Matin, who had agreed, in the interval, to stand by for a call. Fahey signed off and a few minutes later made contact with Matin, who sounded relieved to hear from someone. Very soon the body could be released. Best, he observed, to work through the U.S. Consul in Nice; who would gladly assist in every way.

"We'll be coming your way, Inspector. His fiancée wants him buried over there," Fahey said.

Matin seemed confused. "I believe his fiancée is already here. She's made no mention of a burial in Monaco."

"Is that girl there? Romaine Brook?"

"She will be here for at least a few more days."

Again the wait, and it hung heavy on the line. Fahey narrowed his eyes. "Whatever you do, keep her there and keep her laughing. It works the right muscles, don't you know." he advised Matin. "Till we get over there. Can you? *Merci.*" Hanging up, he had great leeriness about dealing with the police, but there was no option. The bastards had their noses into everything.

Shortly, all the essentials were agreed to, and Fahey, robust with his newest sense of self-worth, and seeing other barriers to surmount, proceeded to fill in Fritzi and Audrey. Talking it over, back and forth, they finally settled on the following night to fly to Nice in France. Fahey lingered long enough for another drink, as he weighed approaches for breaking these latest developments in his life to Wanda. She'd be leaving him for sure, he was certain.

It would never do to bring her along; two women on any foreign expedition—one per arm—was the maximum permissible. A regimental rule, or it should be. Still, it was implausible to think Wanda would succumb to the idea of his larking off to Europe with women she had never met. Heard of, yes, and that was the worst of it Fahey decided. Well, Rhodes; he'd blame everything on Rhodes, and on the mewling and wailing of desperate women who were utterly bereft of others to turn to. No time for consulting the Gypsy on this one. He was on his own, the way he liked it best, and maybe the thing to do was contact Cullis and pound the spike of envy into that good-for-nothing bastard.

They might yank his P. I. ticket but his heart belonged solely, utterly, completely to himself.

Except for Tuesdays and Fridays, when he transferred his affections exclusively to Wanda, and few others, who understood he was only one man with one heart; his long-gone but much-cherished mother, from an early age, had drilled him on the importance of sharing. And he did, limitedly. Which was one of the ways he depended upon to ease his bones through this god-forgotten life that was given to you to see how much suffering you could handle before war was declared.

Chapter Forty-five

"Gin." exclaimed Audrey, fanning out her cards on table, snapping the tricks down with a triumphant gleam in her eyes.

"How terribly impure of you," Fahey observed.

"Six games and that makes the set."

"You've got a mirror behind me somewhere." Fahey smiled as he scratched the stubble of a budding beard. "Never heard of the luck," he added. "Like my Gypsy."

"What gypsy?"

"I told you of her. Head of faculty, and she moonlights as a secret weapon of mine. A national treasure. Going to sell her to the Russian Air Force one day, if the IRS gets out of hand again."

Audrey stacked the cards. "Shall we finish this later?"

"Dropping out on me while you're ahead? Are you without any shame?"

"I'll play if you want to, but I'd rather have more champagne."

Getting up, he went back to the galley in the 787. At 5:20 a.m. celestial time, they were still wide-awake. Fritzi, fatigued, had grabbed a blanket and curled up on a full row of vacant seats in the half-empty plane.

They had drifted into gin rummy, penny a point in view of Fahey's thin wallet. Audrey wanted to drift into something else before they reached Monte Carlo via Nice, thinking actively about the matter until Fahey, her newest servant, returned and handed her a flute of Pol Roget.

"After Monte Carlo," Audrey observed, "I may go on to London. My sons live there. They're twin boys."

"Nippers, eh? How old?"

She told him.

"Who would've guessed." Fahey leaned back, eyeing her. "A girl like you and hardly a wrinkle."

Audrey smiled majestically. "And I'm especially worried about something which won't do any good for my wrinkles."

"Comes with life. Have to trounce our worries, eh?. Fall in love again, then you can grow a new crop of worries." A new idea, then, as he offered, "Have you ever stopped to think how easy it is to be nice to someone until you fall in love with them?"

"No, I haven't. An interesting statement…I'm also being serious."

Seeing she meant it, Fahey let her go on. The lingering suspicions arising at the trial had beset her, she began, then…"I can't bear to have my sons wondering, even for one day, that I had the slightest involvement in the death of Marc Sterne. The boys knew him, of course, and they'll ask things. Will you help me, Alonzo? You know a lot of what happened."

"To my lasting regret, I do. Help you how, love? Point me to the path."

"Can I engage you? After we get back. Will you work for me and look into it?"

"A small problem looms," Fahey said. "My license may be lifted. Might beach me, the sodders." He explained his own predicament, tempted to tell Audrey that Rhodes was at fault. But that wouldn't do at all. Why blame the dead, especially when they were home and dry forever. Rest him, thought Fahey. Give him peace, give him his own private planet and many of those virgins the Muslims keep promising us.

"Could I do something for you?" Audrey was asking.

"Many things." Fahey laughed. "But we'd better wait till we reach Nice. It'll be our glory, my dearest one."

"C'mon…I meant about your license." She took a dainty sip of the Pol Roget. "I've still got friends. I know the governor's wife, Emma. We're buddies. I can always try her," she said, holding her flute precariously.

Fahey straightened her hand; indeed, he was spending an excess of time straightening it. "Thanks, cherub, but there's another hitch. I represented Romaine Brook and so I can't do it for you, if you're against each other."

"What do you owe her? That's over with."

"Question of what they call ethics. I've only caught a slim dose of the ethics disease, but it's in there swinging away all the same."

"Of course, I'd pay you."

"Can't do. I'll find someone for you. A dedicated bloodhound in need of work."

"But I'd like having you," said Audrey, disappointed and showing it.

Fahey barely heard her. His mind was fastened on Romaine. Had she? Rhodes was in good physical shape. Took care of himself, a very agile boyo with fast reflexes. A Special Forces grenadier. How could he have fallen off a cliff?

"Are you about to sleep?"

Fahey opened his eyes. "Thinking of the Tunisian poets again. The Vatican stole their best stuff. Ought to admit it and return it. By chance, are you Catholic?"

"No, well once. Oh, damn. You won't help?"

"Let's first hear the terrifying sagas of Monte Carlo. Then we'll see," Fahey promised her. Sexual tension was coiling in him. He could feel it and wanted to turn this serious talk to the light-hearted variety. No telling the severity of the situation awaiting them in Monte Carlo.

"Alonzo... Fritzi said you can do anything." Audrey's voice, a purr.

"She could've meant this," said Fahey, gently taking Audrey's face with his free hand, then moving himself closer. It was a kiss that became part of his life, to remember always as the first kiss of that minute on that day at 34,000 feet above those exact map coordinates of planet Earth. It elated him. And though it was well past midnight, his night had yet to begin. How to get started, he asked himself; the answer was obvious—unravel her uppermost worry. Ingratiate himself, nourish her hopes, provide succor.

"Exactly, what help are you wanting, *cherie*?"

"We had this houseman-valet. Kardas. His name is Ferenc Kardas, it's Hungarian."

"Him again. I was in court on the day the girl mentioned him."

"I've got to find him somehow."

"Why him? You already have me," replied Fahey, in a severely wounded tone.

"I hope I can have you."

"And you shall, my precious, as soon as we make port."

"Dammit you, be serious, I'm in no laughing mood. I'd like to engage you to go find Kardas, as I said or almost said. He's gone to ground somewhere, raising questions as to why. As if, well—you know—acting like a fugitive. It makes it harder for me, don't you see?"

"Indeed, mam...indeed, I do see...a heartless bounder if ever I heard of one. Hungarians are known for that."

"Not quite all that bad. He never mistreated me or anything—." Saying it, she wished she hadn't made a slip so revealing. "Will you help? You must, won't you?"

"My dove, that's utterly unethical as we've discussed."

"Oh, posh! You can, too. What're your fees, may I ask?"

"My fees, ah, my fees. Well—flexible, it depends."

"On what?"

"My fees, yes…lessee, ah, they could be you. That's it…you…did you know that I've been gazing at the shell of your ear and it's like something only Leonardo could design. You've a perfectly shaped ear."

"We were talking about—"

"—your enticing ear, like those filigreed curves seen in a nautilus. That's the better topic by far, my dream-maker. And then there's your gorgeous front matter. When one is as upholstered as you are…it's an intuitive leap of the senses…it's a hop over the Rubicon and back again…I long for you…"

"Oh God, Alonzo. C'mon…"

"But I am coming on, love."

"I meant it another way, and you very well know it."

"You cannot expect me to sit next to you, with the waft of that perfume that keeps infiltrating me. Like the fragrance of the Persian pink lily, with all its folds and I'm wondering if that lily matches your folds. Legs that're magnets to my eyes. Not to touch those, not to explore the upper region of the thighs that're the guardians of your pistil, not to say—"

"What I say is for you to zip up your mouth, if you don't mind."

"I'd so much rather unzip you. I'm greatly in need of a jutting breast to fondle. If I guess its size, your left one, you must let me have a chance at the right. No two are precisely the same, you see. The odds favor you that I'll get it wrong. Your cup size. Let's give it a go; it's much more fun than gin rummy and all this talking about fees."

Looking at him with a mixture of fascination and alarm, she murmured, "You remember where we are, I trust."

"Our latitude or longitude? I haven't my sextant with me. But I do know where I heartily wish to be. Like to guess?"

"I don't have to guess. What pistol do you mean…guardians of my pistol, you said."

Fahey laughed softly. He was going to make her his, do it by noon tomorrow at the latest. "It's not a gun, love. Anything but a gun. Let me spell it for you—it's p-i-s-t-i-l. In a flower, it's the equivalent of your furry little kitty and all that goes with it."

"Really? Strange name for that. A pistil. I'll remember that one."

"I like it. It's symbolic. Transgenic, too."

"Trans-who…oh, never mind. Aren't you married? Fritzi said you were."

"Astonishing what women tell each other. She actually said that?"

Audrey nodded.

"She's half right, I s'pose. I was married in the Galapagos by a drunken Benedictine. A barefooted boyo with a foot-long prophet's beard on him. No license needed or any of that rubbish. Not done there. The turtles and finches wouldn't stand for any of that, mind. Come to think of it, I'm having hell's own time of it these days with licenses. Paper, that's all it is, and a bunch of brick-brained goddamn clerks with their stamps and ink pads."

"Whooie! You're quite an elliptical talker, Mr. Fahey."

"You're quite an elliptical curve, Mrs. Sterne. Several of them, I've noted. I'd like to begin measuring them. With the, ah, palms of my hands perhaps."

"You're a silly one, you know?" Giggling as she spoke.

"So they claim, even my Wanda does." With a barely muffled sigh, he went on, "The devil with all this, my love. Let's exchange tongue prints. A mouth feast and it'll be the start of us."

"This is hardly the place to—"

Conscripting her, then. Making certain she wouldn't have breath to extend her protest, he pulled her to him. As if a welder's electrical arc had suddenly passed through the cabin, they fused. A flying, wild instant as they struggled to become one body. Still clothed to be sure, but nonetheless a oneness was happening. A Siamese moment.

He was right on her, one mouth hard upon the other. Breaking apart, he laid his head across her exceptional bosom, saying he'd rather perish on the spot than ever be free of her. He would read Percy Shelley to her later, but now, it was to be lip upon lip and then, when gathering new breath, his head taking in the warmth of those cushiony breasts. And at another point, he indicated he'd been surreptitiously studying the hue and texture of her mouth and could tell its native flesh matched that of her nipples and their aureoles. Insisting he must taste her lips again. "A two-for-one thing," he whispered, while gently cupping one breast, and adding, "I must know all about these, love…you've a treasure chest, you see, and I need the full map of it. Like Braille, I must be able to read you by touch alone. And that magazine-cover smile—that's just for your new friend Fahey, isn't it so?"

Fusion again.

She'd always had possessed a largeness of heart, made wide and ready for love, having had a mother and father who ladled out their affections with frugality. She liked men, always had, and they liked her, too. She was a good sport, fun-loving, except when the law was badgering her. But never had she believed a man like this Alonzo Fahey could be piercing her affections, rattling her. He had a patter—a patois—that made her inner workings stutter. Courageously uninhibited, totally without restraints—what kind of man wore a woman's scarf as a belt? Or tucked silk squares up his sleeve? He was no flouncer, of that she was absolutely certain.

Soothing her, then, unwrapping her with a flow of endearments, one being: "Your parents had a flash of highest genius when deciding to sculpt you out of nothing but a spoonful of salts and chemicals. Then you came out of the chute, like a fabled Fabergé egg that had actually hatched…scepters have been tossed aside for a woman like you. You're, ah, historical, that's you. You'll be our regimental adjutant in charge of joy. Made for the job, perfect for it, my loved one."

His hand had gone errant again, very close to her fur-bearing region.

"Somebody's going to come," she warned, pulling her hem down.

"But that's the whole idea." Fahey smiled thinly as the rest of him surged.

"You're im-poss-i-*bblle.*"

"I must have your mouth; immediately…listen, we can get one of those Air France medals...I'll send word up to the skipper. Have a grand ceremony when we land, invite the passeng—."

"A wacko, that's what you are," she murmured, allowing him to roam her again.

"My dearest one, I am here to spread my dreams under your feet like they were flower petals. Dreams for bringing us together. A unity, you see. We'll be a force from beyond Jupiter. Nothing like that Trinity business. We'll be real. When they edit the Bible again, you and I will have two pages at least. I'll see to it, but first, love, we need to write some passages for ourselves. We must lay with each other, Abraham-style, but no daughters this time out."

Pulses of the flesh, then, signaled an oncoming urge to lose herself. In an airplane? What would Julio say? Her last straight thought was that she cared not a fig what Mr. Julio Sterne thought about any of it. None of his goddamn business, not anymore.

"Are you this sexual most of the time?" Audrey asked quietly.

"When I'm around someone like you, I'am. It's genetic, and besides what else could I possibly be? However, I might consider giving up on the others, if you should wish."

"Maybe we should sit apart."

"If you leave me, I'll bellow. More champagne for you, my treasured one? It's top-notch juice. Roget, I think."

"I don't know one from the other. Like penguins, it's all the same to me."

"Let's talk of Sappho…you'd have to be a sworn pelvis-peddler to write poetry like hers. And what do you make of having a father with a name like Scamandronymus. Mine was named Gilead. A two-syllable loafer out of Donegal or somewhere." Feeling the touch of her shifting knee, he urged, "Closer, darling, closer to me, or I'll be contracting pneumonia…yes, love, like that…Jesus, aren't you the splendid one…"

At forty-three, she drew more than her share of stares from wandering male eyes. Now it was Alonzo Fahey's eyes, a full-fledged womanizer for certain. As did any woman, she appreciated admiration, had always known plenty of it, ever since adolescence. Almost always, if finding the attraction to be mutual, it led her to the next bit of guesswork—would Alonzo Fahey be a fireball in bed?

Yet she had reached the quarrelsome throes of middle-age, unsure of when her looks would begin to desert her, that she might at any time start to go dull, be unnoticed, turn broad in the beam. The various and usual worries that ganged up on women at her time of life.

Right this moment, that very thought pestered her, making her hesitate before pushing away his hand that was exploring too liberally under her skirt. Whatever was running through his head? As if she didn't know, as if it hadn't happened before, countless *befores,* though not in airplanes, to be sure, but still, *ah, there, yes*—an agreeable feeling seized her, as that crawling persistent hand slipped between the walls of her thighs.

429

What had he called them? Oh yes, the guardians of her pistil.

Warmed with pleasure, she became a little gauzy, tingling with sensations. Moments later, she became instantly, frighteningly alert when hearing the clatter of dishes in the galley. With a lunging movement, she shoved Fahey aside, knowing she must look a ruin. With wave-like movements, she rolled across his knees, hand-combing her tresses as she strode down the aisle toward the safety of the restroom.

∞

Matin stood behind a glass partition on the upper level of the Aéroport Nice Côte d'Azur. He had previously arranged for Air France's station manager to page Fahey, as the passengers filed into the terminal.

Mid-morning. He hoped to dispose of the Rhodes incident, and turn to other work, a growing mountain of it: constant, unceasing, often urgent.

What would these new Americans be like? Visitors came from all corners, Matin thought. Some for play, others on business, still others wealthy enough live the year round on the Côte d'Azur.

He turned away from the partition and walked toward the escalators.

"*M'sieu Fah-hay M'sieur Fah-hay*, kindly come to the Air France information desk," asked a metallic voice.

Fahey beamed. He had just walked through the entry doors, sauntering along between Fritzi and Audrey, when hearing his name given out in a pearly French accent. "Never leave you alone, do they? See you angels at the baggage."

He headed off for the Air France counter, his black beret perched rakishly over his eyes. Matin stepped forward, introducing himself. They shook hands, Fahey regarding the rotund inspector with delight. A French snooper, he thought. Well-fed and sharp-eyed, who had spotted Fahey at once. He liked his pink jowls and the two food spots on his lapels. Matin seemed a calm customer, and perhaps the sort you could depend on to see the finer points of a problem.

Fahey explained that he and Matin were brothers-in-arms, being that Fahey had given his past services to the Los Angeles Police Department; leaving, he said, when the corruption became too rife to bear for a churchgoer like himself.

Ignoring him, Matin asked, "You are accompanied by others, no?"

"Inspector, I shall be introducing you to the finest, most sought after women in all California. Sun-kissed, they are, like all our oranges. Tell you that for nothing."

Matin made a very slight bow. "They're with you now, is that my understanding?"

"My sentries. Never without them, when traveling abroad."

"I see. Should we find them?"

"They're in conference. Why not put them in their own taxi? They know all about luggage and packing. Purses, too; you could grow watermelons in those purses." Fahey said. "I'll drive separately with you, Inspector, if I may. Clear up a few topics, can we? Is the Brook woman still in hand?"

"She is at the Hermitage, unless she is out walking or shopping. She is confined to the principality, in any event."

"Excellent. I shall return to you shortly."

Leaving Matin, he went to tell the women how lucky they were to be driven into Monte Carlo by themselves. The inspector needed softening up, seemed to have a temper, was drearily long-winded. He'd catch up with them at the hotel; waving a cheery goodbye, he pivoted and went back to be with his newly gained friend.

In Matin's Renault, Fahey rolled down the window. He breathed in the air, testing it for flavor, and asked if Matin would kindly drive the coastal road into Monte Carlo. He wanted to see the sea villages again of Villefranche, Cap Roux, and further up, Cap d'Ail. Slower that way, but he needed time to trowel his way through whatever it was that Matin knew, and was yet to be relieved of.

Or didn't know.

Matin described the sparse details of Rhodes's accident—a plunge onto rocks far below a parapet. A strong wind that day, boats in the harbor were upended, and Rhodes had been drinking wine apparently. Might even have taken ill. In any event, "No one could survive such a fall from that height."

"Do you know who he is, or was?"

"I do now," Matin said. "Your consul in Nice explained."

"What of the autopsy?"

"Nothing unusual at all from the chemical tests. Broken back and a fractured cranium. That's what killed him."

"Was he sick, did you say?"

"Dizziness perhaps."

"Did you know, Inspector, Miss Brook stood trial for murder in Cliff Rhodes's court?"

"Yes, M'sieu," said Matin softly. "She explained it all to me. Quite openly. A very unusual relationship seemed to have developed between them."

"Do you know anything about the young woman? Her background, for instance?"

"I know very little of her. I met with her only twice after the accident. We required her statement and she seemed most forthright. Though we didn't like the fact that she was traveling under someone else's passport."

"She was, was she? Anyone we know?"

Matin gave him the surname: Pachmayer.

"A stranger to me," Fahey said, quietly. "When I first talked to you from California, you said the Brook girl was Rhodes's fiancée. Is that what she told you?"

"Yes. They were expecting to marry apparently, or so she stated."

Fahey, troubled, let his eyes bore straight ahead, as if he were taking a bead on a dime a mile away. Marry, eh?

Circling the small seaside village of Villefranche-sur-Mer, they headed up to the road toward Monte Carlo. Fahey smelled a faint trace of brine in the air. Wishing for rain, hoping it might carry a different fragrance here on this side of the Atlantic.

"Cliff Rhodes was my friend, Inspector."

"I assumed so."

"What if his death was no accident?"

"Ah, but we have no reason to think otherwise. An accident, M'sieu Fahey. A regrettable thing, but that is how we see it."

"But then, supposing it wasn't? You're a cop, Inspector. I was a cop once, as I said. You have to think the worst sometimes. That's another reason I had to get of the profession. Bad for the psyche."

Matin chose not to answer.

"Can we meet tomorrow, Inspector? Say in the morning around eleven or so at our hotel."

"Very good, yes. And with Mam'selle Brook?"

"That'd be best."

"Is there something I should know?"

"Let's wait till tomorrow, shall we?"

"M'sieu Fahey, why is it you want the young woman present tomorrow?"

"Just to say hello. That the marines have arrived, that sort of thing." Fahey pressed, "Have you no personal impressions of her?"

"A most distraught young lady."

"Can you tell me what she told you about the accident? Some of her details? How she answered you and the parts that got you wondering?"

"I had inquired of her what she remembered of the incident. She was very upset, naturally. She stated that this Rhodes drank most of a bottle of wine. Quite tipsy, even. Lurching about and not quite in command of himself out there on that parapet and at the mercy of a powerful wind."

A pause, then, as if Matin was now trying earnestly to remember something, and then Fahey prompted, "Anything more?"

"The coroner has contradicted her. The autopsy revealed only a trace of alcohol in the deceased."

"Think she's been lying?"

"A bit severe, would you not say? A young woman here in Monaco with her affianced. A tragic accident. Trauma makes it quite simple to be confused about events. One's mind is in a tangle and quite easily fooled."

Fahey agreed. Even an entire jury can be fooled. Yet he didn't think Romaine Brook was confused about very much, ever. "What would you say if I told you that this Brook woman is one of the most skilled liars I've ever crossed paths with?"

Matin grunted. Saying nothing, abruptly swerving the Renault into another lane, eyes tight to the road, intent on getting the journey over with. A mile or so went by, and he turned briefly toward Fahey, who, in a brooding mood, was surveying several billion dollars of yachts out there in the glassy surfaced harbor.

"A liar, you said?"

"Wrote the book," Fahey replied. "Non-stop camouflager, that little wench. She's an actress. Good at getting you to believe what isn't so. They get paid for it. You want to watch out, Inspector, for Hollywood women. Take the gold right out of your teeth. My wife wears platinum toe rings. Nuts, isn't it? Mucking up those gorgeous toes with African jujubees. Next thing, she'll be hurling spears at us."

"I see."

"Do you?"

433

"What I meant, M'sieu, is I see possibilities of deceit. Still, I cannot accord with you unless and until I know more."

"She's already masqueraded as a different person. False identity, eh? The thing is, you see, it's a full-time thing. This false identity of hers, wearing a new mask every day."

"You know her well, do you?"

"No, not that well. But the Gypsy's got her figured to the last comma?"

"Perdon?"

"Long story, but I shall elaborate tomorrow."

"We shall explore together, then. Yes?"

"Explore, right. Great concept. We'll do the Magellan thing."

The Renault entered Monaco on the Avenue Prince Albert, rolling through a small park, and then up several more blocks before swinging onto Avenue Kennedy. Almost every street in Monaco was named after some luminary or other: half of them, it seemed, for the local royals. Fahey, intrigued, contemplated a street sign for himself, lettered in gilt, then played one more idea off Matin.

"Let's get the lanterns out, shall we? I'll be Diogenes."

"Diogenes, what of Diogenes?"

"Let's have a look-about, Inspector. We might find there's more to this than we think, eh?"

They'd come to the Place du Casino. Ranks of Rolls and Daimlers everywhere, and, across the way, the Hotel de Paris in splendor so grand it doubled Fahey's heartbeat. Next to that hotel was the Hermitage, where he would be staying with Fritzi and Audrey. Matin pulled into its driveway, easing the Renault toward the curb. He was scowling into the windshield as Fahey got out, thanking him. Matin watched the "ex-cop" bound up the steps two at a time to the hotel's entrance.

Strange, he thought. The whole episode struck him as peculiar, and he hadn't liked the implications of Fahey's questions.

An actress, yes. But a liar?

The passport situation, and then the double assertions—one orally, the other in a signed avowal—that this Rhodes had polished off a bottle of wine before plummeting to his death. The coroner disagreed. Why, then, had she made such an unnecessary statement? To gain what? He had chosen to omit that detail of information in his descriptions to the American Fahey, not wishing to prejudice matters till he knew more of what these three visitors were up to.

Making more problems for him, he suspected.

∞

Fahey found them in the sitting room of a two-bedroom suite; it was a man's room paneled in richly polished walnut. In its center, on a round table, stood a large silver vase of red and white roses. The room itself was large. He could house three or four circus elephants in here, and still find places to sit, admiring of the women who knew a thing or two about standards of living, when traveling.

"We ordered lunch sent up," said Fritzi. "All right with you?"

"What kept you?" Audrey asked before he answered Fritzi.

"Came the long way. Needed a few innings with the inspector. Got a tight mouth on him...one of those. You girls'll have to unsnap his garters..."

"Alonzo," Fritzi warned.

Fahey sat down, noting they had changed into dressing gowns. How women could do it, undress so fast, but you could read a book while they were powdering up. To him, a constant mystery.

"Matin marks it down," he said, "as an accident. No witnesses. So there it is, and that's all he wants to hear. Wrap it up and be done with it." Fahey turned to Audrey. "I had to tell him you were under suspicion about Marc Sterne's death. That's a hand-washer for him. Solely a California matter..."

"Why did you say that?" Audrey complained.

Before he could arrive at an answer, the lunch arrived: grilled langoustine, salad verte, two bottles of chilled Batard-Montrachet. Fahey savored the wine, but ate little, telling them what else he had gleaned from Matin. Needing more time to think on it, he said nothing about Romaine passing herself off as Cliff Rhodes's fiancée. He'd never upset Fritzi if he could avoid it.

Talking away, ladling out opinions, ideas flashing to and fro, he frequently yawned. Audrey was jet-lagged, too, and spoke of a nap, tempting him to inquire if she cared for a companion. He had in mind the little known but sensationally addictive Mumbai massage, a Tantric invention of the Punjab that drove women into eternal sexual longing.

435

He restrained suggesting it, but the vision lingered off and on for the better fraction of an hour.

Caught in her own thicket of thoughts, Fritzi found herself in a state of surprised. She had known Alonzo Fahey for years, yet never seen him like this, so dead-on glum, so recessive and coiled.

Lunch passed, and he left the women to nap while he walked for seven kilometers, absorbing all he could see, in and out of most every street and crevice of the *stadt*. Peering, inhaling, sensing—a thrashing sensation in his mind. Several possibilities entered his thoughts, and it would never do to let even one of them escape.

He had come too far, and paid so little for it. It all must end, the accounts rendered and the missing digits found and then added up.

Matin or no Matin.

ଔ

Waking to the gray of six o'clock the next morning, shaking off his fatigue, anxious to get underway, he waited two hours, read the Paris edition of the Herald, drank three espressos and then called Matin. He wanted to visit the accident scene, could Matin be so kind as to arrange it? With a courtesy copy of the police report, *s'il vous plait*.

An hour later, a young fresh-faced, pink-cheeked young police officer was showing him the ledge at Cap de la Veille. The officer carried a diagram, a freehand drawing of the reconstructed accident scene, and then an English translation of Romaine Brook's version of how it happened. A report of four pages.

Fahey tramped the grounds, examined the area, studied more, and, asked and asked until he had spilled all the questions he could think of at that time of morning.

Not right at all, he thought. Rhodes could drink a camel to its knees. He wouldn't get tipsy on a smattering of wine.

Out on the ledge, Fahey leaned against the wobbly rusted rail that reached only to his lower thighs. He asked the officer to get behind him, then push against him. First, as he faced him, then the second push when his back was turned.

"I would not dare, m'sieur."

"It is mandatory, amigo," Fahey urged. "We are brothers-in-arms. Do it while I hold on to this rail." The officer barely nudged him. "Harder, use the force of a Samson," Fahey demanded. "Give it some arm, son. Be French. *Liberté, Égalité, Fraternité, ou la Mort!* Shove, you mother, or I'll be chatting with your superiors!"

A grab at Fahey's scarf-belt and then another push, the real thing this time. Fahey let go of the rail, but his reflexes were quick enough. His knees buckled, but went *under* and not over the rail.

A wind? Only a wind?

"Once more," Fahey ordered. "Push me again but from underneath my ass. The royal derriere."

The push again, not so hard, but this time Fahey felt the sudden sensation of toppling. His upper torso had suddenly bent dangerously forward before regaining balance. Down below, he saw a slurry of white water dashing across the rocks, some as pointed as steeples.

The young officer's face had paled slightly, believing Fahey had gone mad. "Let's go, *ami*," said Fahey, and they returned to the path leading through the pine woods.

Fahey suspected Romaine for doing something so final and so terrible they would never straighten it out. A girl like her, one for making the light of the day jump around, one of those rare ones. Hard to find even if you knew where to go looking.

"M'sieu is so quiet," said the officer after they had covered a mile in the police car.

"Truth," said Fahey, sounding far away in voice and thought. "I wonder what truth's address is these days."

A quizzical frown from the officer, and then they rounded the corner to the Hermitage.

"I *was* thinking truth must begin in places where they cook with garlic and wine...it frightened me so that I had to go quiet for a time. Don't tell anyone, *ami*. No one will believe you. By the way, have you any information about vineyards up for auction?"

"Vineyards?"

"Nothing overly elaborate. A likeable *vin ordinaire,* it's for the regiment we're organizing. I had in mind something with family crests emblazoned on the label. Perhaps a naked mermaid or two illustrated in gilt under the appellation. It'll be worth money to you, if we find the right grapes."

Reaching the front of the hotel, Fahey got out, profusely thanking the officer. Though assaulted by a rare bout of depression, he took the steps exuberantly, wishing today were an even of the past year and already forgotten.

On the dot of eleven, as agreed, a double knock at the suite's hall door. Fahey, opening it, gave Matin a warm and welcoming look, while instantly changing it to one of mistrust as he glanced at Romaine Brook. She hadn't expected Fahey, and she fell back a pace when he presented himself at the opened door.

"You!" she exclaimed.

"Me." Fahey winked.

"What's he doing here?" Romaine asked Matin, who quietly answered, "Perhaps he will tell us, mam'selle."

Recovering, she said to Fahey, "What fun to see you again…"there's been an awful accident. I suppose you've heard, of course."

Fahey said he had, marveling at her aplomb. Romaine went over to the large round table in the middle of the room and plucked a white rose from a fresh bouquet. She twirled it in her fingers, then sat on a divan near the windows overlooking the hotel gardens.

"What brings you here?" she asked. "In all this?" Her hand swept out to emphasize the sumptuous room.

"Come to see my old friend off," Fahey said. "Going to bury him here by the sea."

"Cliff, you mean?" Romaine looked at Matin.

"Yes," Fahey said. "Needs a proper wake. You can help with the details."

Smiling thinly, she signaled a warning to Fahey with her eyes.

"I asked the inspector to bring you by. I had a question or two for you," Fahey remarked, casually.

"Do I have to?" Romaine asked Matin.

"What harm can there be, mam'selle? You are acquainted with M'sieur Fahey, is that not so?"

"Somewhat, yes."

Fahey started in again, telling Romaine of his visit to the scene of the accident, wanting to get the feel of it, see where his lost friend had perished. It seemed strange that Cliff Rhodes—a man who had once been a highly trained Special Forces soldier—would be taken off by the wind. Any wind, that is, short of a hurricane. "I can't really buy that it's an accident," he said to Romaine, and then, looking at Matin, quickly added: "No offense, Inspector, I'm sure your people are very thorough."

Romaine stood up, smiling dispraisingly, before she said, "If you'd only been with us that day you would have seen for yourself. But I'm so glad you're here, Alonzo. It's nice that a friend would come. I feel so much better with friends."

Standing by the window, she touched the white rose to her cheek. A misty look creeping into her face, and her smile had changed to something innocent and Madonna-like.

"Why were you here with him, Romaine?" Fahey wanted to know.

"I told the inspector already."

"Tell me."

"Cliff and I were going to live here in Europe. Get married probably, though that's none of your business, is it?"

Never misses a beat, thought Fahey, marveling at her agility; must be the quickest mind this side of Jerusalem. "You know, Romaine, or maybe you don't know, I was going to give Fritzi Jagoda away at her wedding. She and Cliff were—"

"Oh, inspector," Romaine gushed. "We've been all through this and it's such a bore. Cliff Rhodes was trying to get rid of that woman."

Matin opened his mouth, but said nothing. He wondered where those other women were, the two he had yet to meet. He wasn't long in finding out. He listened as Romaine rambled on; her back half-turned, she faced the windows again.

Fahey felt a small war about to be declared as he went over to a bedroom door, pushing it open. He beckoned to Fritzi and Audrey. Hearing their footfalls, Romaine wheeled around, her face agape, white as an ice carving now. "God, what is this! What's happening here, Inspector?" The white rose dropped from her fingers. She had no idea the two women and Fahey knew one another.

Fahey, with aplomb, introduced Fritzi and Audrey to Matin who bowed graciously. The moment enshrined itself, its air electrically charged. Audrey sent Romaine a look laced with pity and scorn. They said other nothing to each other, only curt nods. She moved to a place where Romaine couldn't help but see the emerald bracelet around her wrist.

"Cliff sent it back, Romaine," she said evenly.

"Sent what back?"

"This," Audrey raised her hand, the emerald bracelet aglitter.

"I don't know what you're talking about." Romaine's eyes, hard-looking as gun muzzles, swept them all. With one trembling finger, she pointed at Fritzi, who forced herself to look at Romaine.

"See, inspector, that's the woman I told you about. The one Cliff Rhodes wanted to get rid of. She's going to lie to you, so watch out. Be very careful of her."

Matin looked bewildered. It was as if he were witnessing a family argument with no idea of what had started it. He saw Fritzi Jagoda sag a little as Fahey put his arm around her shoulder. Matin cleared his throat and began to ask questions of his own.

Fritzi answered, and Romaine denied Fritzi's replies, with Fahey observing closely. Audrey had become stiff-jawed, livid, her face flushing up to a bright pink. Fahey didn't quite understand why...for he knew nothing of her real history with Romaine. His gaze strayed to Fritzi, who seemed so drawn, thinner and beaten, and, for days now, had been bereft of her ever-present smile.

What could he do? Nothing much, he decided. The women must settle it, do all the rock-crunching by themselves. Waiting for Fritzi to unload on Romaine, he hadn't spotted Audrey slipping away.

ଓ

In one of the bedrooms, Audrey rummaged in her suitcase, and, finding the folder she was looking for, and had almost decided not to bring, she headed back to the parlor, walking through the ignited air till she stood in front of Matin.

"Inspector," Audrey said. "If you'll just listen, I think we can put an end to all this crap," Passing the Las Infantas papers over, she told him: "Those are birth records and official adoption papers...they prove, and I can prove, that I am this girl's actual birth mother. She's never known it before this instant. What happened here in Monte Carlo, well, I don't know, but this daughter of mine is lying and—"

"Oh, that's a good one. *Really!* Don't believe her either, Inspector. It can't be true."

"*Non?*"

"More lies," Romaine blurted. "Anyone can fake papers—"

Matin stopped Romaine with a policeman's look. He saw a dumbfounded stare widen Fahey's eyes before urging Audrey, "Please continue, madame."

"When you go through these papers," Audrey went on, "you'll find out, Inspector, that Cliff Rhodes was this girl's father...*your own father, Romaine*," nearly screaming it at her daughter, "that's the man who died here. And now you want us to believe he brought you here to marry him. You're the most absurd liar I ever met in my life, and I wish to God I'd never heard of you. Ever, ever, never!"

Bravely done, my beauty! For Fahey, his sovereign moment had landed; it was all clarifying now.

Fahey's mind, in its own feedback loop, took him back to that day at Las Infantas; hunting for the identity of Romaine Brook's parents, threatening that prissy nun with a subpoena if she didn't wise up, cooperate. He hadn't ever really known what their records would reveal but, at the time, would've bet most of what he owned that the record's contents would never biologically link Cliff Rhodes and Audrey Sterne to Romaine Brook. Fate's jackpot, the odds astronomical. It had taken a man's life for the facts to come out, so they could be fitted together.

Instantly, he grasped why Rhodes couldn't raise a finger to rescue his private investigator's license; had he, then it'd be another ticket on the bus that goes straight to terminal trouble.

In a slow burn now, his eyes on fire, Fahey rounded on Romaine, ready now to scuff her up. "You're a slick angel, you are...thinking you're pure as this morning's sunrise. You can cut the guff. There're no camera crews here. You killed my friend. You've killed Fritzi's lad. Killed your own father, eh? And look what you've done to your mother. Sister, you're headed straight for the concrete dormitory. Your Kabuki is finito. And do you know what, my little blonde Chiquita? Here's what: I'm on my way over there to wring that fucking neck of yours..."

Seeing the roil in him, her face turned chaotic. She cowered, shoulders slumping. Color fled that semi-famous face that had housed the stratagems of a woman who had withstood pounding after pounding over long months. One too many poundings and now she stood alone as a dark star. Cornered. This wasn't a courtroom. No one to defend her, no rules of engagement, no referee. Surrounded by a ring of hostility, she saw a scattering of four condemning faces, but she couldn't see her own, covered now with a damp sheen.

Her new jury; an enemy she couldn't gull, nor evade.

A muted sob escaped her. Suddenly, a torrent of heaving sobs, the sobs of the ever-lost, ever-forgotten child. Everything suddenly went psychedelic, wildly confusing.

"Speak!" Fahey directed.

A dead silence, then, a silence that portended a newness; perhaps, like the one on the day before God created earth. No one seemed to breathe, no one even moved until Romaine, quick as a leaping wildcat, jumped at Fahey, clawing at him. He grabbed her wrists. She recoiled, pulling herself away as she went feral and wild-eyed. "Get away from me...you godawful people. In-fucking-sane, all of you. You were all in it together. Bastards! How I hate you, hate you!" Snarling the words through her twisted mouth. "Oh, inspector, don't you see—why I had to save myself. She's not my mother. She can't be! And that bitch"—pointing at Fritzi, and fully in a rumpus now, her face streaming tears—"they want you to think my fiancé was my, oh, the cowards, they're out to stop me. Put me away. Tell me I'm crazy! I'm not crazy! I was going to be a star and everything...oh, oh, even Cliff. They got him to go after me. He was going to turn me in...I had to get rid of him. He wanted to have me committed, so I did it, I tricked him and knocked him right over that railing and I knew he couldn't fly...so I got him...*and I got him good didn't I...*"

Fahey heard Fritzi gasp, as he waded in, "You killed that Sterne boy. You did him in, too, didn't you? And lied about it...and lied to Inspector Matin about the killing of your father. Tell us, dammit, and tell us now or I'll be over there to take the skin off your rear."

Her head suddenly jerked, as if yanked by a hook in her mouth. "And I'll do you in, too, you bastard...you're like an abscess," Romaine retorted. "Marc Sterne wanted...he wanted...and he took...I helped him die, and that's what he deserved...got just what he deserved..."

"Oh, he did, did he?" Fahey replied, egging her on.

Matin's eyes filled with disdain and his eyebrows married over his bladed Gallic nose. He spoke into the hushed room slowly, deliberately, then angrily, fixing Romaine with the look of a man who had almost been made a fool of.

"It seems you have lied to us all, mam'selle. At least, you have lied to me and I must warn you that you shall answer for all of your misstatements."

Who was this Sterne, Matin wanted to know? He quickly faced the others, reminding them they stood as witnesses to Romaine's admission: *"I had to get rid of him,"* referring to Cliff Rhodes. Statements must be taken down and signed before the Americans departed the principality. He would return the adoption file, he told Audrey, after a copy was made by a *notaire*.

Turning to Romaine, he said, "You will be placed in custody, mam'selle. You will remain in my presence until the escorts arrive."

All along, Fahey thought, the Gypsy had been right about this perilous schemer. When he returned to California, he'd give her the entire rundown of events that had unfolded here so revealingly in the Monte Carlo patch. What a good think it turned out to be that he had been persuaded to come along to set matters right.

Justice belonged to him today; he'd regale for a month, a penniless month but that was a detail easily brushed aside.

Moving to Fritzi, who was shaking a little, he hugged her with his good arm, nudging her tight to him. A different part of this day was building in his mind. He loosened his arm, beckoning both women toward the hallway. When there, he observed: "Jesus, girls, if I haven't worked up a thirst. You'll never guess what I found out. Napoleon's favorite champagne is called Signature. Honest-to-Christ nectar…let's find us a Jeroboam and let our cups runneth over…" "You can't mean it," Fritzi protested, "you can't. She…well, she killed Cliff. How can we drink champagne to that?"

"Because we must. It's over, dove. It's done with. The bell has rung, can't you hear?"

"What bell?"

"Our bell. The ending bell. This fight's done with. We won. We've got to purge ourselves of that girl. Ostracize her to where she belongs. Why not a little rejoicing? It'll ease things…"

443

Somewhat put off, and put out, Fritzi remonstrated, "But it's not yet noon."

Fahey insisted, "We'll get a head-start on the tourists. Come along, you beauties. *Tout de suite.* We've unpacked enough dirty laundry, done all that we came here for, love," squeezing Fritzi close, "and we'll drink up all those little blondish bubbles and then catch the night ferry for Tunisia. Right across the sea, it is. Gorgeous beaches, the sand like pearls. We'll wear those silken kaftans and go looking for long-lost poets. A scavenger hunt, what of that, my beauties?"

"How can you even think of this," Miffed now and showing it, Fritzi retorted, "He's been gone only a few days."

"Never be thinking along the lines of a fugue, my little firefly. Cliff would've approved, oh, indeed he would have. Tunisia is a gallant place for one's eternal rest...you know that, surely...surely...and Rhodsey would like it a lot. We'll survey the ancient Carthaginian ruins. Hannibal's birthplace, we'll have a look around for that and lay Cliff out under those ancient marble columns, you see, one of those fifty-foot Travertine marble phalluses—"

"Hush, Alonzo, just fr'godsakes please just hush," Fritzi pleaded, placing a moist hand over his mouth.

He spoke through her opened fingers. "You're the one who paid hardest, amigo." Saying it softy, he bent and kissed her nose. Holding fast to her forearm, and, in the same movement, he clasped Audrey's hand, uniting them into a trio. "I can't fix that," he said to Fritzi, except I'll stand with you and for you. Both of you"—he turned to Audrey—"and you'll not have to worry about Kardas again. You're home and dry...Matin will see to that...so what we need, girls...what we must *have* is a bit of the bubbles. Come along. Fahey is buying with your money, be another IOU...give us a few smiles, eh? Later, we'll get to the laughing. Come now, we've put the worst of this day behind us...everything is up to us now...and the Tunisians..."

Only Audrey held back, feeling very drained, weak, and suddenly quite old. Everything, just then, seemed forever lost, seemed a thousand miles off in some unparsed oblivion. Her eyes hurt, felt as if someone was razor-cutting them. Maybe, she thought, she was going blind, the way Cliff Rhodes had been blinded by their daughter, precisely the way Audrey herself had been taken in. For a time, anyway.

What in *bejeezus* had happened?

A long-ago lover dead. A stepson dead. Two marriages gone kaflooey. A confessed killer for a daughter. And now her own self: what kind of mother acts as a prosecutor, offering up irrefutable evidence that will destroy her own daughter?

How could all this be?

How?

Still, it was here in Monte Carlo, a continent away, where the real verdict was told at last.

Buried deep for so many years, the truth—cold, hard, and whole—had finally been outed. How much of all this death belonged on her head?

Her head was abuzz with self-recrimination, but then, out on the street, she lay aside this dreariness as Fahey, escalating again, bedazzled her with his banter. He suddenly halted, standing with them in the middle of a sidewalk as he gazed up at the Monte Carlo sky that seemed bluer than any he could remember, with its sun still climbing toward its peak, telling of the noon-hour soon to arrive.

"Look about you, all this, and it ours," saying it with exuberance, before resuming their journey to no place in particular.

His soul was on the march; pleased with how the day's main task had been handled. Getting justice righted again, getting her feet back in the stirrups, galloping onward to her next battle.

Over and done with, though, at least for today; for the foreseeable hours in waiting, he had two armfuls of loveliness to entertain, and somewhere in this fabled town he'd search out a magnum of the finest champagne findable.

He liked it here, masses of high-end art must adorn these palatial homes. That always meant thieves on the prowl. A healthy market, then, needing him to safeguard things. How exquisite, he thought, as he began to invent Fahey of Monte Carlo, complete with his walking stick he'd forgotten to bring along from California.

Soon as he got the girls squared away, he'd find a printer to do up some business cards. Soon as he got his hands on some money, that is; and soon as he got God smiling again. Maybe Wanda was on top of everything, after all, and there really was One somewhere. Fahey was thinking just then that he'd better find out, in case he needed to put a hex on Cullis.

"Let's give this one a go, and let's be sure to make them remember us.

If they had half a brain on them, they'd let us supervise their courts here," suggesting all this to his charges, while aiming them toward La Chaumière, a five-star watering hole heaped with praise in the Michelin Guide. "When we get ourselves through that door, I'll be needing a kiss from you both, one of you per cheek. Show 'em the Americans are back, fit for any duty these looters can think of...your best smiles too, ladies, some real toothpaste smiles...come along, darlings, it's time we hydrate ourselves..."

And their afternoon was spent exactly that way.

The Author

DAVID CUDLIP holds a master's degree in business administration from Dartmouth College's Amos Tuck School and served in Europe with United States Army Intelligence before entering a business career with the New York private banking firm of Brown Brothers Harriman & Co. Afterward, he was elected a senior vice-president and director of an airline, then went on to become President of Pathfinder Corporation. He also co-founded a privately held company—Datamerx—engaged in electronic in-store marketing services. When living in California, he was an active member of Fictionaires, a group of well-known west coast writers. He now lives in Tryon, North Carolina with his wife, a book-hound herself.

Post A Review

It's easy! If you have an account with Amazon or Kindle Store, follow these steps:
  (1) Go to www.amazon.com
  (2) In the Search Box select Books from the drop down menu
  (3) In the Search Box, enter, in this case, Gun of God
  (4) When the page loads, scroll down to Customer Reviews and choose the button that says: Create Your Own Review. *And go to it!*

If you post a review, and let us know by email to: P3@windstream.net, we'll gladly send you a copy of Pen & Pencil's "The List". It's a compendium of over 200 memorable books in categories such as Fiction, Biography-Memoir, Mystery-Suspense and Nonfiction. The selections were compiled by Georgia Lee Berkley, (a top book buyer at Warwick's in La Jolla, CA) and were more fully augmented by other well-known booksellers, college professors, literary agents, numerous book clubs scattered throughout the U.S. and a hefty array of other addicted readers.

We encourage you to make your own recommendations, should you wish…